THE BLOOD
OF OTHERS

THE BLOOD OF OTHERS

GRAHAM HURLEY

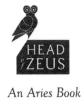

HEAD
of ZEUS

An Aries Book

First published in the UK in 2023 by Head of Zeus,
part of Bloomsbury Publishing Plc

9 7 5 3 1 2 4 6 8

A catalogue record for this book is available from the British Library.

ISBN (HB): 9781801108478
ISBN (XTPB): 9781801108485
ISBN (E): 9781801108508

Cover design: Ben Prior

Printed and bound in Great Britain by
CPI Group (UK) Ltd, Croydon CR0 4YY

Head of Zeus
First Floor East
5–8 Hardwick Street
LONDON EC1R 4RG

WWW.HEADOFZEUS.COM

For
Pete and Marnie Press
with love

'I am tired and sick of war. Its glory is all moonshine... War is hell.'

– General William Tecumseh Sherman
to the graduating class of the
Michigan Military Academy, 1879

Book One

1

SEPTEMBER 1936. NEWCASTLE, NEW BRUNSWICK, CANADA

Hogan could taste autumn in the wind. His friends at Newcastle's high school, the few that he had, told him he was crazy. No one could taste the wind. In New Brunswick, where Canada fell into the North Atlantic, wind was something that mussed up your hair, that blew in your face. It had no business with your tonsils, or the back of your throat, or wherever else you hid those little taste-buds. And besides, autumn was a season, an abstraction, a well-trodden bridge between summer and winter. You could fancy-talk about the rainbow palette of fall colours all you liked but tasting autumn in a blast of cold air? Forget it.

Hogan ignored them all. There it was. He could taste the wind.

That same September was the time he first got to take his writing seriously. He wrote for the school paper, *The Journal*, an easy assignment said those same few friends because he'd set it up in the first place. The word editor sat easily in his mouth. Aside from writer, which spoke to him of a solitary boldness, he considered it the closest description to what he wanted to be, to where he wanted to end up, and he commissioned himself to pen a lengthy piece about Newcastle at the turn of the twentieth century. It ran to nearly two thousand words, celebrated the

3

town's sleepy long-ago charms and occupied one entire edition of *The Journal*.

By 1936, London's *Daily Express* was selling nearly two million copies a day. Its Canadian owner, Max Aitken, was Newcastle's favourite son. He'd grown up in a gloomy Second Empire-style house with a mansard roof and views of the Miramichi River, and Hogan knew that Aitken, now Lord Beaverbrook, was due a visit to Canada that autumn to enjoy the glories of the fall and attend to a little business. And so Hogan waited for the first maples to turn, borrowed two dollars from his grandfather, retyped his story and took the train to Fredericton where Beaverbrook was spending the weekend in a hotel called the Colonial. He had no appointment with the great man but the local Newcastle journalist who'd told him about the visit in the first place said Lord Beaverbrook admired people who took a risk or two.

'Just turn up,' he said. 'This is a guy who loves being surprised.'

And so it proved. The walk from the train station delivered Hogan to the hotel just after midday. Beaverbrook was having lunch with a business colleague but when the waiter placed Hogan's envelope beside his dessert, he took time to scan the contents. Later that afternoon, after waiting in the hotel lobby, Hogan was summoned to Beaverbrook's suite. The mighty press baron, already in late middle age, was tiny compared to the lanky young supplicant but his handshake was firm and his big face had – to Hogan – the properties of a rubber mask. One moment, he looked like a monkey. The next, with his beguiling urchin grin, he was intensely inquisitive.

'How old are you, son?'

'Seventeen, sir.'

'And this was for your paper? *The Journal*? Have I got that right?'

'You have, sir.'

'Good. Great. I started a paper at school, too. *The Leader.* You know why it folded?'

'No, sir.'

'My father caught me working on the Sabbath. Two in the morning in my little bedroom at the top of the house. He was a man of the cloth, son, and I should have had sharper ears. You know the first thing anyone like you should do in Newcastle?'

'Sir?'

'Leave.' Beaverbrook returned the wad of typescript. 'Go away to college for a year or two. Keep writing. And when you get to London, drop me a line.'

Back in the lobby, slightly dazed, Hogan took a closer look at the typescript. Tucked between the first two pages was a card with Beaverbrook's contact details in London. On the back, he'd scribbled a personal note. 'Fine effort. Now you understand why I got the hell out.'

2

AUGUST 1937. ALSACE-LORRAINE, FRANCE

Mid-afternoon found *Abwehr* officer Wilhelm Schultz flat on his belly on the edges of a meadow south of the Luxembourg border. Ten kilometres to the east lay the Moselle Valley. Yet further east were the heavily contested lands of the Saar, returned to the Third Reich only two years before, after its mostly German inhabitants threw their hats in the air and voted overwhelmingly to return to rule from Berlin.

Propped up on his elbows, Schultz's thick fingers tightened once again around his binoculars as the tell-tale signs of *Ouvrage* Molvange swam into focus. *Ouvrage* meant fort. From half a kilometre away, through the thick green curtain of high summer, Schultz could just make out the tell-tale signs of the subterranean complex that stretched deep into these borderlands: the *avant poste* bunkers, surrounded by barbed wire and iron rails embedded upright in concrete; more tangles of barbed wire, draped over a carefully sown minefield; and finally a series of interval casemates, small grey concrete blockhouses with elevating turrets, the metal already a rusty ochre from the drenching winter rains. Link these strongpoints together in clever patterns and you were looking at a long, studded belt of forty-five major *ouvrages* and nearly a hundred of their little cousins that would protect the belly of the motherland. The French called it the Maginot Line and considered their work at an end. The last war had robbed them of an entire generation, but that, according to the politicians in Paris, would never happen again.

Schultz smiled to himself, abandoning the binoculars to roll over and offer his face to the sun. Lately, he'd become something of an expert in the darker arts of fortification. To keep the enemy at bay, to exact a price that no attacking force would ever pay, you needed a great deal of guile and lots of cash. Oddly enough, it had been the Germans themselves, engineers of patience and genius, who'd taught the French how to become moles and burrow underground. Back at the turn of the century, when this area had belonged to Germany, they'd built a ring of forts around Metz and Thionville that had served as a model for the Maginot Line: a complex of underground chambers and passageways, complete with embrasures, blast-proof armoured doors, power distribution plants, and – at the end of the longest, darkest corridors – mortuaries.

Schultz's trade was military intelligence. He'd studied the French installations with some care, and more recently, under a variety of covers, he'd paid the Czech version several visits, returning to *Abwehr* headquarters in Berlin to report on just why an invasion of the Sudetenland could be more troublesome than the Nazi leadership might expect. The Czechs had a decent army, and excellent equipment. More to the point, they'd expended a great deal of effort and reinforced concrete on shutting and bolting Germany's door to the east.

Schultz checked his watch and reached out for his notebook. Tufts of grass were warm to his touch. The French, like any other bunch of soldiers, were creatures of habit. They always sent out patrols in the late afternoon, and now he sat upright scanning a nearby copse of trees before opening the notebook and then fingering his stub of a pencil. Pied flycatcher, he wrote, and a tree sparrow, and a flock of crossbills. Against the latter trophy he added a single exclamation mark, anticipating the conversation to come. Already, he could see movement among the distant trees that softened the low brutal outlines of the *ouvrage*. A patrol of just three figures. Perfect.

They were heading his way, threading a path through the meadow that lay between himself and the fort. They've seen me already, he thought: the big, thickset guy with the battered rucksack, dressed for a day in the country, doing his clumsy best to disappear into the landscape. He was watching them through the binoculars now, single file, each man carrying one of the new MAS-36 rifles, the lieutenant at the front plainly in charge. Much closer, a hundred metres away, the other two broke left and right, jogging heavily through the meadow grass until they had the target of their suspicions surrounded.

Confecting surprise, Schultz lowered his binoculars but didn't bother to get to his feet. It was a lovely afternoon. The sun was still hot. The last thing he intended to expend was unnecessary effort.

'*Vos papiers?*'

The lieutenant was standing over him, his gloved hand outstretched. He had a young face, and a complexion he could probably blame on a shit diet, but the muzzle of the pistol, a metre from Schultz's head, was rock-steady.

Schultz produced his passport from the breast pocket of his shirt. The lieutenant spared it a single glance. The cover, Schultz, always thought, was the colour of the North Sea in winter, a muddy greenish yellow shading into grey, but there was no ambiguity in the spread of eagle's wings over the hanging swastika.

'*Allemand?*'

'*Deutsch.*' Schultz agreed.

'And why are you here?' The lieutenant's German was perfect.

'I watch birds,' Schultz gestured vaguely upwards. 'Birds make me very happy.'

'You're living here?'

'I came from Luxembourg,' another gesture, to the north this time. 'Two hours on foot? Hard to resist in weather like this.'

'And that?' The lieutenant was looking hard at the notebook, abandoned beside Schultz's binoculars.

'That's where I write down my birds. That's where I keep them safe for the journey home.'

Something in Schultz's manner had disturbed the young officer. Schultz could see it in his eyes. Was this tramp deliberately trying to wrong-foot him? By playing the half-wit? The bird-crazy child-man?

'Up,' he said. 'And give me the notebook.'

Schultz got unsteadily to his feet, handed the book over. The soldiers edged backwards, their rifles raised. The lieutenant was studying the pencilled jottings on the first page.

'Pied flycatcher?'

'That was earlier. I'm a lucky boy. They'll be gone in a week or two.'

'And the crossbill?'

'Crossbills, plural. A whole flock of them.'

'Colour?'

'The adults are brick-red. The younger ones a muddy green.' Schultz smiled his obliging smile and flapped his arms. 'Chup-chup,' he was smiling now. 'Chup-chup.'

One of the soldiers rolled his eyes. The lieutenant was leafing through the rest of the notebook. Only towards the very back did he find what he was looking for.

'And this?' He beckoned Schultz closer. Look hard enough at the pencilled lines and it was impossible to miss the brooding cross-hatched presence of the *ouvrage* among the trees.

'The flycatchers,' Schultz murmured. 'That's where they live.'

'In the fort?'

'In the trees. They prefer oak but no one can be choosy these days. Like I say, you need luck in this game. They were noisy as hell this morning. Can't wait to fly south.'

The lieutenant looked up and held Schultz's gaze for a long moment. Then he returned to the front of the notebook and tore out the pages with the bird sightings before folding them carefully into his trouser pocket.

'They're for my youngest,' he said. 'She loves fairy tales.'

They marched Schultz back to the *ouvrage*. Someone must have been watching this modest little drama because the moment they approached the big steel door it swung noisily outwards. At once, as they stepped inside, Schultz felt the chill and damp of life underground. The lieutenant was in the lead again as they made their way down a flight of concrete steps, lit by a line of overbright lamps. Moisture glistened on the bareness of the walls, and Schultz could hear the distant throb of a generator. So far his two escorts had been gripping him, one on each arm, but the narrowness of the staircase made that impossible. At the foot of the stairwell the lieutenant paused in front of a door, fumbling for the notebook before knocking twice.

The door opened and Schultz caught the snatch of a conversation. The guy with the rucksack in the meadow. Some bullshit about birdwatching. Then came a rustle of movement and the scrape of a chair before a figure appeared in the harshness of the light outside. He was tall, much taller than the lieutenant, and he'd buttoned his tunic against the chill of the *ouvrage*.

His rank badge indicated he was a *capitaine*, but Schultz knew that already.

The lieutenant was drawing his attention to the sketch at the back of the notebook. The sight of the pencilled *ouvrage*, not a line out of place, drew a nod from the *capitaine*. Then he looked up.

'*Major* Schultz,' he murmured. 'Has the *Abwehr* lost its wits?'

*

It was nearly dark by the time Schultz finally caught up with Odile. The *capitaine*, after a glass or two of rough red wine from a stone jar and a longish conversation about Hitler's intentions in the east, had released him back to the custody of the young officer with instructions to drive him to the Hôtel de la Gare in Metz.

The journey had taken nearly an hour, largely due to a traffic accident, but Schultz had been untroubled by the silence between them. He knew that the young lieutenant was desperate to find out more about him, about his presence in the meadow, about his status with German military intelligence, about what he was really doing so close to a sensitive military installation, but something about the seeming complicity between the *capitaine* and this *Abwehr* intruder kept his mouth buttoned. Only when he finally pulled the battered Renault to a halt at the kerbside outside the hotel did Schultz's big hand close around his.

'Chup-chup,' he said. 'And thanks for the lift.'

*

Odile was quartered in two rooms on the second floor. A knock from Schultz brought her to the door, and she studied him for a moment before stepping back into the room. The room was still warm and she was wearing nothing but a vest of Schultz's

11

that he'd left in the bedroom of her Paris address only ten days ago. She had Schultz's height, and a little of his presence. The vest extended to the top of her thighs, and her lightly muscled legs – to Schultz – went on forever. In Paris, even some of her friends thought she might have been dealt a few too many male genes, but that had never disturbed Schultz in the slightest. From the moment they'd met, last year in Berlin, they'd wanted to explore each other and now was no different.

Except. Except.

'You'll have an excuse,' she said stonily.

'For what?'

'You said seven at the latest. You said for me to wait in the restaurant. You said we'd eat first.' She tapped the watch on the bareness of her arm. 'It's nearly ten.'

'I got myself arrested.'

'How careless. By whom?'

'Your army. They think I'm a spy.'

'They're right, aren't they?'

'Of course, they are. As it happens, it makes little difference. What's happening here is foreplay. This is a game. Both sides watch each other and if you're lucky it earns you a drink and a decent conversation.'

'And?'

'No matter. I checked with the woman behind the desk downstairs. We can have a whole chicken and the trimmings and a bottle of Château Lafite from my masters to say sorry. I told them not to trouble us for at least an hour.' He stepped forward and cupped her face. 'Does that sound about right?'

She didn't move. Anticipation, thought Schultz, carries the delicate scent of Lancôme, the memory of which he'd carried ever since their first wild coupling the night of Goering's party to celebrate last year's Berlin Olympics. That was when they'd

first met. That was the balmy August evening the gods of the
Third Reich had put their place names side by side at one of
Goering's many tables. At the *Reichsminister*'s banquet, they'd
gorged on a mountain of venison and wild boar and abandoned
the endless round of formal toasts for something a great deal
more personal.

The Germans, in deference to Odile's absent explorer husband
Dominique, had given her a suite at the Adlon, and within hours,
in ways Schultz had barely imagined possible, she'd emptied
him to the point of near exhaustion. For the rest of the night,
setting a pattern that had never changed since, they'd recklessly
exposed other bits of themselves in conversations spiced with
yet more pauses for yet more sex. Schultz was the first to admit
that no fortification in the world could keep this woman at
arm's length. She had a raw physical appetite that was truly
remarkable, a proposition and a challenge that filled him with
the rudest joy.

Now, they sank into bed. An open copy of *The Magic
Mountain* lay on her pillow. She read Thomas Mann in the
original, undaunted by the thickness of the book or the gruelling
perils of the journey to come. Schultz had tried Mann himself,
mostly out of curiosity, but had been forced to concede defeat.
Like Odile, Mann was often beyond either comprehension or
compromise. You saw the world through his eyes, or you accepted
you were probably stupid. Schultz, for his part, was happy to
do the latter, not because he lacked self-belief but because –
in Odile – he found it impossible to imagine a more perfect
relationship. They didn't live together, and they never would.
They didn't anticipate shared breakfasts for the rest of their
lives, because that would be so wholly out of keeping with the
way the relationship had shaped itself. They made love, and they
talked, and they agreed the world was doomed in its craziness,

and then they made love a little more. One day, probably by mutual agreement, it would all come to an end. But not yet.

'So tell me...' She was lighting a cigarette. 'They arrested you.'

'They did.'

'And?'

'And nothing. Those rat holes you've all put your trust in are shit and they know I know.'

'How?'

'Because the guys that are trying to mend them are on our side, always have been. German stock, most of them. One generation back around here, they were in charge. Now they're speaking French again. The French cut corners. They know that. Your people always cut corners. You've got problems with the damp, with condensation, with unfinished cable runs, with munitions storage, with lack of heat. The guys who talk to me are there to make everything better, to make France Boche-proof, and it doesn't cost us much to put them on the payroll. They take the Berlin *Schilling*. They tell us everything. How the new recruits are useless. How most of their dads never came home from the trenches. How their mothers want to put an end to war.'

'And what does all that tell you?'

'Nothing we didn't know already. Dig a hole and close the lid and shut your eyes, you're half dead already. Your next war, when it happens, will be run by the politicians. The Maginot Line is a state of mind, and by the time your generals realise that, it'll be way too late.'

'For who?'

'You. Your lot.' Schultz found her hand under the sheet, gave it a slow squeeze. 'Still hungry?'

3

AUGUST 1939. TORONTO, CANADA

The *Globe and Mail* was the city's leading newspaper. It operated from a handsome white five-storey block of offices which towered over the intersection of King Street and York Street. A five-minute walk towards the Lake Shore took you to a small, intimate, tucked-away bar dedicated to the city's star baseball team, the Maple Leafs.

As Hogan knew only too well from previous errands, Earl Prentiss would be occupying a table towards the back of the bar, beneath a Leafs' shirt once worn by the legendary Ike Boone. To Hogan, who knew very little about baseball, this garment appeared to have an almost religious status. Newcomers to the bar gazed up in awe. One or two of them, braver, even touched it. Prentiss, who made a point of being unimpressed about anything, simply settled at his table and got down to the daily business of lunch.

By four minutes past midday he was already drunk, his eyes glassy, his skinny arm around an overweight woman visibly troubled by the merciless midsummer heat. When Hogan's lanky frame appeared in front of the table, Prentiss did his best to ignore him.

'Phone call from the folks at the Armoury.' This from Hogan. 'That exercise you're covering up on the lake? Scheduled for the weekend? The Royals have brought it forward.'

'Yeah?' The Royals were the Royal Regiment of Canada.

'They're sending a car.' Hogan tapped his watch. 'Two o'clock.'

'Like when?'

'This afternoon. Now, nearly.'

'You talked to these people?'

'The desk took the call. Sent me round.' Hogan didn't move. 'Two o'clock, like I said.'

The two men stared at each other. In his early days on the paper, Hogan had revered this man. The best of his work was outstanding, bending language in ways that Hogan barely believed possible, and a series of long, acutely observed pieces about what it really took to fit into the complicated mosaic that was federal Canada had won a big press award down in New York. Indeed, the presence of a writer like Prentiss on the editorial floor – untroubled by the drumbeat of daily news – had been one of the reasons the eager young tyro from the Maritime Provinces had been prepared to put up with all the lousy jobs that went with his never-ending bid to become a journalist.

Earl Prentiss was proof that the *Globe* cared about talent, about asking the right questions of yourself, about maybe seeing the press of events a little differently. It told Hogan he'd made the right decision to hang in there and bide his time before he, too, could lay hands on a desk of his own and a typewriter and a byline. But now no longer. Prentiss was a lush. He'd pissed his talent down the john. Everyone knew that, and – more to the point – it was months since he'd penned anything worth reading.

Hogan, his message delivered, was on the point of leaving when Prentiss abandoned the woman and fumbled in his jacket and produced a battered leather notebook. He tossed it towards Hogan but it landed short in a puddle of spilled beer on the table top.

'You do it, son.'

'Do what?'

'That shit assignment? Our soldier friends? The fucking Royals? They're yours. Just get the right words in the right order. If it's any good I'll put my name on the end and buy you a drink.'

'And if it isn't?'

'I'll still buy you a drink.'

'But I don't drink. You know that.'

'Sure,' the smile, slightly twisted, was still beguiling. 'So I guess I win either way. You gotta pen? Pencil? Eyes in that fat head of yours? These kid soldiers may be on the boat by Christmas. Watch their every move. Don't take any of the King and Country shit. Abroad's a whole new ballgame and lots of them are country boys,' the smile widened. 'You'll fit right in.'

Hogan hurried back to the office. His afternoon offered nothing but the usual chores – running copy to the typesetters, answering phones, tallying out the bundles of print-warm newspapers before they sped away to various corners of the city – but he knew he couldn't afford to simply disappear. The day's assignments were in the gift of the ageing tyrant known as the Despatcher, who ran the news operation. He ate lunch at his desk, bent over a copy of yesterday's paper, eating baloney sandwiches smothered in mustard.

Hogan came to a halt beside him. Mr Prentiss, he explained, wasn't feeling well. The Royals' exercise had been brought forward and he wasn't able to cover it. Their car would be here at two.

'Yeah?' The Despatcher was still reading the early edition but a hand crabbed left to check reporter availability. 'Shit.'

'Sir?'

'I got no one. The cupboard's bare. Maybe we cover it some other way.'

'They seemed keen, sir, on the phone.' Hogan was inventing now. 'This stuff only happens once a year.'

'Yeah? Too bad.'

'But I could do it.'

'You, boy?' The Despatcher's head at last came up. Hogan grinned his eager Maritimes grin, and then the Despatcher's gaze drifted to the paper, stained mustard-yellow where he'd been turning the pages. 'You really think you can do it?'

'I know I can do it.'

'Prentiss brief you at all? About the Royals?'

'Told me everything, sir.'

A frown, a slow nod, then a dab at his mouth and a gust of baloney as he burped.

'It's yours, son. A thousand words, max. I like your confidence. What else did New Brunswick teach you?'

The car appeared late. Hogan had been lingering at the kerbside for a while. Prentiss's notebook was still sticky from the beer but he used the time to go through it page by page. Expecting jotted thoughts in shorthand, grist for articles to come, he found himself looking at day after day of expenses' claims, most of them charged against entertaining unnamed contacts. It was a thick book, and as the months went by the slapdash references to this bar or that developed a life of their own and Hogan couldn't help remembering the gaunt, wet-eyed figure he'd left in the bar.

'Mr Prentiss?'

Hogan blinked. A black Pontiac Chieftain had ghosted in from nowhere. Hogan bent to the driver's open window. He explained quickly about Prentiss. Touch of summer flu. Sends his apologies. Nothing serious.

'My name's Hogan,' he added.

'Sure,' the driver leaned across and opened the passenger door. 'We need to get going.'

He said his name was Larry Elder. He was a short, compact figure with big, calloused hands and a brutal haircut. To Hogan's slight surprise, he wasn't in uniform. The lake where the exercise was to take place was an hour or so to the north. The men were already embarked and about now, grunted Elder, they would be performing various drills afloat before returning in the late afternoon to storm ashore before the world's press.

'I'm guessing that's me,' Hogan said.

'You'd be guessing right, son. The guys in charge figured it would be good to give Mr Prentiss an exclusive. Shame he can't make it.'

The bluntness of the comment brought colour to Hogan's face. His first instinct was to answer back. Nothing in life had taught him to take an insult lying down but for now he bit his tongue and fetched out the brand-new pad he'd stolen from a desk in the newsroom.

'Larry Elder?' he had his pen poised. 'That's Elder, as in flower?'

Elder spared him a brief look. He had to be at least a decade older than Hogan but there was just the hint of a smile on his weathered face.

'Elder, as in better,' he nodded at the pad. 'Write it down, yeah?'

The next half-hour or so passed in near silence. When Hogan enquired what this particular exercise might do for a soldier, Elder grunted something unprintable about learning to swim. And when Hogan pressed the point, suggesting it might have something to do with the Royals shipping out to Europe, Elder raised an inquisitive eyebrow.

'You got information on that possibility?'

'I'm guessing, is all.'

'Fine. That puts us both in the dark.'

'But there's a war coming, right? Adolf Hitler? Poland?'

'Sure, that's what you news guys are telling us.'

'You think we make it up?'

'I think you have papers to sell. Frighten people enough and they'll dig deeper in their pockets. This place we're going's called Kawartha Lakes. Sounds Indian, right?'

'Right.' Hogan was already writing down the name. Elder waited until he'd finished, and made Hogan read it back to check the spelling. Then he glanced across in seeming approval.

'You know what it means? In the original language? The land of reflections. Pretty, eh? Fitting? Old? Except it was put together forty years ago by some Indian trying to sell it to us whiteys, so I guess that makes it the land of make-believe. I'm older than you, and nastier than you, so a word in your ear. Life's a wagon out of control, son. The trick is never to fall off.'

'Shit.'

'I mean it,' he shot Hogan another look. 'What are you doing now?'

'Writing that down.'

'Why?'

'Because it smells right.'

'*Smells* right? You ever go to school?'

'Yeah. Everyone goes to school.'

'And they taught you horseshit like that?'

'Never,' Hogan tapped the pad. 'I learned the phrase from a hero of mine. Back when he was sober.'

The Royals' exercise was in full swing by the time they arrived. Hogan stood at the water's edge, peering through a pair of borrowed binoculars, underwhelmed by the faraway specks that appeared to be the invasion fleet.

'These are the boats, right?'

'Pinnaces,' Elder grunted. 'Five in all. It was the best we could do. They were shipped up from the city. On flat water like this you're talking twenty men each at a squeeze.'

'They're rowing?'

'Towed. We borrowed speedboats from further up the lake.'

'And when they get here?'

'They'll be landing further down the beach,' Elder gestured to his right. 'We've laid barbed wire and a belt of dummy mines and an iron stake or two to liven things up. MG crews dug in on the flanks.'

'MG crews?'

'Machine guns. Manoeuvres like this are all about flanking fire. The boats land in line abreast. We use live ammunition aimed high to keep their heads down. The wind's a blessing. Blowing from the south, they'll smell the cordite.'

'You ever get casualties?'

'Guys fall over, sure. Lose their footing. Get wet. Get bothered. But usually no one dies.'

'Usually?'

'Usually. Getting a rookie this far costs hundreds of dollars, believe it or not. The army hates wasting money.'

Sobered, Hogan was writing everything down. Elder watched him for a moment, then produced a pack of Du Maurier.

'Smoke, son?'

'No, thanks.'

'Thirsty? I got some beers in the trunk.'

'I don't drink.'

'You don't?' Elder shook his head. 'Any women in your life?'

'My mother.'

'You're kidding me.'

'I mean it. Six of us. My father was out of the story most of the time and she had to cope with all of us for year after year. Any army would have given her a medal.'

'*Six* of you?'

'Sure, and I was the oldest. I guess that was another reason to leave.'

Hogan was watching the tiny fleet slowly getting bigger across the choppiness of the lake. Kawartha, he thought. Coils of barbed wire. Fake landmines. An iron stake or two. The land of make-believe. He swept the binoculars to the right and fiddled with the focus until he found a little nest of helmets that had to be one of the machine-gun teams.

'I get to talk to any of these guys afterwards?' he asked.

'You get to talk to whoever the hell will give you the time of day. I've got some people in mind but never think we're trying to tie you down. Citizen army, right? Everything out there, plain as daylight, right?' Elder reached out for the binoculars, took a brief look at the approaching boats. 'In real life, these guys would be dead meat already. Field artillery? Mortars? Enemy aircraft? Sitting targets, all of them.' He returned the binoculars and shook his head. Hogan couldn't take his eyes off him. So cynical. So dismissive.

'Mind me asking you a question?'

'Go ahead.'

'Does that upset you? The sitting targets stuff?'

'Did once, but dying's like everything. It shouldn't take you by surprise, but it always does. Some guys cope OK. Some don't.'

'And you?'

'Me and death are best friends. Met a while ago and never looked back.'

At Elder's insistence they retreated a little further up the beach as the pinnaces parted company with their tows, pushed out a couple of oars and shook themselves into an extended line abreast. Hogan didn't need the binoculars anymore. He could make out the bodies crouched low as the first of the machine guns opened up, firing high, as Elder had anticipated, then came a low phut of an explosion from one of the boats, and then another, and Hogan watched small black objects trailing brown smoke arc towards the beach, and there was another explosion, even softer, and the boats had suddenly disappeared behind boiling clouds of smoke, scarlet in the wind.

'Neat.' For once Elder was smiling, evidently taken by surprise.

Hogan was still watching the smoke as the crimson curtains began to part. Helmeted figures in full battledress were emerging from the water at the half crouch, many of them starting to cough. The first two men from every boat threw themselves on the coils of barbed wire, making a bridge for their mates who followed. There were no bayonets on their rifles and none of them bothered to drop a knee and aim a blank or two at the defenders manning the machine guns, but Hogan followed their progress up the beach and saw what happened when they got in among the machine-gunners, lashing out with boots and rifle butts.

Hogan, watching through the binoculars again, was a little shaken. Bloodied faces. Men sprawled unconscious. The invaders performing some kind of war dance, scored for adrenaline, and the raw pleasures of conquest.

'You think that was easy?' Elder was watching him carefully.

'I think it was a game.'

'You're right. Now's the time to talk to these guys. They're your age, son. They've never been in a war in their lives but I'm guessing that's about to change.'

Hogan was back at the *Globe* by seven o'clock. Delivery vans were still queuing up at the loading bay at the side of the building for the late edition, but Hogan didn't spare them a second glance. He'd been working in this building for over a year and now, at last, he had real news, a *story*, to impart. This was what he'd come to do. This was what Newcastle's favourite son had *told* him to do. Lord Beaverbrook, he told himself, might even remember their brief encounter back at the hotel in Fredericton. Get the right words in the right order, and I might be shipping east myself.

The day's work at an end, the newsroom was beginning to empty. Ignoring curious glances from a scatter of journalists still bent over their typewriters, Hogan settled at a spare desk, helped himself to half a dozen sheets of plain foolscap, found a box of carbons, wound the first interleaved sheets into the roller and then consulted the notes he'd brought back from the lake.

Thanks to Elder, he'd been given unlimited access to both attackers and defenders. By and large, these were men his own age or even younger, which meant they were barely men at all. Some of them had joined up because they could think of nothing else to do. Others had done their father's bidding. One or two appeared to believe in pulling on a uniform and defending the Dominion. They came from hardscrabble country backgrounds, from huge families in the industrial suburbs, but all of them – even the bloodied defenders – agreed that the afternoon had been well worth it, that getting out on the lake, or digging in on the beach with belt after belt of machine-gun ammunition, was a welcome break from classwork and endless parade-ground drills. One of them, a third generation Royal, had spoken proudly of getting a taste of the real thing. Challenged by Hogan to admit he hadn't been scared by the prospect of live ammunition, he'd simply shrugged.

'I guess it's our job,' he'd muttered. 'That's what we're here to do.'

'Die?'

'Win.'

On the journey back to the city, Hogan had carefully sieved his notes for everything that would sit well on the page, knowing – above all – that he wanted to somehow impart the essence of this strange afternoon of make-believe violence. From time to time in the car he'd lift his head and turn to Elder and check a fact or an impression and, as the journey went on, he became aware that the relationship between them had changed. No longer was the older man holding him at arm's length, hiding behind a series of scathing put-downs. On the contrary, having watched him with interviewee after interviewee, Elder appeared to believe that this gawky infant scribbler might have talent, as well as sincerity. The kids on the beach had opened up. Which meant they'd trusted him.

Moments before Elder had driven away, he'd asked Hogan for his pad.

'What's that?' Hogan was watching the older man scribble a line of digits.

'It's a phone number. It belongs to a friend of mine. Leave a message, and the name of a bar. I need to buy you a proper drink, son, maybe without the pad, this time.'

'Really?' Hogan was delighted.

'Really.' Elder nodded at the line of waiting delivery vans. 'So when do I get the paper?'

'Tomorrow,' Hogan grinned. 'God willing.'

*

Now, beneath a slowly circulating fan in the newsroom, Hogan set to. Already, on the way back, he'd figured out an opening sentence, sharp, declaratory, eye-catching, and beyond that he had a clear sense of direction. The rest – he knew from the countless short stories he'd been writing – would take care of itself, one quote sparking another, plenty of crash-bang colour to make it dance on the page. He wanted to coax his readers to the very edge of the lake. He wanted them to be in pinnace after pinnace as they closed on the defended beach. He wanted them to be crouched over the sights of their rifles. And he wanted them to feel the acrid choke as they splashed through the shallows, the crimson smoke coiling deep into their lungs.

By nightfall, with a solitary journalist still at work at the far end of the newsroom, Hogan was done. He read it through twice, collated the mauve carbon copies, rustled up a stapler and left the top copy on the Despatcher's desk. Home was a single room in a cheap hostel down near the docks. He shared the washroom on the third floor with two stevedores, a Polish butcher and a much older man who appeared to do nothing all day. Exhausted but unaccountably happy, Hogan sank into bed and was asleep within minutes.

Next morning, he returned to work as normal but by noon, on the assumption that his piece might have been read, he made his way to the newsroom. The Despatcher, for whatever reason, hadn't turned up for work. In his place, at the head of the long table, sat a woman Hogan had never met before. She looked Asian. She was wearing a sharp city suit – white blouse, grey jacket and skirt – and she said her name was Mahindra. She also explained that she'd been hired from another major Toronto newspaper, and, more importantly, that she'd just finished Hogan's article.

'This was a first draft?' she enquired.

'It was.'

'Remarkable.'

'Remarkable good? Remarkable bad?'

'Just remarkable. I've marked up just three edits, and that – believe me – is a world record.'

'Today's paper?'

'As we speak. Page 5, all of it. We've used a stock photo, the Royals on Empire Day last year. That's a shame but the writing speaks for itself. What are you working on next?'

Hogan was gazing down at her. Conversations like this were never meant to happen.

'First thing this afternoon, I'm selling tickets for the weekend barbecue. If that goes well, I'll have time to sort the return bundles from last night.'

'You're kidding.'

'I'm not. I'm still an apprentice. The printers downstairs earn a fortune. Maybe that's where I should be headed.'

The woman was shaking her head. She was old enough to be Hogan's mother.

'Wrong,' she was reaching for a phone. 'Leave it to me.'

4

Five days later, with August nearly over, Nazi Foreign Minister Joachim von Ribbentrop returned to Berlin from Moscow. Exhausting days of diplomatic negotiation had hammered out a non-aggression pact pledging the Russians and the Germans not to go to war with each other for at least ten years. Willi Schultz got the bombshell news at the German Embassy in Paris and set out at once for Odile's apartment in rue de la Faisanderie, near the Bois de Boulogne. Summoned to the front door by Schultz's knock, she was very angry indeed.

'You knew about this? What's been happening behind our backs?'

Schultz, who would have dearly loved to say yes, shook his head. He'd never regarded Ribbentrop as clever enough to strike a deal with the Bolsheviks, and thus cover Germany's back until Hitler had the rest of Europe in the bag. The man was a fool, a prisoner of a thousand vanities, no match for the likes of Stalin, but that – just now – was hardly the point. Odile, in common with her large circle of friends, loathed the very idea of Communism, which was why he'd arrived from the embassy to soften the blow.

She stepped very close to him, angry, thin-lipped, not the faintest whiff of Lancôme.

'The socialists want all of us,' she said. 'They want our money, and our souls, and every particle of the lives we've made for ourselves. These people give envy a bad name.'

'I know.'

'You do? You understand? So tell me, please, Herr Schultz, why has this thing happened? Yesterday, your glorious Reich was our best guarantee against *les Rouges*. Hitler hates them. He spent years killing them on the streets and that wretched book of his spells out what else he'd like to do to them. Yet now we learn that this same Herr Hitler has climbed into bed with these animals. Tell me something, is there anyone else he won't fuck? Or are we next on the list?'

Les Rouges. The Reds. Schultz, who'd spent his early days in the Brownshirts seizing every opportunity to batter the Communists, could only nod.

'Regrettable,' he grunted. 'But probably necessary.'

'Necessary for whom? You? Me? Them? Us? Just a particle of sense is all I need, or perhaps an apology.' She was staring at him, her long face drained of all colour. Then she stepped back and nodded at a nearby chair. 'Sit,' she said. Moments later, she'd gone.

Schultz sank into the chair, gazing round at the walls hung with blue brocade, at the carefully chosen mirrors, positioned with a touch of brilliance, at the muted splash of summer colours from foxgloves and anemones, the blooms refreshed every other day. As far as Schultz could gather, the entire house, a much-admired *hôtel particulier*, belonged to Odile but since the departure of her husband she'd elected to live only on the first two floors. Quite where this husband of hers had gone was another mystery. Schultz knew he was an explorer and an anthropologist, and had made discreet enquiries, but aside from a belief that he was probably up the

Nile – Sudan maybe, or Ethiopia – Schultz had drawn a total blank.

Conversations about him with Odile went nowhere. Recently, Schultz had found a man's suits in a wardrobe on the disused top floor, and he judged him to be medium height, with an affection for Scottish tweeds. In the pocket of one of the jackets he'd found a pouch of stale tobacco and a ticket for an unidentified left-luggage *consigne*, but when he'd asked one morning when he might be back, Odile had simply shrugged. Tomorrow? Next month? Christmas, maybe? Never? She didn't appear either to know or care.

Now, with the same abruptness, she was back in the room again, but, looking at her, Schultz realised that he had nothing left to say. Normally, they never parted without agreeing the next tryst, the next opportunity to shut their doors on the world, but with Odile in this mood he knew it was pointless. Beneath the anger there lurked something he'd never sensed before, something altogether darker, and it troubled him that he couldn't make out exactly what it was. Schultz had devoted most of his adult life to exploring motive and consequence, to reading the tiny signals that told him where trust was wasted, but taking one last glance at her as she strode from the room, he realised he was in the presence of a stranger. What had happened between them had plainly come and gone.

Wrong.

'This Poland nonsense.' She'd stopped at the door and turned to look back at him. 'You'll split that poor bloody country between you, you and the Russians. Might that be the plan? Am I right?'

Schultz shrugged, said nothing.

'But that will mean war, *n'est-ce pas*? War with the English. War with us. Don't just stare at me. Admit it.'

This time, Schultz permitted himself the faintest nod.

'And you have a date? When Hitler gives the word and the tanks roll?'

'We always have a date. We're Germans, remember. We hate the unknown.'

'Of course you do. So might you share it with me? This date of yours? Tell me how much time the rest of us have left?'

Schultz got to his feet and studied her for a long moment. Recently he'd been privy to the German war plan, the thick file the *Abwehr* knew as 'Case White', carefully measured doses of extreme violence that would bring Poland to its knees in a matter of weeks. A pact with the Soviets, as he'd immediately realised, would be the icing on the Blitzkrieg cake.

'Well?'

'Well, nothing.'

'You don't think you owe me?'

'I owe you plenty. But not this.'

'A week? Am I getting close here? Early September maybe? Just a nod will do. That's all I need.'

'For what?'

'I have something in mind.'

'You're leaving Paris?'

'*Au contraire*, Herr Schultz. Let's call it a wake, a farewell, not to Paris but to peace. In ways you may one day appreciate, I may even be doing you a favour. Come here...' the beginnings of a smile ghosted across her face '... please.'

Schultz stepped towards her. From the depths of the house came the tolling of the big old grandfather clock she'd stationed at the head of the stairs.

'Well?'

Schultz waited for silence to return.

'By the end of next week,' he offered the ghost of a smile. 'But I never told you that.'

*

The German Embassy was a brisk forty-minute walk away, a handsome assortment of stately rooms looking onto a paved courtyard off rue de Lille. The ambassador, Johannes von Welczeck, had been in post for more than three years now, a turbulent passage in French politics that had given Schultz an intimate working knowledge of the city. Thanks partly to von Welczeck, he knew where the power lay, which members of the right might respond to a lunch or two, and where best to drop invitations when one or other of Berlin's tribal chiefs decided to pay the City of Light a lingering visit.

Odile routinely mixed in company like this, agreeing that most of her friends belonged to what she called *Le Faubourg*, the topmost slice of the Parisian social scene. The resulting conversations, fathered by Schultz, had fattened the files that he stored in the embassy's tiny office reserved for the *Abwehr*, as well as delighting Odile. Schultz knew she boasted about her reach when it came to contacts at the very top of the Third Reich, though he was careful to quash rumours along the Wilhelmstrasse that this striking grass widow had become his lover. I'm rough trade, he'd protest, no manners, no breeding. I brawled. I chased Communists, and some of them I had the pleasure of killing. Whatever talents I might have belong on the streets, not in some fancy boudoir. Wrong, would come the response. That's exactly why women like her can't get enough of you.

Was it true? Making his way back into the embassy, Schultz had decided the answer was probably yes. In truth there was a great deal more to him than met the eye but most of the senior Nazis had their heads up their arses and rarely bothered to take a proper look at creatures as lowly as mere *Abwehr* officers. As for Odile, given their last encounter, he no longer trusted his own judgement.

'You've heard?' Von Welczeck had emerged from an office near the foot of the stairs. He was carrying two cardboard boxes, both empty, and he was looking harassed, his normal composure gone. To Schultz's certain knowledge, the ambassador had spent the past few weeks quietly trying to frustrate the efforts of Britain and France to make their own accommodation with the Soviets, and to see him in a state like this was frankly baffling.

'We've won, haven't we?' Schultz gestured out towards the street. 'We've got these people exactly where we want them. They've pledged to go to war for the bloody Poles but forgot to tell the army. Same with the British. It's a long way to Danzig from Dover.'

'True. But we have to be back in the Reich within days. All of us. Plus everything we can pack in time.' He tossed Schultz one of the cardboard boxes. 'Can you imagine what that's going to entail?'

Schultz slept in a spacious third-floor room in the Hôtel Lutetia, overlooking the busy intersection of Boulevard Raspail and rue de Sèvres. After a difficult winter, he'd grown to love the classy extravagance of the Art Nouveau façades, and a fruitful rapport with the maître d' in the main restaurant had given him bigger than usual helpings of his favourite beef filet with an extra spicy pepper sauce. The maître d's name was Didier, and in return Schultz occasionally fed him harmless titbits of gossip from the higher reaches of the Third Reich.

Now, after a brisk walk from the embassy, he took the lift to the second floor and put a call through to Berlin from the privacy of his room. At this time in the early evening, the *Abwehr* offices in the Bendlerstrasse complex would be beginning to empty but it was mere seconds before a voice answered. Niemayer, he thought, the irreverent young Saxon with a taste for Moabit bars and gipsy music. Much to Schultz's surprise, they'd become good friends.

Calls from Paris were allegedly monitored. Schultz had long ago concluded that the French intelligence services were indolent and generally useless, but just now was no time to take chances.

'Me,' he grunted. 'Busy?'

'What do you think?' Niemayer was laughing.

'That apartment of mine. You've still got the key?'

'Better than that, I'm living there.'

'Good to know. Soon, eh?'

Schultz put the phone down. Life among the Berlin ministries was a permanent gunfight and young Niemayer was quick on the draw. He'd understand exactly the message that Schultz had just passed. 'Case White' is about to be actioned. Expect war in a matter of days.

Now, while he still had time, Schultz needed to check through the list of key contacts he'd acquired over the busy months he'd been in Paris. He kept it in the inside pocket of his jacket and he fetched it out now.

Some of these people he'd disinterred from the weeds of the Third Republic, right-wing politicians mostly, Jew-hating fanatics equally keen to put the Communists against the wall. One recent lunchtime conversation at the Ritz Schultz remembered particularly well. His guest on this occasion wasn't a politician but an aristocrat in his early sixties who belonged to one of the two hundred families which were said to run France. He'd lost an eye at Verdun during the last war and had spent a year and a half as a prisoner on the other side of the Rhine where, among other things, he'd learned a little German. His black eye patch gave him a slightly piratical air, and his admiration for

Général Pétain, the victor at Verdun, was both passionate and unfeigned – as were his views on the France that had emerged from the war.

The spine of the country, he told Schultz, had been broken. Its *esprit*, its fighting spirit, had gone. Paralysed and gutless, today's France was meekly awaiting the arrival of whichever of Hitler's armies decided to put it out of its misery.

'We're wasting our time and we're wasting our money, Herr Schultz,' he'd produced an enormous iron key and pushed it across the tablecloth. 'The wretched thing turns to the right. Give the door a kick or two and help yourself.'

That image, and the memory of the brief conversation which followed, had stayed with Schultz ever since. It spoke of an entitled sense of impatience and despair, a conviction that the nation's future – thanks to decades lost to numberless socialist fantasies – now lay in other hands. The true France, the real France, the old France was far from lost but what it needed was *une rénouvellement*.

'You mean a kick up its skinny arse?' Schultz had enquired.

'Exactly.'

'Administered by whom?'

'Good question, my friend. Are you offering?'

The answer, of course, was yes. Not just to Schultz's titled lunchtime guest but to dozens of other wealthy malcontents beached by what they regarded as the shabby decade now drawing to an end. Most had fortunes to protect. Some talked wearily of moving abroad, maybe to Algeria or Morocco or even Senegal. A handful half closed their eyes and murmured dreamily of *notre patrimoine nationale*. It had been Schultz's job to nod along to this yearning for renewal, for discipline and a return to the old virtues, but no appeal to the national heritage could hide these conversations from the brutal realities of German might and German destiny. One day you'll come for us, Didier the maître d' had confided recently. And we'll have no one to blame but ourselves.

It was that same Didier, oddly enough, who now tapped softly on Schultz's door and handed him an envelope. Schultz studied it briefly, recognising the familiar capital letters. It bore no stamp.

'This was hand-delivered?'

'Yes.'

'By whom?'

'Madame Odile Lescaut.'

'How do you know?'

'She left a message with the receptionist.'

'For?'

'You, Herr Schultz. She said not to worry about a costume. Everything would be taken care of.'

'*Costume?*'

Didier shrugged, said he had no idea, and then departed down the corridor. Schultz opened the envelope. Inside was an embossed invitation to something called *Le Dernier Bal Masqué*. It was to take place the following evening, Thursday 31 August, at 7, rue de la Faisanderie. Costumes were *obligatoires*.

Schultz read the card a second time. The address belonged to Odile, as did the slightly peremptory tone she'd adopted. In the light of their last exchange, he sensed that this wasn't an invitation but a summons. Then his eye was drawn again to the invitation's bottom line. *Costumes*, he thought. Plural. His own, according to Didier, had been pre-selected. How many of them was he expected to wear during the evening? And what clues might they hold to whatever had sparked this initiative of Odile's in the first place? To neither question did he have an answer and then his gaze settled on another word. *Masqué*. Masked. He stared at it and for a long moment he was back in the meadow gazing through his binoculars at the *Ouvrage* Molvange.

Everything in life, he was fast concluding, boiled down to fortification, to camouflage, to sleights of hand, to face coverings, anything – in short – to keep the real world at arm's length. As Europe plunged towards yet another war, you might be wise to become someone else. Either that, or you hunkered down behind metres and metres of poured concrete and prayed to God that the enemy would die of boredom after months of fruitless siege.

Fat chance, Schultz thought, remembering the *ouvrage* again.

*

Schultz made contact with Odile the following morning. In the background, on the phone, he could hear the noise of hammering and when he asked her what was going on, she told him she needed the house to be opened up once again.

'All of it?'

'Of course. Where am I to put a hundred guests?'

What this might entail Schultz hadn't the time to ask. Berlin had ordered the embassy to be ready to leave Paris by midnight, and every corridor had become an obstacle course of filing cabinets, boxes, pictures and maps too big to pack, plus assorted personal luggage. There was still a mountain of unfinished tasks to negotiate and all he wanted from Odile was advice on what time to arrive. Unlike every other guest, he'd still be wearing civilian clothes.

'Half past seven,' she said briskly. 'I'm expecting nobody until eight.'

'And the first of the costumes?'

'For you there's only one,' Schultz caught a bark of laughter. 'And you'll adore it.'

The rest of the day passed in a blur of last-minute meetings to coordinate the imminent evacuation, whatever shape it might take. Schultz put two calls through to Niemayer, trying to steal advance *Abwehr* intelligence on the movement of *Wehrmacht* units poised to fall on Danzig, but on both occasions he got a strange buzzing noise on the line. This in itself was unusual, indicating a total shutting down of normal communications, a sure confirmation, thought Schultz, that 'Case White' was already underway.

This he was able to confirm at a brief private meeting with the ambassador just minutes before he left the embassy for the masked ball. He'd been obliged to share Odile's invitation with von Welczeck, pointing out that it might be the last opportunity to have a serious conversation or two. These were people from the wealthiest corners of the capital, he'd said. Overwhelmingly, they were anti-war, chiefly because war would be the enemy of the share dividends on which they lived, and of the many other blessings that came with membership of *Le Faubourg*. They regarded the pledge to stand alongside Poland as a clever piece of trickery on behalf of the British, who would doubtless defend Warsaw to the last Frenchman. Should war come, and should the Germans find themselves one day back in Paris, then every extra friend that Schultz could make might prove invaluable.

At first, von Welczeck's instinct was to say no. He had the neatest of minds and he was wedded to the minute-by-minute evacuation schedule that his staff had drawn up, and he was determined that his entire embassy would retreat back to Berlin in perfect lockstep. When Schultz pointed out that this might not be possible, that the train or the convoy might have to leave without him, the ambassador pulled a face. At this, Schultz stepped a little closer. Von Welczeck was sleeping badly and it showed.

'You think I can't look after myself, Herr Ambassador? Find somewhere to get my head down?'

'Not at all, Schultz. Madame Lescaut? Your reputation goes before you.' He shrugged and put a thin, pale hand on Schultz's shoulder. 'Good luck. Next week in Berlin, *ja?*'

Schultz took a taxi to rue de la Faisanderie, arriving in time to watch a file of workmen leaving the hastily restored glories of Odile's *hôtel particulière*. She met him at the door. She was wearing a silk blouse in two shades of gold, gathered loosely at the neck, with a pair of blue pantaloons beneath. A black mask studded with diamonds hung from the scarlet sash that encircled her waist, and lipstick, that same rich crimson, added an even deeper bow to the fullness of her lips.

'You're a sailor?'

'I'm a gondolier. Finding Italian musicians isn't as easy as it should be in this city, not under circumstances like these, but friends and money certainly help. Think of Venice, Schultz. We had plans to go there, remember?'

Schultz nodded. It was true. Not just for a week, not even a month, but for a great deal longer. Venice, the city of a thousand mysteries. Venice, the city of Thomas Mann. Schultz had never made much room for love in his life, but even mention of Venice returned him to an earlier, earthier Odile.

'Blame that Ribbentrop,' as ever, Odile could read his mind. 'Blame Molotov. Blame that dwarf Goebbels. You're in bed with the wrong people, Schultz. Venice would have been lovely. Time and opportunity and all those views. Such a pity, eh?'

Schultz could only nod. Beyond the open front door, liveried servants were disappearing towards the big dining room with laden trays. From somewhere deeper in the house came a shimmer of strings and then a long caress from a French horn as Odile's band slipped into a Strauss waltz. The changes of tempo were playful, languor one moment, excitement the next, every expectation challenged and then rechallenged before the music came to a sudden halt, smothered by peals of laughter.

As an overture to possibly a major war, thought Schultz, this took some beating. Had the ball before the Battle of Waterloo struck the same note? Were the English and the French in love with the prospect of a glorious death? Could even music like this soften the violence to come? Somehow, he doubted it, and in any case, the view from Berlin had always been more businesslike. War, most veterans of the trenches agreed, always wrote its own script, and the butcher's bill was the only tally that really mattered.

'Are you coming in?'

Schultz followed Odile into the house. There were decorations everywhere, tricolour-themed, wild explosions of red, white and blue in whorls of silk, and in artfully arranged floral displays: scarlet roses entwined with cornflowers and something delicate and white that Schultz didn't recognise.

'Gypsophila,' Odile again. 'They told me it was impossible to find and they were wrong. They tried to sell me lilies but who wants to dance to the smell of death?'

Who indeed, thought Schultz. They were on the first of the landings by now, and he paused to admire a larger-than-life mannequin posing as Marianne. The keeper of the Republican soul was dressed as a Napoleonic *poilu* of the *Grande Armée*, one of the tens of thousands the great Bonaparte had led across Europe and into the vastness of Russia to cement the glories of the Revolution. Schultz stared briefly at the blue coat, the red-piped collar and cuffs, and the black felt bicorne hat, then reached out and touched the musket with its long blade.

'It's all real, Schultz. But then you'd know that, in your trade.'

'You did all this?'

'I paid for it. Come...'

A second flight of stairs took them to yet another landing. This time, the mannequin was smaller, another woman. She was dressed in rough fustian, wooden clogs on her tiny feet, and might have stepped in from the fields or the cowshed. Someone seriously talented had been at work on the disk of pink that served as her face, and beneath the tangle of dirty hair, Schultz found himself looking at an outdoor face, brightened by eyes that never left his.

'One clue, Schultz.' Odile seemed amused. 'She hated the English.'

'Very wise.'

'I want a name, Schultz. You think this is some kind of joke? Or have I been right all along about you Germans?'

'That we know nothing?'

'That you have no time for history. That for all your glorious music, you have no *soul*.'

Schultz stared at the face a moment longer, then made space for a passing waiter.

'Joan of Arc,' the waiter muttered. 'My wife did the face.'

Schultz turned to grunt his thanks but the man was already halfway down the stairs, carefully balancing his tray of empty glasses on his shoulder. Odile, meanwhile, was disappearing into a neighbouring room. Schultz joined her, aware of the musicians beginning to play again, different tune, different mood, sombre, a hint of darkness before a woman began to sing, her voice low, rich with melancholy. Schultz had heard this music before in the bars of Lisbon. The Portuguese called it *fado*, the music of fate, of longing, of despair.

'What do you think, Herr *Major*?'

Schultz found himself staring at a uniform carefully laid out on a double bed. Ten years ago, it might have belonged to him:

the brown denim shirt, carefully ironed, the corded shoulder boards, the brown kepi, the jodhpur trousers to be tucked into the gleaming knee-high boots, the swastika worn on the left arm.

'Just one thing wrong,' he stepped across to the bed and fingered the four pips on the collar. 'You've made me an *Obersturmbannführer*. I never got past *Sturmbannführer*.'

'A promotion, Schultz. I suggest the phrase is thank you.'

'But you want me to wear this?'

'I do.'

'All night?'

'Of course. The women, especially, will love you.' She tapped her watch. 'Fifteen minutes, Schultz. The SA, as I understand it, were always on time.'

The SA, the *Sturmabteilung*, were Ernst Röhm's hooligan brawlers who'd spent the twenties bossing the streets of city after city in their bid to keep the Reich out of the hands of the Communists. Schultz himself had signed up because he was bored, because he loved a fight, because he was good at breaking heads, but over the busy years that followed, the spilling of so much blood had begun to disgust him, and the more he saw of the Nazi tribal chiefs, the less he liked them.

In the end, the year after Hitler grabbed the Chancellorship, a saviour appeared in the shape of a senior *Wehrmacht* General, the stern-faced Gerd von Rundstedt. It had been Schultz's task to protect him at a potentially violent party rally down in Munich, and afterwards they'd shared a beer. Within a month, Schultz had traded the itchy brown shirt of the SA for the muted grey-green of the *Abwehr*, and since then, his prospects had brightened immeasurably. To join military intelligence meant you had a brain in your head, and no one accused you of cowardice for using it.

'There's a dressing room next door,' this from Odile. 'Plenty of mirrors, *ja*?'

She left the bedroom. Schultz stepped towards the bed and gazed down at the spread of the uniform. It looked the right size, and there were even faint scuff marks beneath the polish on the toes of the boots suggesting they'd once been used in anger. He'd bent to finger the brown shirt. The first time he'd worn a garment like this was mid-winter in a rough Berlin suburb when a mob of Communists were rumoured to be on the march. The SA officer in charge had mustered a group of maybe a couple of dozen to take them on, a mere handful if the rumours were true. Bottles of schnapps had circulated and they'd set off to hunt down the Reds. Looking back, this pathetic little expedition had all the makings of a disaster but when they heard a growl of applause and rounded a corner to find the speaker roaring Bolshevik nonsense they lost no time in laying into the huge crowd.

The odds were hopeless but none of that seemed to matter. They were comrades-in-arms. They'd come to strike a blow for the Germany that had been betrayed. Most of them were drunk. They carried hardwood nightsticks, clubs, empty schnapps bottles. One or two of the older men, from the same boxing club, wore knuckledusters. Schultz was no stranger to violence, but this was bloodshed on a dizzying scale. He remembered the splintering crack of teak against bone, the fear on a man's face when he fell beneath a volley of blows, trying to shield his head and groin from the blur of boots, the taste of blood in his own mouth when a thin, spotty youth landed a lucky shot. The rally disrupted, bodies prostrate on the freezing cobbles, Schultz and his mates retreated in goodish order and got properly drunk in a bar they trusted. It had been, everyone noisily agreed, *fantastisch*.

Schultz slipped out of his suit and tried the shirt. A perfect fit. Next, he pulled on the jodhpur trousers, tightened the leather belt and reached for the boots. A little tight, perhaps, but nothing that wouldn't surrender to the evening's revels. Straightening his back, pushing out his chest, his right hand reached at once for the swastika armband. It felt familiar beneath his fingertips. He slipped it onto his left arm, pushing it up beyond his elbow and then taking some care to make the final adjustments. It was a buried reflex, an automatic check that put a ghost of a smile on his face. Even now, a decade later, he couldn't escape the insanity of those Berlin nights.

Just the kepi to go. Next door, in the dressing room, there were mirrors. Now he needed to re-meet this figure from his past, renew the old acquaintance, make sure that the intervening years hadn't betrayed him. The door to the dressing room was half ajar, and the moment he stepped in, the light from the bedroom fell on a full-length mirror. Schultz paused, staring at this familiar stranger, then put the kepi on, tightened the big belt a notch, and finally threw himself a derisive *Heil Hitler*. It was done. He was a Brownshirt again, a seasoned brawler. Clever Odile.

'Impressive.'

Schultz froze. A hooded figure was sitting in deep shadow in the corner of the room. Schultz stared at him for a long moment, wondering whether he was looking at a ghost, then he found the light switch on the wall. The figure in the chair was trying to smile. Gaunt face. Early middle age. Hints of someone vulnerable inside.

'I'm a Benedictine, Herr Schultz,' he gestured down at the black robe, then fingered what looked like a prop from a theatre set. 'And this is unglazed terracotta. Holds half a litre. The monks favoured water but a night like this...' He shrugged, holding out the mug. 'Help yourself.'

'You've been watching me?'

'I have.'

'Who put you here?'

'Our Odile. She thinks we might become friends.'

'Why would she think that?'

The smile at last widened. On his lap was a small artist's sketchpad.

'You want to take a look? It's rough, I know, but under the circumstances...' He shrugged again. 'My name's Gasquet. But you can call me Lucien.'

Schultz couldn't remember the last time he'd been cornered like this. Survival was his trade. You covered every angle, anticipated every surprise, let no one close. Yet here he was, dressed as a pantomime thug, talking nonsense to a Benedictine monk.

He took the sketch. A handful of pencilled lines had caught him semi-naked beside the bed. It was very accomplished, better than any mirror: the breadth of his shoulders, the depth of his chest, the first signs of a belly above the heavily muscled thighs.

'It's yours. It's a present, a token of my regard. You're a handsome man, Herr Schultz, as Odile promised. Keep it. Frame it. Check yourself out from time to time.'

'You do this for a living?'

'I do lots for a living. I'm a child of the theatre. I write. I direct. I make mischief. Please...' He offered the sketch again but Schultz shook his head and settled for the terracotta mug. One sniff told him it was grappa.

'Venetian brandy, Herr Schultz. Odile can be more than difficult but she gets the little details right. On a night like this, believe me, that matters. Will it be war in the morning, Herr Schultz? You against me? Or will we both be spared for something better? Kinder?' He smiled. 'More intimate?'

Schultz, who recognised a proposition when it was offered, said he didn't know, hadn't the first idea. The grappa had burned its way down to his belly and at once he felt a great deal more relaxed, more mellow, less angry at himself, at letting his guard down like this. Everything Odile did had a purpose. So where did this bizarre figure fit in?

Schultz fetched another chair from the bedroom, made himself comfortable. He wanted to know what had possessed this man to dress up as a monk.

'You know anything about a painter called Caspar David Friedrich?' Gasquet asked. 'German Romantic? Beginning of the last century?'

'Nothing,' Schultz gestured at his own uniform. 'I'm trouble on the streets. I'm beer and bloodshed. Picture galleries are for the dead and the nearly-dead. Caspar David who?'

'Friedrich. He did a picture he called *The Monk by the Sea*. All he gives us is a tiny little figure in the biggest, emptiest landscape you can ever imagine, nothing but ocean and sky and just a hint of clifftop. People hated it. And they hated it because they couldn't understand it.'

'So what did it mean? What was it about?'

'You, Herr Schultz. And me. And all of us. In the huge void, in the huge otherness, we're nothing. That's what this tiny speck of a monk signifies. Some people are baffled. Others are frightened. You, I suspect, would understand.'

'Why do you say that?'

'Because Odile assured me it was true. She says you still pretend to be the hooligan you're not. She also says you're a quick study.'

'In what regard?'

'Is that a serious question? When we're talking about *Odile*?'

Schultz held his gaze for a moment, then shook his head. Sex, he thought. The woman was obsessed.

'Then I'm flattered,' he muttered. 'What else did she tell you?'

'She told me you often play the dog.'

'Dog?'

'Sniffing around those forts of ours. Marking your territory. Leaving all that German scent. Might I ask you a question, Herr Schultz? One combatant to another? Will the Maginot Line do the job?'

'I'm afraid not. It was built for the wrong war.'

'Meaning?'

'Meaning there are ways round it. That's why God invented maps, Monsieur Gasquet. A man of the cloth, I'm surprised you need telling.'

Gasquet at last struggled to his feet, smoothing the wrinkles from his robe. A leather purse and a pair of iron keys hung from the knotted white rope around his slender waist, and once he was able to get a proper look at the face inside the cowl, Schultz realised he was older than he'd thought. Mid-forties. Maybe even more. He sensed that this man was serious about a proposition, about locking the door and going to bed and keeping the rest of the party at arm's length. His very presence in the dressing room told Schultz that he was reckless, as well as greedy for a new conquest, but it was maybe the uniform that stayed his hand. Ironic, Schultz thought, that a brown shirt and a pair of shiny boots can save me the trouble of keeping my arse to myself.

'One more thing about *The Monk by the Sea*,' Gasquet's coy smile suggested he was sharing an intimacy. 'People said it took your eyelids away. Why? Because Friedrich gives you no perspective, no way into the picture, none of those little tricks to make you feel better about the world. Understand the big nothing and you understand there's nowhere to hide. Ever.' He paused. 'Could you live with a painting like that on your walls? *Could* you, Herr Schultz?'

Schultz reflected on the question for a moment or two, wondering why it seemed so urgent, and then nodded.

'Yes,' he said. 'I could.'

'Excellent. That means you're a listener, Herr Schultz, which makes you very rare indeed.'

'Because I'm a German?'

'Because you're a man,' Gasquet smiled again and stepped a little closer. 'Are you telling me no, Herr Schultz?' He pulled a face. 'Because that would be a waste, as well as a shame.'

Schultz held his ground. Ten years ago, he'd have beaten this man to a pulp. Now, he said he was glad of his brief company, and meant it. Maybe later in the evening they could get together, attack the grappa again, have a serious chat about Caspar David Friedrich, but in the meantime he had a million people to meet, all of them – like the Maginot Line – heavily camouflaged.

Gasquet nodded, not bothering to hide his disappointment. Then he laid a thin hand on Schultz's arm.

'Odile was right.' He'd visibly brightened. 'Dressed like that, this party is yours for the taking.'

*

And it was. By now, dozens of guests had appeared and most of them had lifted their costume ideas from childhood or travels abroad. There were lots of Pierrots, and circus clowns, and other troupes of wandering players, and as well – much to the musicians' delight – gust after gust of the Venice Carnivale pushed in through the big front doors: chalk-white faces with blackened eyes beneath extravagant hats, dresses heavy with brocade, plunging necklines full of later promise, vast skirts worn centimetres above the ankle, and everywhere there were masks.

A lot of these people, thought Schultz, must know each other so intimately that nothing can disguise their real identity. Couples met and re-met on the wide sweep of staircase, or in the space cleared for dancing, or they swooped on the laden tables for another glass of champagne, a second scoop of caviar. With conversation and gossip went laughter, at first playful, later anything but. Odile's Paris, the Paris of *Le Faubourg*, the Paris of limitless wealth and limitless appetite, had come to forget the approaching war. Danzig, one woman told Schultz, sounded like a disease, something scrofulous and deeply unpleasant you'd do your best to avoid. Who on earth wanted to fight the Germans again? Especially when dressed like the divine Schultz?

Conversations like these went on for hours. He bumped into them at every turn. Maskless, he was relying on his old gruff self, on his schoolboy French and heavy accent to woo the women and piss off the men. Odile was right, and so was Lucien Gasquet. For all the hours these women must have spent in front of the mirror, what really appealed to them was the rough, ungentle presence of someone from a very different corner of the world out there, someone for whom the word indelicate meant nothing, someone who demanded – and largely got – respect.

With one woman, though, it didn't work. Looking back, Schultz suspected she had to be Jewish. He'd been watching her for a while. Unlike the splashy extravagance that surrounded her, she favoured restraint. Her dress looked medieval, a dark green full-length top revealing a decorous fall of creamy silk beneath. At the table that served as one of the bars, she and her partner drank only water. They were often locked in conversation, their heads bowed. She was an attractive woman but there was an impatience, or perhaps irritation, when she shook her head at ceaseless invitations to dance. Shortly before midnight, when rumours of a fireworks display drew revellers towards the tall windows, Schultz met her face-to-face. She looked him up and down, and then took a tiny step forward and slapped his face. A woman nearby gasped. Two men roared with laughter. Someone else clapped. *Quel théâtre*, murmured his wife. Clever Odile.

Schultz fought the temptation to rub his cheek. His assailant hadn't been joking. Whatever she knew about the Brownshirts hadn't ended well.

The woman's partner was demanding an apology. His French was perfect but Schultz caught just a trace of a German accent.

'An apology from me, you mean?' Schultz enquired.

'Of course.'

'For what?'

'For everything. For the whole damn shame of it. Your country is a rat's nest. It's infested. My wife suspects you may have fleas.'

'And you share that belief, Monsieur?'

'Of course.'

'So would you like to repeat it?' Schultz nodded at the window. 'Outside perhaps?'

'To what end?'

'Excellent question, Monsieur. We Germans have our reputations to protect. I'll probably have to kill you.'

Another stir of laughter, more uneasy this time. Then the growing circle of spectators parted and Odile appeared. She took Schultz by the arm and led him towards the wide sweep of the staircase.

'Top floor,' she murmured. 'Third door on the left,' she was smiling. 'Guests of mine have forgotten their manners. Would you mind?'

With that, she was gone again. No explanation. No scold for upsetting her guests. Just, as ever, firm directions.

Schultz made his way up the staircase, aware of the attentions of the crowd below. Some of the women were pointing at him. Others were tugging at their partners' gaudy sleeves. Then came the first of the fireworks, the rat-tat-tat of an opening salvo that offered the darkest promise for the days and nights to come, and the garden outside was suddenly flooded with light from the huge starburst that followed.

Glad to be alone again, Schultz finally made it to the top floor, pausing at the balustrade to peer down. He'd had a comfortable amount to drink, he knew that. He'd done his best to follow what he imagined might be Odile's script, to charm the ladies and unnerve the men. This, in its way, had been a pleasure, playing a role he thought he'd abandoned forever, but now the sheer press of wealth and privilege had begun to sicken him.

These people live in a world of their own, he told himself. Whatever happens tomorrow, and over the weeks and months to come, they'll doubtless survive. Because money, real money, is weightless. It's a passport to do exactly as you please, to whomever you please, and dismiss the consequences. He shrugged, aware that this put him among the hated Communists, but the prickle of outrage thickened into disgust and by the time he paused on the top corridor, counting the doors that receded towards the window at the end, he was debating whether to bring this bizarre evening to a halt, to abandon whatever mission Odile had in mind and simply leave. Tomorrow, God knows, would be busy enough. Did he really need yet more complications?

Then came a scream, quickly stifled. Schultz stopped, listened. The third door on the left was barely metres away. He paused. He could hear movement inside, footsteps, whispered conversation, something urgent, then another scream – muted this time – followed by laughter.

Schultz tried the door. The merest pressure told him it was locked. He took a step backwards, then raised a leg and kicked savagely at the door jamb. The heel of his boot splintered the wood and he felt a hot surge of satisfaction as the door swung open. Frontal assault, he thought. Never fails.

Inside was a bedroom. A figure he recognised lay sprawled face-down on the bed. The black Benedictine habit was rolled up to his waist, and a small mountain of pillows had hoisted his white arse. His legs were spread, one costumed man on each, and two others, both dressed as bishops, held his arms. Between his legs, another figure was kneeling on the counterpane, dressed as a cartoon nurse. The champagne bottle was halfway up Gasquet's arse and there was fresh blood everywhere, scarlet against the whiteness of his hairless thighs.

The nurse was looking round and Schultz realised he'd seen this man before, earlier in the evening when he'd been a tournament jouster, freshly muddied from the lists. An hour later his chest was overpadded, and his swarthy face was thick with rouge, but he hadn't bothered to shave off his moustache and greying goatee. Now, he pulled the bottle out, seized it by the crudely broken neck, and then lunged at this uninvited stranger. Schultz feinted to the left to catch him off-balance and kicked him hard in the groin. He folded at once, gasping with pain, curling on the floor at the foot of the bed with one bloodied hand half raised in surrender as Schultz set about him. One of the other men tried to come to his aid. Schultz shot him a look and told him he was next. An exchange of glances, and the room was suddenly empty.

Schultz hadn't finished. It took him barely thirty seconds to kick the man to death, blows and stamps to the head mainly, and afterwards he felt a whole lot better. Then he helped Gasquet off the bed, mopping his bloodied thighs with a towel from the neighbouring bathroom. The man was whimpering with pain now. Coaxing him towards the door was impossible, and in the end, Schultz slung the thin body of the Benedictine monk over his shoulder, his trophy good deed for the evening, and made his way back down the corridor. By now, the fireworks display had come to an end, and Odile's guests were treated to a fresh entertainment as Schultz stepped carefully downstairs. The nearest hospital, he knew, was barely a kilometre away.

As he reached the ground floor, he met a surge of applause. This was more theatre. This was yet another of Odile's amazing party tricks. Who better to kidnap a man of God than an SA brawler? The first man Schultz met face-to-face was staring at the trail of blood that patterned the bottom staircase.

'Last rites?' he enquired.

Schultz pushed past him, then paused and turned round.

'You've a car outside?'

'I have, yes.'

'Then come with me.'

'I might not want to.'

'You have no choice, my friend. When you get back, you might take a look upstairs. Top floor. Third door on the left.'

The man turned towards his wife, looking for any excuse for this sudden nightmare to end, but Schultz drew him back again. The uniform, he realised, gave him real authority.

'Talk to those musicians,' he was looking at the wife this time. 'We need a change of mood. Tell them *fado* might be good.'

5

Three days later, with dawn at the window, George Hogan was awoken at his hostel in Toronto by a double knock at the door. When he finally managed to unbolt it, a messenger from Western Union handed him a telegram. *Chamberlain has just declared war on Germany*, it read. *We conference at nine o'clock.*

We?

As the messenger clattered away down the stairs, Hogan read the telegram a second time, fighting a rising tide of excitement. This could only have come from Mrs Mahindra, the newly arrived replacement for the old curmudgeon everyone knew as the Despatcher. In barely a week, in a man's world, she'd turned everything in the newsroom upside down. Hogan knew this because many of the older hands had told him so. They said she was decisive, and brave, and full of bold ideas, and in the light of this sudden outbreak of editorial enthusiasm Hogan's only regret was his own absence from the third-floor newsroom where she held court. After her applause for his piece about the Royals' exercise, he'd been half expecting a place of his own at the hallowed table, but so far it hadn't happened. At least not yet.

Hogan glanced at his watch and began to get dressed. Today was Sunday, and in the light of Mrs Mahindra's abrupt summons, Hogan knew he had a problem. For longer than he cared to remember, he'd been a staunch Baptist. The calling had been part of his early youth, an obligation that his implacable mother had laid on all her unruly brood. Full immersion, at her insistence, had awaited each of her children on their eighth birthday, and in this respect Hogan had been less than lucky. He'd been born in early February and memories of his baptismal dunking in the Miramichi River, still choked with rafts of drift ice, would never leave him. His mother had been waiting on the freezing pebble beach with the threadbare towel he'd always associated with high-summer swimming.

'Keep the faith,' she'd whispered fiercely as she rubbed him dry, 'and the Lord will watch over you.'

Since then, Hogan had rarely missed a Sunday service, sharing a bench with more and more of his siblings as they, too, became Baptists. At first it had felt like a chore, but skipping chapel was a risky business and would likely earn you a maternal tanning with a freshly cut switch from the willow at the bottom of the garden. In this respect, as in many others, his mother had been unforgiving but, as Hogan got older, the creed and a succession of Baptist ministers had begun to take the place of a father he'd barely known. More promising still, the Bible had become a source of real fascination.

Hogan had never doubted that life spoiled you for stories but here in its many New Testament incarnations was the best of them all. Only last week he'd been reading yet again about Golgotha, about the sheer indignity of ending your days hanging from a cross on a brimming rubbish tip outside the city walls, and his eagerness to imagine himself there, to turn those last six hours into an act of reportage, had sparked a long conversation with the minister in the downtown College Street chapel.

Since arriving in Toronto, Hogan had never missed attendance at the Sunday morning service. Today, though, had to be different.

Major European powers would soon be at each other's throats. Canadian bodies and Canadian blood would doubtless be on the line. Just now, just here, was his prime allegiance to his Maker? Or to Mrs Mahindra?

He was at the *Globe* offices in time to queue for a coffee. Every chair at the long table that dominated the newsroom was already taken, and when Mrs Mahindra appeared to call for order at one minute to nine, Hogan was obliged to remain standing. There followed a brisk volley of assignments for the senior hands in the newsroom: major interviews with federal spokesmen in various Ottawa ministries, plus special attention to what the French-speaking Quebecois might do. The emphasis here, Mrs Mahindra insisted, was the probable date when Canada might herself declare war. Canadians were prickly about their independence from London, but no one doubted for a moment that the country would follow English armies into battle. The only real question that mattered was when.

Heads nodded round the table and there followed a series of what Mrs Mahindra termed 'second-order issues'. They had to do with food supplies, with the defence of Canadian territorial waters and airspace, and with the likely need to ship vast quantities of food to the motherland, should German U-boats try and enforce a blockade. From the edges of this charmed circle of *Globe and Mail* insiders, Hogan could only marvel at his luck. Not only was he watching history in the making but, in the shape of Mrs Mahindra, the paper truly appeared to have stumbled on someone uniquely able to rise to the occasion.

She was brisk, organised and astonishingly well informed. She wore the same sharp grey jacket and skirt over a white blouse and lifted her head from time to time to check faces around the table over the top of her black-framed glasses. Conversation after conversation over the last year had confirmed a prejudice against women at the higher levels of Canadian journalism, yet here was Mrs Mahindra – an *Indian* for mercy's sake – visibly impressing even the greyheads in the room.

She brought the meeting to a halt shortly after half past nine. To Hogan's disappointment, his name hadn't featured in the drum roll of assignments, and as journalists around the table reached for their telephones, he was thinking of maybe catching the end of the morning's service. The College Street chapel was a ten-minute walk away. No one would notice if he crept in at the back and found an empty bench. Then, from nowhere, came the lightest pressure on his arm. Mrs Mahindra. She had an armful of papers, and her glasses now hung from a black cord around her neck.

'This way?'

Hogan followed her through the mill of journalists eager for more coffee, and heads turned to watch as she led him into an empty office and closed the door.

'I had a call from London about an hour ago.' She hadn't bothered to sit down.

'About what?'

'You, George. I took the liberty of sending them your piece about the Royals.'

'Them?'

'A gentleman named Robinson. People in the know call him EJ. He runs the *Daily Express* on behalf of Lord Beaverbrook, whom I gather you've met. What EJ needs now is another piece to shed light on what fighting Canadians think about the prospect of war. It's a reasonable request, and one I'm glad to share. Two bites of the apple, George. One in London, and one here. By tomorrow morning, please. Nine o'clock again. No more than fifteen hundred words.'

She offered him what might have been a smile and stepped towards the door before briefly turning back.

'One other thing, George. Why are you living in a hostel? You need a telephone. If this thing turns out the way we all want it to, I'll be glad to help. OK?'

Hogan held her gaze. All he could manage was a nod. Then she was gone.

Fighting Canadians? Hogan knew exactly where he had to start. He stole back into the newsroom. More than a week after his visit to the lake to watch the Royals storming ashore, he still carried the number Larry Elder had given him. To fix a meeting, all he had to do was phone.

To his slight surprise, he found himself talking to a woman. She had a foreign accent and she appeared to be discomforted by a stranger's voice, but the conversation warmed the moment he mentioned Larry Elder.

'You know Larry?'

'A little, yes.' Hogan explained briefly about the excursion to the lake. He was a news reporter. He'd like them to meet again, in a café maybe. Could she pass a message?'

'No need,' she laughed. 'He's here with me.'

There was a silence on the phone, then the rasp of Elder's voice.

'You the guy I drove out to Kawartha Lakes?'

'I am, yeah.'

'Liked the piece, liked it a lot. You're not as dumb as you look.'

'Thanks.'

'I mean it. I even showed it to Juanita here.'

'And?'

'She loved the picture.'

It was Hogan's turn to laugh and when Elder asked why he'd called he said he needed help.

'What kind of help?'

'I need to lay hands on a fighting Canadian.'

'What the hell does that mean?'

'I guess someone with combat experience, someone who's been in a war, someone happy to talk about it.'

'You mean someone old? The last war? Vimy Ridge? First Canadian Division?'

'That might do it, though it might help to be younger. Either way, it has to be abroad.'

'You mean Europe?'

'Yep.'

'A live war? Frontline?'

'Yep.'

'Then that would be me.' Elder must have stepped away from the phone for a moment. Hogan could hear a brief murmur of conversation in the background. Then Elder was back again.

'Midday,' he gave Hogan an address. 'Juanita's cooking. Come for lunch.'

Hogan rode the streetcar to a stop five blocks from the address. It turned out to be a tall, brick-built property that must once have been a warehouse. Elder's directions took Hogan to a ground-floor unit at the rear of the building. Access from the street led into the gloom of an unlit corridor. Much to Hogan's surprise, it was newly swept and featured a vase brimming with wildflowers on the low table beside the numbered door. There was even the stub of a candle in a puddle of hardened wax.

His knock brought Elder to the door. Barefoot in the heat, he was wearing shorts and an Argonauts T-shirt. He peered down the corridor and then told Hogan to come in. At once, Hogan could smell garlic. Elder led him into a smallish room dominated by a stove, a kitchen sink and a table. The table had been laid for three, nothing but a knife and a fork each, plus thick glass mugs. After nearly a year at the hostel, Hogan felt instantly at home.

'This is Juanita. She's Spanish, from Teruel. Two reasons why she cooks the best tortilla you'll ever taste.'

Juanita turned briefly from the stove, brushing a wisp of greying hair from her face. She was a handsome woman, late middle age, sturdy, big-boned. She was wearing a plain black cotton dress which may once have belonged to someone else because it was a little tight round the waist and shoulders. When Hogan said hello, she simply nodded before returning to a pot of something green, bubbling on the stove.

On the wall above the table hung a huge black and red flag. The flag was torn in one corner and the whiteness of the wall showed through a neat line of holes across the middle.

'The flag of the anarchists,' this from Elder. 'A little souvenir from Barcelona.'

Hogan nodded. On the opposite wall were a couple of posters, creased and travel-stained. One of them featured a heroic bunch of crudely drawn riflemen defending a trench beneath the slogan *No Pasarán!*

'This was the Spanish Civil War?'

'Yeah.'

'But isn't there a law against Canadians fighting abroad?'

'Sure. There is. Coupla years back.'

'And you still went? Enlisted? Joined up?'

'I did. Little office on Spadina. Most of the guys were Finns and Ukrainians, plus a whole bunch of Commies. Some of them I still see from time to time. You can get a lot off your chest in a war, believe me. Especially if you survive.'

'But how come you took me out to the lake the other day? How come you're with the Royals? After breaking the law?'

'I'm not with the Royals. That was a favour for a pal. He's a Major, gets me to talk to the new guys from time to time, tell them the way it is, the way it feels when it's for real. The day I drove you out, the regular escort had gone sick.'

'This pal pays you?'

'He does. Coupla bucks from time to time. Nothing on paper.'

'But he's a serving officer?'

'Yeah, I just said.'

'And you're telling all this to *a journalist*?'

'Sure. And you know why? Because you want to hear the rest of it. Spain. Teruel. That shit fucking winter. The tens of thousands who ended up dead. You get it all, my friend, but I never told you. However you dress it up, whatever fancy tricks you play, that's your call. I'm just here to tell you the way it was.'

'I don't get to name you?'

'No fucking way.'

'So how do I know it's true?'

'You listen, my friend. And then you be the judge of what happens next.'

Hogan nodded. He was looking at Juanita again, trying to guess how much English she really understood.

'This man saved my life,' she didn't turn round. 'You should trust him completely.'

Elder was busy prising the top off a bottle of Rolling Rock.

'You gonna take one of these?' He licked a curl of spume from the open neck of the beer and offered it to Hogan.

'Water's fine.'

'You kidding me?'

'I don't drink. I think I mentioned it before.'

'*Never?*'

'Never.'

'That's gotta change,' Elder offered the bottle a second time. 'Just one for the Sabbath, comrade? Temptation for a thirsty man? Put that abstinence of yours to the sword?'

Again, Hogan said no. Elder, he was beginning to realise, didn't need a car to be in the driving seat.

'Mind if I sit down?' Hogan nodded at the table.

'Shit, no. This is where Juanita takes over. We're married, by the way. Meet Mrs Elder.'

The tortilla, as promised, was delicious, as was the mess of steamed chard that went with it. Hogan sorted through a list of adjectives and decided that only one of them did the meal justice.

'Unctuous?' Juanita was careful with the word, seeming to like it.

'Gooey,' Elder was wiping his plate with the heel from the cut loaf and lifted his head to gaze at Hogan. 'So where do you want to start? You're looking at a guy who's spent most of his life in the roughhouse. Some folks can live with the shit we make for ourselves but not me. Nothing turns out right without a fight. One moment me and a bunch of guys are making life tough for folks like that bum Kozminski. Next, I'm in the office at Spinosa lying about everything that might get me into even more trouble and volunteering to kill Fascists. Kozminski is a Fascist, too, but killing him would have been awkward. Sign up for Spain, and you can kill as many Kosminskis as you like, and maybe even get yourself a medal if it all works out. No contest, yeah? *No pasarán*, right? So we go to New York. We ship to France, we take the train south, we walk across the Pyrenees, and we report for duty.'

He lifted a huge clenched fist, ignoring a cautionary glance from his wife, then took a long pull at the bottle. Emmanuel Kozminski was a widely hated boss in the Toronto garment trade who chased union reps from his premises and gouged his workforce for every last cent. The *Globe*, according to Prentice, had once run a long campaign against him but to absolutely no effect.

'You went to Spain because of Kozminski?'

'I went to Spain because of justice. Nice idea in theory but when someone gives you a gun and a bunch of ammunition you figure it might make a difference.'

'And did it?'

'No way. But at least we tried, and I'm guessing that's what really mattered. Fifteenth International Brigade. Mackenzie-Papineau Battalion. Great bunch of guys. By the time we went to war I could order a beer in both Finnish and Ukrainian. Solidarity, right?' At this point, the plate pushed aside, his tone changed. He wanted Hogan to come with him as the Mackenzie-Paps found themselves alongside fellow crusaders in this war to the death. The training, he said, was a joke. If you were lucky – and most weren't – you got a blanket to go with the gun and the bullets, and even the elements of a uniform that might fit, and – most important of all – a pair of decent boots. You did a little practice shooting, but not too much because bullets were rationed, and so-called fucking instructors with not a day's combat experience between them listed ways the lie of the land could save your life. Dead ground. The cover of trees or rocks. A field of waving corn in high summer. Then, thanks to another of God's conjuring tricks, it was suddenly winter, and colder than a witch's tit, and you found yourself in the back of a broken-down old truck bucketing through the mountains to a town called Teruel.

'This was when?'

'Back last year. Coldest damn winter since whenever. If the Fascists didn't get you first, then you found the snowdrift of your dreams and never woke up. Either that, or you lost bits to frostbite.'

'Bits?'

'Noses were popular. Hands, feet, anywhere exposed. Your flesh dies, goes black, and the rot never stops. One of the Finnish guys compared it to capitalism. You lose a toe, then a foot, then the whole damn leg, and pretty soon there ain't one particle of you left. That wind in winter is pitiless. We had it bad because we were living rough.' He turned to Junita. '*Querida?*'

Hogan made a note of the word, meaning to check it later.

'Darling,' Juanita was looking at Hogan's pad. 'It means darling.'

Elder's wife-to-be, it turned out, had been struggling to survive while Franco's troops battled with the Republicans. Most of the time she lived in unheated basements, along with hundreds of others, getting colder and hungrier and more desperate by the day. The water had frozen in all the pipes and it was too dangerous to forage for wood for fires, and the children and the old were beginning to die. Somehow you got used to sleeping with the unburied and then came the day the Republicans stormed into the city and began to toss grenades down into the basement cellars.

'That's you?' Hogan was looking at Elder.

'Me. Sure. Because that's war. Happened that Juanita's little cave was spared. She spoke a little English. Her son was fighting with our guys. She hadn't seen him for months, thought he was dead. We found him fighting with the Army of the East. Fine boy. Handsome, like his mother.'

'So what happened?'

'In Teruel? The Republicans, that's us, had whipped the Fascists' sorry asses. Big mistake. Throw in a hundred thousand men, which is what we did, and you're never going to lose. By the time us Internationals arrived, mid-January, the Reps had killed all ten thousand of the Fascist bastards in Teruel, not a man left standing. What no one had figured was Franco, the Fascist leader. The guy's brave, sure, but he never got the big picture. He's a peasant at heart. What matters isn't blood, or even victory, but *tierra*, land, mother earth. What you have, you hold. And what you don't want are headlines telling the world someone's stolen what's yours. Teruel was a shitty little place, poor as hell. No one with a brain in his head cared a damn about it but it was the provincial capital and that mattered. And so Mr Franco put a bunch of armies together and blew the whistle, and after that we were as good as dead. They came from the north, down the river, and then they marched through the suburbs and this time we were the besieged. They threw tanks at us, and Italian heavy artillery, and we had the Condor boys for company during the day and believe me that's serious bombing. By now we'd run out of everything – most of all bullets – and that concentrates your mind. Some of us broke out before it got personal and the Fascists did a bit of extra killing, but many didn't. Last time I saw a Ukrainian he was on his knees in front of some Moroccan *Regulares* bastard who was about to shoot him. A sight like that you never forget. I knew the guy, loved him in a way, but I had no bullets left and without bullets you're a dead man. The war had turned to shit, like wars do.'

Hogan nodded. The sheer force of this account, so laconic, so ultra-violent, had shaken him. He still needed more detail, the small print of the nightmare that had been Teruel, but at this precise point he wanted to press Elder on two points.

'And the civilians?' he asked.

'Most of them were evacuated. Little New Year's Eve present. Two hours to leave with as much of your life as you can carry.'

'And Juanita?'

'She stayed. With me. Even carried a fucking rifle. Not that they worked good in that kinda cold.'

'And the point of it all? We're talking weeks? Months?'

'Two months. The town, like I say, had never been a picture postcard but there were fine buildings, and folks had scraped a life, and in summer it must have been OK, but by the time we'd gone, there was nothing left. I remember the day I first arrived and took a proper look at it. Even then the town felt a hostage to winter, and the mountains, and us, but after the Fascists came back a second time, and the pair of us had a proper go at the place, there was *nada*. All the decent buildings, they'd all gone. The battle was pointless from the start. All that violence led to nowhere but a bunch of rubble. That battle took a hundred and forty thousand killed and wounded. To the victor the bones? Until it happens in front of your eyes, you'd never believe it.'

Hogan scribbled himself yet another note, Elder's final thoughts rendered in faultless shorthand. For the sake of clarity, he read the quote back, unable to account for the smile that ghosted across his host's face.

'I've said something funny?'

'Not you, son. Me. It's not like I can ever change any of this shit. I can't. Neither can you. Neither can anyone. Write it down. Make sure you use it. Soldiers need to understand that, need to know exactly what kind of craziness they're heading into, but even that's a waste of breath. Shit happens. The next war has started already. One day soon we're going to miss that neat line of trenches where all that horrible stuff happened in the last war because this one will be knocking on your own front door.'

Another quote, even better. Material like this belongs on a tombstone, Hogan thought. What price civilisation? Or forbearance? Or good works? RIP.

Returning to the beginning of Larry Elder's war, he explored the experience a second time, trawling for those moments of perfect recall that badge the best and worst of times. The morning when the freshly arrived volunteers of the Mackenzie-Paps launched their assault uphill against the gun emplacements and steel tank traps of a defended position. How men bent double against the machine-gun fire and the gradient, against the smack of hot metal and the suck of gravity. How an awkward gallop slowed to a heavy climb uphill, bayonets fixed, every last sense attuned to the angry whine of passing bullets. How some men were hit. How some men fell. How some men died on the stony, unyielding earth before they'd had a chance to draw breath.

Moments like this, Elder muttered, taught you more than any goddam training course. The need for cover, for manoeuvre, for the blessings of a merciful God, and as well the need for those split-second decisions that become the one guarantee that you might survive until sunset, might see the dawn of another day. In the thick of battles like these, he said, nothing mattered except the need to kill. That, of course, was exactly what any General relied on. If you got to the enemy first and you killed enough of them, then you might – just – force him to his knees. After which, the peace would belong to someone else.

'Like who?'

'Like the fucking politicians. They spill the blood of others and you know what? They still fuck up.'

The blood of others. Yet another half-line of shorthand in Hogan's book. At last, his job done, he knew he'd arrived at the only remaining question that possibly mattered.

'So how do I know that any of this is true?' He put his pen down and closed his notebook.

'Whaddya mean?' For the first time since they'd met, Elder looked disturbed.

'I can't use your name. We can't run a photo. What you've told me is incredible, and that's a compliment. It happens that I believe every word but that's because I want to. I can make it work on the page, as well, but that's not the point. My boss is unforgiving. That's why she's my boss. I need collateral, I need to meet someone else who knows you well, someone who can tell me it's all true. Trust is a wonderful thing, Larry, but hey...' He gestured at his pad. 'Just a name, maybe?'

Elder didn't reply, not at once. Then he glanced at his watch and got to his feet, checking in his pocket for spare change. He said he had a call to make. Privacy demanded he use the call box across the street. Without waiting for an answer, he was gone and Hogan reached for his pad while the clump-clump of Elder's footsteps disappeared down the corridor.

'You really think he's lying?' Juanita's murmured question hung between them for a moment before Hogan shook his head.

'Not me. I believe him. But like I said, I have to be sure enough to convince others. I know it sounds silly but they're not betting on Larry, they're betting on me. You understand what I'm trying to say?'

Juanita nodded, said nothing. Then she got to her feet and left the room and Hogan heard her rummaging in some drawer or other before she reappeared with a single photograph. She placed it neatly beside Hogan's empty plate. She had some brandy. It was Spanish. Would he like a glass? Just a small one? Just a taste? For maybe a toast?

'A toast to who?'

'Him,' she nodded down at the face in the photo. Someone youngish, unshaven, maybe mid-twenties, maybe older. The smile seemed unforced and revealed an uneven line of teeth. He was wearing a beret of sorts, flat-topped, black, and the shot had been taken against a background of mountains cloaked by a gathering mist.

'My son,' she said. 'His name was Jaime.'

'Was?'

'He died at Teruel. He was one of the *Dynamatistas*. He carried bombs to throw at the Falangists. One of them blew him up.'

Hogan was staring at her. So calm, so matter-of-fact. Was it this loss that had led to her marriage to Elder? And had a new start, a new continent, bandaged the wound? These were questions he knew he should be asking but something drew him back. He looked at the photo again, declining the brandy. The young Jaime was Spanish, but from what little Hogan knew, a face like that could have belonged in any of the International Brigades, regardless of nationality. He was white, he carried the scars of winter fighting, he could use a little sleep and a decent meal. But, all too sadly, he was dead.

'I have an idea,' Hogan said at last. 'You might think this is crazy.'

'Tell me.'

'I'll be writing this article when I get back. I know they'll want a face to put with it.'

'Not Larry's.'

'Not Larry's.'

'So...' Her eyes settled on the photo. 'You think maybe...?'

'Jaime? I do, yes. But I'll need a little more about him...' he tapped his notebook '... for your son to become part of Larry's story.'

Juanita thought about the proposition for a moment or two and then gestured for Hogan to pick up his pen. For the next half-hour, without a single prompt, she talked about life in pre-

Civil War Teruel, how it had been for herself and her family, how her husband had been the first to die at the hands of the Falange, how her daughter had been raped and then killed before the battle for Teruel had even started, and how her son had joined the Republican Army of the East as a direct result. There followed a detailed, pitiless account of surviving those terrible months of winter, followed by the decision she'd had to take when the moment of evacuation arrived.

'I stayed,' she said. 'And it made me whole again.'

It was shortly after this that Elder returned from making his call. Outside, he said, was a green Buick. At the wheel was a close friend of his called O'Donovan. He was a Major with the Royals, the officer who'd put various assignments Elder's way. The two of them were close buddies. There was nothing Elder had told Hogan that O'Donovan didn't know already. If Hogan had the time and the inclination, he'd be happy to go through the story quote by quote. On the other hand, the pair of them might agree on a shortcut.

'Like?'

'Meet the guy. You'll like him. Shit knows...' a cold smile '... you might even trust him.'

And so Hogan said his farewells, pocketed the photo, and re-emerged into the clammy embrace of an early fall afternoon. A tall, slim figure in uniform was sitting, as promised, at the wheel of the Buick. When Hogan paused beside the open passenger door, he declined the invitation to get in. Instead, he asked for a card.

'You mean ID?'

'I mean a contact number.' Hogan paused. 'Though an ID might be useful, too.'

The ID was standard military issue. Major Frank O'Donovan, Royal Regiment of Canada. The card contained two phone numbers.

'The bottom one is best,' O'Donovan had the steadiest eyes Hogan could remember. 'You have a question for me?'

'Just one. Larry has told me about what happened in Spain. By midnight, I'll have written it up. You mind me giving you a call?'

'You mean tomorrow?'

'I mean midnight. Or maybe earlier if it goes as well as I think it might.'

Stooped beside the window, he held O'Donovan's gaze. Then the older man checked his watched, rubbed his long face, and shrugged.

'Strange times,' he said. 'Hell, why not?'

Hogan was back at the *Globe* within the hour. Sundays normally belonged to the handful of reporters who kept the paper going over the weekend but the outbreak of war had changed everything, and there was no space at the news desk. Mrs Mahindra appeared. She seemed to be thriving under the pressure of events.

'Well?'

Hogan gave her a brief account of the interview he'd just conducted. Punchy guy who fought with the Mackenzie-Paps. Terrific detail. Love interest in the shape of a Spanish wife he'd rescued from the carnage.

'You're telling me he brought her back?'

'Better than that. She cooked me lunch.'

'So how did he get her past Immigration?'

'They got married in Paris. She showed me the certificate. Neither of them would go into details but it obviously got them into the country. One problem, though. He doesn't want to be named. Or photographed. Otherwise the Mounties will be knocking on his door.'

'So what do we do? Anyone can invent a story like that. This is a newspaper, remember. Facts, George. Names, dates, details.'

Hogan nodded. He'd been expecting exactly this.

'Just give me an office,' he said. 'And let's see what happens.'

He worked solidly for nearly three hours, crouched over a typewriter in a borrowed office next to Mrs Mahindra. In mid-evening, she brought him a mug of coffee with a plate of cookies she'd found from somewhere, a gesture not lost on the scatter of reporters at the news desk. By now, Hogan had worked and reworked the story until it filled five and a half pages. There were still cuts to be made, emphasis and key quotes to be added, and he knew he needed a break before tackling the final paragraph, but to his relief she didn't demand a look before he was properly through. Instead, she said she had to get home.

'First thing tomorrow?' she asked. 'You'll be done by then?'

Hogan nodded, barely spared her a glance, said thanks for the cookies. After she'd gone, he had another read-through before making yet more changes. In essence, his plan had been simple. He'd used Elder's account of his baptism of fire at Teruel to plunge the *Globe*'s readers into the grimness of combat. This story had no room for heroism, or glory, or any of the other civilian fantasies about foreign wars. It was about a bunch of guys who'd arrived to fight for a cause, and one in particular who'd left with none of his preconceptions intact.

Thanks to the weather, and the unforgiving chemistry of high explosive, this unnamed, faceless volunteer had emerged from those winter months a meaner but a wiser man. He'd watched a working city demolished brick by brick, stone by stone, until nothing was left. He'd been witness to acts of violence large and small, atrocities wrought on women and children, and for none of them could he offer any rationale.

Teruel, in short, had been a terrible warning. Modern combat was brutal, unsparing and, above all, efficient. Men died in their tens of thousands. Neither the battlefield nor the basement left you anywhere to hide, and death was rarely anything but ugly. These were the cold facts, incontestable, the one legacy of a war the Mackenzie-Paps had lost. The taste of defeat was bitter but somehow you had to cope. All wars produced winners and losers, always had, always would. But at Teruel, something in civilisation had died, and from now on, in all likelihood, things could only get worse. We're Canucks, Elder had muttered towards the end of the interview. We know bad things happen, but never on a scale like this.

Hogan finished the last cookie and tried to wrestle the final paragraph to the mat but somehow it wouldn't happen. He knew at this point he needed a break, and so he gathered up his various drafts, slipped them into a folder, and took the streetcar back home, getting off several stops before the hostel to walk a little and clear his head.

An hour later, back in his room with his ancient second-hand Remington, he knew it was done. He sat back for a moment, rubbing his eyes, then gathered the final draft before hunting for dimes for the public phone on the corner of the street. It was nearly half past eleven. God willing, O'Donovan would still be up, still waiting.

'You're done?'

'I am, sir.'

'Is this going to take a while?'

'I've got thirty cents. If it's OK with you, sir, let's see how it goes.'

It was dark now, and Hogan began to read, following the lines of typescript with the help of a nearby streetlight. By the time he'd fed his last dime into the slot, he was barely at the top of page three.

'You've got a problem there, son?'

Hogan explained about running out of money. O'Donovan said he understood.

'It's a great read so far. Phone the operator. Reverse the charges. I'll pay for the rest of the call.'

The line went dead and Hogan stared at the phone a moment, swamped by something close to relief, then dialled zero. The operator re-established the line to O'Donovan, and Hogan began again at the top of page three. Ten minutes later, after a pause while he apologised to a woman patiently waiting to make a call, Elder's story was at an end.

'That's it?' O'Donovan wanted to know.

'That's it, sir. Finito. Curtains close.'

'And Larry didn't want to be named?'

'No, sir.'

'I'm not surprised.' There was a brief silence on the line. 'You've done a great job, son, and best of all is the way you've turned him into a kind of ghost. He could be anyone, any of those guys who shipped out there. That makes it all the more powerful. At least from where I'm sitting.'

'But you think it's all true?'

'I know it's all true.'

'How, sir? You mind me asking?'

'Not at all. Larry and I are close. I've met some of his buddies. Most of them were at Teruel, too, and all their stories match. In a court of law, I guess you'd call that corroboration. One other thing while you're there? Off the record?'

'Of course, sir.' Hogan was doing his best to ignore the woman outside.

'Larry has been fighting this battle for years. Way back, when we first met, he'd be at rally after rally, waving the flag, collecting for various causes. He was a Communist then.'

'No *pasarán*?'

'Exactly. But Larry being Larry took all this stuff to extremes. He was a decent boxer, light-middleweight, and he fought bare-knuckle, too, for serious stakes. One time, he killed a man. Turned out the guy already had a problem, but Larry didn't know that. But here's the thing. Every cent he earned in those fights went to the cause. It might be some housing issue. It might be medical care for folks with no money. It might be a pair of shoes for kids in winter. He's a good man, son. And you've done him ample justice.'

Hogan carried the thought back to the hostel. O'Donovan had suggested only one change, to the designation of a Fascist tank, and Hogan was happy to make it. The next morning, he rose early for a final read-through before taking the streetcar downtown. Mrs Mahindra was back in her office, the phone to her ear. Hogan left his final draft on her desk, along with Juanita's photo of her dead son, and then paid a visit to the big basement room that archived the *Globe*'s collective memory. The librarian in charge at weekends was a tall, spinsterly woman from the prairies who, it was rumoured, rarely saw daylight. She'd always had a soft spot for Hogan but when he asked her about bare-knuckle fighting back in the early thirties, she pursed her thin lips, then shook her head.

'You've got a name in mind?'

'Guy called Larry Elder. I think he may have killed someone.'

The librarian got up and went through a couple of drawers. None of the index cards helped with either bare-knuckle fighting or Larry Elder but she directed Hogan's attention to an older archive, in case he'd got the dates wrong. Hogan spent the next half-hour or so working slowly backwards through the late twenties but drew a blank. By the time he was back upstairs, Mrs Mahindra was off the phone.

'You've read it?'

'I have,' her hand briefly settled on the typescript. 'This isn't at all what I was expecting but that says more about me, than you. You write like an angel, Hogan. I can see this guy. I can hear him, smell him. I don't need a photo, or even a name. Just your guarantee that he's not kidding us along.'

'He's not.'

'This is you speaking?'

Hogan shook his head. He'd readied O'Donovan's card and now he offered it to Mrs Mahindra. She reached for her glasses and peered at it.

'He's been through it, this guy?'

'Every word.'

'And?'

'Phone him. You don't have to believe me.'

She gazed at him for a moment, and then shook her head.

'I'm buying in,' her hand settled on the typescript. 'And so will London. You must have worked half the night. Anything you need?'

Hogan had half anticipated this question. In his heart he knew he'd put something special and important on the page and O'Donovan's reaction had confirmed it. Now, it seemed, he owed Larry Elder a very big thank you.

'There is one thing,' he said. 'You were right about a telephone.'

'In that hostel of yours, you mean?'

'Yep.'

'Then leave it to me. When are you next due to pay rent?'

'The week after next.'

'And is there a notice period on the room tenancy?'

'One month.'

'Then cancel now. We'll pay the two weeks and find you somewhere else.'

'Like where?'

Mrs Mahindra gazed at him for a long moment, then shook her head.

'Patience is a virtue,' she was smiling now. 'But you Baptists know that already.'

6

By December 1939, three months later, Paris had come to life again. The *bouquinistes* had returned to their freezing pitches on the *quais* beside the river. The acres of chairs and tables along the major boulevards, abandoned so abruptly at the outbreak of war, were as busy as ever. And a young policeman, caped against the icy rain, was doing his best to sort out the mad swirl of traffic on the Place de la Concorde.

True, it was suddenly chic not to wear evening dress, and titled hostesses in the 16th *arrondissement* were writing handsome cheques to the army of charities that had sprung up in anticipation of the coming horrors, but the brutal fact remained that there wasn't quite enough war to go round. Disappointment? Perhaps. Relief? Undoubtedly. *Les Boches* had set a brisk pace in Poland, especially over Warsaw, and it was a comfort to wake up every morning to find the pale Parisian sky still empty of the dreaded Stukas. The war, in the end, would doubtless come to France. But not quite yet.

It was at this point – on a wet, windy morning ten days before Christmas – that Odile Lescaut and Lucien Gasquet stepped into a train about to leave from the Gare de l'Est. The tickets for the first-class compartment had been Odile's little *cadeau* to tempt Gasquet aboard. The indulgence bought them comfort and warmth for the half-day journey, and she assured him that everything would be taken care of once they crossed the border and flung themselves on the tender mercies of the Luxembourgeois.

All Gasquet had to bring with him was a supply of black charcoal sticks, a pad of heavyweight cartridge paper, ideally 42 x 59 cm, plus his favourite easel. Waiting for him at a hotel in Luxembourg City was someone she referred to as 'the client'. He was, Odile said, well placed, a person of undeniable influence. He was also handsome and vain enough to commission a portrait in charcoal, something simple in black and white. In a letter she showed Gasquet on the train, he seemed to favour an almost Japanese purity of line. Gasquet, who knew a great deal about calligraphy and had spent some time in Kyoto thanks to his interest in Noh theatre, was delighted by the prospect of the trip. All the uncertainties that accompanied *la drôle de guerre* were beginning to unnerve him. Living alone in Paris, he told Odile on the phone, it was impossible to dismiss this joke of a war.

Lunch on the train was served shortly after they left Reims. The proffered menu proposed filet of beef with an assortment of accompanying vegetables, or grilled plaice with wild samphire, sauteed potatoes and herb butter. Gasquet asked the waiter whether they might serve *pommes purées* instead of the sauteed potato with the fish. The waiter looked briefly troubled and then promised to enquire. Today's on-board chef was evidently Polish, a burden – he murmured – that wasn't entirely the poor man's fault.

Left to themselves again, Odile was curious about the mashed potato. As far as she remembered, Lucien was always ravenous for anything that had seen hot fat.

'Not yet,' one thin hand settled on his stomach. 'They repaired most of me but I still have to be careful.'

Odile, discomforted, muttered an apology. Thanks to Wilhelm Schultz, Gasquet had been on the operating table within an hour of arriving from August's masked revels in rue de la Faisanderie. Over the course of two operations, they'd first stemmed the blood loss and then sewn up the worst of the damage in his back passage. Odile had paid several visits, arriving with armfuls of books and the kind of right-wing newspapers she knew Gasquet enjoyed, but after that she'd laid the whole episode to rest. The detectives investigating the death of M. Babineau had taken statements from his friends who'd fled the scene on the third floor before the violence began but the fact remained that no witness to the beating itself appeared to exist. Ex-Brownshirt Willi Schultz, alas, was nowhere to be found. Sensibly, along with the entire German Embassy staff, he'd packed his bags and left.

'It still hurts?' Odile was keen to make amends.

'Shitting is a nightmare and farting is something I try and avoid. I've found a doctor who can work miracles with certain lotions, and he's handsome, too, but that simply makes it worse. One day, he tells me, I'll be open for offers. It's a lovely phrase, and an even nicer thought, and well worth the money I'm paying him, but he tells me my best friend should be patience. We've had a dalliance or two, me and patience, but in all honesty I'm not sure it's going to come to anything. Wine is something else that doesn't agree with me but that I can live without.'

'Whereas...?'

'Exactly. It's strange, isn't it, how abstinence can confirm the person you really are?' Gasquet shrugged, gazing out of the window, and Odile murmured her agreement before returning to her magazine. She'd cabled the train's arrival time first thing this morning, receiving an acknowledgement within minutes.

Twenty-six minutes past five. Luxembourg City. Platform three.

She spotted the bulky presence of Wilhelm Schultz the moment she stepped down to the platform. He was wearing a coat she'd never seen before, black leather, new looking, nearly ankle-length, and he lifted a hand in greeting as the platform filled with arriving passengers. Gasquet was the first to extend a hand, wrestling awkwardly with his easel and his bag. As a writer/director, and occasional actor, he'd acquired a certain reputation among the people who really mattered in the world of Parisian theatre. Queer, certainly, and thin-skinned, and reckless with his emotions, but also a man with a visible neediness: to be wanted, to be someone of influence, above all to *matter*. Odile could see it now, in the way he grasped Schultz's big hand, in the way he closed the gap between them, oblivious to the swirl of passengers heading for the concourse.

'You saved my life,' he said. 'Without you, my friend, I'd be dead.'

Odile had never seen Schultz wrong-footed and it amused her to watch him extricating his hand from Gasquet's, keen to bring this exchange to an end.

'Journey OK?' Schultz was looking at Odile. 'You managed to lay hands on a compartment?'

'We did. Thanks for the thought.'

'*You* paid for that?' Gasquet, staring at Schultz, gestured towards the departing train.

'My masters paid.' A thin smile. 'Welcome to Luxembourg.'

Schultz summoned a cab to take them to the Hotel Kons, four storeys of brutal modernism in the middle of the city. Schultz, aware of Odile's disapproval at the look of the place, promised good food and impeccable service. *Oberst* Zimmermann, he explained, had been living here for three days and had half fallen in love with it.

'This is my client?' Gasquet had recognised the name from the letter.

'He is,' Schultz was checking his watch. 'He's been in the saddle for most of the afternoon, and he'll be taking a pastry or two about now. The man eats properly later.'

After booking in and leaving Odile to take the lift to her room, they found Zimmermann in the hotel's restaurant, occupying a table beside the window. The last of the daylight fell on the soft grey-green of his *Abwehr* tunic and he glanced up as Schultz and Gasquet approached. Lean face, hair swept back from a high forehead, a golden signet ring on the little finger of his left hand. He looked, in a word, distinguished.

A waiter organised a chair for Gasquet but the Frenchman waved him away. He was looking down at Zimmermann, his head cocked at a slight angle, his eyes half closed, an overtly theatrical pose that put what might have been a smile on Zimmermann's face.

'Perfect,' Gasquet murmured.

'What is?'

'The light. The setting. Everything. I should fetch my easel and start at once.'

'You want to draw me *eating*?' Zimmermann gestured down at his plate.

'I want to capture your spirit, your essence. Draw in charcoal and you can seize the moment. I did something similar with Herr Schultz here. As it happened, he wasn't aware of my presence and maybe that helped.'

'Was he eating, too?'

'On the contrary, he was half naked. That tells you everything you need to know about a man. The body, the way you stand, the way you breathe, is the soul made flesh.'

'Naked?' Zimmermann's gaze had settled on Schultz.

'I was getting changed, Herr *Oberst*. It was a masked ball. I dressed in SA brown and forgot my manners. The women loved me. The men less so. In fact, some of them took liberties. That, Herr *Oberst*, turned out to be the kind of mistake you only make once. Am I right, Gasquet? Are your insides up to one of these delicious pastries?'

Gasquet pulled a face and shook his head before settling carefully on the chair. He wanted to know everything about *Oberst* Zimmermann. He wanted to know about his passion for horse riding. He wanted to know what he was doing here, a week before Christmas in a Luxembourg hotel. And he wanted to know, above all, about his plans for France.

'So when might we expect you?' he asked. 'And should I find a stable for your horse?'

*

Odile and Schultz met later at a smoky downtown bar. Gasquet, she said, had lost no time falling for Zimmermann. At best, she thought, half a day at the easel, making multiple passes at an image they'd both be happy with, might generate the beginnings of something interesting. What she'd never anticipated was this.

'Should I take the man at face value? Do you?' Like Schultz, she was drinking *Weissbier*, and like Schultz, she was disappointed in Lucien Gasquet. Too obvious. And far too theatrical.

'Gasquet's an actor,' Schultz grunted. 'That's where he comes from. That's what he does. Face value means nothing.

Zimmermann eats at a much bigger table. In Berlin, he has the pick of the prettiest boys. The Gasquet I saw this evening will be nothing but a passing snack. He's too old. He's damaged goods. And he's far from pretty.'

Odile scowled. When she was angry, she always reached for a cigarette.

'Getting him here was your idea.' She was looking for her lighter.

'I know. These days it's easy to be wrong.'

'You don't think it will work? Be honest, Schultz. Take a leaf from our book. Leave just a little room for doubt.'

'Very funny.'

'I mean it. You need to hold that famous nerve of yours. Tomorrow the poor man may calm down.' At last she coaxed a flame from her lighter, sucked greedily at the cigarette and expelled a long plume of smoke. 'So tell me about the handsome *Oberst*.'

Schultz eyed her for a long moment, and then shrugged.

'He used to have a big desk at the *Abwehr*,' he grunted. 'That's where we first met. He had a natural flair for intelligence work. In my trade you have to have an instinct for weakness, for how best to unlock a man. It's nothing you can teach, it's instinctive, something you're born with. In the wild, Zimmermann would have been a wolf, hunting alone. Beneath the looks and the charm, he's feral, he's a predator. He made *Oberst* before he was thirty. On the Bendlerstrasse, that had never been done before.'

'So what happened?'

'He got himself noticed. Gerd von Rundstedt? Does the name mean anything?'

'Nothing.'

'He's a *Generaloberst*, that's one below *Feldmarschall*, proof that the *Wehrmacht* still has a brain as well as a conscience. He's a Prussian, so Hitler doesn't entirely trust him, but he's probably the best we've got. Last year, he took us into the Sudetenland without spilling a drop of blood and retired soon afterwards. Hitler was never to his taste but when the call came to sort out the Poles he had no choice but to obey. The soldier's oath has a lot to answer for.'

'He led the invasion?'

'He did.'

'And you're suggesting that was bloodless, too?'

'The man took the entire country in less than five weeks. Unlocking the doors and letting us in would have been wiser. The Poles only have themselves to blame.'

'And Herr Zimmermann? He was in Poland, too?'

'He was. Rundstedt had extracted him from the Bendlerstrasse. He covered Rundstedt's back in the Polish campaign and now he's got an even bigger desk in Koblenz. He's putting together an intelligence service for Army Group 'A' because Rundstedt trusts nobody. Rundstedt works from the same headquarters. They have offices on the same floor. They talk daily, and Zimmermann attends every conference. Rundstedt hates surprises of any kind, especially home-grown, which is probably wise. Nothing feeds the ambition of our leaders quicker than an easy victory, and it's Zimmermann's job to keep these animals in their cages. He plays the wolf to perfection, and he's very good at it.'

'And Gasquet?'

'The lamb. To the slaughter. Wrong choice, I'm afraid. Arse in tatters. Way too old. My fault. Best you put him on the train tomorrow and leave Zimmermann to get on with the war.'

Odile nodded and reached for her drink. Then her gaze returned to Schultz.

'Koblenz?' she murmured. 'Should that tell me anything?

Schultz smiled, said nothing. Koblenz lay to the north, an easy drive from Luxembourg. Odile hadn't finished, not quite.

'You remember the Hôtel de la Gare? Metz?'

'How could I forget? A whole chicken afterwards, and a half-decent red? The blessings of peace, eh?' Schultz lifted his stein, 'Here's to Château Lafite.'

'You said you'd spent the day in the field. You told me about getting arrested. *Ouvrage* Molvange? Am I right?'

'Yes.'

'And maybe a look at the rest of the Maginot Line? Isn't that what you do? Isn't that what Zimmermann does?'

'I get the facts on the ground. Zimmermann is the clever one.'

'And this Rundstedt?'

'He turns it into another victory.'

'By taking on the forts?' A vague flap of her hand. 'By wiping them out?'

Schultz gazed at her for a long moment. He had no intention of answering a question like that, not even to Odile. At length, he emptied his glass and glanced at his watch.

'We should make your trip worthwhile,' he suggested. 'Before everything gets too difficult.'

To Schultz's slight surprise Odile agreed. They returned to the hotel, pausing briefly beside the entrance to the bar where Zimmermann and Gasquet were occupying a table in the far corner. Gasquet had his back to the door but Zimmermann spotted Schultz at once, the faintest nod of acknowledgement and what seemed to be a genuine smile. The pair of them looked relaxed, and when Gasquet leaned forward, orchestrating some story or other with flamboyant gestures, both hands, Zimmermann laughed. Odile saw it, too.

'Maybe we're wrong,' she said. They were heading for the stairs.

'I doubt it. Zimmermann's an actor, too. It comes with the territory. At his level, nothing is ever what it seems. It might be wise to remember that.'

Odile's room was on the top floor. Earlier, she'd taken a nap and the bed was already turned down. Schultz lingered by the door, trying to kid himself he could smell Lancôme in the heat from the big radiators, watching Odile rummaging through the contents of her suitcase. The bottle of Lafite lay beneath a couple of folded dresses.

'Sit.' She gestured at the bigger of the two armchairs.

Schultz ignored the invitation, and wandered towards the window, gazing down at the thin dribble of traffic slowing for the dimly lit intersection below. He'd used this hotel on a number of occasions recently, chiefly for meetings with a French stonemason working on the chateau at Sedan. There was nothing that happened on the banks of the Meuse that escaped this man's attention, and a sizeable family debt had delivered him into Schultz's hands. He had a passion for wild boar, hunted in the vast forests of the Ardennes. He was good company and some of their lunches lasted deep into the afternoon while he went through his many notes and photographs.

A pop of the cork told Schultz it was time to sit down. Odile had readied two glasses.

'We need to talk about the man you killed,' she said.

'Why might that be? We're at war, remember. One more body? Who's counting?'

'That's hardly the point. All my friends assume we're next on the list and you won't find anyone in Paris who isn't trying to lay hands on a German dictionary. April? May? That same room at the Hôtel Lutetia? You really think the city belongs to the French anymore?'

'Paris deserves to be shared,' Schultz grunted. 'It needs our care and attention. Both will be a pleasure, as I'm sure *Oberst* Zimmermann agrees.'

'He'll be there? Part of the occupation?'

'Without doubt. He speaks good French. He knows his way around a menu. He enjoys an evening in the theatre. There isn't a major gallery in Europe he hasn't visited. Rundstedt will find him somewhere suitable to pitch his tent and ask him to take the city to his heart.' Schultz loosened his tie. 'Which is rather the point.'

'You mean Gasquet?'

'Of course. In an ideal world they become lovers. That would please me very much. All kinds of possibilities. Will it happen? Somehow I doubt it, but stranger things have come to pass.' He raised his glass. 'Here's to the gods of charcoal...' he frowned '... and fucking.'

Odile didn't move. Her glass remained untouched.

'His real name's Babineau, Camille Babineau. His mother's Italian, from Napoli, which I imagine accounts for his nickname. Most people I know called him *Il Polpo*. Tentacles everywhere. Fingers in every pie.'

'This is the man I killed?'

'He is. He was a criminal in a suit with a lovely estate in the Touraine and friends from the darker corners of Montmartre that even you wouldn't want to meet. Doing to France what you did to Poland may be a chore, but your problems won't end with the victory parade. The police won't bother you. *Au contraire*, one of them told me they regard what happened as a favour, but I gather that revenge is a way of life in Napoli.'

Schultz nodded. In these moods, Odile could bring a chill to any room, even this one.

'So what do you suggest I do? Call the party off?'

'Downstairs, you mean? With little Gasquet?'

'I was thinking Koblenz, with Rundstedt. I'm due there tomorrow afternoon. We Germans have a codename for everything. The next step is *Fall Gelb*, "Case Yellow". One of the countries on our list might well be France. Do I advise the *Feldmarschall* to pop the paperwork back in the envelope? Pay Hitler a visit? Offer his apologies? Suggest our sainted Führer takes a quiet year or two in the Austrian Alps? Herr Zimmermann, for one, would be disappointed. Me, too.'

'You'll be part of it? Back in Paris?'

'Almost certainly. Every loyal servant deserves a bon-bon from time to time, and mine will be Paris. You're right, incidentally, about the Hôtel Lutetia. I left a couple of bags with the maître d'.'

Odile at last took a modest sip from her glass, then cupped her hands around it.

'You're cold?' Schultz asked. 'In *this* room?'

'No.'

'Angry?'

'Of course.'

'At me?'

'At all of you.'

'Us Germans?'

'You men. I used to like men, my husband in particular, even my little brother when everything was going his way, but something happens, maybe something chemical, when you all get together. I went to a great deal of trouble over that party, getting people in, opening everything up, inviting the right mix of people, insisting on all those costume changes, then Babineau and those monkeys set about little Gasquet, and there's blood on the sheets, and more blood on the floor, and suddenly my gangster friend is dead.'

'You sent me up there.'

'I did. You're right.'

'And you dressed me for the occasion.'

'Yes.'

'As a Brownshirt, an SA hooligan.'

'Yes.'

'So was that some kind of joke?'

'In a way, yes.'

'You never thought people like me really existed? Out on the streets every night? Hunting for Reds to kill? Or maybe you thought you'd take a chance with that? Trust my better nature?'

'I thought I knew you.'

'And?'

'I didn't.'

'In what respect?'

'You mean it. All the violence, all the bloodshed, that comes easily to you. You're good at it. Killing someone means nothing to you. You want the truth? That frightens me. You want another truth? It appalls me. And one last thing? The most shameful of all?' She nodded towards the bed. 'It excites me.'

*

Schultz and Odile were late to breakfast next morning. The restaurant was about to close and both Zimmermann and Gasquet were on their feet beside their abandoned table. Whatever had happened last night appeared to have transformed Gasquet. Yesterday's nervousness, the fretful pallor of a man out of his depth, had quite gone. Instead, the gauntness of his face seemed to glow with a deep satisfaction, a kind of inner peace that Schultz himself had rarely seen in the mirror.

'Come...' Gasquet murmured. 'We'll all go up together.'

Zimmermann glanced at his watch and shook his head, but Gasquet put a hand on his arm and insisted. A couple of minutes, he said. Maybe less. Zimmermann shrugged, attaching himself to the party as all three of them followed Gasquet to his room. Both windows were wide open, and apparently had been all night.

'Could you ever live with heat like that?' Gasquet wanted to know. 'We certainly couldn't.'

Odile was studying the bed, the blankets thrown back, the bottom sheet patterned with drying blood, but what drew Schultz's attention was the easel. It was set up in the very centre of the room, the big sketchpad unrevealed. Gasquet stood beside it, the master of ceremonies awaiting his cue. He had eyes only for Zimmermann, who was still lingering by the door. Schultz had always admired his talent for adjusting to the demands of every situation. When required, he could command attention, charm everyone within earshot, dominate a conversation or a conference without ruffling a single feather. Just now, he was close to invisible.

At length he nodded, and with the barest flourish, Gasquet flipped the front cover from the sketchpad on the easel, revealing the charcoal sketch beneath. For a long moment, there was silence. Through the open window, Schultz recognised the busy chatter of a distant steam train, but his eyes never left the sketch.

Gasquet had drawn Zimmermann naked. He was standing in quarter-profile, just a hint of the bed behind him, a moment of time perfectly caught in a handful of charcoal lines. This was the stillest of still lives, a pose that reminded Schultz of a statue he'd once seen in a Berlin museum, but something remarkable had happened, something celebrated in the Greekness of Zimmermann's stance, his perfect balance, the flatness of his stomach, the tiny suggestion of a smile on his face, how comfortable he was in his skin. A work like this told Schultz more than any photograph, any movie camera, could ever capture. This handful of charcoal lines, seemingly so artless, so casual, so spontaneous, had somehow trapped a deeper truth. It was about trust and contentment and – yes – conquest.

Odile was the first to find her voice. She'd always had difficulties with the notion of praise.

'Astonishing,' she said quietly, then looked round at Zimmermann.

'*Perfekt*,' he murmured.

7

CHRISTMAS EVE, TORONTO

By now, Hogan had acquired a nickname at the *Globe and Mail*. Watching his meteoric rise over the autumn, promotions prompted by a series of feature articles building on the success of his remarkable piece about the fighting at Teruel, he'd become the Miramichi Express, the unstoppable talent from the far reaches of the Maritime Provinces who seemed to have turned every journalistic cliché on its head.

This was a scribbler who kept himself to himself, who had no interest in after-hours gatherings at the bar across the street, who didn't even *drink*, for God's sake. That the boy knew how to write was never contested. Even Earl Prentiss agreed that the paper was nursing a serious talent. But what made this slightly awkward youth uncomfortable company was his absolute refusal to bow the knee – or even acknowledge – the pecking order in the newsroom. Older journalists muttered darkly about his churchgoing on Sundays. One guy in particular, who reported from the outer fringes of psychiatry, thought he might be schizo. Only the few women allowed access to a typewriter knew better. Mrs Mahindra, they said, trusts him enough to give him house room. That should tell us everything.

It was true. Mrs Mahindra's stewardship of the paper through the autumn had brought her the security of a three-year contract as the editor of the *Globe and Mail*. With the contract went a substantial pay rise. Mrs Mahindra's husband, thanks to a nimble business brain, was already a wealthy man. His firm, Impex Mahindra, trading in imported Indian and Persian goods, had kept his family afloat through the years of Depression, and had now earned a fortune. To celebrate his wife's new position at the *Globe*, Sammi had bought her an early Christmas present to grace the family mansion out in Lawrence Park North, and when Mrs Mahindra arrived at the paper's annual Christmas Eve party she brought a series of photographs of what she called the new love in her life.

The newsroom was already crowded with journalists. Sales had been climbing steadily since Canada had joined the war, and the management were only too happy to contribute mightily to the evening's revels. Barrels of beer from a local brewery were readied on a long table while balloons in Maple Leaf colours hung from the ceiling. Prentiss meanwhile – already drunk – was holding court from a chair in the corner.

'Gather round, my children.' Mrs Mahindra had abandoned her usual business suit for an Indian sari in the deepest mauve. Now she put the first of the photographs on the news desk and beckoned her charges closer. The photo showed a bath installed on a black and white checkerboard-patterned floor. The bath occupied the corner between two walls and the far end was compartmented by a tall enclosure. A vertical row of eight taps ran up one side of the compartment, and visible within this space was a shower head.

Mrs Mahindra, who was drinking soda water, demanded guesses. What was this thing? Had it landed from Mars? Was it a German secret weapon? What did it *do*? A collective murmur offered a series of suggestions, most of them unprintable. Mrs Mahindra's gaze went from face to face, shaking her head, then decided to offer a clue. The second photo was dominated by the same bath, but this time the shot included two girls, both of them on the cusp of womanhood, both of them gorgeous, both of them swathed in towelling robes. One of them had stationed herself beneath the shower head, while the other was posed beside the line of taps, a playful smile on her lips, one shapely leg artfully revealed.

'My lovely twins,' Mrs Mahindra was beaming. 'Meet Aruna and Naaz. Naaz is the naughty one. She used to be frightened of her mother but for this shot I had trouble getting her to wear the robe at all.'

This news was greeted by whistles from the assembled scribes.

'To Naaz!' went the toast. Glasses were raised around the table, then Prentiss called for order. These last two months Mrs Mahindra had exiled him to the *Globe*'s Montreal office from where he'd been filing a series of glum pieces about fallings out among the Free French in Quebec, and it was an open secret that Prentiss deeply resented the posting.

'Let's ask Miramichi,' he was having trouble getting out of the chair. 'He should know. He damn well lives there.'

A roar of approval greeted the suggestion. Heads turned, looking for Hogan. He was standing at the back of the crowd, nursing a glass of tomato juice. Only this morning he'd put the bath to good use but a single glance from Mrs Mahindra told him not to answer.

'Wish I could help you, guys.' He grinned. 'Keep guessing.'

'You gotta crush on Naaz? Or maybe Aruna? Which one's the sweetest to you?'

The question from Prentiss sparked a roar of laughter. Even Mrs Mahindra thought it was funny.

'Tell them, George,' she said. 'Tell them what they've got you for Christmas.'

'I can't. It's a secret. Except it includes some kind of special soap. Seaweed? Have I got that right?'

Whistles, this time, and a shouted insistence on total disclosure.

'Envy I can handle, guys.' Hogan was beginning to enjoy himself. 'It pays to know when you've hit the mother lode.'

'They put you to bed at night?' Prentiss again. 'Read you stories? Tuck you in?'

'Only at weekends. And only afterwards.'

'After what?'

'That would be telling,' Hogan raised his glass. 'Here's to Montreal. Better luck next time, eh?'

For those still sober, the comment was an open declaration of war, but Prentiss's star had faded, along with his liver, and in any case the faces round the table were enjoying themselves too much to bother with a washed-up drunk.

'Have you taken Naaz home yet, George?' Prentiss wasn't giving up. 'Introduced her to the folks?'

'Every weekend, my friend. And she can handle the nightlife, too. Dancing till dawn? Then a twirl or two on all them floating logs? Take my word for it. The girl's a natural in the wild. Born for it. Even the moose fall in love with her. Heck...' he raised his glass again '... who wouldn't?'

The roar of applause at last shut Prentiss up. He collapsed slowly backwards, allowing unseen hands to guide him into his chair, while Mrs Mahindra asked one of the sports reporters to broach another barrel of ale. For his part, Hogan hadn't moved. En route to find a tap for the barrel, the sports jock paused briefly beside him.

'You aced the bastard,' he murmured. 'Happy fucking Christmas. You deserve it.'

Sammi Mahindra had sent his driver to pick up his wife and his lodger. Hogan sat in the back of the limousine, beside

Mrs Mahindra. At her insistence, he'd been occupying a suite of three rooms at the rear of the handsome faux-nineteenth-century mansion in Lawrence Park, one of the city's choicest areas. The biggest of Hogan's rooms had its own telephone and a fine view of the grounds at the rear the building, including the newly laid tennis court, and at Mrs Mahindra's suggestion, Hogan had been more than happy to use the room as a study. The rest of the accommodation served as sleeping quarters and a kitchen/diner but stepping into the house itself Hogan was only metres away from one of the property's four bathrooms, which happened to contain the new toy. Back in the newsroom, the woman who ran one of the weekend features pages had finally given it a name.

'It's for hydrotherapy,' she'd guessed. 'All those taps? You get sprayed and pummelled and spoiled every which way.'

The woman had been right, and now, in the back of the limousine, Mrs Mahindra was musing about her husband's generosity. At first she'd assumed the present was for her use only but within days her husband was using it more than she did.

'He calls it his Ganges,' she told Hogan, 'but that's because he's a romantic. He tells me water is a gift from the gods. It makes him feel reborn. It makes him feel *powerful*.'

Hogan smiled. Moving in with the Mahindras had been a gamble – for him as well as them – but the life they'd made for themselves had impressed him deeply. Even by Toronto standards they were very rich, and yet they never flaunted their money, never took it for granted. Hogan knew for a fact that hundreds of thousands of dollars a year were remitted back to the subcontinent in support of various causes, and there was a small army of beneficiaries much closer to home who owed their survival, especially in winter, to cheques written over Sammi Mahindra's signature. The way husband and wife made their money work for the poor sometimes reminded Hogan of Larry Elder. Elder had literally fought to put bread in the mouths of the city's hungry, and had the scars to prove it, but in their own unflashy style the Mahindras were no less generous.

'We're going to miss you, George.' Mrs Mahindra gave his knee a motherly pat. 'The girls especially. Remind me about the boat. The first week in January? Have I got that right?'

'Sure. I have to be in New York by the 6th. The boat sails the following day. Some of the Royals will be on board, which is great. Especially Frank O'Donovan.'

'The guy who OK'd the Teruel piece?'

'Exactly.'

'And EJ?'

'We talked on the phone again the day before yesterday. He says he's found me somewhere to live in London. I get a desk of my own in Fleet Street and an assignment to something he's calling Dominion News. He sends his best, by the way.'

'And what about those folks of yours back home? Disappointed you can't make it for Christmas?'

'Not at all. New Year's Eve was always more important in our family.'

'Good,' she nodded, patting his knee a second time. 'Christmas was something new to us when we first arrived but now I guess we couldn't do without it. Naaz wants you to carve the bird, by the way. I said you'd be delighted.'

That night, unusually, Hogan dreamed. It began with a fitful set of images, like a movie half glimpsed through spread fingers, crazy jump-cuts that at first made no sense. Then, still dreaming, Hogan tried to bring a little order to this chaos, baiting a line and casting it deep into the waters of his subconscious, curious to know what might end up in his keep-net, and as he lay there in the darkness he began to enjoy himself.

Back in the chill of early autumn, with the big maples already shedding their leaves, Sammi Mahindra had hired a tennis pro to coach the twin girls on the new court. He had a Ukrainian accent and claimed to have played Wimbledon over a couple of seasons and he appeared for long weekends in his dazzling whites to urge both girls to stop giggling and start playing. Gazing out from the desk in the warmth of his study, Hogan had marvelled at the man's patience and guile, and at the speed with which the twins began to take him seriously.

Their sixteenth birthday fell at the end of October and Sammi wanted to stage a modest tennis tournament for their closest friends to celebrate the occasion. The Mahindra gene demanded victory, of course, but by the time the invitations went out Hogan had no doubts that winning was a one-way bet. And so it proved.

Both girls attended the same private school. It was exclusive, and single-sex, and when the weekend of the tournament arrived Hogan was very happy to run the all-day juice bar. Now, in his dream, the court was empty, the playing done, and his little bar was mobbed by a small army of leggy girls. Then came the moment when he had to award the tournament trophy. There was only one of them – for the overall winner – but Hogan made a neat little speech for the sake of the watching parents, talked boilerplate drivel about shared endeavour, and ended up awarding the trophy to the twins. Sammi had invested in a big silver cup with two handles. At Hogan's insistence, the girls seized one handle each as Sammi raised his camera for the souvenir shot, but in the dream they only had eyes for Hogan.

Both of the Mahindra twins, he knew, were curious about him: about what he got up to in that big downtown office of Mummy's, about how different he seemed, so buttoned up, so remote, so provincial, yet so utterly sure of himself. On one occasion, Aruna – quieter, more reflective than her showboat sister – had knocked on the door of his study and tried to find out more. He'd offered her the spare chair beside his desk, pushed his Remington to one side and told her to play the cub reporter, to fire away, any question in the world.

This invitation, he knew, had intrigued her. She'd wanted to know how it had been back home for him. She wanted to know about his brothers and sisters and whether he'd ever gotten bored at school. And most of all – a question she blamed on Naaz – she wanted to know whether he'd ever dated. Amused, Hogan had told her the truth. He'd had few friends of either sex. Had he ever dated? No.

'Not ever?'

'No.'

'And now? When you're grown up?'

'No.'

'Why not? What's stopping you?'

'Nothing.'

At this point, the remembered conversation had bled back into dreamtime, and he was suddenly treading the boards in the theatre of his imagination, and the study door had burst open – no knock this time – to reveal Naaz. She, too, wanted to know about his girlfriends, about whether he thought he was handsome, about how far he'd go on a first date. Like her sister, Hogan knew that Naaz was still a child in a woman's body but she was bursting with impatience, determined to know him better, eager to try herself out, and so she pushed her sister aside, and perched on Hogan's bony lap, and cupped his face, and told him she'd fallen in love.

'With?'

'You, dummy. How come you never noticed?'

After that, the images had become blurred, and less certain. Naaz may have stayed on his lap, she may not. Aruna may have stormed off in a sulk or said something vicious about her grab-everything sister. Either way it didn't really matter because the timeline fell apart, and it was nearly a decade later, and the twins were up for another award, this time in showbusiness.

In Hogan's dream, they were both actresses, and they wore identical dresses that sparked roars of applause from the huge audience. The awards took place in a vast exhibition hall filled with tables under a spangly ceiling. The evening was scored for power and money and it was evident from the start that the birthday girls from Lawrence Park had become the toast of North America. They graced magazine covers. They lent their names to body lotions and fancy cocktails. In the way of the Mahindras, they'd become rich, and famous, and then richer still, and at the awards ceremony Hogan found himself sharing a table with their husbands.

'I knew these ladies once,' Hogan told them. 'Does that still give me kissing rights?'

'Bullshit.' The nearest of their husbands had the face of Hogan's father. 'In this life you pay for everything.'

In this life you pay for everything. Hogan awoke with a start. He was lying on his back, his eyes wide open, every nerve tuned for the slightest movement. He'd heard something out in the corridor, a tiny scuffing noise. It was still dark, the wind stirring in the big maples, flurries of snow in the air through the double-glazed windows. He lay still for a moment, his brain still fogged with the mysterious presence of his father at the awards ceremony. Then came the scrape of the bedroom door inching open, just feet from the bed.

Christmas Day, he thought. Might this be Santa Claus? In person?

The Mahindras kept the hall lighting on all night and now Hogan could see a shadow, utterly motionless, on the carpet.

He studied it for a long moment, and then recognised a scent that Mrs Mahindra often wore around the office. She must have helped herself from her mother's dressing table, he thought. This wasn't Santa Claus at all. This was one of the twins.

The shadow moved, crept closer, bent over him while he told himself this was still a dream. Then he felt a stir of colder air as she lifted the blanket, and then the sheet, and slipped into the bed beside him.

'Naaz?'

'Aruna.'

'You know what time it is?'

'Late. Early. I don't care.' She began to unbutton his pyjama top. 'You mind at all?'

'Mind what?'

'Me. Doing this.'

Hogan didn't know what to say. Should he play the adult, tell her no harm done, send her back to bed? Or was this the moment when he stepped out of himself and enjoyed whatever might follow?

'One favour? Just one?' Aruna's face was inches from his, her eyes huge in the darkness of her face, a hint of toothpaste on her breath. She was wearing a thin nightdress and he could feel her pulse quicken as she pressed against him.

'This favour,' Hogan murmured. 'What is it?'

'Kiss me?'

'Sure.' Hogan obliged. It felt more than good.

'I've had a crush on you forever. We both have.'

'I don't believe it.'

'It's true. Ask Naaz. She'll be along in a minute.'

'Three of us? In this bed?' Hogan stifled a laugh.

'Don't worry,' Aruna was kissing him now. 'It'll be great.'

And it was. Naaz arrived shortly afterwards, noisier, stark naked. She joined them in bed, ignoring her sister's cautionary finger on her lips, taking the lead in exploring Hogan from head to toe. Aruna kept whispering that this was their surprise Christmas present, something they'd cooked up between them, a memory he might care to take across the ocean, a kooky way of telling him how much they'd enjoyed having him around.

Aroused, Hogan didn't quite know what to make of it. He'd never bedded a woman in his life, let alone made love, but after a while he realised that this wasn't a grown-up interlude at all. On the contrary, he'd become the invited guest at a Mahindra nursery game conducted with a kind of gleeful innocence.

The girls poked bits of him they especially liked, shared opinions about the length of his toes and the faintest suggestion of hair on his bony chest, discovered where he was most ticklish and most responsive, grew briefly fretful about a scar on his leg he blamed on a logging accident, cooed over the dusting of freckles on his forehead, and told him he had the eyes of a holy man, a playful reference to the much-thumbed Bible he kept at his bedside.

Hogan, in short, might have been a favourite uncle who'd strayed into the company of toddlers determined to clamber all over him, but when they finally agreed it was time to leave, it was Naaz who pulled the sheets back, took a last look at his naked body, and then planted the wettest of kisses on his still-erect cock.

'That's the one you take to England,' she was laughing again. 'Never forget us.'

Book Two

8

LONDON, FEBRUARY 1942

Another winter, two years later.

Hogan had become a regular at the Beaver Club. It lay in a side street off Trafalgar Square in the shadow of Admiralty Arch and it offered a reminder of home for the thousands of Canadian troops who'd shipped over at the outbreak of war. For a handful of coins, you could get a bath, or a shave, or a shoeshine. The canteen, ever busy, had good eats and if you were after something lighter there was a soda fountain and snack bar nearby. Barely a month into the New Year, you could even pick up the remains of the Beaver Club Yuletide offers. 1/6d. would buy you a stuffed white rabbit with rather fetching pink button eyes.

'Tempted?'

Hogan, the rabbit in his hand, glanced round. He hadn't seen Frank O'Donovan since they'd crossed the Atlantic together and the intervening years had given him a leaner, harder look.

'I'm late. I'm sorry.' O'Donovan extended a hand.

Hogan had secured a table in the back corner of the canteen. He and O'Donovan queued for plates of gristly meat pie and O'Donovan acknowledged a wave or two from neighbouring tables as they sat down.

'They made you a Colonel now?' O'Donovan was in uniform, and Hogan had checked out the shoulder tabs.

'Lieutenant-Colonel. Just the one pip.'

'Makes you feel any different?'

'Makes me feel old.' O'Donovan was looking round. 'This place always reminds me of a ballgame. You'd never dream these guys are here to fight a war.'

It was true. After the bombshell of Pearl Harbor and America's declaration of war, the news had steadily darkened. First the noose of the U-boat blockade in the Atlantic drawn tighter and tighter; then one defeat after another in North Africa; and now the Japs putting Singapore to the sword. Only yesterday, in the *Daily Express* newsroom, Hogan had seen long columns of Brit prisoners filing into captivity, chilling black and white images wired from the ever-obliging Foreign Ministry in Tokyo. Yet to sit here, among the cigarette smoke and the laughter, you'd never suspect that the country had its back to the wall in these blackest of days.

'You rode the Blitz OK?' O'Donovan had abandoned his plate.

'The place where I'm living never took a direct hit. I guess that makes me lucky.'

'The East End, right?'

'Right. How come you know that?'

'I read the *Express*. I bought it at first because I knew you'd signed up but after a while it became a habit. You write a lot about the East End. You bring the place to life, what's left of it.'

Hogan acknowledged the compliment with the faintest smile. Crossing the Atlantic, he and O'Donovan had spent a lot of time together. Hogan had been happy to share his plans with the older man, and happier still to have become friends, and meeting again he sensed that none of that mutual trust had gone.

O'Donovan was still mystified about Hogan's living arrangements. 'You told me on the boat they'd found you a place in Bloomsbury. Canucks are hopeless with foreign cities but that ain't the East End.'

'Bloomsbury cost me a fortune. The *Express* is fun but when it comes to wages at my level they're mean as hell. The place they'd found me was way more space than I ever needed so I headed east. I'm on my fifth bike, incidentally. Twenty-five minutes to Fleet Street on a normal day, way longer after a heavy raid. You get a hard time if you turn up late, so when it was really bad, I was leaving at dawn.'

'And the other bikes?'

'Three stolen. One died of abuse. Some mornings this war feels more than personal. The bomb craters appear overnight, and the bigger ones can eat you alive.'

O'Donovan laughed. So far, he said, he'd spent most of his war on the south coast teaching farm boys from the prairie how to read properly, and city boys how to dig trenches and lay barbed wire. Down in Kent and East Sussex they'd had front row seats for the Battle of Britain but even that hadn't lived up to the billing.

'Ours, you mean? On the paper?'

'Yours, and everyone else's. The wireless. Those Churchill speeches. Tune in, and my guys expected something out of the movies, but most of the dog-fighting happened way up, contrails on sunny days, sometimes the odd parachute. You think about it later, and I guess that's the way it's bound to be, but then the Blitz comes along, night after night, and in their tiny heads my boys are queueing for train tickets to London, wanting to get stuck in. Take them off to war, and all they get is bored. That's a direct quote, by the way. Not one guy, but half a dozen.'

'They really want to get themselves blown up? They're that crazy?'

'They're young. They know nothing. I guess it's the same thing.'

Hogan nodded, using a crust of stale bread to mop up the last of his gravy. In truth, especially to begin with, the Blitz had terrified him. First the wail of the sirens, then the drone of the approaching aircraft, and finally the measured tread of exploding bombs as they crept closer and closer. Where they fell, who they killed, seemed utterly random, the unluckiest ticket in the lottery of your worst nightmare, and crouching in the backyard shelter with the rest of the tenement, your eyes closed, a prayer on your lips, Hogan often thought about Larry Elder, and how right he'd been. Peel away all the bullshit about courage, and sacrifice, and multiple heroics, and war was a dish you'd never want to taste again.

Hogan tried to share the thought with O'Donovan but knew he wasn't really getting through. O'Donovan, after all, was a soldier, and in his trade it didn't pay to think too hard about the small print.

'You could have moved some place else,' O'Donovan pointed out. 'Live by the docks and you're gonna get a hard time. No surprises there.'

'You're right. And after a while you sort of get used to it. You know what you should tell your guys? That war, my war, is a pain in the ass. The electric fails and there's no coal to be had so you're living in three pullovers. The phones are always dead or dying. The movies close early and the theatres have all shut. The pub's your only option but the price of beer is outa reach and in any case I don't drink.'

'So why go to the pub at all?'

'In winter it's warmer, and they always have a piano, and people like to sing along but the dark nights are a problem because the bombers come early and walking back you have to dodge all that falling shrapnel. I'm living in a place called Limehouse. There's ack-ack everywhere. If the Germans don't drop a bomb on you, it'll be your own guys who get you killed. Here...' Hogan dug in his pocket and produced a heavy sliver of pitted metal, the edges razor-sharp, wrapped in a handkerchief. 'That one nearly did for me last week. Missed me by inches. When I picked it up it was still hot. This is February, remember. Can you believe that?'

O'Donovan was looking at the heavy splinter of shrapnel from an anti-aircraft burst. After a while he reached forward and touched it. Hogan had seen something similar in a Greek Orthodox church he'd once visited in Toronto, an old lady on that occasion, genuflecting in front of an ikon. There'd been something in her eyes that spoke of abject surrender, not to violence in this case but to God. Again, watching O'Donovan, Hogan was tempted to table the thought but in the end he buried it.

'You mentioned a proposition,' he said instead, 'when you telephoned.'

'I did. You're right.'

'So how can I help?'

'My guys deserve a little recognition. They're feeling neglected. The locals down our way are middling OK, no real problems. The girls are all over us because we have money and that can get awkward with some of the Brit fellas, but the older folk remember the last war and they understand respect, so on the whole, we get by.'

'You want me to write about that? About the boredom? About getting by?'

'I want you to write about a guy I'm guessing you'll remember. The guy with no name. Our man in Teruel.'

'Larry Elder?'

'The very same.'

'You're telling me he's over here?'

'Right. And he sends his regards, which I guess is one sign this country is getting to him. The Larry we knew back home never bothered with courtesies like that.'

O'Donovan smiled and glanced round before beckoning Hogan closer. Elder, he said, had gotten sick of sitting the war out in Toronto. Two days after the Japs bombed Pearl Harbor he'd made contact with a guy from Pittsburgh he'd shared a trench with in Spain. FDR had just declared war on Germany and Elder wanted to be part of it.

'But he hates war. He told me.'

'He hates what war does. Being a spectator is even worse.'

Volunteering in Canada, said O'Donovan, still risked exposing his service in Spain, and so Elder took the train south and threw his hand in with an American unit who could use a little of that Spanish Civil War experience. They'd taken a good look and liked him well enough to ship him across with the first wave of GIs. His precise status had never been altogether clear, and Elder had immediately made life tougher for himself in a roughhouse brawl defending a woman in a Dorset pub. Thanks to Elder, one of the two guys bothering her – a GI from South Carolina – was unlikely ever to walk again, but Elder had shown no remorse. Sure, he'd broken the guy's neck. Of course, an injury like that had consequences. But didn't the local ladies deserve better from their loudmouth guests, invited or otherwise?

'So what happened?'

'Conversations at staff level. That's big potatoes but just now none of us have got much else to get excited about. Naturally, I spoke up for Elder, told them what a firecracker the man was, and by the end of the afternoon I'd agreed to look after him.'

'You're telling me he's with the Royals now?'

'He is, for our sins and hopefully for the enemy's, too. The guy's ungovernable. Nothing's changed. My boys love him already.'

'You're telling me he's made a difference?'

'I'm telling you nothing's changed. The man has views on everything, and it starts with just what we should be doing when we get down to fighting this war.'

'You've given him a rank? All that experience?'

'No way. We've bought him on approval.'

'And you're assuming you can ever send him back? Full refund? I'm not sure I believe any of this, Frank. In Toronto, they'd still make him as a criminal. By going to Spain, he broke federal law. That's jail time, isn't it?'

'You're right. And that's exactly what he says. He was always canny, and nothing's changed. He's leaning on my better nature. He's telling me he belongs inside the tent rather than out. And looking round here, my friend, I have to tell you I'm in full agreement.'

O'Donovan gestured at the nearby tables, and Hogan could only agree. The last couple of years, he knew, had changed him. He felt tougher, wiser, less forgiving, but he still knew how to get alongside a prospect, and win his confidence, and empty him of enough to sustain a story for the inside pages. Looking around now, the canteen tables seemed to recede forever, young faces stabbing at their plates, trading gossip, looking up to share a joke. Had any of these guys bothered to ask themselves about that winter in Teruel? Did they even know, or care, where it was?

'So what's the proposition,' Hogan asked again. 'What do you want me to do?'

'I want you to come down to Winchelsea. Take a look at what we've been tasked to do. Draw your own conclusions. Then it might be wise to spend a moment or two with our Larry.'

'It's OK to use his name now? Take a picture?'

'That's his call, not mine. All I know is what happened last time. The piece you wrote woke us all up. You're gonna tell me that was Larry's doing, Larry's little war, but that's only half the story. You waved the magic wand, my friend, and that tells me you understood the guy. Larry likes you, and that's because you took him by surprise. Not face-to-face exactly, but later.'

'On the page, you mean?'

'Yeah. And that's why we need you both again.'

'To do what, exactly?'

'To wake us all up.'

Hogan pushed his chair back from the table and folded his arms. The Teruel article had gotten him to London, had secured him a desk at the *Daily Express*, had given him the confidence to buy a broken-down old bike and wobble into the grubby depths of the East End. There, to his slight surprise, he'd stepped into a real understanding of what had fuelled Larry Elder's anger, and that discovery had given him his first real taste of manhood. The father figure at the awards ceremony in his long-ago dream had been more right than he knew. In this life, you pay for everything.

'There's a problem,' Hogan said slowly. 'My boss? Lord Beaverbrook?'

'You told me about him on the boat coming over. Maritime Provinces? Same hometown? Same view of the same river?'

'Sure. And now a cabinet minister. This is a guy who never has enough pies to stick his fingers in. He rides herd on the politicians, on businessmen he doesn't trust, on us as well. He has energy to spare and a thousand ideas a minute. Every single one of them gets a hearing because that's what he demands. Back last summer, when we were suddenly friends with the Soviets, Churchill made him Minister of Supply and sent him off to buddy up with Stalin. Word in the office says they were peas from the same pod. Stalin demanded the earth, and Beaverbrook set to. He's out of town for day after day. He patrols the production lines, kicks anything that moves. Last week there was a shortfall on sanitary towels to send to Russkie women. The factory owner blamed snow. I wasn't there but Beaverbrook blew up. You want me to tell that to the Russians? Our allies? You think they don't know anything about fucking *snow*?'

Hogan, who very rarely cursed, didn't even bother to apologise. Instead, he bent into the table again.

'You're right about him coming from the Maritimes, Frank. Off the coast, there's a famous wave. It comes from nowhere and it's huge and I used to wait for the right conditions and then go down to a particular bunch of rocks where it happened and wait some more. Once you saw it, you never forgot it. Us locals called it "The Rage" and that's exactly what we now call the boss. Not The Beaver. Not Mr Impatient. The Rage. Two words that get to just who this man is. The Rage. That, he says, is how you win wars like this one. You break down doors, and kick the furniture to pieces, and take shit from no one. And from where I've been sitting, I guess he's probably right.'

O'Donovan offered a slow nod, then a shrug.

'So where's the problem you mentioned?'

'It's time, Frank. None of us ever have enough of the stuff and neither does The Rage. The Russians have got to him. Stalin's got to him. The Russkies are bleeding bad and they need more than boatloads of tanks and diapers. Stalin's demanding a second front, a landing for our boys in France, anything to thin out those German divisions in front of Moscow, and The Rage is waving the Red Flag like the crazy he is. It's a crusade really.

Second Front Now. Flags, posters, rallies, the lot. Working where I do, you have to sign up, and for whatever reason The Rage has assigned me as part of the team. That means lots of travel, lots of trains with nowhere to sit, long hours in the freezing cold, no room for anything else in my life. God knows, it may all stop tomorrow. That's what it's like on a Beaverbrook paper but for now he's got two million-plus readers in the bag, and Joe Stalin on the phone, and the worker ants scurrying the length and breadth of the land. I'd love to say yes to coming down to Winchelsea, but you may have to be patient.'

O'Donovan said he understood. Then he glanced at his watch and stood up. Regrettably, he had a longstanding date at a nearby club with a buddy from Montreal. As far as the Royals were concerned, he simply wanted Hogan to know that he had free run of any of their training camps. Plus unlimited access to Private Larry Elder.

'I love the idea of The Rage,' he was smiling. 'It would fit Larry like a glove. Something else, too.'

'Like what?'

'Larry's a quick study and he knows all about that movement of yours. Second Front Now. Better still, he thoroughly approves.'

*

Hogan had locked his bike to a line of railings across the road from the Beaver Club. He'd returned briefly to the canteen to reclaim his stuffed rabbit, and now he tied it to the handlebars and skirted Trafalgar Square before setting off towards the river. It was a cloudy night and there was rain in the air, and he knew a night like this would keep the *Luftwaffe* away.

Traffic was thin in the darkness along the Embankment. Hogan dismounted and stood beside the wall, gazing down at the stir of the rising tide. He knew it was an image that wouldn't leave him for hours, the current signalled by nothing but sundry bits of rubbish, ghostlike, heading upriver. On similar nights like this, when he knew that a raid was unlikely, he sometimes wandered down through the maze of narrow streets where he lived until he got to a particular spot beside a Limehouse pub. An alley offered access to the water via a tiny apron of muddy beach, and he knew this stretch of the river well enough to picture the nearby docks in the darkness.

Hogan shared his tenement house with two other lodgers. One of them was a woman called Evie. It turned out that she was much younger than she looked, and she had a little girl, a scrap of a child with blonde curls and a lisp. She'd met and married a Greek sailor who was away for long months on Atlantic convoys. When his ship returned, it berthed either in Liverpool, or Glasgow, or in these same upriver docks, and because Evie had friends among the stevedores she always knew when her hubbie was due back.

So far, Hogan had yet to meet him but photos of Yannis were impossible to miss if you paid Evie's little sitting room a visit. In the photos, he was a big man, wild looking, handsome, with black curly hair and a toothy grin, and the moment Hogan had first glimpsed him he knew at once that he belonged to that community of nomads you'd find in any docklands hostel. Only this morning, moments before he'd pushed his bike into the street and set off for work, Evie had emerged from her room to tell him that Yannis's boat was due within the week. From somewhere, God knows how, she was going to get flowers and something nice to eat and drink. She'd taken a shine to Hogan, and she'd made him promise that he'd call by to lift a glass or two.

Now, Hogan set off along the Embankment. His route home skirted the Tower of London, passing deserted terraces that must once have been grand. Like similar properties in Belgravia and Knightsbridge, areas that Hogan also knew well, they'd long been abandoned by their owners. Laying hands on staff, above all a decent cook, was now close to impossible and these families had decamped to the big city-centre hotels like the Ritz and the Dorchester where a lot of money could still put something grander on the table for the rich.

Hogan pedalled on. It was impossible to miss how quickly these buildings surrendered to damp and neglect and the general air of shabbiness that seemed a badge of a war like this: ruined stucco, peeling plaster, blast-damaged windows patched with linen or cardboard. In the next block lay a small urban park but here the war, for once, had done Londoners a favour. All the iron railings had been ripped up, leaving the pale, sodden turf available for anyone to take a stroll.

Beyond Tower Bridge, the city abandoned its airs and graces, enveloped by the East End. Here the bomb damage was everywhere, side streets cratered, rubble roughly piled at the kerbside, the faint whiff of escaping gas, and the stronger sweetness of ruptured sewers. Hogan could hear the crunch of broken glass beneath his tyres, and as he braked beside the entrance to a tube station he recognised yet again the ghostly remains of the posters that had gone up that first winter when he'd settled in the East End. *Be a Man*, went the slogan, *Leave a Space for Women and Children*. You found the posters everywhere, all over the network, and the joke that did the rounds of the *Express* newsroom during the darker days of the Battle of Britain suggested they should have been printed in German.

Past the station, he counted the streets on the left. An air raid warden stepped into the road and demanded to know where he was going.

'Home.' Hogan fumbled for his press pass.

The warden produced a flashlight and examined it. Under the tin hat, he had the face of a bank manager.

'It's late,' he said. 'Is this journey really necessary?'

Hogan muttered something about how news was perishable, how you had to nurse the best stories into print, why they had to be fresh for next day's breakfast tables, and then he shielded his eyes as the flashlight came up to illuminate his face.

'Where do you get an accent like that, sir?'

'Canada.'

'You're telling me you volunteered to come over? Out of uniform?'

'Yes.'

'And you live round here?'

'Number 14,' Hogan nodded down the road. 'Crofton Street.'

'So why would you ever do that?'

Hogan held his gaze, then shrugged. The flashlight wavered for a moment and then dipped a little until it found the rabbit, still attached to the handlebars.

'And that, sir?'

'A present. For a friend.'

It was true. Moments later, the flashlight was off and the warden had waved Hogan on his way. He pedalled into the darkness, mindful of a shouted warning about the next big bomb crater in the road, only partially filled. Hogan swerved, missing it by inches, one hand reaching for the rabbit.

Crofton Street lay on the right. The door to number 14 had been salvaged from a local bombsite after a near-miss had splintered the original, and it had no lock. Hogan pushed it open and bumped his bike into the narrow hall. The old man who lived upstairs had been cooking cabbage again, and the stink hung in the cold air.

Hogan bent to take off his cycle clips, and then his fingers tugged at the knot that secured the rabbit to the handlebars. Tomorrow morning, first thing, he'd leave it at Evie's door. Her little girl would love it. He'd nearly teased the knot out when he heard a movement in the darkness. Then a door opened, and a pale disc of face appeared. It was Evie, and the moment she stepped towards him he sensed she'd been crying. The back of her hand was wiping one eye. Hogan glimpsed a handkerchief balled in the other hand.

Hogan stared at her, then abandoned the rabbit and opened his arms. First the *Globe*, and now the *Express*, he thought. You don't get this far without scenting the imminence of something terrible.

'Yannis?' he murmured. It was barely a question.

9

PARIS, THREE DAYS LATER

After a great deal of thought, Schultz had come up with a plan. This French Gestapo, Zimmermann had mused yet again. These people are totally out of control. They have the backing of the *Sicherheitsdienst*, they have no manners, and they think we have no memory. Unless we invite them to think otherwise, the *Abwehr* – your *Abwehr*, our *Abwehr* – is doomed. Do what you can, Schultz, and report back.

Like Zimmermann himself, Schultz nursed an impatience with the eternal turf wars that were the price of belonging to the Greater Reich. Traditionally, the gathering of military intelligence had been the job of the *Abwehr*. That was where both Schultz and Zimmermann had earned their spurs. Military intelligence was an elastic phrase and in the last years of peace Zimmermann had wasted no time in expanding the reach of the agents and analysts in the Bendlerstrasse.

Then, in the opening months of the war, Himmler's rival SS empire had scored a famous victory on the Dutch border in the shape of two luckless British agents lured into a trap at Venlo. Under interrogation, Himmler's Gestapo had sweated countless names out of them and rolled up an entire network. From that moment on, said wiser heads in the upper reaches of the Bendlerstrasse, the *Abwehr*'s days in the Nazi sun were numbered.

Not because they lacked the talent or the application but because Himmler had the ear of his master. The *Sicherheitsdienst*, he told Hitler, is the Intelligence Service the Reich deserves. And to prove his point, he advised his master to look no further than Paris.

Hitler adored Paris. He'd visited it just once, on a cloudy June morning in 1940, a bare two days after his armies had brought France to its knees. The roads south were still choked with refugees but the boulevards of the capital itself were empty. In the early morning Hitler had been driven from viewpoint to viewpoint, trailed by a newsreel crew, and the resulting footage had been screened in cinemas across the *Heimat*.

Homeland audiences applauded the sight of their Führer visiting the Opera House, La Madelaine and the Trocadero, from where he gazed down the long boulevard that led to the Eiffel Tower. There were more stops on this brief tour but what had always struck Schultz, who'd seen the footage countless times, was the expression on Hitler's face. He couldn't quite believe that he was the master of this astonishing city. He was bewildered by the French refusal to put up a decent fight and bewitched by everything he was seeing. He was back on his waiting Focke-Wulf Condor by nine in the morning, and he never returned.

That left a void in Paris that Himmler was only too eager to fill. Nazi tribal chiefs were demanding French booty and the *Abwehr* was only too happy to offer its services. Schultz had helped set up the *Otto Buro*, requisitioning a taskforce to empty premises abandoned by the capital's richer Jews. Laden trucks motored to a rail yard in the north of Paris, and it was one of Schultz's jobs to tally the seized belongings that daily made their way to Germany.

Then had come new bees to the *Abwehr*'s honeypot, led by a career gangster called Henri Chamberlin. Schultz had met him in the early days, recognising at once how this burly ex-jailbird could help. He had a range of skills, most of them violent, and he held no beliefs in anything but money. He'd deliver for whoever paid him most, and when the property seizures multiplied and re-multiplied, the German authorities – delighted – realised they had a real success on their hands. This, after all, was a Frenchman. He understood how to squeeze the last sou out of his beleaguered countrymen, and he never cared how many throats he cut on the way to a serious fortune.

By now, Schultz knew the *Abwehr* had a problem. Chamberlin, aided by Himmler's rival SS, was recruiting thousands of convicted criminals into a gang that was swelling by the day. These were murderers, rapists, racketeers, hoodlums and kidnappers and all it took was a phone call from Chamberlin with SS backing to free yet more of them from jail. Schultz had done his best to sound the alarm, to tell anyone who'd listen that Chamberlin recognised no authority but his own, but his early warnings fell on deaf ears. The booty trains headed for Berlin were getting longer and longer, and worse still – thanks to their tireless gangster – the SS in Paris were growing bolder by the day.

And so Henri Chamberlin found himself installed in a smart apartment building on rue Lauriston where he parked his white Bentley and held court in the uniform of an SS *Hauptsturmführer*. People he met for the first time were impressed by these trappings of Nazi power but those on the inside – including Schultz – knew better. Henri Chamberlin had become a robber baron, ruthless, insatiable and widely feared, which suited the SS rather well.

Schultz had walked the two kilometres from *Abwehr* headquarters at the Hôtel Lutetia, enjoying the fitful winter sunshine on his face. Number 93, rue Lauriston was a heavily guarded four-storey building in a wealthy quarter south of the Arc de Triomphe. Schultz had been here on a number of occasions recently, mainly social calls to briefly show his face at one or other of Chamberlin's lavish parties after his own return from a posting to Kyiv. The salons on the first floor, with their high ceilings, attentive butlers, profitable conversations and endless supplies of champagne attracted guests from every corner of Odile's *Faubourg*. With them came a fashionable scatter of actors, professional sportsmen, musicians, cabaret singers and other metropolitan luminaries. Schultz had once pushed into one of the lavatories to the rear of the first floor to find Maurice Chevalier with his trousers around his ankles, enjoying a quiet cigarette.

Schultz had neither the taste nor the patience for company like this, which won him few friends among Chamberlin's entourage, but he'd now paid enough visits to view mutilated bodies at the mortuary in the Pitié-Salpêtrière Hospital to recognise the building's real function. Across the capital, Chamberlin's gang was known as *La Carlingue*, or 'The Cabin'. The top floor of rue Lauriston housed a suite of barely furnished rooms reserved for torture. The screams of men and women who'd crossed Chamberlin and his lieutenants were said to keep the neighbours awake at night, while gunshots from the basement signalled the moment when *La Carlingue*'s victims were put out of their misery. Even Odile regarded violence on this scale as excessive.

Now, Schultz crossed the road and approached the two guards at the main door of number 93. They both wore the black uniform of the SS, and the older of the two men carried the rank of *SS-Scharführer*. When Schultz paused on the pavement, his *Abwehr* uniform raised the faintest smile.

'You have an appointment, Herr *Major*?' Bavarian accent.

'I have a meeting.'

'With?'

'Monsieur Chamberlin'

'Monsieur Chamberlin isn't available. I'm afraid he's been called away.'

'Really? We talked on the phone less than an hour ago.'

'Monsieur Chamberlin is a very busy man, Herr *Major*. May I suggest you lift the phone again? Tomorrow, perhaps?' He shrugged. 'Or maybe the next day?'

Schultz held his gaze, then pushed past. The door eased open under his weight and he found himself in the spacious lobby which served as a reception centre. A desk in the corner was dominated by a wall map of France, the area under German occupation a darker shade than the rest. South of the Loire, the French were governed from Vichy.

'Herr *Major*?' The figure behind the desk, a much older man, was wearing a light suit and his accent suggested he was probably French. Schultz barely spared him a glance as he stepped into the hall and made for the stairs, hearing the scrape of a chair as the older man got to his feet.

Schultz was already halfway up the stairs. The walls were hung with framed photographs of footballers from a selection of the top French clubs, with a heavy emphasis on Olympique de Marseilles. Odile, to Schultz's surprise, was a football fan with a special *tendresse* for a star midfielder known as 'The Black Pearl'. Schultz was glancing at him now as he clumped onto the first-floor landing, the young Moroccan in the striped shirt, stretching for a ball, perfect balance, intense concentration.

'Herr Schultz...'

Schultz paused. He recognised the voice, thickened by the two packs of Gauloises Caporal he was said to smoke a day. Pierre Bonny had been a respected police inspector in Paris before corruption charges put him in prison. Released three years later, he'd now brought a little much-needed discipline to the mayhem that had been *La Carlingue*, and one of his many assets was a command of basic German.

The older man on the desk had summoned one of the SS guards in the street, and both were mounting the stairs. Bonny dismissed them with a cursory wave of his hand.

'Follow me, Herr *Major*. My apologies in advance.'

Bonny led the way to the second floor. Chamberlin, Schultz knew, occupied a windowless office in the very middle of the corridor. The gangster boss of *La Carlingue* had a healthy interest in his own survival, and the office had been lined with steel as a further bid to keep unpleasant surprises at bay. Bonny had a key. Inside, the stale air was laced with something heavy and acrid. Chamberlin, Schultz concluded, also smoked Gauloises.

'Here, please...' Bonny indicated two armchairs in the corner of the room. The low table between them was cluttered with a spread of magazines, empty cups, a brimming ashtray, plus a small vase stocked with orchids.

'Henri has been called to the Majestic,' Bonny sighed. 'Stulpnagel's staff again. That man has not the first idea of the pressure we're under. You'll have seen yesterday's demands from *Reichsminister* Goering?'

'No.'

'It's mainly fine art. The *Reichsminister* has the list we acquired from the Louvre. The French, sensibly, have buried most of it in the countryside but somehow Berlin expect us to find the ones he's selected, dig them up, brush them down and send them north.'

Schultz shrugged. The Majestic Hôtel served as *Wehrmacht* headquarters in Paris, a happy combination of luxury suites and fine dining for *General* Stulpnagel's small army of staff officers.

'We had agreed a meeting,' Schultz said again. 'Chamberlin gave me no indication that he wouldn't be here. I know it's a small courtesy, but a phone call would have been enough. God knows we all have far too much to do.'

'Of course, of course. Just tell me how I can help.'

Unlike his hooligan boss, Bonny understood the value of an apology and a listening ear. Chamberlin, to Schultz, had always looked like a thug and the big face in the *Abwehr* files had been further coarsened by good living, while Bonny, behind the thick glasses, might have passed for an academic, or perhaps a senior civil servant. Unprompted, he said he was here to soothe Schultz's ruffled feathers, to broker a brief peace between the warring organisations, and Schultz was almost tempted to believe him.

Almost.

'We understand that you're putting money into a play,' Schultz said. 'Bernard Shaw. *Pygmalion.* Is that true?'

'Not we. Not me. Chamberlin. He's been fucking too many actresses lately, and one of them's got under his skin. She wants to play the flower girl, Eliza Doolittle, and she loves orchids which is another reason why Chamberlin is making the play happen. Mention orchids and the man gets silly. He says he's trying to bring French and German audiences together but when did Henri ever need a justification? Guilt normally passes him by. I'm not sure he even knows what it means.'

'Is the play fully cast? Do you happen to know?'

'I gather it's not, but they're starting rehearsals next week.'

'Then he should make time to audition an actor friend of ours.'

'He has a name, this friend?' Bonny had produced a pen and a small notebook.

'Lucien Gasquet.'

'You mean *der kleine Korken*?' Bonny glanced up. For once the smile looked genuine.

The little cork. Schultz had never heard the phrase before but had to admit it did Gasquet more than justice: the born survivor, negotiating the foaming rapids and treacherous undercurrents that had become life in occupied Paris. Much to Schultz's delight, the little cork's affair with Zimmermann had blossomed, and lately they'd moved into a requisitioned apartment a bare five minutes from rue de la Faisanderie.

'Gasquet produces as well,' Schultz said. 'In fact he's just done another Shaw play, *Saint Joan*. Crap like that's irresistible if you're after an evening of heavy clues. The brutal invader? The English goddams from across the Channel? All dressed up to represent us Hun bastards?'

'You watched it?'

'No. I'm a simple man, Monsieur Bonny. This stuff I pick up from Gasquet. To get a part in *Pygmalion* he needs to impress Chamberlin and maybe the actress he's fucking. All I want is a date and a place and I can make that happen. Gasquet loves orchids, too, if you think that might help.'

Bonny nodded, held Schultz's gaze for a moment, and then went to Chamberlin's desk. From a drawer, he produced a sizeable appointments book and flipped ahead through the coming days and weeks until he went backwards again and settled on a date.

'February 2nd?' He named a theatre. 'Maybe late afternoon?'

'That's next week. How late?'

'Half past five? He's put "read-through" here. That could be Gasquet's opportunity. Chamberlin told me yesterday they're still looking for a Professor Higgins.'

Schultz nodded, making a note of his own. It would be dark by the time the audition was over, which would be perfect for the plans he'd laid. He looked up again. Bonny was back in the armchair. Evidently, he had something else on his mind.

'You mind a word of advice, Herr Schultz? Assuming we're on the same side?' Schultz said nothing, gestured for him to carry on. 'That guy you killed way back. The day before war broke out.'

'Babineau?'

'*Il Pulpo.*'

'What about him?'

'You might need to watch out for yourself, take more than the normal precautions.'

'We're talking about the police?'

'Christ, no. You did them a favour. Babineau was half-Italian. He was also from Naples, which makes it much worse. He had mafia connections going way back and two of these reptiles arrived at the Gare Montparnasse last week. Sadly we've lost track of them since but we don't think they came for the museums. Italians are like kids. They get sentimental for all the wrong reasons.'

'Meaning?'

'Meaning next month was Babineau's birthday. He would have been fifty. The family believe they should honour his memory.' The smile again, but colder this time. 'Maybe you need to join the dots, Herr *Major, n'est-ce pas?*'

Schultz considered the proposition then nodded and said he was grateful. Should this intelligence be true, then it was impressive. Small wonder *La Carlingue* had rebadged itself as the French Gestapo, he thought. Employ a small army of criminals and jailbirds and you infiltrate every corner of this city. With Himmler's backing, Chamberlin and Bonny had been happy to join forces with the old enemy and there was doubtless a great deal of money to be made, to everyone's mutual advantage.

'I hear that Chamberlin's due a new working name,' Schultz grunted. 'Lafont? Am I right?'

'You are, Herr Schultz,' Bonny got to his feet and extended a hand. 'And we think that's probably a good sign. I happen to know that we've delivered far more than any of your people in Berlin ever expected, and for once we're not talking fine fucking art.'

Rue de la Faisanderie was a brisk ten-minute walk from rue Lauriston. Less than an hour ago, Schultz had suspected that Zimmermann was right, that the *Abwehr* in this city was in deep trouble, and now he knew it was probably worse than even Zimmermann had thought. On the phone, Chamberlin had never had any intention of opening his office door to the likes of an *Abwehr* Major. He may have been elsewhere in the building. He may, God knows, have genuinely been called away to the Hôtel Majestic. But what was certain was the role that Bonny had been deputised to play. Try and make a friend of this *Abwehr* dinosaur. Try and open his eyes to what's really happening here in Paris. And if that doesn't work, try and scare him.

Schultz paused at the intersection that would take him into rue de la Faisanderie. It was here, more than two years earlier, that he'd kicked a man to death. He'd done it because Odile's masked ball had tested his patience to breaking point, and because he was a little drunk. Dress a man in what had once been his first skin – the brown shirt, the belt, the polished boots – and don't be surprised by what might happen next. In Berlin, he'd done his best to beat Communists to death because they were helping themselves to what remained of the old Germany. At Odile's house that evening, it was theft of a different order but theft nonetheless. There were certain liberties you could take, but Gasquet's ageing arse wasn't one of them.

Odile's door opened on Schultz's second knock. Expecting Odile herself, Schultz found himself looking at a tall young black figure with a dazzling smile and impenetrable French. The spotless white shift extended to below his knees, and a colourful silk scarf was heaped around his slender neck.

'Odile?' Schultz enquired.

The question triggered a regretful shake of the head, a gentle gesture with his right hand, and another volley of fiercely accented French. Then a second figure appeared, and Schultz was aware of bony white fingers lingering briefly on the bareness of this youth's forearm. Schultz had never seen anyone so black before.

'Gasquet,' he grunted. 'Are you inviting me in?'

A whispered instruction from Gasquet despatched the young black into the depths of the house. Odile, he said, was out for the day. A coffee, perhaps, and maybe a croissant hot from the oven? Moments later, Schultz was following Gasquet into the big kitchen. Outside, through the tall windows, the sunshine had disappeared and snow was falling from a leaden sky.

'So who is he?' Schultz nodded at the open door.

'We call him Conso. He's a present from Odile's husband. Dominique's still out in Somalia and he suspects we're having a hard time.'

'Conso? What sort of name is that?'

'It's short for *consolation*. Dominique found him in the bazaar in Addis Ababa. He posted him to Algiers with the Tuareg, and a family friend put him on a boat to Marseilles. After that she lost track of him but happily he's here now. Odile insists that *consolation* really means a kind of tonic, a pick-me-up, and I have to say she's not wrong. He's a beautiful boy, both inside and out. Beautiful nature. Beautiful everything. Have you ever seen a face like that? Odile thinks God cast him as a woman and then changed his mind. It's been a pleasure to share him.'

'And Conso? He has any views on the matter?'

'None at all. Novelty in this city has become hard to find, Herr Schultz. Even German street patrols are impressed. Conso has cheered us all up, especially Odile.'

'She's sleeping with him?'

'Of course. She says he's returned her to the wild. The day this war ends, and we take our sticky fingers off Africa, is the day she ships out with him, back to Ethiopia, back to the heat and the light. Believe me, gratitude is too small a word.'

'To her husband?'

'To Conso. You know Odile. She's impenetrable. She lives in the darkness of her own soul. Can you imagine any man breaching those walls? Coaxing her out? Into the sunshine? That's what this boy has done. He's truly remarkable.'

'And you, my friend? You share that sunshine?'

'Of course. I was never frightened of pleasure.'

'And Zimmermann? He knows…?' Schultz gestured vaguely towards the door.

'More than that. He's had a taste or two of our good fortune, as he should. Conso is someone we all celebrate, even you my friend, should you feel the need.'

Schultz nodded, said it was a generous offer, changed the subject. Henri Chamberlin, he said, was looking for an actor to play Professor Higgins.

'I heard.'

'You know his money has gone into *Pygmalion*?'

'Everyone knows. He could be almost human, making a gesture like that. Why's he doing it? What's in it for him?'

'An actress called Mimi. Chamberlin can't help himself, can't stop fucking her, so we think you ought to try for the part. Chamberlin wants to audition you next Thursday. His girlfriend is the one you really need to impress but Chamberlin will be there, too. He knows what she can do to a man, and he doesn't trust her in company.'

'Very wise. But why me? Why do I need another Shaw play on top of *Joan of Arc*? One, believe me, is quite enough.'

'That's not the point, my friend. We need to get Chamberlin into that theatre and the promise of you on stage can make it happen.'

'But why? Am I missing something here?'

'Not at all. Chamberlin virtually alone in that theatre? Unprotected? Unsuspecting? He doesn't care who he hurts, and he's made a lot of enemies. You'd be doing the Resistance a very big favour.'

'You're going to kill him? Chamberlin?' Gasquet was looking alarmed.

'Have him killed.'

'Why?'

'Because he's an ugly piece of shit, and because we need the Resistance to start taking you seriously. You're one of them, remember. That's what they should be thinking. That's what we *need* them to think. And thanks to Zimmermann you have better access to what's really going on than anyone else they'll ever meet. Just as long as they trust you.'

'But why? What did Chamberlin ever do to me?' Gasquet was whining now, a child trapped by circumstance with nowhere left to go.

'Those aren't questions you should be asking. All we want you to do is attend the theatre with something to say for yourself. You need to treat it as a real audition. You need to *want* to be Professor Higgins. After that, everything will be taken care of.'

'You're going to shoot him?'

'Have him shot. The Communists have been trying since we went into Russia because Chamberlin's seriously pissing them off. It's my pleasure to offer a target they can't possibly miss.'

'But Chamberlin works for the Germans, for the Gestapo. In this city, he *is* the Gestapo.'

'Of course.'

'So what happens when they come knocking at my door? Afterwards?'

'They won't.'

'But how do I know that?'

'Ask Herr Zimmermann,' Schultz was looking at the tall black figure who'd reappeared at the open door. 'When he's not too busy.'

10

Looking back, Hogan would be perplexed and slightly shocked by the workings of fate. He'd never attached the slightest importance to 14 February. Valentine's Days had come and gone, back in the Maritimes, and he'd ignored them all. He'd never bought a card, never spared the displays in the candy shop even a passing glance. True, that last year at school, before he turned his back on Newcastle and the Miramichi, he'd once received a huge card in shocking pink. The card was unsigned, except for a line of pencilled kisses, and it had made his eldest sister hoot with laughter.

'Who have you upset?' she'd asked, a question that had stayed with him ever since. In truth, the list was very long, and almost exclusively male, and the fact that it might have come from a girl with some kind of crush had never occurred to him.

'So who are you dating, Miramichi?'

Hogan had been summoned to the general manager's office. On the *Daily Express*, E. J. Robertson was widely acknowledged to be the proprietor's presence on earth. Back home in Toronto, he'd been working at a city centre hotel when he'd caught Beaverbrook's eye, which was why he was known on the paper as 'the Bell Hop', but now he served as the ballast that kept

Beaverbrook honest, and he'd done a fine job in translating crisp reporting and daring layouts into astronomical circulation figures. Robertson rarely bothered with working journalists as lowly as Hogan, which made this morning's summons all the more puzzling.

'Me and dating are strangers, sir,' Hogan was looking at a line of cards on the shelf behind Robertson's desk. One was embossed with a plump heart in scarlet satin.

'Any reason I might understand?'

'I doubt it, sir,' Hogan shrugged. 'No offence.'

'You prefer men?'

'Not that way.'

Robertson nodded, studied Hogan a moment longer, and then opened a file of cuttings. Upside down, Hogan recognised some of the headlines the subs had attached to the copy he'd brought back from the Second Front Now movement. The most recent piece had included a brief interview with an ex-staff journalist now tasked with organising a series of giant rallies across the country. Under thirty thousand, he'd told Hogan, and I lose my job. Imagine trying to fill Trafalgar Square, every single square inch. This is politics, not football. The man lives in a world of his own.

The man, Hogan had assumed at the time, was The Rage. And it turned out he'd been right.

'You'll be glad to know The Beaver very much approves of this copy of yours,' Robertson tapped the file of cuttings. 'But serving at our master's pleasure was never going to be a simple proposition. God, how I loathe those dinner parties. He threw another one last week. Mountbatten was there, and Noël Coward, and the usual riffraff from Mr Churchill's circle of toadies, and now the boss wants someone whose head won't be turned to find out what they're up to. Coward has consented to an interview. Denham Studios is out in the sticks. I'll get Jenkins to drive you. That man's a sucker for the movies.'

'Denham Studios, sir?' Hogan was lost.

'Yep. I'm told they're shooting some key scene or other this afternoon. I gather it involves lots of smoke and water. Mountbatten has been invited, which might be interesting.' He paused. 'HMS *Kelly*? Name mean anything?'

'I'm afraid not.'

'Sank off Crete last year. Check the cuttings. Not our finest hour, despite any opinions Mr Coward might have on the matter. Good luck, son. You're expected for two o'clock. Find out what the bastard's up to.'

'Mountbatten?'

'Noël Coward.' A thin smile. 'So remember the date and watch that arse of yours.'

*

It was already late morning, but Hogan knew he had to check the cuttings library. The front desk was manned during the week by a divorcee from Ealing called Sheila who was rumoured to have been a beauty queen at the Clacton Butlin's before the holiday camp was handed over to the military. Judging by yet another display of Valentine cards, she was a popular girl.

'Fourth cabinet on the left,' she smothered a yawn. 'Lovely man, that Lord Mountbatten. So handsome, so bloody attractive, never a single hair out of place. If he was a dessert, I'd have seconds.'

Hogan spent an hour with the cuttings, wondering why this man had passed him by. The name wasn't unfamiliar, far from it. Hogan knew that he was of royal blood, that his connections extended to Buckingham Palace and probably beyond, and that he'd married a fortune, but what came as a surprise was the sheer volume of press he seemed to have attracted.

In photograph after photograph, Sheila's favourite dessert had offered himself to Fleet Street's finest snappers: the sculpted head, the immaculate side parting, the shoulders back, the line of medal ribbons across the broadness of his chest. If you were looking for hope in these beleaguered times, Hogan thought, then here it was: defiance, and courage, and fortitude all made flesh.

But there was a great deal more to this story, and as he dug deeper, Hogan began to keep a tally of the number of times HMS *Kelly*, his Lordship's first seagoing command, had so nearly come to grief. An encounter with an enemy mine at the mouth of the River Tyne. Storm damage early in 1940. A collision with another destroyer just two days after her return to sea. And then a brief battle with the Germans off the Norwegian coast before limping home after a torpedo hit her amidships. In all, at a significant cost in lives, HMS *Kelly* had lurched from disaster to disaster before German dive-bombers had finally sunk her off the south coast of Crete.

On his way out of the cuttings library, Sheila called his name. She wanted to know more about his interest in Mountbatten. When Hogan briefly explained about his trip out to Denham, her eyes widened.

'You're going to meet him? Face-to-face? *Talk* to him?'

'That's the plan.'

'Christ,' she shook her head. 'You men have all the luck in this bloody world.'

Jenkins was one of Beaverbrook's team of chauffeurs and insisted on leaving central London early in order not to miss anything at the studios. Thanks to his addiction to movie magazines, Hogan was able to pump him about the filming. Noël Coward, it seemed, had come across the story of HMS *Kelly*'s final hours and had decided that here was an opportunity to raise the nation's spirits. On the face of it, Hogan could think of no good reason why losing a ship should be anything but bad news but by now he'd been in the country long enough to recognise the national addiction to disaster.

Two years back, the Germans had chased most of the British Army out of northern France, but by some strange magic the evacuation that followed had become a kind of victory. The English bone had been torn from the teeth of the hated German *Hund* and Hogan had found himself shaking his head in disbelief at the headlines. Many of them had adorned the front page of his own paper. MIRACLE AT DUNKIRK, his favourite had read. WE LIVE TO FIGHT ANOTHER DAY.

Do we? Just now, Hogan found that hard to believe. The news from the Far East and North Africa was getting ever gloomier, while the shelves at the grocery stores were bare. Beer in the pubs cost a fortune and ration cards, it was rumoured, would soon be buying just a handful of the calories you needed to survive. Where Hogan came from, food on the table was something you took for granted, yet only yesterday at his desk in the newsroom he'd begun to make enquiries about getting a share in an allotment. Lovely idea, the woman on the phone had told him, but the queues stretch round the block. MIRACLE AT DUNKIRK, he thought glumly. WE LIVE TO STARVE ANOTHER DAY.

Jenkins delivered him to the Denham Studios in the middle of the lunch hour. The main lot between the huge hangar-like structures was empty, apart from a line of scenery flats carefully stacked against one of the studio walls and protected from the weather. By now, thanks to Jenkins, Hogan knew that Noël Coward had lent his scripting skills to Mountbatten's account of losing his ship. HMS *Kelly* had been there to embark British troops on yet another evacuation, but Stuka bombs had quickly broken the destroyer's back and sent her to the bottom. According to the latest magazine account Jenkins had read, Mountbatten owed everything to his magnificent crew, whom Coward was only too happy to put on the nation's cinema screens.

'It can't fail,' Jenkins had told Hogan in the car. 'It's a wonderful story.'

Really? At last, they'd found their way to the canteen. According to Jenkins, the heroic loss of *Kelly* was the only movie in production, and most of the tables were occupied by extras dressed as sailors. Many had visited the make-up department for daubs of oil and pretend burns. Some of the uniforms had been ripped, and one of the younger diners sported an ugly wound that appeared to be still bleeding. One entire table, longer than the rest, had been reserved for young matelots swathed in makeshift bandages, heavily bloodstained, and one of them was bent over a bowl of soup, the sling for his broken arm carefully folded beside his script.

Looking round, Hogan was amazed by the artifice and the make-believe. Only last year, a real destroyer had foundered under a torrent of bombs. Men had been killed and injured. Yet barely months later, accompanied by a decent lunch, it was happening all over again.

'Hungry?' Jenkins was at the counter.

Hogan nodded. Unlike the Beaver Club, the studio canteen ran to proper joints of meat, carved in front of your eyes. The accompanying vegetables hadn't been boiled to death, which was unusual, and there was a choice of potatoes. Hogan went for two thick slices of lamb, carrying his laden plate carefully to a nearby table. Moments later, a uniformed officer appeared at the main door and clapped his hands. Heads lifted around the canteen and a figure Hogan had been studying only hours ago in the cuttings library stepped into view.

There was the scrape of dozens of chairs as diners rose to their feet. One or two of them saluted, and the gesture quickly spread across the canteen. In the flesh, *Kelly*'s real-life commander was undeniably impressive. Mountbatten was taller than Hogan had expected, and his open duffle coat revealed a naval uniform as he began to move from table to table, shaking hands, patting shoulders, pausing for a murmured word or two. As he came closer, Hogan caught the essence of these brief conversations. Marvellous, he kept saying, wonderful, and every movement, every gesture, carried a slightly regal sincerity that put a smile on face after face.

This was the battle-scarred Captain who'd led his men into battle and here he was again, in their hour of need, lifting spirits, spreading good cheer, telling them how well they were doing. Mountbatten, in short, had become part of this world of make-believe, of smoke and mirrors, yet there was something so compelling about his performance that Hogan, too, was beginning to lose his bearings.

He beckoned Jenkins closer. Mountbatten, barely feet away, was bent over the next table.

'These men actually served with him?' Hogan whispered.

'Christ no, son. They're bloody actors.'

After lunch, a studio executive took Hogan and Jenkins to the main set, a vast space dominated by an enormous water tank. There was still a chill of winter in the air, and Hogan could smell the acrid tang of fuel oil. The steel platform at the far end of the tank was occupied by three cameras on wooden tripods, and a small group – mainly men – was huddled beneath one of the huge lighting stands, heads bent over an open script. Mountbatten had disappeared by now, but the extras from the canteen had gathered at the other end of the tank. They looked, thought Hogan, disconsolate and a little cold, which probably suited the next scene rather well.

'Mr Hogan?'

Hogan glanced round at the proffered hand. She was small and vivid, her hair cut short. The red coat offered a welcome splash of colour among so many uniforms and the leather gloves felt soft when Hogan shook her hand.

'You got a spot of lunch OK, Mr Hogan?' Husky voice, lovely smile, hints of mischief.

'Lunch was great.'

'You're more than welcome. My name's Annie.'

Hogan introduced Jenkins and asked what might be happening next.

'We're rehearsing a big scene that slots into the sinking. The bombs have fallen and the Captain has ordered Abandon Ship. You're talking to a woman, Mr Hogan, so the detail is a bit foggy, but I gather this afternoon is about close-ups. Does that make any sense? From where you're standing?'

Hogan smiled, watching Jenkins as he wandered towards a knot of extras and fell into conversation. Having this woman briefly to himself was something of a relief. War, he thought, was overwhelmingly scripted for men.

'And the interview?' he asked. 'With Mr Coward?'

'Today's turning into a bit of a disaster. He's just spent lunchtime on a rewrite. If all goes well we might find you half an hour after the rehearsals but I'm afraid Mr Coward is a moving target. Think positive, Mr Hogan. They serve afternoon tea at four. Scones and all the clotted cream you can eat.'

'So the interview might not happen? Is that what you're telling me?'

'Love and war, Mr Hogan.' That smile again. 'Absolutely nothing guaranteed.'

She peeled off a glove, reached up and plucked something from his jacket. It was an artless gesture, totally spontaneous, and Hogan found himself looking at a tiny feather in the palm of her hand. She examined the feather more closely before sharing it with Hogan.

'You know what my mother used to tell me? She said this comes from a baby, a little chick, and she used to call it angel dust. It was a secret between us. I had to swear I'd tell no one. This early in the year is unusual but maybe it's a sign of spring.'

Hogan nodded. He was still looking at her hand, so small, so delicate, perfect nails lacquered the same shade as her coat.

'You work for the studios?' he asked.

'Christ, no. What makes you think that?'

'You said "we". *We're* rehearsing a big scene.'

'I meant his Lordship. He has a way of taking over everything that crosses his path. Hence *we*.'

'We're talking about Mountbatten?'

'The very same. Lord Louis. I'm a private in his little army but most days it's fun. He can't get enough of Mr Coward at the moment, as you might imagine. He's given the man an important chunk of his life, and he loves what's happening with the movie, but he needs to know that every last detail is right. We spend far too much time on his bloody set, believe me, but normally it isn't as cold as this. His Lordship tells me I need to toughen up and when I look for the twinkle in his eye it isn't there.'

'Maybe you should fight back.'

'I do. I tell him I'm not on his bloody boat and I never will be. He thinks that's funny because he thinks it would make me a better person and it took me several days to realise he meant it. You want another secret, Mr Hogan?'

'Try me.'

'We call him the Presence, because that's exactly what he is. It's a compliment really. He's everywhere, all the time. Big things? Little things? They all matter hugely to him. Some days it's like working for God. Other days, he can be a pain in the bottom.'

Hogan nodded. With the Coward interview maybe in doubt, he needed another trophy to take back to the *Express*.

'You're with Mountbatten a lot?'

'I'm part of Combined Ops. That's his baby. He likes to think of us as a family, and that's nice, so yes, we all see quite a lot of each other.'

'Combined Ops?'

'Top secret, I'm afraid. Ultra hush-hush. Breathe a word and I'd have to put a noose round your neck and find a tree.'

'But you could slip in a good word? On my behalf?'

'Why would I do that?'

'Maybe to get me some kind of interview?'

'With his Lordship?'

'With the Presence,' Hogan was frowning. 'Could you make that happen?'

For a moment, Hogan thought he'd gone way too far but then he was looking at the hand extended again, still ungloved, the softest touch of flesh on flesh.

'Interesting proposition,' she said. 'I'll do my very best.'

Filming the close-ups in the water tank stretched deep into the afternoon. Hogan had never been on a movie set before and he was fascinated by the endless takes and retakes, by the painstaking attention to lighting, and camera movement, and getting the half-submerged actors in exactly the right configuration. Each take called for a roughish sea, which meant cranking up the wave machine. Normally, the water was at least lukewarm but there were problems with the studio's boiler which had failed completely overnight and so the water was stone-cold.

Once the wave machine was up to speed, it splashed everywhere, and as a thick, oily smoke curled over the tank, the actors did their best to fake terror or blind despair, but the

longer he watched, the more Hogan began to understand that
precious moment when everything came together – a shouted
line, a despairing gesture, a bigger-than-usual wave that engulfed
the action. That was the cue for the director to shout 'cut', and
then 'print', and for watching studio hands to haul the soaking
cast out of the tank and rub them dry and present each actor
with a mug of hot cocoa before his next immersion.

The director was Noël Coward, and Hogan watched him
closely as he briefed his actors, gave them line notes, then
debated the coming sequence with his cinematographer. Like
Mountbatten, he was very obviously in charge, the centre of
everyone's attention, but this was authority of a different order.
He was a thin figure in a black polo-neck sweater and he had
none of his Lordship's easy grace. On the contrary, he was the
first into every conversation, insisting on this point or that,
scolding an actor who'd fluffed a line, offering a slightly arch
compliment to the technician in charge of smoke effects, riding
a wave of fidgety impatience in a bid to finish the afternoon's
work before retiring to watch the previous day's takes. Twice,
his ever-roaming eye settled briefly on Hogan, and after his
assistant had declared the day a wrap, he climbed carefully
down to the studio floor, shot Hogan a look and tapped the
watch on his wrist.

'A bare twenty minutes, alas, but let's make the best of them…
shall we?'

They talked in a back office. Signed publicity stills were
pinned to a huge corkboard, and Hogan recognised faces he'd
last seen in the Art Deco splendour of the Odeon in Leicester
Square. Greta Garbo, he noticed, had the careful hand of a
schoolgirl trying to impress.

'That's rare, believe me.' Coward had noticed Hogan's interest.
'She never signs for anyone, and never gives interviews. Fifteen

thousand letters a week from fans, and she burns the lot. Why did she oblige on this occasion? Who knows. Maybe it's a fake. After all, that's what this place is for...'

'Make-believe?'

'Fantasy. Fakery. Comfort. Solace. In peacetime, Mr Hogan, the cinema is a place to weep. Nowadays, there are all too many real tears and so we must conjure something a little different. You're going to ask me how this latest adventure of mine came to pass but first I must offer a confession. I had the faintest brush with the movie business a while back, a role in a film called *The Scoundrel*, and it was then that I realised that every movie set is a temple dedicated to cheating. Write it down, Mr Hogan. Cheating. Artifice. Clever lighting and endless patience. If you want the truth, I worship in a different temple. Care to hazard a guess?'

'The theatre.'

'Exactly. Good writing. Performance. Clever set design. The casting of a certain spell. Does any of this make sense?'

Hogan nodded. He'd never been to the theatre in his life but Jenkins had acquired a ticket for *Blithe Spirit* only a couple of months ago and held Noël Coward in awe as a direct result. Clever plot, he'd said. Brilliant dialogue. Audience rocking in the aisles. Now, back in the world of movies, Coward had changed tack.

'For this movie I was courted,' he nodded towards the set beyond the door. 'A little deputation arrived, a bunch of people not without influence in this wicked world. They wanted me to make a propaganda film. Happily, I was due to dine with Dickie and Edwina the following evening, and he told me about losing poor *Kelly*. After that, the movie wrote itself. It must be the same in your trade, Mr Hogan. You pen something half-decent, something that takes you by *surprise* on the page, and your heart leaps. Am I getting warm here? And might you like a cigarette?'

Hogan declined the offer. There was something icy in this man, the care he took to showcase his undeniable eloquence, every trait, every gesture so carefully measured. Another Presence, Hogan thought, determined to choreograph every second of his waking life.

'Dickie? Edwina?'

'The Mountbattens, dear boy. Everything worthwhile in this country begins and ends with the monarchy, and here's a very good example. You're looking at someone who truly admires our Senior Service. If I'm to render Dickie's story on the silver screen, then I owe his crew a duty of care. Our first working title was *White Ensign*, serviceable enough but it raised just a scintilla of doubt in the Admiralty, so naturally I came up with something a little different. Happily, they loved *In Which We Serve*, and they were equally supportive when I shared the script with them. Not just that, either. Ronald Neame is a cameraman of genius, and in David Lean I have the best cutter in the business. Get the right team, the right script, plus minute attention to every detail, and you're looking at something really special. I've promised Dickie a rouser, and that's exactly what he'll get. But you know what?' He leaned forward and touched Hogan lightly on the knee. 'Dedication like that is wasted on our masters.'

He sat back again, letting the observation settle between them, offering no further clues. Hogan fought the temptation to enquire further but failed completely.

'Masters?' he asked at length.

'MOI, dear boy. Ministry of Information. You've no doubt had dealings with these people yourself. They have no imagination, no guts, not the first idea of what really makes a difference on the screen or the stage or even in that paper of yours. They're gaggers and smotherers. They exist to choke the life out of anything with the merest spark of promise. You want to know what they said about Dickie's magnificent tale? About my script? They told me, and I quote, that *it will be exceedingly bad propaganda for the Navy as it shows one of HM's ships being sunk by enemy action.* Can you believe that? Be honest, please.'

Hogan was smiling. Dunkirk, he thought. Another triumph plucked from disaster.

'So what did you do?'

'We submitted that same script to Bertie. Happily he adored it. Not only that but he went into print, put words on paper. The exact phrase he used with respect to the Navy is written on my heart. He thought I'd captured the spirit of those brave folk who man our ships and keep us safe. Captured, Mr Hogan. Seized the essence of, the *truth* of. Now that doesn't happen by accident, a fact wasted on those fools in the Ministry.' He reached for a cigarette, and then shot Hogan a sudden smile. 'And so thankfully the show goes on. You can write that down, too, if you so wish.'

Hogan ignored the invitation, leaving his pen beside his notepad. Instead, he had another question.

'Bertie?' he asked.

'His Majesty the King, dear boy. In this country, if you want things to happen, one does nothing by halves.'

In the end, the interview extended to nearly an hour. Hogan did his best to turn it into a conversation, sensing that this martinet would respond best to someone who took a risk or two, and the gamble paid off. Noël Coward obviously loved the whiff of mischief, of the temptations of the unexpected question, and when Hogan began to lead him into the weeds of showbusiness he was very happy to respond. What it really took to bring a theatre audience to its feet. How bitchy people could be when a success put your name in lights. How an ancient country like Britain, fifty million people who should have known better, were still bound hand and foot by a class system that served no one but the rich. The latter whispered confidence brought a smile to Coward's pursed lips.

By now, given his inquisitor's accent, and perhaps his sheer youth, he seemed to view Hogan as a fellow outsider and, with the interview nearly done, he fell to musing about the virtues of camouflage.

'You need to be kidding people,' he murmured, 'all the time. Regardless of your antecedents, you need to become someone else. Maybe that's why it helps to be an actor, or maybe that's why one becomes an actor in the first place. You should try it, George.' That smile again. 'Might do you a power of no-good.'

This was the first time Coward had used Hogan's Christian name, and it felt like a compliment, or perhaps an invitation to an intimacy or two.

'I've done exactly the opposite,' Hogan confessed. 'Deep down I'm a hometown boy from the Maritimes, and I guess I always will be.'

'Religion? Does that matter?'

'It does.'

'You believe in God?'

'I do, yes.'

'Which brand? Are you a Catholic? A southpaw? Or perhaps something more exotic?'

The question was deliberately provocative, and Hogan coloured slightly before admitting that he was a Baptist.

'Golly. That's full immersion, isn't it?'

'I'm afraid so.'

'For life?'

'Yes. It happened to start in a river but that meant nothing at the time. Immersion turns out to be forever.'

'And you believe it?'

'I do.'

'Because it helps?'

'Because there's no other way. Not if you want to stay you.'

'And that's important?'

'It is. As long as you're straight with yourself.'

'No fibs?'

'Small ones. None that matter.'

'Any dancing?'

'Not that I can remember.'

'And God marks your homework? Every night when you say your prayers?'

'God watches. Which is probably more important.'

At this, Coward nodded, as if unsurprised. Then he leaned forward.

'One last story, George, this time for your ears only. As a little boy, I'd sit in the corners of railway carriages and sob my heart out in the hope that someone would take pity on me and perhaps give me tea at Fuller's. To my recollection, only two clergymen ever rose to the challenge. One of them talked to me for a long time and told me to trust in God and everything would turn out right. The other pinched my knee and gave me sixpence. Of the two, I infinitely preferred the latter. So what does that suggest?'

'About you?'

'About life, George.' He glanced at his watch and pulled a face before getting to his feet. 'It tells you to keep fibbing, and to keep taking risks.' He extended a cold hand. 'You've made our little chat a pleasure, George. Just one other thing.'

'Sir?'

'The young lady you impressed this afternoon. Dickie's girl.'

'You mean Annie?'

'I do, yes.' He was fumbling in his pocket. 'She asked me to give you this.'

Hogan took the proffered note, smoothing out the creases. There was no message, just a phone number. LAN 7667.

Hogan looked up, aware of the intensity of Coward's gaze.

'I happen to know that's her personal number, George, and it happens to be St Valentine's Day. Good luck, my friend…' a tiny squeeze of Hogan's shoulder '… and for God's sake learn how to *dance*.'

11

Schultz had never heard of *El Diablo* but had near-unlimited faith in *Oberst* Hans Zimmermann. Just now, summoned early to his office in the Hôtel Majestic, Schultz was nursing a cup of remarkably good coffee, happy to let Stulpnagel's intelligence chief finish his briefing.

'This is someone who came to us a couple of years ago. He's Spanish. He turned up here in the winter of 1940. We were still new to the city, still getting used to the French, still trying to stay friends. Even you, Schultz, have to admit that isn't easy.'

Schultz nodded, said nothing. He'd first been posted to Paris in the late thirties. Even in peacetime, the French often seemed to be living on a different planet.

'*El Diablo* means "The Devil",' Zimmermann continued. 'The guy served with the Nationalists during the Civil War. I'd love to tell you that he's got Fascism in his bones but that wouldn't be true. He'll fight for whoever pays best.'

'Like Chamberlin?'

'Exactly. Though he and *La Carlingue* have fallen out.'

'Over?'

'Money. Always money.'

'So why The Devil?'

'He got himself blown up in Madrid. He was in the city as a spy for the Nationalists and one of our Condor Legion bombs brought down half a church on top of his head. If you're trying to picture him at prayer, Schultz, don't bother. He still believes that churches offer the best firing positions for a sniper but on this occasion he was wrong.'

'Damage?' Schultz was still thinking about *El Diablo*.

'Terrible facial injuries, deep wounds poorly stitched. His nose is a mess, his mouth leaks, and his left eye has stayed half shut but he can still use a sniper rifle with the other one. This isn't someone a girl would take home to mama and his Spanish passport doesn't help.'

'A recent photo?'

'The number, Schultz.' Zimmermann ducked his head to notes on the desk. '3266607. It's the sixes that count, all three of them.'

'The mark of the Antichrist?'

'Exactly. Hence *Diablo*. He's a big man, two metres tall, carries a bit of weight. There's no missing him, especially the face. He once told me he even frightens the animals at the zoo.'

'Does he have a real name?' Schultz was looking at the passport. Zimmermann was right about the face. Viewed from any angle, it was truly grotesque.

'Carlos Ortega. I gather they named him after some nettle or other.'

'Who told you that?'

'He did.'

'And you've seen him recently?'

'Yes. He's made an enemy of Chamberlin so he's touting for trade. We took him to the ranges at Vincennes just to make sure.'

'And?'

'Ninety-three per cent bulls at one hundred metres with a little crosswind from the east.'

'But we're thinking indoors.'

'I know. You've done the recce?'

'Of course.'

'And?'

'Thirty-six metres, line of sight.' Zimmermann's hand settled on the passport. 'One other thing. Canaris used him in an operation down in Spain. Operation *Felix*.'

'Trying to get the English out of Gibraltar?' *Admiral* Wilhelm Canaris was the head of the *Abwehr*.

'Exactly. It never happened, of course, but that wasn't Ortega's fault. Canaris had the gravest doubts about him because the man's far from invisible, but he took us all by surprise. He's clever. He was speaking reasonable German within months of working with us and he turns his appearance to his own advantage. He's also headstrong and very brave. He's costing us a fortune by the way and we need to know it's money well spent.' Zimmermann extracted what looked like a map from the file at his elbow. 'He's expecting to meet you this evening. Père Lachaise. Eight o'clock. The tomb of one of the Rothschilds. I've marked it with a cross on the bottom. The nearest exit is on rue de Repos and I've arranged for the gate to stay unlocked until nine. See what you think.'

Schultz spent the afternoon with Odile. Thanks to Conso's many talents, Schultz was no longer required in her boudoir but lately the sheer *ennui* of the occupation had settled on her like a physical weight, and the endless days with their endless repetitions had taken her to a place in her head that she barely recognised. *Ennui* was a term she used with some precision. Sometimes, she said, it felt like a minor irritant. Other times, especially at the end of a long, long winter, it took you to the very edges of despair. On days like this, endlessly bleak, *ennui* didn't begin to measure up. *Anéantissement*, total annihilation, was much closer.

Money, she was beginning to realise, couldn't insulate you from this feeling of utter helplessness, an acknowledgement that her own life, and the lives of others she counted as friends, lay in the hands of strangers. Uninvited, the Germans had helped themselves to the best of France – to its treasured buildings, to its choicest meats and fish and cheese, to its finest wines. Walk anywhere in Paris, and familiar views – much cherished – were disfigured by Nazi banners and *Wehrmacht* signage erected for the benefit of tens of thousands of troops assigned to keep the French in line.

These so-called guests, so loud, so rich, so *powerful*, had taken over the best of the cafés and the restos. Roaring drunk by mid-evening, they thumped the café tables and stamped their boots and sent a torrent of marching songs across squares where once you could hear the nightingales sing. That was bad enough but those with a working knowledge of German reported that later, before the Chain Dogs ordered them back to barracks, they did their best to offload their homesickness and their guilt on the prettier Parisiennes silly or desperate enough to give them a hearing. These aren't men at all, they reported back. Most of them are boys.

Schultz left rue de la Faisanderie after nightfall. Odile accompanied him to the door and unusually she drew him in and offered her lips for a kiss. They'd been sharing a bottle of earthy red for most of the afternoon, and Schultz could taste the Midi in her breath. For a moment Schultz thought she was frightened and when he asked, she nodded.

'Of course I'm frightened,' she said.

'Of us?'

'God, no.'

'Then of what?'

'*Le vide.*'

Schultz nodded. He understood the word only too well, largely because she was beginning to use it so often. *Le vide* meant the emptiness, the bottomless nothing that defeat and occupation had left at every door in France. Odile, for all her wealth, and for all her Fascist talents in bed, had found herself as helpless, and adrift, and bewildered as everyone else. A life worth living, she'd told him barely an hour ago, had become a proposition entertained only by criminals and the insane. In the former group any Frenchman could name thousands, while the latter – somewhat to her surprise – was in danger of including herself.

'*C'est le grand rien,*' she'd murmured as she turned away and stepped back into the house.

The big nothing. Schultz nodded to himself, tugging on his leather gloves. Gasquet's Caspar David Friedrich, he thought. And the monk on the edge of the void.

*

Père Lachaise cemetery was some distance away but Schultz was happy to walk. The dimly lit streets were as empty as ever and his *Abwehr* uniform with its peaked officer's cap protected him from the occasional *Wehrmacht* patrols. Barely metres from rue du Repos, a group of three soldiers finally brought him to a halt.

'*Papieren,* Herr *Major?*'

Schultz studied the outstretched hand for a moment, then produced his *Abwehr* pass. After a cursory glance, the Lieutenant in charge asked whether he needed any help.

'Kind of you to ask,' Schultz grunted. 'The answer is no.'

'Père Lachaise?' The officer nodded at the nearby entrance. 'You're visiting the dead? At this time of night?'

'I'm visiting the nearly dead,' Schultz wanted his pass back. 'Goodnight, gentlemen.'

The Lieutenant studied him for a moment, and Schultz knew he was intrigued.

'The nearly dead, Herr *Major*?' He offered a cold smile. 'That could be anyone in this fucking country.'

Schultz watched the patrol clump off into the darkness, and then turned towards the rusting iron gate at the end of rue du Repos. He'd been to the cemetery only once before, to rummage for a cache of documents allegedly hidden by a *résistante* who'd attracted the *Abwehr*'s attention. On that occasion, Schultz had been impressed by the sheer size of the place, but the muddle of tombs crowding onto the gravel paths in a riot of bad taste offended his sense of order. Back home, the deceased were often happy with a plain black tombstone inlaid with the barest information because a good Protestant death required no more, but here in Père Lachaise, the dead still demanded attention.

The gate, as Zimmermann had promised, was unlocked. Schultz pushed through, and paused for a moment, glad for the warmth of his greatcoat in the damp, windless chill of the night air. The Rothschild tomb, according to Zimmermann, lay beneath a plane tree beside the pathway to his immediate right. He stepped towards it, uncertain which of the tombs belonged to the banking family. Look for a green door, fancy fretwork, inset in a kind of portico, Zimmermann had said. He'd mentioned the family's crest, too.

Crest? Fretwork? Schultz was still easing slowly from tomb to tomb when he sensed movement. At first, he'd assumed the hunched figure on the nearby slab was part of the weird theatre of this place, but now the figure had come to life, getting to his feet, kicking bits of gravel from his boots, one large hand stifling a yawn.

'You're late, Schultz,' the rasp came from deep in his chest.
'That boss of yours said half past seven.'

'Wrong. He told me eight.'

'Who cares? Here, my friend. A toast to the dead.'

Schultz was looking at a metal flask in the hand extended
towards him but made no move to take it.

'You're Ortega?'

'*Sí.*'

'Can you prove it?'

A chuckle, this time, then the other hand producing a box
of matches from the depths of his pocket. He was dressed like
a navvy, stained overalls, leather belt, trouser bottoms secured
with binder twine.

'Care for a look?' He struck a match and held it level with
his eyes, the flame throwing a flicker of light over the big man's
features. Zimmermann had sketched the damage that had taken
Ortega out of the Civil War, and the passport photo hadn't lied,
but in the flesh, especially in a setting like this, the Spaniard's
face made Schultz physically recoil. His scalp, latticed by a web
of poorly sutured wounds, was bare except for a single tuft
of black hair. His injured left eye had drooped, cushioned by
the livid flesh of his pitted cheek, and the diagonal slash of his
mouth seemed to lack a lower lip. Most bizarre of all, another
tuft of hair had mysteriously appeared on the wreckage of
his nose.

Nightmare figures like these had emerged from the trenches
of the last war, whole faces lost to high explosive, and metal
masks had been hurriedly engineered to cover the worst of
the mutilations, but Schultz sensed already that this man was
different. He had no interest in disguising his wounds. On the
contrary, his was a declaration, a challenge thrown at the feet
of passers-by. Come across me in the Métro, or on the street,

and you'll look the other way. Meet me here, among the dead in Père Lachaise, and I'll be the perfect fit, just another grotesque eager for a conversation.

'*El Diablo*, eh?' A throaty chuckle. 'You get it now, Schultz? You believe me? Or do you want to see my papers?'

The match guttered and died and Schultz at last reached for the flask. Already he could smell the thin black-market spirit that masqueraded as cognac.

'To Madrid,' Ortega grunted, watching Schultz tip the flask to his lips, 'and the rest of that evil bloody winter.'

They talked for perhaps half an hour, sitting side by side on the marble slab, emptying the flask. Schultz offered an account of the job he had in mind, reduced to the barest details. An audition was to be held in the Théâtre Edouard VII in a couple of days' time. The theatre would be empty apart from a small group associated with a production of a play called *Pygmalion*.

'This includes Chamberlin?'

'It does. He's putting up the money.'

'Then he'll have protection. He moves nowhere without it. Three guys, sometimes four.'

'His girlfriend's there, as well.'

'Mimi with the huge tits?' Ortega's smile revealed a line of broken teeth. 'You want me to kill her, too? Another thousand Reichsmarks, my friend. Less ten per cent if you pay in advance.'

Schultz shrugged, said nothing. So far, even Zimmermann wasn't aware what he really had in mind.

'We have access to the theatre from nine in the morning. The audition's due for late in the afternoon. I can also take you there the previous day. There's a box above the upper circle that might do very nicely. You can operate from the space behind the back wall and the sight-lines are near-perfect. It's dark up there. No one will see you.'

'And afterwards?'

'We get you out.'

'We?'

'*Abwehr* volunteers. Men I trust.'

'I'll need more than *Abwehr* volunteers. These people have long memories. I'm a hard man to hide, believe me, and I don't want to go underground like some bloody mole, so there has to be a way of taking care of that. Chamberlin dead will put a huge price on my head. This place gives me the creeps, by the way. Can't we find somewhere better to talk?'

At Ortega's insistence, they walked down through the empty streets towards the river. Schultz was in no hurry to offer more details about the audition and in any event Ortega had something else on his mind.

'You killed a guy,' he muttered.

'I've killed a number of guys.'

'Babineau? The arse bandit? Or don't you Germans have a memory anymore?'

'Ah...' Schultz was taking his time. 'You mean the one they call *Il Polpo*?'

'I do. They're coming for you. I know these people. They're good. They'll hurt you and they'll take their time. If you're really lucky they might kill you, but never count on it.'

Schultz nodded. They'd reached the Parc de Bercy and he could smell the Seine beyond the nearby *quais*.

'You're trying to sell me protection?'

'I'm telling you I can deal with them.'

'How much?'

'A lot. We can start talking at ten thousand Reichsmarks but it may go a lot higher.'

'You're buying these people off?'

'I'm putting a bullet in their pretty heads. Italians are hopeless with money. They'd spend it in a week and still come looking for you.'

Schultz nodded, and said he'd think about it. On the *quai* beyond the *parc*, overlooking the water, Ortega led him to a favourite bench.

'You come here often?'

'A little for the view. Mainly for the conversations.'

'With whom?'

'Women. Always the women. Men avoid me. It takes a woman to settle down and pat my leg and tell me everything's going to be just fine. Some go way further, mainly the older women. Their menfolk are in Germany with the STO. They have a big bed at home and their needs don't stop with the ration book. The ones with a conscience are the best fucks because they think they're doing me a favour.'

'And the others?'

'The others want to take me to a priest. Full confession. They assume that no man has a face like mine without getting himself in deep shit with the Almighty. Forgiveness of sins, my friend. Happy ever after.'

Ortega laughed softly in the darkness. The *Service du travail obligatoire* kidnapped Frenchmen of working age and hauled them off to German factories where they'd work day and night for the greater glory of the Reich. Schultz had interviewed a number of STO widows, all of them aligned in one way or another to a Resistance network and knew that Ortega's story was probably true.

'You like this city?' Schultz asked.

'I love it. I loved it from a distance first. French guys I knew in Madrid were crazy about Paris and at first I put it down to homesickness. The French can be like the Italians, all kids at heart but moodier, then I started listening harder, and watching them when they all signed up with the Republicans, and I realised they meant it. City of Light, right? Views to break your heart?' He leaned forward on the bench, his big fist to his mouth to smother a bout of coughing, then told Schultz to thump his back. Schultz did his bidding.

'Harder.'

Schultz obliged.

'Harder still.'

'You've got a problem in there?'

'Don't ask. Wrecked on the outside. Fucked where it matters. Before I went to Madrid, I was with the *Nacionales*. On the way to Badajoz, we smoked *kif* on the march, rolled with tobacco and shit knows what else. Those North African *Regulares* had lungs of iron. Me? I loved the *patois*. I loved the way they fought. But I should have left their tobacco alone. You know what they used to say about life? It's the smallest things that kill you.'

'And the battle?'

'At Badajoz? It was a massacre. We swallowed those guys whole. Some of them we shot when we kicked their doors in. The rest we took to the bullring. Fuck all left.' Ortega fell silent a moment, then gestured down towards the arches of the nearest bridge. 'That'll happen here, too, now the Americans are in the war. The Americans own the world. One day they'll turn up and chase you guys back to Germany. Meantime you'll have wired everything worth blowing up, just to spite the bastards. War is the real enemy, my friend, and anyone with a brain in their heads knows it. Not Fascism. Not Communism. Not any other bloody ism you can dream up. Just war. *Comprende?*'

Schultz nodded, said nothing. He was beginning to like this man with his ruined face and his hard-won wisdom, and – more importantly – he was beginning to take the offer of protection seriously.

'So how would it work?' Schultz asked after a while. 'Let's assume you've killed Chamberlin. *La Carlingue* come looking for you. You need to get out of town. What about my Italians?'

'We trail your coat.'

'What does that mean?'

'It means we take them to the very end of some railway line or other, somewhere in the country, somewhere hours and hours away from this place, and then we deal with them.'

'We?'

'We.' That smile again, and a heavy hand on Schultz's thigh. 'Trust me, Herr *Major*. It'll be much cheaper.'

12

Hogan waited until he'd typed up his interview with Noël Coward before phoning the number he'd passed on. Reading through his notes, he marvelled at the way even minor observations now seemed pre-shaped for inclusion on the page. This was a man, he concluded, who really understood the arc of a story well told, of how a tiny indiscretion could hint at a larger mischief, of the value of names so casually dropped: Edwina, Dickie, and finally the King himself. Was this jobbing playwright and songsmith really on first-name terms with Bertie? Did he turn up at the Palace when the pressure of work permitted for a light midweek supper and a glass or two of port from the royal cellars? And might his precious film indeed rouse the nation to yet greater efforts when all else was crumbling to dust?

To these questions Hogan had no answer but he could still hear Coward's mannered drawl in his head, and in the end he was happy to let the article shape itself. Robertson scanned it quickly, and cautioned Hogan once again to guard his arse.

'He liked you,' he said. 'God knows why.'

Downstairs in the newsroom, one of the duty subs took a sterner line. The meat of the story, he insisted, lay in all the obstacles the Ministry of Information had put in Coward's way.

Who had authored the quote about 'bad propaganda'? Had Coward volunteered a name? And if so, might Hogan put in a call to find out whether all this stuff was true? Hogan knew the question was pointless, partly because Coward had refused to impart the name, but mostly because the whole thrust of the story was his connection – through his revered Dickie – to the King.

'In this country, it matters who you know,' Hogan pointed out. 'With the right friends in the right places you can get away with anything.'

'And that's it?'

'That's everything. Coward knows it. Mountbatten knows it. That's why he got away with so many accidents at sea. That man cost us a fortune in repairs and ended up with blood on his hands.'

'Blood?' The sub's head came up. 'Whose blood?'

Hogan briefly tallied HMS *Kelly*'s chequered history before she finally succumbed to German dive-bombers. Men blown apart, drowned, lost at sea.

'So why isn't any of this in your piece?'

'Because my piece is about propaganda, about turning a disaster into a call-to-arms. Coward was never in the Navy. He never had command. All that blood and treasure lies at Mountbatten's door, not his.'

'So why not interview him?' The sub had returned to Hogan's copy, marking it up with the stub of a pencil.

Hogan let him get to the end of the paragraph, then checked his watch.

'Good question,' he said. 'I'm about to try.'

Hogan put two calls through that same afternoon. On both occasions, the phone rang and rang but no one answered. When he leaned back in his chair and closed his eyes, all he could remember was the feel of flesh on flesh, and the sight of those perfectly lacquered nails, and her gamine smile when she looked up at him. Tonight, he told himself. By eight o'clock, she'd have made her way home.

He gave the operator the number from a borrowed phone on the bar at a pub called the Mudlark in Limehouse. He'd tried two nearby boxes, but one had succumbed to blast damage, and the other had been crowbarred in the search for cash. By the time the operator had made the connection, a gaunt stevedore whom Hogan knew by sight had rolled up his sleeves, taken a pull at his pint, and settled at the piano. What he lacked in technique he made up for with brute strength.

'Hello?' That same voice.

'Hi,' Hogan yelled. 'It's me, George. We met at—'

'Who? I can't hear a thing. Where on earth are you?'

'I'm in a pub. It's George. The journalist. Denham Studios? Noël Coward?'

'Gotcha. George with the angel dust. You've got a pen, George? Something to write on?'

Hogan made a note of the address she gave him, telling him to come round. Tonight was evidently perfect. No extra company. No competition. Just the two of them. Hogan began to read the address back to her but already the operator was on the line, asking whether he wanted to place another call.

By now, most of the drinkers in the pub had gathered round the piano, swaying in time to the music. Hogan had never much liked 'We'll Meet Again', but the plump woman at the pianist's elbow had a lovely voice and Hogan sensed the hint of a tear when he caught the barmaid's eye. He beckoned her closer.

'Expecting a raid tonight?' he asked.

'You ain't heard?'

'No.'

'Bomber's moon, love. Not a cloud in the bloody sky.'

Hogan managed to hail a taxi on Whitechapel Road. The cabbie asked where he was going and told him to get in. There were rumours of a big raid, he said, and he was off back home to Camden Town before things got sticky. Dropping Hogan in Gower Street would almost be en route.

'That makes you lucky, son. Where did you get that accent?'

The journey passed quickly. Hogan, folded into the back of the taxi, found himself quizzed on life in the Maritimes. The conversation, as ever, revolved almost exclusively around food and he was still describing the contents of his mother's fish chowder when the cabbie came to a halt outside a dark four-storey brick terrace that seemed to go on forever. A pound note produced a handful of change, and Hogan found himself alone in the blackout as the taxi disappeared around the corner. Crossing the pavement, he went from door to door peering over the iron railings until he found 77. Bottom bell, she'd said. Ground floor.

She'd opened the door before he'd had a chance to ring the bell.

'Where have you been?'

'Home.'

'Where's home?'

'Limehouse.'

'Christ, you get two medals. One for Limehouse and another for laying hands on a taxi. Come in. And don't tell me you aren't hungry.'

She was wearing a stained pinafore over a white blouse, and she shook water from her hands before disappearing into the depths of the house. Hogan hesitated a moment, wondering why any woman would wear a scarlet beret indoors, then followed her into a dimly lit hall. Spotting an open door, he knocked once and stepped inside. He found her in a tiny kitchen, bent over a saucepan. The space beside the cooker was cluttered with items Hogan hadn't seen for years: a bottle of olive oil, a big triangle of Gruyère cheese, black pepper, two heads of garlic and a newly opened bottle of dry Vermouth.

'What's this?' He was pointing at the remains of a thick, slightly tarry sauce in a chipped glass jug.

'Beef stock.'

'*Beef* stock? Where on earth did you get that?'

'Work. Be nice to the right people and you'd be amazed how generous life can be.'

'This is Combined Operations?'

'Combined Ops, yes. Want a taste?'

She offered him the wooden spoon, and then laughed.

'What's the matter?'

'Don't be so cautious. We're at war, remember. Be brave.'

Hogan, slightly ashamed, took a lick at the liquid on the spoon. He could taste the depth of the beef stock, and the sweetness of the bubbling onions, and something else he said he couldn't put a name to.

'Describe it.' She was reaching for the Vermouth.

'Smelly,' he said. 'Spicy. Quite nice.'

'Minced garlic. I went mad and used three cloves. My mother would never forgive me.' She paused, quizzical. 'You've never had garlic before?'

'Never.'

'So what do you eat in that building of yours? I thought the *Express* spared no expense?'

'Sandwiches, mostly. Lots of Spam. An egg on a good day. Occasionally bacon.'

'Their choice?'

'Mine. There's fancier stuff but it costs the earth.' Hogan's gaze returned to the pot. 'That's lovely.'

'It's my mother's recipe. We used to have it every weekend. My father always demanded a roast on Sundays, but my mother insisted on proper food first. It was a kind of stand-off, really. She was French. He was anything but.'

The bottle of Vermouth was uncorked. She poured a generous slug into the saucepan and gave the onions a vigorous stir with the wooden spoon. Then she dipped a finger into the mix and gave it a long reflective suck.

'Not sure,' she was frowning. 'Second opinion, please.'

She bent over the saucepan, and then turned round and extended the glistening finger. Hogan held her gaze a moment, then opened his mouth. She was right about the Vermouth. The taste was coarser, and slightly metallic, but that was hardly the point.

'Have I upset you?' Her face was very close now.

'Far from it.'

'Too much?'

'Not at all.'

'You lie, you lovely man. The soup is buggered but who cares. My fault. Too much Vermouth. Too much excitement. Top drawer for the cutlery, Mr Hogan. There's a table to be laid next door and you'll find a bottle of Sancerre in a bucket in the bathroom. Coldest room in the house.' She dismissed him with a slightly imperious wave of her hand, and returned to the saucepan, adding pinches of black pepper as Hogan rummaged in the drawer.

'We need forks?' he had a fistful of knives and spoons.

'Sadly not. I'm feeling guilty enough as it is. Soup is all we have I'm afraid but as my lovely mama used to say, soup is everything. You know the French for ambrosia? *Ambroisie.* The food of the gods. We live in hope, Mr H. If all else fails, you can blame little me.'

Ambroisie. The food of the gods. Hogan stepped next door with the cutlery, savouring the taste of the word in his mouth. *Ambroisie*.

The living room was a decent size and put his Limehouse digs to shame. A small leaf table was positioned in the middle of the carpet, two wine glasses readied at either end. Hogan laid the knives and spoons and then gazed around. Two years of barging into strangers' lives had taught him how to hunt for the essence of an interviewee from a handful of clues – the choice of wallpaper, the presence of books and knick-knacks, a folded newspaper or a rack of much-read magazines, family photos on the mantelpiece, maybe a print or two hanging from the picture rail – but this room had a bareness that was unusual.

No pictures brightened the creamy whiteness of the walls. The standard-issue shade hanging from the ceiling rose reminded Hogan of the newsroom at the *Express*. The coal scuttle beside the waiting grate was empty, as was a grey metal waste-paper bin. Not a trace, in short, of the normal clutter and muddle of a busy domestic life. Except for a stand of early daffodils in a glass vase beside the wireless, this might have been somebody's office, barely lived in, tidied daily.

Propped against the vase was a letter. Hogan peered at the address. *Miss Annie Wrenne, Flat 1, 77 Gower Street, London.*

'You like my daffs? I stole them from the park round the corner. You have to pounce first thing else they've already been liberated.'

Hogan glanced round. The beret had gone, and now she was wiping her forehead with a drying-up cloth, demanding to know why he hadn't laid hands on the wine.

'The bathroom's that way.' She nodded at the door. 'I tried to get the bloody stains off but they wouldn't budge.'

Stains? Hogan wanted to know more but already she was back in the kitchen. He turned once again to the envelope propped against the vase. Glasgow postmark. Careful capital letters. He gazed at it a moment longer, and then made for the bathroom. The wine bottle was sitting among a puddle of melting ice cubes in a bucket in the bath. The enamel of the bath was heavily stained and when he looked harder Hogan could see fine traces of abrasion. The hand basin was also stained and Hogan's gaze lingered on the scatter of make-up on the nearby shelf: a deep crimson lipstick, a tube of some cream or other, a little powder puff of the kind he remembered his mother using on very special occasions, plus a tiny bottle of perfume with barely a trace left inside.

Hogan glanced at the door, and then loosened the top of the bottle, lifting it to his nose. Lemons, he thought. And a hint of honeysuckle. And sunshine. And something else deeply promising he couldn't quite put into words.

Minutes later, they were settling at the table to eat. Following Annie's cue, Hogan let his crouton settle in the rich broth until the crust of cheese was soft enough to yield to his spoon. Mouthful after mouthful confirmed that she was a cook of genius, a compliment he was more than happy to share.

'Great,' he kept saying. 'Just great. Where I come from, they'd be queueing at your door. Your father was a lucky man.'

'Really? God knows how, but he found a perch in the Diplomatic Corps. You'd think that would give him a certain *politesse* but you'd be wrong. In his book, praise of any kind was a weakness. Keep people on their toes. Never weaken. That sort of tosh might win wars but it never did much for my mother, or even me for that matter. Food was food. As long as it was hot and kept him regular, all was well. Ours was a quiet house, as you might imagine.'

Hogan, happily surrendering to seconds of onion soup, wanted to know more. Brothers? Sisters?

'Neither. My mother produced me, my father took one look, and that was that. This is my mother speaking, not me. She's French, as I mentioned, and my real name's Agnès. Soft "nye" in the middle, like 'Anyes'. You want to try it?'

'Anyes,' Hogan murmured. 'Does that sound OK?'

'That sounds perfect.'

'Anyes,' Hogan said again. 'I like it.'

'Like it how?'

'The taste of the word in my mouth,' He smiled, then tried it again. 'Anyes.'

'The *taste* of the word? What does that mean?'

'Easy. It sits just here, in the roof of the mouth. Anyes. It's like a chewy wine gum,' he was grinning now. 'Black has always been my favourite. You?'

'Red. Always. No contest.'

'Because?'

'They're always first out of the bag. God knows why but that's the way it is. Bassett's were my favourite as a kid.' She paused a moment, pursuing a fragment of crouton with her spoon before looking up. 'You ever play the making-it-last game?'

'Never.'

'Twenty-eight minutes was my record. That's nearly half an hour. A friend of mine once told me you have to surrender to the moment, but never hurry it on. She was older than me and much wiser and it was years before I twigged what she really meant. You find that, too?'

Hogan held her gaze, then coloured slightly and changed the subject.

'So why Annie? Shouldn't I be calling you Agnès?'

'Technically, yes. In practice, no. My mum settled on Annie and after that there was no way back so Annie I became.'

'You like it? Prefer it?'

'Pass on both. It's a name, that's all. It happens I agree with you. Agnès is a lovely sound, more a blessing than a name, and maybe one day I'll go back to it, but not yet.'

'So you were an only child? Have I got that right?'

'You have, Mr H. Just the one of me.'

'Did you ever feel lonely?'

'Not at all. *Au contraire.* My mother and I were best friends, which was just as well. When I was a baby, my father parked us by the seaside for a summer. That way, we could never bother him. As it happens, my mother loved the place and so it became our home.'

'Anywhere I might know?'

'I doubt it. Does Puys ring any bells? *La belle Normandie?*'

'No.'

'Dieppe?'

Hogan shook his head. He had a dim recollection that it might be served by some ferry or other but that was that.

'Puys is a tiny village on the Channel coast, an hour on foot from Dieppe. Chalk cliffs, terrifying views down from the top, stony beach, good swimming if you happen to be a polar bear. My father had access to a lovely house through a friend in the Foreign Office. It was a couple of minutes up from that same beach. It was cheap as hell so my father bought it. Thanks to my mother I spoke good French but the place was thick with Brits who'd liked it enough to settle so I was spoiled for company. Later in the piece my father insisted on a posh girls' boarding school near Maidenhead but in every way that matters I grew up in France. On bad days, I still think the best bits of me are *Dieppoise.*'

'Meaning?'

'French. Norman. Headstrong and chatterbox and smelling ever so slightly of fish.' She laughed, poking around in her soup for the last soft pebble of cheese. 'My first proper boyfriend was a fisherman. On the rougher days he'd take me to sea and put me to the test. In some ways he was a bit like my father. In others, he was utterly wicked and utterly delicious. I owe that man a great deal. He taught me everything about what really matters. His name was Marcel and I often wonder what's happened to him since.'

'How old was he?'

'Twenty-seven.'

'And you?'

'Seventeen. His father had drowned at sea and he'd inherited the boat. It was nothing grand, a tiny thing really, but he'd installed a mattress down below which, to say the least, was a playful gesture.'

'So what did he teach you?'

'He taught me about what matters and what doesn't. He also taught me how to laugh, which turned out to be the key to pretty much everything.'

'Including the mattress?'

'Of course. The French always contend that laughter is the best aphrodisiac, and they're right. I never knew that until I met Marcel, but it was fun learning. I think that was what he liked about me. I made him laugh. From his point of view, that turned out to be a bit of a blessing.'

'How come?'

'He'd married a staunch Catholic, and I got the feeling smells and bells didn't do it in the boudoir.' She smiled at the memory and lifted the bowl to her lips, draining the last of the soup.

'And your mother? She's still in Puys?'

'Cornwall. Little village inland from Mevagissey. It was my father's idea. This was back before the war but he could see which way Mr Hitler was heading. My mother didn't really want to leave France, but he insisted. The next thing he did was abandon her but I'm not sure she ever noticed. He'd been absent in every way that matters for years.'

'And he's still alive? Still around?'

'So I understand.'

'You never see him?'

'No.'

Hogan was watching her carefully. This woman's background was fascinating but just now he had something else on his mind.

'Tell me about Mountbatten,' he said.

'What's he got to do with anything?'

'I'm just curious, that's all.' He gestured at the empty bowls. 'I'm guessing that most of this must have come with his blessing.'

'You're wrong. The man doesn't know how to boil an egg. Food doesn't really interest him, as long as it turns up on time.'

'And laughter?'

'Another blind spot. He can be generous to a fault but he takes himself very seriously indeed. I think it must be the German in him. The Brits are good at irony, and the French aren't bad either, it's one of the things we do really well. Just now it helps to be able to laugh at yourself but my boss never really got the knack. Time matters, his precious schedule matters, and all the smaller vanities matter even more. This is a man, Mr H, who designed specially embossed buttons for his servants' livery, who insisted on a bespoke shade of blue for his precious Rolls. There wasn't quite enough legroom, by the way, so he got the beast specially lengthened. What that cost him would keep my mum in onions and Sancerre for the rest of her life.'

'You said boss.'

'I did.'

'You work for him? Exclusively?'

'I share him with a handful of other worker bees. He loves to have people around him, *his* people, and that's another little *trait*. He needs to put his smell on everything because the one thing that really matters is control. Day and night, no matter what he's up to, he's always on the bridge of his own ship. I'm sure you saw it at the studios. He needs to be bent to that little tube they yell down. And you know his favourite command?'

'Full ahead.'

'You're right, full ahead, foot to the floor, don't spare the poor bloody horses,' she reached for his hand, gave it a squeeze. 'You're very clever, Mr H, much brighter than you like to make out. You also know how to listen to a woman, which is rare, and if you can bear a compliment, you know exactly which questions to ask.'

'I'm flattered.'

'No, you're not. I'm guessing this war must have hardened you. Either that, or active service on that rag of yours. Might I be right?'

'On both counts,' Hogan nodded. 'Yes.'

'And are you a believer?'

'Meaning?'

'Do you offload on God from time to time? Maybe every Sunday to keep yourself in credit?'

'Why do you ask?' The notion of credit made Hogan laugh.

'Because Mr C marked my card.'

'Mr C?'

'Noël Coward. He thinks there might be something holy about you, something a little forbidding. He thinks you need to loosen those stays of yours and since you haven't touched your wine, I probably agree.'

'But that's because I don't drink.'

'Yes, you do.'

'Is that an order?'

'*Au contraire, Monsieur H.*' She leaned forward and cupped his long face between her hands. 'It's a promise.'

They were in bed when inner London took a deep breath and the chorus of sirens reached for the scariest notes. Annie, curled across Hogan's chest, stroked his hand and told him not to be frightened.

'This is a movie,' she whispered. 'This is the bit when the baddies get their wicked way.'

'Too late,' Hogan gave her tiny hand a squeeze. 'I'm doomed already.'

'And is that a bad thing?'

'Not at all.' The pale disc of her face was inches away. 'Where's the nearest shelter?'

'Goodge Street tube.'

'And do you ever use it?'

'Never, unless I'm seriously fed up and need the company. Tonight? No chance, I'm afraid. Does that bother you?'

'Not in the least. That God of mine tells me that death can be a blessing. I've never really believed it until now. Choose your moment, and you'll die a happy man? Ridiculous.'

'Really? Is my work done here?' She kissed him softly, the way you might send a child to sleep. Then her tongue was in his mouth again and he felt himself stirring under the single sheet, and he heard the softest chuckle as she ducked her head and slipped down between his thighs and took him in her mouth. Instinctively, he began to move but she stilled him with her other hand, reappearing briefly to murmur something about patience and wine gums, and he lay back, waiting for the familiar throb-throb of the approaching bombers, wondering idly whether any of the bombs might have their names on it.

Their names.

He smiled in the darkness, realising that he truly didn't care, that this amazing woman had done something wondrous with the wiring that had always held him together, that she'd been clever and dextrous and reckless enough to recognise the person he'd so carefully – religiously – kept locked away all these busy years. He admired her for it. He loved her for it. And above all he wanted it never to stop. She was right, he thought. Patience – or maybe surrender – is all.

She was teasing him now, her head back between his thighs, her busy tongue fluttering here and there like a trapped bird, and in the far distance, away to the east, he heard the low percussive thump of the first explosions as the bombs began to fall. Limehouse, he thought with just a twinge of guilt.

Evie and all the other tenants in the street would by now have retired to their Anderson shelters, just an arch of corrugated iron and maybe a layer of earth and sandbags between you and oblivion. He'd spent the evening with Evie only last night, playing with her tiny daughter, trying to cheer the pair of them up after the news about Yannis. I loved that man, she'd told him, and that can only happen once.

Hogan had done his best to persuade her that she was wrong, that happiness was a gift dispensed by God's benevolence, by God's endless mercy, and now – with the memory of his own voice still in his head – he realised that he'd been wrong. Happiness is far from passive. Wait for God and you might be waiting your entire life. Happiness is here and now. Happiness is conversation across two empty glasses. Happiness is peeling away a stranger's secrets until only the essence remains. The bottle empty, she'd taken him to her bed, just a little drunk, and it had felt the most natural thing in the world.

Now, the *Luftwaffe*'s giant boots were coming ever closer, the house beginning to shudder under a series of near misses. Out in the street, he could hear the tinkle of glass as windows blew out. Then came the heavier impact of tiles and masonry and a sudden blaze of light beyond the blackout curtain, the entire house shaking with the blast. His hands felt for Annie's head, a protective gesture, wholly instinctive. You don't have to do this, he was trying to say. We can put our arms around each other, and close our eyes, and resign ourselves to the sweetest of deaths because everything else is nonsense, but again she gently pushed his hands away, sucking and sucking until he could hold on no longer.

When he tried to withdraw, she shook her head and sucked a little more, and then came another bomb, and a third, and he abandoned all control as the terrace rocked in the blast waves, and suddenly her head was still, and there was movement under the sheet, and her face appeared inches from his own. She was wiping her mouth. She was smiling. She whispered something about another bottle, something really special, and she kissed him before slipping out of bed in the darkness and disappearing into the hall.

Hogan lay back. In the distance, growing louder by the second, he could hear the bell of an approaching fire engine. He pictured the firemen readying their ladders and their hoses. He imagined the drifts of smoking rubble that awaited their attention. He wondered about the broken bodies they'd come to disinter. And without the faintest trace of shame, he realised once again that he didn't care.

'Agnès,' he whispered to himself, hearing the creak of the door as she came back to bed.

13

Five days later, Schultz collected a car from the *Abwehr* barracks in Vincennes and drove to an address in the depths of Montmartre. The last time they'd met, Ortega had referred to his three rooms above a repair shop as his 'lair', a doff of the Spaniard's cap to his nickname. This morning *El Diablo* was nursing a major hangover. Schultz, surprised, had somehow assumed that this ruin of a man was immune to anything so mundane.

'Why so early?'

Ortega had resettled himself in a battered leather armchair beneath a poster of Stalin. Someone, Schultz presumed *El Diablo*, had further mutilated the pockmarked face with a stick of charcoal, crudely smudged around the narrowness of his eyes, with ugly black cross-hatching elsewhere. Looking from one face to the other, Schultz wondered whether Ortega had taken a good look in the mirror before attacking the leader of the Communist bloc. Close the curtains, dim the lights, properly restore Ortega's ruined nose, and the two men might have been brothers.

'Good night?' Schultz gestured towards the litter of empty bottles beside the big wireless. It was tuned, Schulz noticed, to Radio de España, a new outlet that was broadcasting from Madrid.

'The woman drinks like a Pole. Three hours ago she was still dancing.' Ortega rubbed his face and gestured vaguely at the square of faded carpet, cratered with cigarette burns. 'One day, if I ever find the time, I'm going to put her in the circus.'

'She's still here?' Schultz gestured towards the door.

'Gone. I checked just now when I woke up.'

'Gone where?'

'God knows.' He paused, frowning, as if something had just occurred to him. 'Chamberlin?'

'He's due at the theatre around five this afternoon. I have a key.' Schultz tapped his watch. 'We need to take a look first.'

The Théâtre Edouard VII was ten minutes away, near the Palais Garnier. Schultz recognised the two Renault saloons parked across the road. A couple of his men in one, three in the other, all of them in civilian dress.

'Who are those people?' Ortega was rubbing his good eye again.

'*Abwehr.* Colleagues of mine. It might help to take precautions.'

'Why?'

Schultz studied him for a moment. The night's drinking had given Ortega's ruined face a blotchy puffiness that took the grotesque into another dimension, and the stench of his breath prompted Schultz to open the driver's door.

'Come.' He nodded towards the pillared arcade that housed the theatre's entrance. Zimmermann had already briefed him on the layout inside. The caretaker's name was Caryl. He would be leading the way to the staircase that offered access to the lower dress circle and the one above. At the very top of the staircase, Ortega and Schultz would be taking a left and then looking for the second door into one of the private boxes.

Minutes later, with Ortega sweating neat alcohol, they emerged into the box. The stale air carried the scent of perfume and cigars, and when Schultz's eyes had accustomed themselves to the gloom, he stepped towards the brass rail and looked onto the rich crimson bowl of the theatre beneath: dozens of rows of seats, of creamy plasterwork and then the wide gape of the empty stage. The caretaker had switched on the house lights and two of the *Abwehr* men, as instructed, had settled into seats in the fourth row. One of them, looking up, acknowledged the lift of Schultz's hand.

'That's where Chamberlin will be sitting?' Ortega had joined Schultz.

'According to the caretaker, yes.'

Ortega nodded, narrowing his good eye, framing one of the *Abwehr* men with a circled finger and thumb. A grunt told Schultz he was content.

'Easy,' he said. 'I'll need to go back for the weapon.'

'We've got one in the car. A Mauser Karabiner 98. Oiled, checked over and ready to go.'

'No,' Ortega shook his head. 'There's only one weapon I trust and it's under my bed. I meant to bring it but I didn't. Blame the wine. Blame my thirsty little friend. Blame who you like but that's what I'll be using. You want the job done properly? You want the man dead? Leave it to me.'

Schultz held his gaze. This, he knew, was the moment he had to come clean.

'You're not going to kill him,' he said softly.

'I'm not?'

'No. You're going to be up here. You're going to have a weapon. You're going to look the part. But then my guys are going to intervene.'

'And do what?'

'Arrest you. Drag you away. The more noise, the more fuss, the better, but no blood, no shots fired, nobody dead. Think of it as a piece of theatre.'

Ortega, Schultz could see, was trying his best to make sense of this sudden development but his fuddled brain simply wouldn't oblige.

'You're telling me I don't get to kill the bastard?'

'Correct. You don't even get to pull the trigger.'

'Why not?'

'It's complicated. For your sake and ours it's best you don't know. We're giving you a role. It doesn't demand much. All you have to do is play along. Might that be possible? Or shall we call the whole thing off?'

Ortega was considering the proposal.

'It'll cost you,' he muttered finally.

'How much?'

'Double the agreed fee.'

Schultz laughed. Already, they were paying him ten thousand Reichsmarks.

'An extra thousand,' Schultz offered.

'Five thousand.'

'Two.'

'Four.'

'Two and a half. My final offer.' Schultz nodded at the door. 'Else you'll be walking home with no fee at all.'

Ortega brooded for a long moment.

'Done,' he said finally. 'But I still need my own weapon.'

'Why? You're an actor now. Killing the man can wait for another day.'

'Sure, my friend, but what you're asking me now is different. I have to be comfortable. I have to mean it. I need my own props. It's the smallest favour. All you have to say is yes.'

Schultz drove him back to Montmartre and collected the sniper rifle. The blanket he'd used to wrap it was slightly oil-stained, and the moment it appeared Schultz recognised the long barrel of a Soviet Mosin–Nagant. Ortega treated the weapon with near-reverence. He said it had cost him a fortune on the black market. The scope had four times magnification and was effective to three hundred metres on a still day. He'd used it in anger on a number of occasions here in Paris and so far it had never let him down. On any job, he said he felt naked without it. Hence the trip back to his dingy rat hole on rue Myrha.

'Something else, my friend.' They were on their way back to the theatre. 'What happens after this little game of yours?'

'We take you away. Keep you safe.'

'Chamberlin gets to see me?'

'We'll be giving you a balaclava. *Monsieur Invisible.*'

'*Inconnu?*'

'Even better.'

'And after that?'

'You go away and spend the money.'

'And Chamberlin?'

'The *Abwehr* have just saved his life.'

'For twelve and a half thousand Reichsmarks?' Ortega was staring at him. 'You think he's that precious?'

'Not him, Ortega. Someone else.'

Lucien Gasquet arrived at the theatre half an hour early. He was dressed in the robes of a fifteenth-century bishop, a bible clutched to his skinny chest, and from the private box Schultz watched the caretaker help him onto the stage. Gasquet dismissed him with a wave of his pale hand, advanced to the front of the stage and peered out at the empty rows of seats before making the sign of the cross. Then he went down on his knees, kissed the rough boards and began to mouth something inaudible.

'What's he doing?' The expression on Ortega's face might have been a frown.

'Rehearsing. Take it from me, the man's a bag of nerves.'

Gasquet was on his feet now, seeming to wrestle with the delivery of a particular line, then came a rustle of movement at the back of the theatre and the caretaker reappeared with a group of men. Schultz counted them. There were six in all. Chamberlin was the first down the aisle, leading a woman by the hand, pushing the caretaker to one side. The boss of the *Carlingue* was wearing a full-length leather coat, unbelted, while the woman was dressed for spring.

'That *puta* Mimi,' Ortega grunted. 'I should be killing her, too.'

He'd settled in the darkness at the very back of the box, the sniper rifle cradled in his lap. From time to time, his big hand ran up and down the polished wood of the stock, a gesture – thought Schultz – both respectful and fond. Outside, in the dimly lit corridor, his *Abwehr* colleagues were awaiting their cue: two sharp knocks on the already-open door, plenty of noise, a torrent of cursing, then the would-be assassin hustled down to the bigger of the waiting cars via a side exit known only to the management. Ortega was a big man, hard to handle, but timing would be all-important. Two minutes max, Schultz was insisting. Not a second more.

By now, Chamberlin had taken a seat five rows back from the stage with Mimi beside him, and one by one his escort joined them, gazing round at the empty theatre, plainly impressed. Ortega, still at the back of the box, had pulled on the balaclava and Schultz was aware of his good eye watching a particular individual, the figure who'd come in last. He was an Arab, dark-skinned, and moved with an easy grace. Unlike everyone else in Chamberlin's party, he was checking every part of the theatre with some care.

Schultz eased himself backwards, sharing the darkness with Ortega as the Spaniard raised his rifle for a closer look at the Arab. Once he'd found him in the telescopic sight, he muttered something to himself and then made a tiny adjustment to the focus.

'What's wrong?'

Ortega ignored the question. He was chuckling now, a reaction that began to unsettle Schultz, but Gasquet was at the very front of the stage having a shouted conversation with Mimi, who'd got to her feet. She was offering him the benefit of a rehearsal first. Only then would he be expected to deliver his audition piece for real.

'And if you like the rehearsal?' asked Gasquet. 'Its spontaneity? Its *truth*?'

'Then we'll let you know.'

Mimi resumed her seat. Two of the *Carlingue* were sharing some joke or other, probably about Gasquet, but Chamberlin silenced them with a look. Then, on Mimi's cue, Gasquet fingered the wooden cross hanging from his neck, peered into the depths of the theatre beyond the nest of heads, and began to declaim.

'*Who has turned this dairy maid's pretty head?*' he piped. '*The answer is the devil, and for a mighty purpose for he is spreading this heresy everywhere...*'

Schultz had no idea how long this passage of Gasquet's would last. In a final conference with Zimmermann only last night, he'd agreed not to trigger Ortega's arrest until Gasquet had hit his stride but listening to him now, Schultz could hear a nervousness in his delivery, stress misplaced in line after line, snatched breaths upsetting the gathering force of the bishop's rage. The speech

Gasquet had chosen came from *Saint Joan*, another of Bernard Shaw's plays, and Bishop Cauchon was determined to bring the young upstart to her knees.

'*What will the world be like when venerable, learned, pious men are thrust into the kennel by every ignorant labourer or dairy maid whom the devil can puff up? It will be a world of blood, of fury, of devastation...*'

Better, thought Schultz. Much better. He'd stationed himself beside the half-open door and a final glance at the group in the stalls told him that Gasquet had at last captured their attention. Then he heard something else, an unmistakeable click as Ortega worked a round into the chamber of his weapon. Schultz swore softly, looking behind him to find out why, but Ortega's thick finger was already tightening on the trigger. Then came the lightest intake of breath, the rifle steadied in the sniper's big hands, followed by a deafening report that echoed around the theatre and brought Gasquet to a halt before he bolted for the shelter of the wings.

'*Scheisse.*' Schultz was on his feet now, reaching for the door, but the waiting *Abwehr* men were already storming into the box. Three of them grabbed Ortega, who gamely roared a series of obscenities but made no attempt to resist as he was manhandled outside into the corridor. Schultz, wrong-footed, heard them dragging Ortega away, then turned to stare down at the scene below.

Two of the *Carlingue* were hurrying Chamberlin up the aisle towards the rear exit, while the others were bent over the body of the Arab, sprawled across two seats. Half his face had ceased to exist thanks to the exit wound and Mimi was staring at gouts of blood, the deepest crimson, that had sprayed across the whiteness of her blouse. Explosive ammunition, Schultz thought. For a lot of money, you get the very best.

Schultz left the box. His route to the side exit took him past a line of dressing rooms and then a costume department. Pausing briefly beside a suit of medieval armour to kick at a door that had stuck, he was trying to assess the damage. Chamberlin, thankfully, had emerged intact but the key question remained. A small fortune should have bought Ortega's unquestioning compliance in this little piece of theatre. Yet, for whatever reason, he'd still pulled the trigger. Why?

*

'I know that man. He's an Arab. He's a snake. We go back years. I've lost count of the woman he's had off me.'

'Your women?'

'My women. Women who made my life a little sweeter. Women he'd toss away after a couple of nights. Sure, one or two would come crawling back to me but whoever wants a slice off a cut loaf?' Ortega shook his head. 'A reptile like that? I should have killed him months ago.'

By now, it was early evening and Schultz had at last caught up with Ortega at a house the *Abwehr* used just west of Paris. Neuilly-sur-Seine was safe because it was monied and because it was much favoured by senior *Wehrmacht* officers, often with their mistresses in tow. Neuilly was where you went if you were in need of a decent meal and a classy fuck, and just now Neuilly was where Ortega was renewing his affection for a decent bottle of Château Lafite.

Schultz removed the bottle and put it to one side. An hour with Zimmermann back in the Hôtel Lutetia had convinced him that the chaos of the audition might, after all, work to the *Abwehr*'s advantage. Military intelligence had cracked a bid by a vengeful, out-of-control marksman to wreak havoc among the ranks of the *Carlingue*. They'd arrived at the theatre too late to save the Arab's life but early enough to make sure that Chamberlin remained intact. The marksman was now in *Abwehr* custody, and it would fall to *Oberst* Zimmermann to decide his fate.

Agreed, the SS would doubtless try and seize him but the word on their lips should be *danke*. Thank you for keeping an ear to the ground. Thank you for getting to the theatre in time. And thank you for saving Chamberlin's life. The legendary head of the French Gestapo had fallen into a carefully baited Resistance trap. Only the *Abwehr* had been alert enough to foil the bastards.

'You're telling me the actor guy was part of all this? Bait for *La Carlingue*?'

'I'm telling you the Resistance owe him a very big favour. But for us, Chamberlin would have a bullet in his fat head.'

'So what happens to him? The actor guy?'

'We've taken care of that already. The *Carlingue* will come looking but he's long gone.'

'And me?'

'Word will get round, my friend, balaclava or no balaclava. That was an explosive bullet? A dum-dum?'

'Of course. That's what you paid for.'

'We paid for you to behave, to take orders, but that's a different issue. If I was Chamberlin, I'd be recovering the bullet, taking a good look, drawing a conclusion or two. Marksmen of that quality are rare, even in a city like this. We need to get you out of Paris, my friend.'

Ortega nodded. The proposition seemed altogether reasonable. 'Any idea where?'

Schultz nodded, then reached for the bottle.

'Dieppe,' he grunted. 'You'll love it.'

Book Three

Book Three

14

A small flotilla of nineteen boats, including three destroyers, left the Cornish port of Falmouth in the early afternoon of 26 March 1942. A retired naval Captain living on a headland outside Coverack studied the departing warships through binoculars. What especially intrigued him was one of the three destroyers. He'd been aboard HMS *Campbeltown* only last year at the invitation of her Captain. The ex-US Navy vessel, previously the USS *Buchanan*, had then sported four funnels. Now she had only two, both raked aft. Mystified, the watcher on the clifftop tracked the ships until they disappeared into the gathering mist.

Two days later, in pitch darkness, the convoy was suddenly illuminated by German searchlights on both banks of the Loire estuary. The huge dry dock at Saint-Nazaire, vital for the repair of German capital ships, was eleven minutes steaming away. At 01.34, under heavy fire, HMS *Campbeltown* rammed the dock gates.

Assault teams of Royal Marine commandos clambered from the embedded destroyer and began to blow up installations and equipment around the dry dock. Royal Navy motor torpedo boats at sea, meanwhile, were attacking other targets. By daybreak, fierce opposition from German troops ashore began to take a toll among the commandos, many of whom had fanned out into the town. At noon, four and a half tons of high explosive packed into *Campbeltown*'s bow erupted, killing an inspection party of German officers aboard plus hundreds of nearby soldiers and civilians.

The explosion put the dry dock out of commission for the remainder of the war, but the price paid by the raiders was high: of the 612 men embarked at Falmouth, only 228 returned home. Losses on this scale were softened by the gazetting of eighty-nine medals, including five awards of the Victoria Cross. Jubilant accounts of the raid fed a growing public hunger for good news married to heroism, and leading the wave of applause was the *Daily Express*. NAZAIRE DOCK GATE HAS VANISHED read the following day's headline.

To some at Combined Operations, this spectacular conjuring trick exactly met the organisation's wildest expectations. They were in business to catch the enemy off-guard, to hit him where he least expected, and that's exactly what they'd done. Others, including Annie Wrenne, quietly shared their misgivings with their loved ones. His Lordship spills much blood, she confessed to Hogan. He's also agreed to give you an interview.

Nearly two weeks later, on a cold spring morning, George Hogan found his way to the headquarters of Combined Operations, a neat Georgian building hidden away in Richmond Terrace, a cul-de-sac off Whitehall.

To Hogan's surprise, there were no guards at the entrance to the building, not even a lone sentry. He pushed the door open and stepped inside. A young Lieutenant behind a desk made a note of his name and lifted a phone. A woman in a WRN uniform shot Hogan a dazzling smile as she hurried past with an armful of documents. His brief conversation over, the Lieutenant was nodding at the nearby staircase.

'First floor,' he said. 'Someone will be up there to meet you.'

It was Mountbatten himself. He emerged from a nearby office, clad against the chill in a Navy-issue sweater. Hogan noticed the heavy gold braid on the shoulder boards.

'George?' Mountbatten's handshake was firm and brief. Hogan, wondering whether a salute might have been in order, followed him through an anteroom where two more WRNs were attacking their typewriters. Purpose, Hogan thought. And yet more smiles.

Mountbatten's office was airy and bathed in light now that the early mist had lifted. A biggish desk was dominated by a wall map. The coast of continental Europe extended from the tip of Norway to the Bay of Biscay, and scarlet marker pens had highlighted three locations, one in Norway and the other two in France.

'This is retrospective, of course.' Mountbatten had noticed Hogan's interest. 'The one at the top was Operation *Archery* back in December. We descended briefly on Vaagso. Deeply satisfactory, if I might say so. We blew up a munitions factory and retired in good order. No one saw us coming but the Germans poured troops into Norway afterwards, which was the whole point of the exercise. Anything to help the Russians, eh?'

Hogan was already making notes but Mountbatten stayed his hand.

'No need, George. We have a typed summary one of my girls will give you later. Our next outing was the Bruneval raid. The RAF were getting worried about attacks on their bomber streams. The boffins needed to take a look at a particular piece of German radar kit and we were only too happy to oblige. Surprise is everything, George. The Germans barely had the time to fire a shot. Then there's Saint-Nazaire...' A perfectly manicured forefinger found the scarlet cross on the mouth of the Loire. '... a bigger operation, much more ambitious, but I'm sure you'll know about that. All this is enemy territory, of course. We're thieves in the night. We steal across and try the doors and make a general nuisance of ourselves. So far, I'm very glad to say it's working rather well but in this business one is always the servant of circumstance. Ours is the duty, as they say. But events, alas, belong to God.'

He waved Hogan into the spare chair and settled behind the desk. The sun was streaming through the big window and one hand was shading his eyes to take a better look at his young visitor.

'I love your country, George. I spent a while in Washington last year and we have good friends in Los Angeles. Americans have the happy knack of making things happen and it's a pleasure to find ourselves in the same business.'

'I'm Canadian, sir. From the Maritimes. A little town called Newcastle.'

'Ah, from whence cometh the good Lord Beaverbrook. I can't imagine that can be a coincidence, George. Might I be right?' He dismissed his mistake with a boyish grin.

Hogan shrugged, mumbled something harmless about being lucky, and finally opened his notebook. A conversation with a defence expert in the newsroom had yesterday wised him up about the sheer novelty of Combined Operations.

'I understand they gave you matching promotions in the Army and the Air Force,' Hogan was checking his notes, 'when you took this job.'

'That's true. The only one that matters, of course, is the naval rank. To be the youngest Vice-Admiral since Nelson is no small honour, believe me. There are disadvantages, too, of course. One finds oneself in the councils of the mighty, and often I have to say it pays to be nimble, as well as diplomatic. When it comes to laying hands on certain kinds of tactical support for our little expeditions some of my colleagues can be less than biddable. This country is cursed by little wars of its own, and many of them you simply can't afford to lose.'

'Why's that?'

'Because we're spilling blood, risking men's lives. You take precautions, of course. Precautions in the planning, and precautions long before that when we put the men through training. Becoming a commando, George, doesn't happen by accident. Ever heard of Achnacarry? It's up in Scotland, way past Fort William, wild as hell, utterly godforsaken, truly miserable. We can send you up there, give you a taste of what makes a Royal Marine. Everything in this building begins and ends with these men of mine. My job is a bit like commanding a ship at sea. If you don't cherish your crew, if you don't value them, depend on them, drive them to their very limits, then nothing good will ever happen. They know that, and I do, too. They know I'll ask the impossible and settle for nothing less. They also know I'll take care of them through thick and thin. That's the essence of leadership, George. What did you make of Noël's little show, by the way? Out at Denham?'

For a moment, Hogan had lost the thread. He was thinking far too hard about HMS *Kelly*'s multiple accidents and the lives this man had lost at Saint-Nazaire but then he remembered the scene in the canteen at the film studios, and the afternoon he'd watched Noël Coward at work.

'Fascinating.'

'And Noël? I understand he gave you an interview. Pearls of wisdom? Grist for that mill of yours? Edwina and I dined with your boss only recently. I fear the Russians have stolen his soul. He can talk of nothing else but Stalin and all those tanks he's after but just now I imagine that might be what we all need.

Forty thousand in Trafalgar Square last month? The Second Front Now business? Am I right, George?'

'You are, sir. I was there.'

'And?'

'People believe him.'

'You mean The Beaver?'

'I mean Stalin. Russians are dying in their tens of thousands. If they ever sue for peace, we all know where Hitler will be looking next.'

'Quite, George,' the figure behind the desk gestured at the map behind him. 'And that's why we need to keep the wretched Germans on their toes. Every time we turn up and leave our calling card they have no alternative but reinforcement. Someone very shrewd at the Palace told me yesterday that we're in the business of humiliation. We land in Norway and France and God knows where else and make fools of them. Men in penny packets, just a handful, but the *right* men, with the *right* attitude, and *right* equipment. Very few people thought any of this could ever be possible but it's been a pleasure to prove them wrong, and you know where the biggest thank yous come from? Moscow, George, because every German wasting his days on the Atlantic coast is one German less on the Eastern Front. Strategy, George,' he tapped his head. 'Have confidence in the big picture and then leave it to us mere mortals to fill in the bits that need a splash of colour. A pleasure, dare I say it. Ask anyone in this building. And a privilege, too.'

His phone began to ring, and he answered it at once, bending into the conversation, his voice lower. Hogan, pretending to study his notes, was listening hard, trying to imagine who might be at the other end, and gradually it dawned on him that this was no ordinary call, not business at all. He was privy to a different Mountbatten, not the vigorous man of action but someone softer, kinder, almost playful. At length, with a mock sternness, he counselled more homework and perhaps an afternoon in the saddle, before bringing the conversation to an end.

'Lilibet,' he was beaming at Hogan. 'She's always on the line. Sometimes I think she takes me for her real father, though Bertie, of course, would probably be aghast.'

Bertie? Lilibet? Slowly it occurred to Hogan that this was yet another boast. Bertie was the King. Lilibet was his sixteen-year-old daughter. Here, in short, was a man with a finger in every pie, royal or otherwise.

Mountbatten, oblivious, was in the middle of a story about a long-ago Christmas he'd shared with the royal family at Sandringham. The point of the story should have taken him to a much younger Princess Elizabeth, a mere child at the time, but somehow he became waylaid by his prowess at the wheel. The roads empty, an accomplished driver could make it to King's Lynn and back in slightly under twenty minutes. Mountbatten was happy to confirm he'd done it in fifteen.

'And that's with a light dusting of snow, George, though you must never breathe a word,' he spread his hands, a gesture close to applause. 'No one believed me when I got back to the estate, but that doesn't make it any less true. You know what's easiest to handle in this life of ours?' He was grinning now. 'Envy.'

With a warning that time was fast running out, the interview continued. Hogan made a brave attempt to secure a hint or two about future targets for Combined Operations but was treated to a brisk lecture about the absolute need for secrecy. It seemed that Mountbatten had recently been drawn to Sun Tzu's treatise on *The Art of War* and was glad to confirm that keeping the enemy off-balance was key to a successful encounter. You should appear when least expected, at a moment of your own choosing, and know exactly what you want to achieve. No less, no more.

'Wind, Forest, Fire and Mountain, George,' he was tallying each word on the fingers of his left hand. 'Fast as the wind, silent as a forest, ferocious as fire and implacable as a mountain.' He nodded at Hogan's notebook. 'You want to write that down? And promise not to send it to Berlin?'

There came a light knock at the door, and it was at this point that Hogan lifted his head from his notepad to watch Annie come in with a tray of tea. She offered Hogan the faintest nod, apologised for being late and warned against the biscuits.

'I'm afraid they're beyond redemption, sir,' she said brightly. 'Even the mice won't touch them.'

Mountbatten was on his feet, glancing at his watch.

'George, meet Annie Wrenne. I'm still trying to understand why she's still with us but thank God she is. Annie, this young man works for our friend The Beaver. So far, it appears to have done him no harm at all.' He stepped round the desk, ignoring the tray. 'Time, I'm afraid, waits for no man, least of all me.' He extended a hand to Hogan, then shot a glance at Annie. 'I'll be at Downing Street if you need me. Thankfully, Winston has a lunch with Maisky so it shouldn't take long.' He nodded down at the biscuits. 'Help yourselves. I suspect our young man needs feeding.'

Mountbatten swept from the room, leaving Hogan gazing at Annie. A couple of hours ago, back in Gower Street, he'd served her breakfast in bed, a single orange, cherished for days, carefully segmented.

'Maisky?' he queried.

'The Soviet Ambassador. He pulls your boss's strings. I'm amazed you need to ask.'

'Just checking.'

'You lie.'

'Always.'

'Well?' She nodded at the empty desk. 'Was I right?'

'You were,' he beckoned her closer. 'He knows nothing about us?'

'Nothing. I told him the interview request came from a friend of mine on the paper. That's sort of true, isn't it?'

Back at the *Daily Express* building, Hogan returned to his desk to find a note telling him to report to the BH. BH was newsroom code for the Bell Hop, or E. J. Robertson. Hogan took the stairs to the fifth floor, where Robertson's secretary told him to go straight in. The general manager was careful to leave all day-to-day decisions on the paper to the editorial team but news of Hogan's coup in securing the interview with the Head of Combined Operations had evidently reached as far as Washington, where the paper's proprietor – at Churchill's insistence – was still cooling his heels after resigning from the cabinet as Minister of Production.

'He wants you to telephone him, son. If that sounds like good news it probably isn't. My only advice is be prepared.'

'For what?'

'He wants a clue to where this bloody war is going next and he thinks Mountbatten might know. Did you ask him, as a matter of interest?'

'You mean Combined Ops? Their next outing?'

'Of course. The Americans are pressing for a landing in force on the Cherbourg Peninsula. They're calling it Operation *Sledgehammer* and given the time and effort The Rage is devoting to his Russian friends, we obviously think it's a fine idea. The Americans want it to happen this year, with a breakout once we've made ourselves at home, but it seems our military don't agree, and neither does Churchill. They're calling it Project

Crazy. Not enough men. No boats. Big problems once we get there with resupply. Most of this stuff goes over my head but The Rage is going to want answers.'

'I haven't got any, sir. I know lots about driving fast, and about what it takes to become a commando, but that's about it. Combined Ops have landed twice in France so far, so that might be a clue.'

'Nothing else?'

'Nothing.'

Robertson nodded. He was gazing at the telephone, calculating the time difference with the eastern seaboard. Beaverbrook, as everyone in the building knew, worked brutal hours, rising every morning at six. Just now, according to Robertson, he was in a borrowed villa on an island off the Georgia coast, furiously working on a radio speech he was due to deliver coast-to-coast from New York.

'He broadcast to the Canadians a week or so ago,' Robertson grunted. 'It was the usual stuff, how the Empire needs to lend the Russians a hand, but no one's fooled, least of all in Downing Street. The Reds have kidnapped him. He's running a foreign policy of his own. He knows all about the practical problems but he doesn't care. I shouldn't be telling you this but there are people around Churchill who think our lord and master fancies his chances.'

'As?'

'Prime Minister. It's gossip, of course, and mischief, too, but neither comes as a surprise. Make the call, son. Give him whatever comfort you can.'

Robertson asked his secretary to raise the number on the transatlantic exchange, and Hogan drew up a chair at her desk next door. Minutes later came the rasp of the familiar voice.

'EJ?'

'Hogan, sir. George.'

'The Miramichi Express? Good to hear you, son. You've seen Mountbatten? Talked to him?'

'I have, sir, yes.' Hogan offered a brief account of the interview at Richmond Terrace.

'And that's all? That's it? This is a guy with lips even looser than me. Friends in Washington tell me he wants to be in charge when we finally invade, and I believe them. The Americans love him, incidentally. All that class, all that breeding, all those fucking *connections*. He rolls the Yanks over, Hogan, and I got that from a source I'd trust with my life. You're really telling me he said nothing about any of this?'

'I am, sir, yes.'

'Then maybe you weren't listening properly. No clues at all? Nothing about Roosevelt? George Marshall? Young Eisenhower? These people think the sun shines out of that man's royal arse. In fact they're due a visit any time now, and you know where they're headed? You got it, son. Richmond goddam Terrace, where Mr Combined Ops will bang the gong for the Second Front and tell them how clever he is. That's all I want, son. Just a confirmation, the merest whisper, that he's got something tasty up his sleeve which might mean another outing for those precious commandos of his. I've watched that man for years. If there's glory on offer, there's no way he can resist it. Maybe you should go back. Maybe next time round he'll like you better. How did you grab that interview in the first place, incidentally? I'm curious to find out.'

'I asked nicely, sir.'

'In person?'

'Definitely.'

'To the man himself?'

'I'm afraid not,' Hogan was thinking about *The Art of War*. 'He hates full frontal assaults, prefers to take the enemy by surprise.' Hogan paused a moment, wondering if he'd gone too far, but then there came a click on the line and the voice of the transatlantic operator. The Rage had evidently returned to his early breakfast.

15

Schultz took the call mid-evening in his room at the Hôtel Lutetia. There were just four hours to go before Babineau's fiftieth birthday expired at midnight, and he was impressed by the Italians' impeccable timing.

'How many?' Schultz bent to the phone. The call had come from Didier, his faithful maître d'.

'Two, Herr Schultz. They say they have something for you in the car. To be honest I—'

'Ask them to come up,' Schultz cut him short.

'*Monsieur?*'

'You know the room number: 307. All will be well, Didier. I guarantee it.'

Schultz ended the call. Ortega was asleep, at the mercy of some dream or other. From time to time he grunted, ox-like, his huge frame prone on the bed, a thin trickle of saliva escaping from his ruined mouth, and Schultz watched the tiny tremor behind one eyelid before he stepped over and shook the Spaniard awake.

'They're here,' he grunted.

Ortega was on his feet in seconds, rubbing his good eye. For a big man he moved with surprising grace. He had a Luger automatic tucked inside the waistband of his trousers, another to hand on the low coffee table. Both magazines were fully loaded.

'Dum-dums?' Schultz was looking at the pistol.

'No need. This kind of range, who needs the mess?'

'You want me to answer the door?'

'I want you next door in the bathroom. You've seen enough of me today. This should be simple.'

Schultz shrugged and retreated to the tiny bathroom. He'd spent the day trailing his coat in various Paris locations, trying to flush the Italians out. Ortega had been in close attendance throughout and Schultz had been impressed by his talent for keeping the lowest of profiles. In the Théâtre Edouard VII he'd consented to wear the black balaclava. Out in broad daylight, he'd simply disappeared.

Schultz settled on the lavatory. He had a weapon of his own, a short-recoil Walther P38, and now he eased a round into the chamber. Over the recent weeks, ever alert, he'd learned to trust Ortega with his life, a faith he'd never extended to any other human being, but he knew more than enough about the workings of fate to assume absolutely nothing. In the unlikely shape of *El Diablo*, he'd found the near-perfect bodyguard, a killer able to tease the darkest possibilities from any location. The man was feral in the way he could sniff the wind, plot the angles of approach, interpret a sudden stir in the tide of pedestrians on a Parisian boulevard. Faced with a couple of Italians reckless enough to stage a revenge killing on *Abwehr* turf, he was entitled to consider the job already done. Two men dead on the thick nap of the Lutetia's carpet? Easy.

But they didn't come. At length, Schultz emerged from the bathroom and phoned Didier.

'They drove off, Herr Schultz, a couple of minutes ago.'

'Did they ever get out of the car?'

'No. Some kind of quarrel, I think. Italians, like you said.'

Schultz nodded and thanked him before hanging up. Tomorrow was a busy day and he'd been depending on getting the Italians out of the way. Their second thoughts about the Hôtel Lutetia doubtless meant another attempt. Maybe tomorrow. Maybe later. Whenever it might happen, the train ride out of the city couldn't wait. He had meetings arranged, questions to be answered, plans waiting to be laid.

'You want me to stay the night?' Ortega gestured at the big double bed.

'Christ, no. Nine fifteen at Gare St Lazare. The Dieppe trains leave from platform five.' Schultz gestured towards the door. 'Bring a change of clothes. You might be there a while.'

Ortega nodded, smothered a yawn with the back of his big hand, pocketed the spare Luger and left. Schultz listened to the clump-clump of his footsteps as he wandered away down the corridor, and then came the squeak of metal on metal as he opened the doors to the waiting lift.

It was still barely nine in the evening. Schultz's room doubled as an office, and he spent nearly an hour at his desk reviewing the prospects for tomorrow's visit to Dieppe. Zimmermann had agreed that – on paper at least – the choice of the fishing port was perfect for what both he and Schultz had in mind. What mattered now was making sure that news of the prospects on offer reached the right ears.

The key to that operation was Lucien Gasquet. His near-success in tempting the boss of the French Gestapo into the crosshairs of a professional assassin had won him the admiration of key figures in the biggest of the nascent French Resistance networks, based here in Paris, and it simply remained for Gasquet to confirm that the town and the harbour were virtually undefended, a source of concern to his German lover but an oversight that the occupation authorities seemed in no hurry to rectify.

True, the recent Führer Directive number forty had alerted commanders in France and Belgium to prepare for the likelihood of enemy landings. Given Stalin's incessant demands for the opening of a second front, he could hardly do less. But whether or not the sleepy town of Dieppe qualified for the attentions of Organisation Todt, experts in the black arts of fortification, remained to be seen. It was Schultz's task tomorrow to explore the many possibilities offered by what Zimmermann was already calling the Dieppe situation, a prospect that brought a smile to Schultz's lips. An early night, he told himself, wondering what had become of the luckless Italians.

He awoke nearly three hours later, the room in darkness, unsure what to make of the noise he'd heard. He lay quite still, every nerve stretched tight, waiting for it to happen again. Someone at the door? A scrape of something in the lock? A stir of movement outside in the corridor? The leavings of some dream or other, spilling out of his sleepy brain? He'd no idea.

Then, as he fought the temptation to drift away again, there came another noise, unmistakeable this time, a throaty grunt, oddly familiar, and moments later a second voice, maybe a woman, and a gasp of pain. Schultz was out of the bed by this time, the Walther he kept beneath the pillow secure in his hand. He stepped slowly towards the door, feeling his way in the darkness.

It was Ortega, definitely. How come he was still in the hotel? Schultz was trying to map the situation from the few clues he had. Ortega's voice, low, angry, was a string of curses. *Puta.* Whore. Anything for money. Any trick you cared to fucking name. Schultz was smiling now. He could picture the big face inches from hers, the fine mist of spittle his broken mouth seemed unable to contain, the rich expletives heaped on his latest target.

Very slowly, Schultz unbolted the door and opened it, the gun still in his hand. Sprawled on the carpet was a woman he recognised. She was a regular at the hotel, half French, half Romanian. She was younger than most of *les collabos horizontales*, and way prettier than any of them, and for money and other favours she was more than happy to service a number of *Abwehr* officers. Schultz had never had the pleasure himself, never felt the need, but she was said to be dextrous and playful and more than happy to stay the night. Recently, thanks to a quiet order passed by an eager client near the very top of the organisation, she'd virtually had the run of the place.

No longer. Ortega had his big knee placed on her chest, and one hand was cupping her face. The weight of his body made it hard for her to breath and however hard she tried she couldn't move her head. Her eyes were wide, watching Ortega's every movement as he produced a knife, testing the blade against his ruined face before reaching for her ear.

'Don't.'

Ortega, for once, had been taken by surprise. He froze for a moment, then gestured at the gun beside the woman's body.

'She came for you, *hombre*,' he muttered. 'The *puta* needs better manners. Maybe not the whole ear. Maybe just half.' His attention returned to the terrified face beneath him. '*Comprende?*'

The woman tried to kick him, tried to wriggle free, but failed. Schultz bent quickly and retrieved the revolver. It was a little Beretta, much favoured by the city's army of whores. It was hopeless over any kind of distance but at point-blank range, with Schultz asleep in bed, it would have done the job. The Italians, he thought. For a fee she couldn't possibly turn down.

Schultz, in his vest and underpants, was aware of the woman's eyes on his body.

'All night,' she offered. 'Both of you. No charge.'

Schultz and Ortega exchanged glances. At least the woman had a sense of humour.

'Well, *hombre*?' Ortega at last eased the weight on his knee.

Schultz opened the door a little wider, then told Ortega he'd make the call.

'We get her locked up,' he said. 'And come back for her next week.' He paused. 'So how come you knew she was after me?'

'I didn't. I waited downstairs. I watched and when she turned up I followed her. I know the Italians. I fought with them in Spain. People get them wrong. Once they're in the mood, they never give up.'

*

By noon next day, Schultz and Ortega were in Dieppe. The *Wehrmacht*, Schultz knew, had occupied the Hôtel Royal on the seafront, which was said to have a fine canteen. For a handful of Reichsmarks, Zimmermann had told him, you could fill your belly with plates heaped with local meat and vegetables, and there was normally fresh fruit and limitless Normandy cream to follow. Ortega needed no persuading after the long, slow journey north on the train but Schultz had other ideas. The Tout Va Bien café was said to be popular with German troops. No better place for a midday beer.

The café overlooked a stretch of the harbour. As in Paris, Schultz thought, the Germans had cocked their legs and left their scent on their new trophy: long Nazi banners hung from public buildings, signposts in heavy Gothic script showed the way to military installations, and every public clock was set to Berlin time. Stern notices warned the population of the consequences of civil disobedience and everywhere there were young soldiers in *Wehrmacht* grey who were so obviously enjoying this peaceful seaside resort they'd suddenly come to own. Off-duty, they were still in uniform but many of them spent their pay in local shops. They moved in groups of three or four and many of them carried purchases wrapped in newsprint. The ones from the local butcher were already seeping fresh blood.

Schultz stood in the bright spring sunshine, gazing across the water at a line of fishing boats secured against the harbour wall. None of them sported the tricolour at their stubby masts because the national flag had been banned throughout the Occupied Zone and Schultz sensed that Goebbels would love a film set like this. It spoke of the unending reach of the Greater Reich. It confirmed mute obedience on the part of the French, and implacable resolve by their new captors, and it served as well to remind even the English that nowhere on earth was immune to the attentions of the men in *Wehrmacht* grey.

Schultz shook his head and turned away, thinking of Odile and her recent attack of *ennui*. How the France she loved had been stolen from under her nose. How there was nothing left but *le vide* and a bottomless sense of loss. Schultz was glad to be out the bubble that was Paris but there was something about a scene like this that didn't agree with him either. He'd willingly volunteered his own modest talents to try and add a little self-respect to the exhausting business of being German, but it was days like this that made him feel just a little uncomfortable. Conquest, in the end, was theft. And there was no Führer Directive that could ever change that fact.

Ortega had the remains of his face upturned to the sun. He was standing five metres away, plumb in the middle of the pavement, and Schultz was aware of the stir of mawkish interest in his companion. Ortega, for his part, seemed oblivious.

Schultz had noticed on a number of occasions that he paid no attention to his image in the mirror behind countless bars, or to his reflection as he passed the plate-glass window of a shop front, and it was the same when they finally stepped into the Tout Va Bien café. Every table except one was occupied by German soldiers, most of them absurdly young. They had the heedless arrogance that came with conquest, and after Schultz had ordered a couple of beers one of them leaned across and tapped Ortega on the arm.

'What happened?' he asked. 'What did you do to upset her?'

The question raised a slightly uncertain laugh from the neighbouring tables as others looked at this mountain of a man and wondered what might happen next, but Ortega merely shrugged.

'A church fell on my head,' he grunted. 'Never trust in God when you most need him.'

The comment cleared the air. Another German picked up Ortega's accent and wanted to know more. The Spaniard obliged, tossing them a couple of choice morsels from the fighting at Badajoz, and his subsequent winter in Madrid, and then Schultz intervened to steer the conversation in another direction, and suddenly the young garrison soldiers were talking about the rigours of January in a dump like Dieppe, and how quickly things could change when spring arrived and the sun came out.

April, they all agreed, had put a smile on their faces. At last they were showing decent movies at the Kursaal cinema in rue Aguado, and the food at the Hôtel Royal had definitely improved. Better still, Madame Lili, who ran the brothel next to the fish market, had imported some real lookers from Rouen, and had so far resisted the temptation to raise her prices. In short, business was good for the Germans and the locals alike, and the coming summer held nothing but the richest promise. Given the size of the Greater Reich, there were certainly worse places to sit out this bloody war, and the more they heard about life on the Eastern Front, the more they thanked God for their good fortune.

'And what about the English,' Schultz asked. 'The Americans? You don't think they might turn up one day? Ruin the party?'

Schultz's question was directed at a blond youth with a Hamburg accent. In reply, he offered a firm shake of his head.

'It won't happen,' he said. 'And even if it ever did, we'd kick their arses and send them home to mama.'

The promise raised a roar of approval from nearby listeners. Fists crashed down onto table tops. Beer danced in chipped glasses and suddenly the entire café was on its feet, bellowing a pre-war marching song Schultz recognised only too well. The last time these words had been on his lips, he'd been chasing Communist scum up darkened alleys in Berlin, prior to beating them senseless.

*

A little later, after plates of imported *Blutwurst* between thick slices of local bread, Schultz and Ortega took a walk through the narrow streets of the town's centre. The warmth in the sun had sent Dieppe's winter wardrobe back into storage and most of the women, especially the younger ones, were dressed for the coming of summer: loose cotton skirts, neatly pressed blouses, open sandals, even the makings of a simple picnic in the frayed wicker baskets on their arms.

The beach, though, was off-limits. Schultz and Ortega stood beside the two lines of barbed wire, taking stock of what they could see while they awaited the arrival of an approaching *Wehrmacht* patrol. The town had been built in the valley of a river that emptied into the harbour, and the rash of seaside villas had spilled inland as Dieppe began to flourish as a tourist resort. In the distance, right and left, tall cliffs fell sheer into the lapping sea. The cliffs dominated the apron of grey beach before them, the whiteness of the chalk patterned here and there by thin brown stains of vegetation.

Schultz was in uniform and the sight of his *Abwehr* pass prompted a nod from the patrol's *Leutnant* when Schultz sought permission to examine the beach more closely. One of the patrol donned gloves and hauled the barbed wire back, letting Schultz and Ortega through. Yet again, no one could take their eyes off the Spaniard.

The beach shelved steeply in wave after wave of grey pebbles towards the lapping tide. Schultz scrambled awkwardly down until he was standing at the water's edge.

'Well?' He gestured round. 'Pretend you're attacking. Imagine you're coming in from the sea. What do you make of it?'

Ortega had stooped for a couple of the pebbles before joining Schultz. One of the pebbles was the size of a tennis ball, the other was smaller, less round. He weighed them both in his hand for a moment, and then stamped hard, feeling the bank of stones shifting bodily beneath his weight.

'This beach will eat them alive,' he grunted. 'Even if they bring tanks.'

'Especially if they bring tanks,' Schultz said. 'Think of the weight. You're right. The tanks will dig themselves in.'

A biggish wave appeared from nowhere and Schultz stepped up the beach. Machine-gun posts were under construction along the promenade, sited to hose lethal fire onto the beach where he was standing.

His long summer days before the war, quietly exploring the French Maginot Line, had taught Schultz a great deal about the science of fortification, and he knew at once that this little seaside town was virtually impregnable. A torrent of machine-gun fire from every conceivable landward angle. The longer reach of mortars and artillery from the neighbouring clifftops. In short, a blizzard of scalding lead that would stop any invader before he even set foot in the town. *Ouvrage* Dieppe, he thought.

Ortega agreed.

'A machine-gunner's wet dream,' he was gazing at the workmen pouring concrete along the promenade. 'Give these guys enough ammunition and you wouldn't see the beach for bodies. We had a couple of positions like this at Badajoz. The Reds had no option. They were queuing up to be killed.'

Schultz nodded. Beyond a wide expanse of grass behind the promenade was a line of hotels. Windows in the upper levels had already been sandbagged for snipers and machine-gunners, while the big casino at the western end, its walls camouflaged with green and brown paint, had been turned into a fortress with the emplacement of what looked like a 37mm gun at the building's entrance. Better still, bookending the kilometre of beach, was a sizeable castle, ancient, thick-walled, virtually impregnable. From here, a handful of marksmen would be spoiled for targets.

Schultz stepped back through the double barbed-wire barrier and approached the *Leutnant*. He wanted to know what happened along the coast, both east and west.

'Cliffs, Herr *Major*, and then more cliffs. OK, you've got the odd river, and the chance to maybe mount some kind of thrust off the beach, but the lie of the land has always been our friend here, and that makes us feel very, very safe.'

The lie of the land, thought Schultz, a simple truth that surely even the British would have to acknowledge. So maybe, after all, they wouldn't come. Maybe they'd simply respect the geography of the place and tear up whatever plans they might have laid. This conclusion, so obvious, so rational, gave Schultz just the smallest twinge of disappointment. When he asked the *Leutnant* where he might find the local commander of the garrison, he pointed back towards the town centre.

'Ask anyone for the school,' he said. 'It's west of the town square.'

Schultz set off to find the school, leaving Ortega to enjoy the sunshine. He knew already that the Dieppe sector of the coast was the responsibility of the 571st Infantry Regiment, part of the much bigger 302nd Division. According to Zimmermann, it was understrength, with barely 1,500 men defending nearly sixty kilometres of coast, while the seafront in the town itself was held by only a single company of around 150 men.

Schultz found an officer at a desk at the back of the school. A smell of chalk dust and much-thumbed books still hung in the stale air, and a collection of toys had been tidied into the far corner of the room. It was a tribute, thought Schultz, to the *Abwehr's* hard-won reputation that the mere presentation of his pass could secure an interview with the regimental adjutant.

Kapitan Linder was a tall officer in his late thirties, his seamed face already tanned beneath the crescent of white left by his cap, and he listened patiently while Schultz outlined his interest. He wanted to know exactly what plans had been made to defend the town in the event of attack from the sea, and he wanted – above all – to know about timelines.

'You mean when they might come?' A Saxon accent.

'Exactly.'

'Meaning you think they will?'

'Meaning anything's possible.'

'You've been down to the beach? Seen what we're up to?'

'Of course.'

'And you still think they might risk it?'

Schultz nodded, adding nothing more, committing everything to memory as Linder described the walls of *Wehrmacht* grey that would keep the town in German hands should the British ever be foolish enough to mount any kind of challenge. He admitted at once that he needed more troops. The garrison was presently undermanned but he'd been promised reinforcements, most of them probably Polish. In the meantime, hundreds of Dutch and Belgian workers had been shipped in to strengthen the seaward defences. Houses along the seafront had been designated for demolition to open up interlinking fields of fire, and plans were underway to seal off the streets that led into the town centre.

'In case the English arrive in strength?'

'In case they bring tanks with them.'

'And on top of the cliff?'

'*Cliffs*, Herr *Major*,' emphasising the plural. 'We have 175mm gun batteries, all of them protected. Firepower like that can stop most landing craft even getting to the beach. We're turning this place into a mincing machine. Only butchers can appreciate what we have in mind.'

Schultz nodded. It was a compelling image, an entire stretch of those endless grey pebbles converted into an abattoir.

'And air support?'

'We're blessed, Herr *Major*.' He gestured at the big map tacked to the blackboard. 'The *Luftwaffe* are promising us more than three hundred aircraft. The Abbeville boys from Jagdgeschwader 26 are flying Focke-Wulf 190s now. They can be with us in less than twenty minutes, and by the time the RAF arrive, those English pilots will be trying to save every spoonful of gas. At

Abbeville they're talking about a turkey shoot, and I suspect they're not wrong.'

'And timing?' Schultz enquired. 'You have thoughts about that, too?'

'It has to be summer,' Linder said at once. 'The weather after September you can never predict. Sometimes you're looking at waves the size of houses, but after May it all quietens down. The fishermen know that, but along this coast you're still the prisoner of the tides. Anyone wanting to land needs a big spring tide to bring them way up the beach but that means a full moon so it might help to have cloud cover. But clouds suggest wind, which you definitely don't want, so there's another problem. Midsummer, it gets light early, as well, so you'd need to be off the coast by four in the morning. It all sounds so simple, Herr *Major*, but thankfully it isn't. The weather and the tides can be our friend. Maybe two opportunities in any month. Maybe none at all.'

Schultz nodded, taking his time.

'But what if the English make the wrong assumptions about the place? What if they think you're here for the taking?'

'But we're not.'

'I know, but that's not my question. Every war is shaped by expectations, by what the enemy *thinks* might happen, and sometimes that has to be based on assumptions. So what happens if we take certain steps...' Schultz shrugged '... to doctor those assumptions, to sweeten them, to suggest that maybe your defences aren't as perfect as you've just described? What happens if the British think they have negligence, as well as luck, on their side?'

'Negligence?' Linder looked briefly shocked. 'You're suggesting...?'

'I'm suggesting nothing, Herr *Kapitan*. I'm simply offering a thought or two. The English might find the prospect of a landing, even a brief period of occupation, immensely attractive. The promise of a prize like that, especially with their war in its current state, could be overwhelming. Think of the headlines. Think of the glory. You want something badly enough and you'll tell yourself any lie to make it happen. All I'm saying is that we can help make that lie sound almost plausible.'

'How?'

'By spreading false information. By concocting a story that isn't even half true. And then by feeding it into those Chinese whispers that we know will finally reach British ears.'

'We're talking about the Resistance?'

'We are, Herr Linder. Convince the right network, people the British have learned to trust, and you start to spread that big fat lie that some of them have grown to depend on.'

'That this place is here for the taking?'

'That Dieppe is undermanned, poorly defended. Not because of any oversight on your part, Herr Linder, because we know already that's not true, but because there are people on the other side of the water who want, or maybe *need*, to believe this shit of ours.'

Schultz was studying the figure on the other side of the desk. Linder was bent over a pad, scribbling himself a note Schultz couldn't read. At length, he looked up, and there was just a hint of admiration in his smile.

'You're in the intelligence game, Herr *Major*, and it certainly shows.' The smile broadened. 'I've always wondered what the *Abwehr* do to earn their corn, and now I know.'

*

That evening, Schultz booked himself into a hotel overlooking the harbour while Ortega paid a visit to Madame Lili's nearby brothel. Schultz had invited the town's mayor to share a dinner at the *Abwehr*'s expense. Nothing formal, he'd assured the mayor's secretary. Half past seven, if that's convenient.

René Levasseur was an agreeably relaxed *Dieppois* in his early forties who'd been obliged to master enough German to sustain an hour or two's conversation. He seemed to sense something unusual in the battered figure across the white linen tablecloth and he readily confirmed what Schultz had learned already. Yes, the town had been more than happy to find accommodations for the influx of labourers working on the seaward defences. Yes, there was talk of a possible visit from the English across the Channel. And, yes, there were plans afoot to evacuate local kids to families in the Auvergne. This would happen, he said, by June at the latest though he was personally convinced that the English would never appear.

'Why on earth not?'

'Because there'd be no point. What would they want from this town of ours? What would they *do*? OK, we still have invasion barges the Germans never used tied up in the inner harbour. I suppose they might tow them home with them. But what other use could we ever be? Apart from broaching a bottle or two and cooking them a decent omelette? Invasions are meant to be forever, Herr Schultz. This would be nothing but a day trip before you Boche fine them for trespassing and chase them away.'

'We'd kill them,' Schultz pointed out. 'Not all of them perhaps, but most.'

'I know. I'm being ironic. It's a weakness of ours, I'm afraid, but under the current circumstances it makes us feel a little better.'

There was more than a hint of reproof in the calm mayoral smile, but Schultz held his gaze for long enough to remain on speaking terms.

'It's a delightful little town,' he murmured. 'When all this nonsense is over, I might come back here for a holiday.'

'In which case,' a tiny nod of Levasseur's head, 'you might be welcome.'

'You really mean that?'

'I said might, Herr Schultz. Indulge me a little more. The only certainty in my country is the existence of doubt.'

Schultz was preparing for bed when he heard the lightest tap at his door. After last night he was taking no chances and he reached for the Walther P38. Happily, it was Ortega. Schultz unlocked the door and poured him a brandy from the bottle he'd purchased downstairs. Ortega smelled of fish.

'Well?' He gestured towards the darkness outside the window. 'Any surprises at Madame Lili's?'

'Plenty, *hombre*, all of them good. They both came from Le Havre. They must put something in the water there. Lots of stamina and a trick or two I've never come across before.'

'They?'

'Henrietta and Danielle. Were they really sisters? That's what they told me but who believes anything they hear in the whorehouse?' He frowned, looking at the shirt buttons open down the broadness of Schultz's chest. 'You're going to bed?'

'I am, yes. Any reason why I shouldn't?'

'Come with me. A little present. Maybe even two.'

'You're taking me back to the brothel? Madame Lili's?'

'Sadly not. Though we have Madame herself to thank.'

'For what?'

Ortega wouldn't say. Schultz rebuttoned his shirt, reached for his jacket and followed Ortega down the stairs and out into the darkened street. One alley led to another, the cobbles slippery underfoot with slop from the fish market. At last, at the end of a narrow cul-de-sac, Ortega brought Schultz to a halt beside the remains of an abandoned Peugeot 402. The wheels had been stolen and someone a while ago had tried to set the little car on fire.

'In the back, *hombre*.' Ortega had produced a lighter. 'Take a look.'

Schultz bent down and peered inside. Then came the scrape of a flint and a spill of light and Schultz found himself looking at two bodies, one of them heaped untidily on the other. Only one face was visible, a neat hole above his right eye.

'Your work?' Schultz glanced over his shoulder.

'Mine, *hombre*. Our Italian friends. They must have followed us onto the train this morning. Their mistake was visiting the brothel. Madame hates Italians but I'm guessing they didn't know that.'

'You shot them? In the fucking *brothel*?'

'I did them here, beside the car. I led them a little dance and they thought they had me cornered. Yet another mistake.' A flash of broken teeth in the darkness. 'You owe me money, *hombre*. Reichsmarks will be fine.'

16

Only slowly did the details of Operation *Myrmidon* begin to seep out of Combined Ops headquarters. Even Hogan, who'd virtually moved into Annie's ground-floor flat in Gower Street, was denied a glimpse of an expedition that had gone so disastrously wrong.

It was the second week in April, and Annie had returned to Gower Street late in the evening, riding a wave of excitement generated by a bunch of very senior American commanders who'd descended on Combined Ops HQ in Richmond Terrace.

'They loved us,' she dropped her bag at Hogan's feet. 'They loved the set-up, they loved his Lordship, they loved the whole thing. In fact they loved it so much they took us out to dinner. George Marshall? That nice General Eisenhower? We went to Claridge's. We had the run of the menu, anything we fancied. Have you the first idea what fillet steak costs these days? Can you remember what it even *tastes* like? For that kind of money, I could pay for the bloody invasion myself. With change to spare.'

'Might you have a date?' Hogan, realising she was drunk, mimed a pad and pen.

'For what?'

'The invasion.'

'Ah...' She reached up for him. 'Take me to bed, Mr H. Do your worst, then ask me again, but nicely next time.'

Hogan did his best to oblige but knew at once it wouldn't work. Her kisses were sloppy. She had a fit of the giggles. Then she rolled over and fell out of bed. He reached down to haul her back but it was too late. She was already fast asleep.

She awoke an hour before dawn. Hogan had draped a blanket over her to tide her through the night but now she pushed it away and climbed in beside him. When she complained of a headache, Hogan said he wasn't surprised.

'How much did you have?'

'I lost count. I think it was the novelty. When was a girl last offered four refills of Moët before the dinner wines even arrived? This war's been fun since the Yanks signed on. Hands across the ocean, eh? *Vive* Roosevelt.'

She rubbed her eyes, stifled a yawn and lay back on the pillow. Hogan had spent a couple of hours the previous afternoon in the company of a disgruntled Royal Marine commando with a lot to get off his chest. He'd been cashiered after an incident aboard a ferry called the *Princess Beatrice*. According to this ex-bootneck, 6 Commando had been one of two units spearheading yet another Combined Ops raid. *Myrmidon* had called for a landing in south-west France. Three thousand troops would storm ashore and wreak havoc among road and rail transport into Spain, but the ship had grounded on a sandbar at the mouth of the River Adour and been forced to withdraw. In the view of Hogan's source, the whole trip had been a shambles. A month at sea with nothing to show for it? Planners who'd failed to check out the estuary approaches? No wonder he'd taken it out on one of his luckless officers. With no other target available, the bloody man had only himself to blame.

'Does that sound about right?' Hogan enquired. 'Or has this guy made the whole thing up?'

'Why ask me?' Annie's eyes had closed again.

'Because you work there. Because you'd *know.*'

'And supposing you're right, do you really think I'd tell you?'

'You might.'

'Because you get to fuck me so often?'

'Because you're still drunk.'

'But that's taking advantage, isn't it?'

'Of course it is.'

'And you've no regrets, Mr H? No conscience? What's happened to that sober, God-fearing Baptist person I invited into my bed?'

Hogan, gazing at the pale disk of face in the darkness, could only shrug. It was true. Half a lifetime seemed to have sped by since he'd last settled on one of those hard Baptist benches, and the truth was that he wouldn't have missed a single moment of the days and nights they'd spent together. Mad evenings in bed, cheating the increasingly infrequent raids. Wild experiments with French cooking thanks to the fancy ingredients she liberated from the pantry at Richmond Terrace. Weekend expeditions by train or bus into the remote Home Counties countryside.

On one of these outings, deep in woodlands near Tring, they'd come across an old tramp trying to revive a fire he'd built. Annie had foraged for drier twigs and knelt by his side, coaxing a flame from the dampness of the leaves. They'd fallen into conversation. The tramp was a shy man, solitary by nature, but Annie had blown on the embers of his life, and by the time they left him they knew a great deal about the wife who'd betrayed him, and the grown-up kids he never wanted to see again. For Hogan, that long afternoon had been a masterclass in empathy, and on the journey home he'd told her so.

'If you ever give up on Mountbatten,' he'd said, 'you could always become a priest. That poor guy found himself in the confessional, and that was thanks to you.'

Now, she was properly awake, returning to bed with three aspirins and a glass of tepid water. Still drunk? Probably. But in the mood, it seemed, for a proper conversation.

'I'm serious, George.' She rarely used his Christian name.

'About what?'

'Taking advantage. Sometimes I get the feeling I'm just another contact in that big fat book of yours, your shortest cut to the great and the good. Are there compensations? Should a girl be grateful for proper rations? Of course she should, but maybe that's not quite enough.' She swallowed a tablet, then another. 'Do I hear a yes?'

'You hear nothing. I don't know what you mean. The guy I mentioned was talking about *Myrmidon*. I asked you whether any of it was true, but you wouldn't give me an answer. That's not a problem. It's not even a disappointment. If friends of mine asked about you, I'd have very little to say, but that's fine too because everything between us is present tense. Everything just happens and that's the way I love it.'

'But you don't have any friends, any real friends. At least that's what you told me last week.'

'That's true but I know you. I think I know you very well, and that means you count as a friend and maybe a lot more. I know you here, and I know you now, and that's plenty, believe me.'

'But is it enough? Be honest.'

'It's plenty. I mean it. Anything else would be greedy.'

'You're not interested in my past? Where I might have been? What I might have done? Other men in my life?'

'Of course I'm interested and one day I guess you might tell me. I know about your mother down in Cornwall and the father you never see and your fisherman lover and those summers you spent wherever it was, but in my trade the rest would barely make even a paragraph.'

'That sounds horrible. Am I that shallow? That empty? Should I be upset?'

'Not shallow. No way empty. Just mysterious.'

'A blank page?'

'A mystery.'

'And that's what you like? What you want?'

'I want all of you and in God's good time I might one day get it. Until then...' Hogan touched her face '... I love you this way.'

She nodded, catching his hand, seeming to understand. Then she reached up for him and kissed him gently on the lips.

'I love your simplicity,' she murmured. 'At first I thought you were hopelessly naïve, a kid in long trousers with a lovely grin, but that isn't true. You know exactly who you are, what you want, what you *need* to want, and in men – believe me – that's very rare. I spent hours around that table in the hotel last night, Mr H. I watched those grown-ups talking, posturing, playing their little games. The power they have defies belief. Most of us can barely imagine it. One mistake, one wobbly line on the wrong map, and thousands might die. That should give them pause for thought but somehow it doesn't, and if you're after a proper confession I find that truly terrifying.'

'Was Mountbatten there?'

'Interesting question. Of course he was there. The Americans insisted. He knows the King. He knows everyone. He plays papa with the Heir Apparent. He's the house guest at Christmas. All this stuff is window dressing, but it makes him the star attraction. The Americans arrive in London, and they take a good look round, and they spend a little time in Downing Street, and all they ever hear is the word "no". No, we can't invade France this year. No, we can't afford the material or the men. So, yes, you'll have to take the clipper home and wait a year or two until things change. But then along comes his Lordship with his charm and his contacts and his fancy titles, and these Yanks of ours suddenly find themselves speaking a language they at last understand. They don't trust us, Mr H, but his Lordship comes from a different part of the wood.'

'He's at least half-German,' Hogan pointed out. 'Should that matter?'

'Not in the slightest. They treat him like one of their own. As far as they're concerned, he's a Yank, honorary or otherwise. There's another thing about Americans, too. They're not afraid to fail. An operation goes wrong, it's no big deal. The important thing is having the balls to try it in the first place. Mountbatten knows that and it makes him very happy. Older Generals, Admirals, whatever, might not be so brave.'

Hogan nodded. The first grey light of dawn had appeared at the edges of the blackout curtain.

'He told them about *Myrmidon*?'

'Of course not.'

'Did you? In your cups?'

'Come here,' she began to straddle him. 'That's the silliest question you've ever asked me.'

*

Afterwards, when they awoke again, she announced she wouldn't be going into work.

'Why not?'

'There's someone I have to meet.'

'Combined Ops?'

'Sort of. Half and half.'

'Combined? Or Ops?'

'Don't ask. You could take me to lunch afterwards. I'd like that.'

Hogan reviewed his day. In the morning, he was due at an editorial conference about upcoming projects for the summer.

Mid-afternoon, he'd agreed to meet Frank O'Donovan again. His Canadian Second Division were still kicking their heels at various locations across southern England and O'Donovan was running out of ideas to keep them out of trouble. Hogan, uncomfortably aware that he'd been neglecting his fellow countrymen, knew it was time to deliver on his promise to interview Larry Elder but knew as well that the piece would be a tough sell in the newsroom. Nothing, after all, had happened and just now there was precious little sign that anything ever would.

'The Fighting Cocks,' he said. 'One o'clock OK?'

*

She was late. The West End pub was popular with rehearsing thesps from nearby theatres who broke for a sandwich at midday and Hogan had secured the last vacant table. He'd brought the morning edition from the newsroom and he spread it on the table while he waited for Annie to join him.

Lead story on the front page announced that the RAF had dropped a huge bomb on Essen. German troops, meanwhile, were landing on the Crimean Peninsula, while French Resistance forces had attacked German headquarters at Arras. Hogan turned the page. Unusually, mention of the paper's proprietor had been relegated to an inside page.

Beaverbrook's coast-to-coast broadcast from New York, it seemed, had been a smash hit and he was rumoured to be flying back any day now. Hogan gazed at the smudged newsprint. Gossip at the *Express* only this morning suggested there were moves afoot to give him a job in Washington. An appointment as the UK's Ambassador, heavily favoured by Churchill, might keep The Rage out of mischief.

'A big gin? Can we manage that?'

Hogan glanced up. 'We' he liked. The last time he'd seen this woman she'd still been in bed as he left for work. Now she was wearing a smart suit he'd never seen before. It fitted her perfectly, turning heads the length of the pub, and he wondered again where she'd been.

'Someone important?'

'A bit, yes.'

'Just the two of you?'

'Yes.'

'Should I be worried?'

'*Au contraire*. Just trust me for once. Tonic if they've got it, please. And maybe the usual splash.'

At the bar, Hogan stipulated a double Gordon's and added the dark red bitters himself. This was a routine they'd adopted most evenings at Gower Street, and he knew exactly the balance she liked best in a pink gin.

Back at the table, he began to suspect she might have been crying. Her eyes were red, and slightly puffy, and she seemed unaccountably nervous.

'You OK?'

'No, since you ask.'

'Want to tell me why?'

'No.'

'You're sure?'

'I am, yes. Maybe one day but not now.'

'That sounds pretty final.'

'Does it? We hope not.' She rummaged in her bag for a handkerchief and blew her nose. When Hogan presented the chalked slate that served as a menu, she shook her head.

'I'm happy with this,' she was looking at the gin. 'Then I'll go home.'

'You want me to come with you?'

'No, but thanks for the offer.'

She relapsed into silence, staring into nowhere. Hogan tried to raise a smile with a story from the newsroom but it didn't work. By now, he'd recognised at least two of the faces at neighbouring tables from the showbiz columns on the paper. One of them, a youngish woman who'd recently starred in a Noël Coward play, offered him the beginnings of a smile.

'She's making eyes at you, Mr H.' She got to her feet, the gin untouched. 'I'm in the way here, aren't I?'

Hogan shook his head, asking her to sit down again, maybe have something to eat to settle her stomach after last night, but she shook her head. Then, with a final glance towards the actress, she left.

Hogan brooded for most of the afternoon, trying to tease some sense out of her sudden departure. O'Donovan, thankfully, had left a message cancelling their rendezvous, and after a lengthy session with tomorrow's news editor, Hogan was back at Gower Street by early evening. He found Annie in the bath, making the most of an inch or two of tepid water. She was reading a book, and she seemed better, more cheerful.

'I tried to phone you earlier,' he said. 'But the phone doesn't seem to work.'

'I know. I'll report it tomorrow. Sit,' she nodded at the side of the bath, then lodged the book between the taps. 'You drank the gin, I hope.'

'Every last drop.'

'You lie, Mr H. The day you stoop to spirits there's no hope for the world. I owe you an apology, by the way. You shouldn't have to live with a hysteric, especially after buying me that big fat Gordon's.'

'Is that what you are? A hysteric?'

'No, far from it. We all make mistakes I'm afraid, even me, but I might have something in the way of compensation. Are you ready for this?'

'For what?'

'For my big, big secret? Just you, little me?'

'Try me.'

'But no telling? No passing it on? Even to people you trust?'

'I promise.'

'Cross your heart? Pray to that god of yours?'

'You have my word.'

'Say it again.'

'I promise.'

She nodded, evidently satisfied, then pulled a face at the dribble of lukewarm water she managed to tease from the tap.

'You were right about *Myrmidon*,' she said. 'After Saint-Nazaire, it was a total flop. His Lordship, as you might imagine, plays to win. He needs to restore a little of his reputation, he needs a headline or two, he needs to be *noticed*, and so we'll all be working like mad on another wheeze. He's calling it Operation *Rutter*. We're talking maybe six weeks' time. This has to do with winds and tides and lots of dead Germans.'

'He's got somewhere in mind?'

'Of course.'

'And are you going to tell me?'

'I am,' her hand settled briefly on his. 'It's Dieppe, Mr H. His Lordship thinks it's the perfect choice and naturally we all agree.'

*

It fell to Odile to host Lucien Gasquet's meeting with the Resistance. The request came directly from Zimmermann, whom she'd grown to like as well as admire, and it was Schultz who explained the sequence of trains that would bring Gasquet to

Odile's door. Since the audition at the Edouard VII, Gasquet had been living in an apartment requisitioned by the *Abwehr* out in the western suburbs, safe from the reach of the *Carlingue*. In the interests of what he lightly termed 'conjugal rights', Zimmermann paid him the occasional visit, but he and Schultz had agreed that now was the time to move the Dieppe situation forward.

The choice of the Resistance middleman was the key to everything. For the ruse to work, the information had to come from a network already trusted by the various agencies in London, and in the shape of an ex-teacher called Michel Aubert, Schultz knew he'd found his man. Thanks to circumstances it had taken Schultz weeks to fully understand, Aubert had aligned himself with a network based in the engine sheds out at Saint-Denis. These men, mostly hardline Communists, had carefully built a series of cells in the aftermath of last year's invasion of the Soviet Union, imposing a structure and a discipline that had so far resisted all Gestapo attempts at penetration.

Aubert's own speciality was analysis, testing offered information against known facts on the ground. Hence his presence in Odile's drawing room. A tall man, in serge trousers and a leather-patched corduroy jacket, he was now awaiting the arrival of Lucien Gasquet.

Odile met the actor at the door, shocked by how thin he'd become. Gasquet, visibly nervous, told her the trains had been hopeless but didn't think he'd been followed, though these days you could never be sure. When he looked beyond her into the depths of the house, enquiring hopefully about Conso, Odile told him that the young Somali had returned to Marseilles. Paris, she said, had finally let him down. Too cold, too grey, and – with a touch of adolescent frankness – too exhausting.

Gasquet followed her through to the drawing room. Aubert, sitting beside the window, got to his feet and extended a hand.

'Bishop Cauchon,' his voice, like his touch, was light. 'A privilege to meet you.'

The greeting caught Gasquet off-balance. Only yesterday, out in his apartment, Schultz had coached him through the next hour or so, insisting that it was just another piece of harmless theatre, but Gasquet's audition in the Edouard VII had shaken him badly and he knew enough about the Communists to be seriously alarmed. These people never took prisoners. If this story of his didn't hang together, he could expect no mercy.

'You know about the Edouard VII?' he asked.

'Everyone knows, M. Gasquet. In certain circles, drinkers toast your health. Chamberlin is a gangster and a thug. Live by the gun, die by the gun. Just a shame the *Abwehr* saved his life.'

'Indeed.'

'And brave on your part, too. How on earth did you lay hands on the sniper guy?'

'I didn't. I was simply asked to attend the audition.'

'By whom?'

'I've no idea. It was a voice on the phone.'

'You did it for money?'

'I did it for France.'

'You didn't ask any questions?

'I knew it involved Chamberlin. He has a weakness for Bernard Shaw, or maybe Mimi, or maybe both.'

'You know Mimi?

'Only by reputation. She used to be a decent actress.'

'And now?'

'She's a joke. She's moved into directing. That says more about Chamberlin's money than any talent of hers, believe me.'

'Yet you were happy to be there?'

'Not entirely. But a wise man never crosses the *Carlingue*.'

'So it wasn't for France at all? Is that what you're telling me?'

'On the contrary. I have very little courage, Monsieur, but I truly hate what's happening to us. We're on our knees. We're supplicants. With Saint Joan, it was the English. With us, it's the Germans. The sooner they're gone, the better. So,' he shrugged, 'you do what you can.'

Aubert held his gaze for what felt like an age, and then nodded.

'So tell me about your friend Zimmermann.'

'Hans? He's maybe the exception.'

'A decent German?'

'Yes.'

'And you were living with him?'

'I was, yes, until that wretched audition. Now I spend most of my days hiding from the *Carlingue*.'

'Because they think you betrayed them?'

'Because they want to kill me.'

'And Zimmermann?'

'We meet when we can.'

'For?'

'Sex, mainly. And a little conversation. We also share a passion for Viennese apfel strudel if you think that's important.'

'And pillow talk? Peering into this man's soul?'

'That, too.'

'So tell me what secrets he might be sharing. Information that might be of interest. You can do that?'

'Of course.'

This, Schultz had told him, would be the question that flagged Gasquet's path to the heart of the interview. Offer a series of titbits first. Stumble on Dieppe later, almost by accident, like an afterthought. Gasquet had recognised at once that this was sound advice, and had spent most of the night rehearsing his lines, but now – aware of the unwavering gaze on his face – he was close to panic.

'Take your time, my friend. Just tell me about this Hans Zimmermann of yours, what upsets him, what alarms him, what he'd like to change.'

Gasquet nodded, swallowing hard. Was he right to sense an edge of menace in this stranger's voice? Had he already dismissed this story of his? Gasquet shrugged, then frowned, suggesting what he hoped came across as intense concentration. He described Zimmermann's despair at all the battles lost and won with Himmler's SS, at his impatience with some of the directives from his *Abwehr* bosses in Berlin, so hopelessly remote, at his bewilderment over the never-ending quotas of looted goods he was supposed to be despatching to the *Heimat*, and just recently his frustrated bid to put flesh on the bones of the latest Führer Directive.

'This is number...?'

'Forty. Strengthening the Reich's coastal defences. Hans believes the war in the east is sucking Germany dry. Hitler appears to think that the English may mount attacks to relieve the pressure on Stalin. The irony, of course, is that no German troops are available to put up any kind of fight. Why? Because they're all in Russia. This, believe it or not, keeps Hans awake at night. I tell him it shouldn't, but it does. He says the cupboard's bare, and he's probably in a position to know.'

'So where might we be thinking?'

'That's what I asked him last time we met.' Gasquet was warming up now. He'd followed Schultz's script to the letter and the sudden appearance of a notepad on Aubert's lap told him he'd at last caught this man's attention.

'The obvious places are the best defended,' Gasquet said.

'Meaning?'

'Calais. Boulogne. Dunkirk. Hans says it takes no effort for the English to get there which is why the best divisions the

Germans can muster are already allotted. It's other places that worry him.'

'Has he named any?'

'Yes, Abbeville for one, but there's a big airfield close by which seems to make a difference.'

'And where else?'

'Le Havre. It's a huge port, of course, and already well defended.'

'And that's it?'

Gasquet paused, frowning again, having a think.

'Yes,' he said. 'No. Wait. He mentioned Dieppe. He told me he once holidayed there as a kid and it made an impression. Huge cliffs. Nice little harbour. Lots of English.'

'And?' Aubert's racing pen had come to a halt.

'And?' Gasquet feigned confusion.

'He mentioned its defences?'

'Yes. The phrase he used was so-so. Plenty to work on if you had the opportunity.'

'But?'

'No troops worth the name.' Gasquet shrugged. 'Does that make any sense?'

17

It took Hogan nearly a month to properly digest the news about Operation *Rutter*. Beaverbrook returned to London at the beginning of May, despatching a barrage of memos urging his exhausted staff to make yet greater efforts on behalf of the beleaguered Soviets. After the icy torments of a Russian winter, with little movement on either side, spring had triggered a new fighting season, sending German armies across the endless steppe towards the Caucasus Mountains and the oilfields beyond. Access to limitless oil, Beaverbrook warned, might well bring the war to a close on Berlin's terms. All hands to the pump.

Fresh demands took Hogan the length and breadth of the kingdom, attending rallies, testing public opinion, knitting together interview after interview in a bid to placate his hyperactive proprietor. By and large, he detected a real sympathy for the Russians, especially among the big industrial cities in the Midlands and the North. This war, Hogan had decided, was turning into a great leveller, breeding a huge citizen army pledged to a fairer division of the spoils, once the Germans were finally beaten.

No one doubted that this dream, one day, would come true and people were honest enough to acknowledge that the Americans, with their vast assembly lines and limitless wealth, would be the ultimate guarantors of victory, but it was equally clear that Yank money in Yank pockets was beginning to turn the working population against the ever-growing army of GIs. For British men, especially, the invasion of young Americans was far from welcome. These kids were too spoiled, too rich, and far too pushy when it came to local woman, and Hogan took care to assure anyone prepared to listen that Canadians, unlike their noisy southern neighbours, knew how to behave.

This was a distinction that Annie was the first to acknowledge. Hogan was back from his travels in Gower Street maybe one night in three and he became aware that their lives together had knitted and settled down. After telling him about Operation *Rutter*, and the surprise awaiting the good citizens of Dieppe, her lips appeared to be sealed. She'd handed him a big fat story and made it clear that the subject was now taboo. For his part, whenever he found an hour or so to call his own, Hogan made discreet enquiries with specialists on the paper who might have an opinion on the subject, but was puzzled by their response.

One or two, younger than the rest, thought that any landing in force deserved a round of applause while older, wiser heads, especially those with first-hand knowledge of this stretch of coast, failed to see the military logic behind a landing. The place was too small to offer decent pickings, while the geography promised nothing but grief to an invading force. A couple of dozen Boy Scouts could defend the place, said one saloon bar general. What on earth would be the point?

Hogan, who'd never set foot in France, could only nod sagely and scribble himself a note. For one longish evening in the flat, more silent than usual, he began to wonder whether Annie had deliberately planted word of *Rutter* as a piece of disinformation, a skittish hare that would lead her eager paramour down all kinds of rabbit holes. A ploy like this, he told himself, would simply add to the rumours and scuttlebutt behind which Combined Ops liked to hide its real motives, and Annie Wrenne – ever loyal – might have been happy to thicken the confusion. Would she really do that? Would she ever treat him as simply a pawn in a bigger game? He hoped to God that the answer was no. By now, this extraordinary woman – so vivid, so *alive* – had come to occupy the very middle of his life, but then came the moment when a chance discovery came to Hogan's aid and he began to sense a way forward.

It was the second week in May, and he'd come directly to Gower Street after an exhausting journey south. He'd had to stand in the corridor of the train for the entire journey, the air thick with cigarette smoke while the endless stations crawled past, every platform crowded with yet more servicemen. One of the casualties of this war had been any notion of personal space, of just a breath or two of fresh air, and all he wanted now was a wallow in the bath.

The flat was empty. Hogan dropped his bag, stripped in the bedroom, and padded next door. Only last week, God knows how, Annie had laid hands on a bag of pink bath salts and after he'd coaxed a tepid stream of water from the tap, Hogan began to look for them. The cupboard under the sink was empty except for a bucket and a bundle of rags but there was another cupboard, smaller, on the wall above the tiny hand basin. The bath salts were on the bottom shelf, the bag secured by an elastic band, but what got Hogan's attention was the book she'd taken to reading and rereading.

It was in French, *Le Grand Meaulnes* by Alain-Fournier, and Hogan began to flick through it, wondering what it might take to master a language like this. Then, towards the back, he found a black and white photograph that seemed to serve as a bookmark. It showed two ranks of fit-looking men, all seated, all in uniform, gazing rather stiffly at the camera. In the background lay a biggish house, lightly turreted, behind a bank of shrubs, and when he turned the photograph over he found a carefully handwritten note on the back. *Commando Basic Training Centre, Achnacarry*, it read. *November 24th 1941.*

Achnacarry? The name stirred deep in Hogan's memory and finally took him back to the interview he'd conducted with Lord Mountbatten in his office at Combined Ops headquarters. Achnacarry was up in Scotland. Achnacarry was where a bunch of unforgiving instructors gave you a thorough shake and turned you into a serving commando. Achnacarry, in short, was the living nightmare you'd do best to avoid.

Smiling now, glad of his comfortable perch in Fleet Street, Hogan took a closer look at the photo, realising that someone had ringed a particular face in the faintest pencil. He was sitting in the front, five away from the end of the row. Hogan peered harder, and then carried the photo across to the window for a better look. He was young, lean, and unlike his buddies he had a smile on his face.

Hogan glanced up, wondering who on earth he might be. Had Annie acquired this book from some second-hand shop? And, if so, had the photo already been inside? Or was the pencilled ring her own? Or maybe the work of the man himself? To none of these questions could Hogan muster an answer, then – moments before he prepared to step into the bath – he remembered the envelope he'd noticed on the mantelpiece that very first time Annie had brought him back to the flat. The envelope had carried a Glasgow postmark, and Glasgow might well be on the way to Achnacarry.

Hogan glanced at his watch. Five to five. Annie was rarely home before six. Winding a towel around his waist, Hogan started on the bedroom. He knew that Annie kept her personal possessions in one of the drawers in her dressing table, but when he looked he could find no trace of the letter. Guilty now, battling a growing sense of shame, he went through the rest of the drawers. Apart from handfuls of silk underwear, a passport and a collection of letters from her mother, nothing.

Curiosity led him to check the passport. The stamped photo showed a younger Annie Wrenne, unsmiling, longer hair. She'd been born in a French location he didn't recognise but the real surprise was her age. He'd always imagined her to be in her late twenties but her birthday – 23 October 1909 – put her at thirty-two, a full decade older than Hogan. He eyed the photo a moment longer, and then his gaze strayed to the scatter of silk underwear before he carefully replaced the passport and shut the drawer.

Next door, in the living room, he tackled a line of books he knew she raided in the evening when there was nothing on the wireless, but again he drew a blank. The only room left was the kitchen. Tucked into a corner of the work surface beside the stove was a row of cookery books. Most of them, once again, were in French but towards the back of a slender volume of dessert recipes, he finally laid hands on the envelope. He gazed at the handwriting, recognising the careful capital letters on the back of the photo, and then he checked the postmark. Glasgow, 1 December 1941, just a week later.

Another glance at his watch. Ten past five. By now, the water in the bath would probably be cold but he didn't care. The back flap of the envelope, with its smear of glue, had reaffixed itself. He laid hands on a knife and slipped the blade beneath the flap, easing it free. Inside, he found nothing but a postcard-sized image of a body hanging from the severed bough of a tree. The etching was in black and white. Watching the body was a figure dressed like a cavalry man, slouched beside a stone pedestal.

He was wearing a moustache and a Russian-looking hat and below the image was a line of text: *Los Desastres de la Guerra*.

Hogan gazed at the card for a long moment, and then turned it over, finding a line in what he took to be Spanish. He stared at it, trying out the words one by one, wondering whether he was even close to getting it right. *Cuando el amor no es locura, no es amor.* He tried it again, a little faster. For reasons he couldn't fathom it felt right, *tasted* right. A third time, and he knew it would be easy to memorise.

'*Cuando el amor no es locura, no es amor,*' he murmured. Followed by a single kiss.

Locura? Amor? Hogan was still staring at the line when he heard the turn of a key in the building's front door. By the time Annie had let herself into the flat, and found him semi-naked in the kitchen, Hogan had resealed the envelope and returned it to the recipe book.

'Hungry?' She was taking in the scene.

'Starving,' Hogan was gazing at a photo of a fruit compôte. 'You don't have a couple of peaches by any chance?'

*

Hogan phoned O'Donovan the following day, using an empty office off the main newsroom. It was still early in the morning, not quite eight, but he'd managed to track O'Donovan down. According to his aide-de-camp, the Royals' Lt-Colonel was occupying room 308 in a requisitioned hotel on the Isle of Wight.

'O'Donovan. How can I help you?'

Hogan bent to the phone. First things first, he thought.

'The Isle of Wight, Frank?'

'Correct.'

'Why?'

'Are you guys always this blunt?' O'Donovan was laughing. 'This is wartime, George. Everything's a very big secret.'

'I'm just conscious of your time, Frank.'

'That's very thoughtful of you. We're on business, George. Someone's given us a reason to be here at last, thank God.'

'To do what?'

'That I can't tell you.'

'How about I come over? Do that interview with Larry Elder?'

'That might be tricky. I'll have to take advice.'

'Call you back?'

'Better had. Ring the same number this afternoon after half past four. Room 306, by the way, not 308.'

The line went dead and Hogan looked up to find Sheila, the archive queen, at the door. She'd found some cuttings on the siege of Leningrad that Hogan had requested.

'Where's the Isle of Wight?' Hogan asked. 'Any ideas?'

Next day, Hogan took the train to Southampton. O'Donovan had cleared the interview with Frank Elder but strictly on the condition that it contained nothing about the Royals' current deployment. No mention of the Isle of Wight. And absolutely no hints about what might possibly follow. Hogan's copy was to be submitted to the regimental adjutant, thoroughly checked, and then telexed direct to the *Express* newsroom.

'Stray off the reservation, George,' O'Donovan had warned, 'and life might get extremely tough.'

'Like how?'

'It starts with boiling oil, and after that you're on your own. Bring an overnight bag, by the way. You owe me a decent dinner.'

At Southampton, Hogan left the train and walked through a wasteland of bombed-out streets to the makeshift pontoon that was serving as a ferry terminal. A fussy little steamer carried him the length of Southampton Water and across the Solent until they berthed at a town called Cowes. The weather was glorious, real warmth in the sun, fat seagulls feasting noisily on broken mussel shells at the water's edge. O'Donovan's aide-de-camp met him on the quayside and walked him to the waiting Jeep.

'American?' Hogan was looking at the state of the vehicle. Even the tyres looked immaculate.

'If it's new and it works, it has to be. You're in luck, Mr Hogan. It's been raining all week. This is the first time I've had the top down.'

Hogan grinned, pumping his hand. Toronto accent, he thought, similar age. They left Cowes and drove south across the island. Hogan, whose knowledge of the British Isles was largely limited to the darker corners of the big industrial cities, was enchanted by the peace and the beauty of the place: hedgerows heavy with late spring blossom, fidgety clouds of tiny sparrows, distant views of chalk uplands, even a glimpse of a distant buzzard.

'Care to tell me where we're going?' The Jeep had come to a near-halt behind a tractor.

'Place called Freshwater Bay. Believe it or not, the guys are living in a holiday camp. After a year under canvas in Winchelsea, they're still in shock.'

'But what are they *doing*?'

'Fitness drills first thing. We're doubled up across the board, no exceptions, so that means at least an hour of throwing yourself around. After that, we send them on a three-mile run. Most mornings, we're on the cliffs, and most afternoons, too. Next week we'll be bringing the LCAs round. Opposed landings. Lots of bangs. Lots of getting wet...' Abruptly, spotting his chance, he pulled out and passed the tractor, giving the farmer a cheerful wave before shooting Hogan a look. 'Should I be telling you all this?'

'I've no idea. LCAs?'

'Landing craft assault. Men in full battle kit, ammo, sidearms, mortar bombs, the lot. They have to sign a docket saying they know how to swim and that's where the problems begin. Some of these guys are country boys, never seen the ocean in their lives, but hell, who's gonna be counting?'

'Counting what?'

Another sideways glance. The ADC had donned a pair of tinted aviator glasses against the glare of the sun and he looked, to Hogan, like a movie star.

'Enough,' he grunted. 'You'll get me shot.'

Minutes later, they arrived at the holiday camp. The board at the main gate had been shrouded but the roped tarpaulin had come loose and Hogan could read the word 'Brambles'.

'That's Brambles Chine,' the ADC had found his voice again. 'Peacetime, you'd probably be paying a fortune for this.'

He parked the Jeep outside a hutment with anti-blast tape across the windows and dug a radio from the clutter of equipment in the back of the vehicle. The Lt-Colonel was evidently on a nearby beach assessing his men's performance as they fought their way up the chalk cliffs. He and Hogan took a well-trodden path out of the rear of the camp and Hogan wondered just how many boots had been this way since the Royals' arrival.

A couple of hundred yards, and the path dipped to the left, and Hogan was suddenly looking at a view full of sea. From somewhere close came shouts from an instructor urging his men to greater efforts, and Hogan caught a despairing yell as someone on the cliff face missed their footing.

'They're roped up? These guys of yours?'

'Sure. For now I guess that's best practice but a coupla days' time they'll be doing it bareback.'

'Bareback?'

'No rope. Where these guys are headed, speed will be the essence. You insist on a rope, you probably book yourself a bullet. Simple choice.'

'Shit.'

'Exactly, and that's another problem. The drinking water in these parts is no good, don't ask me why. A lot of the men have got trench mouth from washing out their mess tins. The rest spend far too long on the john.'

Hogan nodded. 'Trench mouth' would sit well in the opening paragraph.

'There, buddy. Look.'

The ADC had come to a halt, pointing at a sheer face off to their left, and Hogan paused to watch the khaki-clad bodies fighting for handholds on the crumbling chalk as they inched their way towards the top of the cliff. Below them, on the strip of beach, a tiny figure was gazing up, his binoculars raised, studying the men's every movement, and Hogan felt a sudden wave of sympathy for young recruits like these, some of them flatland prairie boys born and bred, strangers to vertigo and the terrifying suck of gravity. No physical challenge, he thought, could be worse than this. Except, perhaps, the presence of other men, well dug in, determined to put a bullet through their pretty heads.

The ADC had exchanged waves with the figure on the beach.

'That's O'Donovan,' he grunted. 'I guess I better take you down.'

The interview with Larry Elder took place in the late afternoon in a curtained room in one of the chalets back in the camp. O'Donovan, evidently at the insistence of Divisional HQ, sat in to monitor proceedings but Larry Elder paid him scant attention. Months in uniform had shed what little weight he'd had to spare and he'd acquired a snake tattoo that encircled the length of his right forearm. Hogan had taken the trouble to prepare a list of questions he'd shared with O'Donovan but, once again, Elder showed little interest in following any agenda but his own. What mattered just now, he told Hogan, was that training was suddenly for real, that what you learned on those goddam cliffs might save your life once the shooting started, and that even the boneheads in the regiment were showing signs of understanding the plot.

'Our job is to wise these guys up,' he rasped. 'Make them join the dots. War is war and every next thing I learn about the Krauts tells me they're fucking good at it.'

'*Our* job?'

'They made me Corporal a couple of weeks back. That means I can shout at anyone now. Makes a difference, believe it or not.'

Hogan looked at O'Donovan for confirmation, and got a ghost of a smile.

'Cpl. Elder's been testing us every which way since we took him on,' he murmured. 'Best thing all round is to make it official. This man's got a mouth on him, as you know. Might as well use it.'

The thought put a smile on Elder's face. He wanted to know where the Royals were headed after the Isle of Wight, and he was looking at Hogan.

'No idea, Larry. That's not a question I can answer.'

'Can or will?'

'Both. All the loose-lips shit? I'm a journeyman reporter. Nobody tells me anything.'

'Sir?' Elder was looking at O'Donovan now.

'I plead the Fifth.'

'No fucking comment? Talk to my lawyer? What kind of leadership is that? Has to be cliffs, am I right? Has to be chalk?

Am I on the money? Because otherwise we're all wasting our time.'

O'Donovan said nothing. Hogan had put his pencil down, wondering why this man was so ungovernable, so *angry*, but Elder hadn't finished.

'France, yeah? Some place across the Channel? Keep going south until you can *smell* the bastards? Am I getting warm here? Or do you Brits have somewhere else in mind?'

This was a direct challenge, and Hogan knew it. In a way, he'd become an honorary Brit, working for a London newspaper, English by adoption, but still his hands were tied. In his heart, given what Annie had told him, he suspected Elder was probably headed for Dieppe but there was no way he could share that knowledge.

'I'm just here to talk expectations, Larry. I don't have a name for you, or even a vague destination, but I'm sure all of that will happen in God's good time. Just now, I want you to tell me how you feel.'

'How I *feel*? What kind of bullshit is that? I feel the way anyone feels going into a fight. It could be a boxing ring. It could be a dirt alley back of a grog shop. It could even be a fucking battlefield. Either way, unless you're stupid, you take care to get in shape, here,' he gestured at his new tattoo, 'or better still up here.' A bitten fingernail settled briefly on his forehead. 'Everything, my friend, begins with conquest, and that includes fear. You want me to say I'm frightened because that's what turns all of you guys on because you think it sells more papers, but the fact is you're wrong, all of you, not about the papers and all them readers, but about the fear. Get frightened, even the littlest bit scared, and that war of yours is over, along with probably your fucking life. There,' he nodded at Hogan's pad, 'write it down. War kills. Fear kills. And then tell me you're buying me dinner.'

Hogan nodded. This was vintage Elder. He scribbled down the quote about fear, then his head came up again.

'You still speak Spanish?'

'Yeah.'

'Happy to translate?'

'Try me.'

'*Cuando el amor no es locura, no es amor.*' The line wouldn't leave Hogan alone.

'Wow,' Elder whistled. 'Shit accent, *hombre*, but even you can't spoil a tease like that. You know where it comes from? Calderón de la Barca. Greatest poet in the world. Playwright, too. Where did you get it? Who wised you up?'

'It came from a friend.'

'And she loves you? This friend? Makes life good for you?'

'Just the translation, please.'

Elder held his gaze, and then slapped his thigh and laughed.

'Sure, buddy. *No problema.* It means "Love that is not madness is not love". How's that to get you through the darker nights? Happy now?'

O'Donovan, it turned out, had plans to drive Hogan back to the hotel in Cowes where they kept a decent table, but at Hogan's suggestion they took Elder to a local pub overlooking the sea. It was run by a fisherman's wife and the day's catch had just arrived on the rising tide. Hogan insisted the meal was on the *Daily Express*, and he made his way through a huge plate of hake and chips while O'Donovan and Elder abandoned their ranks and swapped stories about the old days on the waterfront in Toronto. When Hogan enquired about homesickness among these men's charges, O'Donovan admitted that the last couple of years had been tough. The men hadn't enlisted for long periods of boredom punctuated by the occasional drunken run ashore but now, he insisted, their spirits were high. Elder, a little to Hogan's surprise, nodded in agreement.

'This is the honeymoon,' he said. 'And nothing feels sweeter.'

'And later?' Hogan was trying to press him.

'Later, my friend, it will feel very different.'

Elder left them shortly afterwards, returning to the camp. Without pausing to ask, Hogan bought two more pints at the bar and carried them back to the table.

'You've learned how to drink?' O'Donovan was looking at the cloudy ale.

'No choice, I'm afraid.'

'Care to tell me more?'

'Not really. Except I never knew what I was missing.'

'You mean the drink? The alcohol?'

'That, too.'

Hogan ducked his head. He wanted to know whether O'Donovan had ever been to the Commando Basic Training Centre at Achnacarry.

'I have, yes, just a couple of weeks back. A bunch of us Canucks flew up there. Combined Ops wanted to show the place off.'

'This is Mountbatten?'

'Of course. The sainted Lord Louis. The guy's a real operator. The guys all love him.'

'You stayed a while?'

'Three days. That was plenty. Afterwards I ached for a week. Why do you ask?'

Hogan had thought about bringing the photograph but had decided against it. The last thing he needed just now was an awkward conversation with Annie, should she find it missing. Where's my photo? What have you done with it?

Now, Hogan scribbled a date on his pad and tore the sheet off before presenting it to O'Donovan.

'November 24th? 1941? What *is* this?'

Hogan did his best to explain. Guy in the front row. Fifth from the left. Presumably some kind of passing-out parade. Might Donovan have a contact up in Achnacarry? With access to the original photo? Someone who might put a name to the face?'

O'Donovan took another glance at the date and then looked at Hogan again.

'This is important?'

'Yes, I think it is.'

'Personal, or professional? You mind me asking?'

'Not at all. Personal. In fact, very personal. Should that make a difference?'

'Sure, it makes all the difference. That pen of yours?'

Hogan passed the pen across. 'Front row,' he said again. 'Number five from the left. A name is all I need.'

18

Three weeks later, early June, two figures on Dieppe station met *Major* Wilhelm Schultz off the late-morning train from Paris. One of them was *Kapitan* Linder, the regimental adjutant with the 571st Regiment charged with defending the port. The other, wearing a fisherman's smock and a pair of working trousers, was Ortega.

At Linder's insistence, they were driven straight to his office in the local school. Linder had a lunchtime appointment at Divisional headquarters further inland and could spare only an hour before his departure. Schultz took him aside as they left the car in the playground, enquiring whether Ortega should be present while they talked. Linder was evidently surprised by the question.

'But of course, Herr *Major*. He's one of us now.'

'You're paying him?'

'In kind. He gets to eat and drink anything he likes at a small list of selected restaurants, and Madame Lili has been more than accommodating. He also goes to sea with some of the fishermen and helps them sell the catch. He has a gift, that man of yours. He can make a friend of anyone.'

Schultz nodded, said he was glad to hear it, and followed Linder and Ortega into the school. Nothing, it seemed at first glance, had changed. The same map on the same blackboard. Even the same toys neatly piled in one corner. Then his eye was caught by another map, smaller, that offered a carefully drawn bird's-eye view of the town's beach in front of the harbour, and of the coast that extended perhaps eight kilometres west and east. Various locations were colour-coded, and lines radiated from each, either laterally along the beaches or out to sea. According to Linder, this was the latest snapshot of the town's defences, with arcs of interlinking fire designed to hose a torrent of hot lead onto any force reckless enough to attempt a landing.

'Carlos will show you later,' Linder, settled behind his desk, was aware of Schultz's interest. 'His pass takes him anywhere and he's on first-name terms with all the key commanders. Am I right, *hombre?*'

Ortega nodded, said nothing. His big hands were rummaging among the contents of his tiny classroom desk until he found what he was after, a comic book featuring a colourful collection of Stone Age cavemen hunting a variety of enormous carnivores. Oblivious to anything else, he leafed through until a happy grunt signalled where he'd left this little adventure.

'Herr *Major?*' Linder was tapping his watch. 'You mentioned something about our Resistance friends on the phone. Hérissé? The flyer they call Dutertre? Am I right?'

'Yes,' Schultz nodded. 'From their point of view, I'm happy to say they're probably looking at a disaster.'

'Probably?'

'With luck, yes.'

Hérissé, Schultz explained, belonged to a network called *La Confrérie de Notre Dame.* The network was run by a former film producer who operated under the codename *Colonel Rémy.* Rémy had caught the eye of MI6 in London, who held the quality of his intelligence in high esteem, and his standing with the British spooks had been further enhanced when Hérissé had supplied him with exhaustive details of a new German radar installation on the cliffs near Bruneval. This information, said Schultz, had seeded the recent raid conducted by Combined Operations.

'Combined what?'

'Operations, Herr Linder. It's a newish organisation in London. It's run by one of the members of the royal family. His name is Louis Mountbatten. He's related to more or less everyone of any importance, and his task is to make life tough for the likes of you and me. Keep us on our toes. Bloody our noses. This is a man desperate for glory and that's exactly what Hérissé was able to offer. Combined Ops dropped on the radar station back in February, helped themselves to lots of equipment, and barely lost a man. That operation was near-perfect and gave Mountbatten the taste for more. That's why Hérissé was here in March.'

'In person?' Linder was looking surprised.

'I'm afraid so. The best of these people are invisible, and that includes Hérissé. As far as we know he spent two weeks here, moving from safe house to safe house, and built an entire dossier. Calibre of guns, battery positions, the location of pillboxes, anti-tank barriers, anti-tank guns, even where to find those military HQs of yours. In other words, the complete plan. There was far too much to transmit by wireless and so he got on the train to Paris to hand the dossier over to another ex-flyer, a guy called Roger Dumont, who'd courier it to London. They were due to meet at a restaurant on rue d'Anjou but on his way to the station Hérissé witnessed a collision between two of our vehicles and was detained to give details. That meant he missed his lunch, which in turn meant that he had to return the following week. Same restaurant. Same time. Happily, we'd arrested Dumont that very morning, and Hérissé was finally obliged to hand the dossier over to yet another *résistant*. It may get to London in the end, but somehow I doubt it.'

Linder nodded, then gestured towards the window.

'Everything? You're telling me he saw *everything*?'

'He did. He's very thorough. He's trusted. And if that dossier was to end up in the hands of British intelligence, I suspect they'd think twice about coming. But that's hardly the point, Herr Linder. The wretched man was despatched here. He was tasked and sent. And that probably means our suspicions are right.'

'We're next on the list? After Bruneval?'

'After Saint-Nazaire, which was another Mountbatten triumph, and after a little disaster down south, which he's keen to forget. A successful landing here will wipe the slate clean, restore his Lordship to his former glory. My suspicion is that he can barely wait. Unless, of course, *Colonel* Rémy decides to take another look at your porcupine of a town.'

Linder began to make notes. Schultz watched him, saying nothing. At length, his head came up and he shot a look at Ortega.

'Carlos? What do you think?'

Ortega looked up, his finger anchored on a page featuring a caveman with a giant club.

'Any strangers here, I'll know within a day,' he grunted. 'People tell me everything, often without knowing.'

Linder departed for his meeting at Divisional headquarters while Ortega carefully returned the comic book to the desk. Schultz, meanwhile, was reviewing the map of the town's defences on the wall. The longer he studied it, the harder it was to believe that any organisation, no matter how well equipped, would risk a landing. He'd made exactly the same point to Zimmermann, only a couple of days ago, but his boss had dismissed his qualms.

'It was your idea to bait the trap, Willi,' he'd pointed out. 'And I suspect that luck of ours may hold. I have it on good authority that Gasquet's little *amuse-bouche* has made it through to London. This isn't the *Rémy* outfit, but another trusted network. They're telling the British that the place is virtually undefended, that they'll be pushing at an open door, and it seems that the Brits are all too eager to believe them. In war, it pays to know the enemy, what makes him tick, why he can suddenly abandon sweet reason. That, Willi, is being kind. In this instance, they may be making the bloodiest of mistakes, and it's certainly not our job to dig them out of their own shit.'

Now, in the classroom's dusty sunlight, Schultz recounted the conversation for Ortega's benefit. The Spaniard listened hard, then shrugged, got to his feet, and shot a glance at the old school clock on the wall.

'A beer first, *hombre*,' he suggested. 'And then a little tour to make you a happy man.'

Two hours later, Schultz was on the clifftop at a village called Le Petit Berneval, six miles to the east of Dieppe, peering down at the high tide lapping at the grey pebbles. The single ravine leading up from the beach was blocked with barbed wire and mines while behind him lay a heavy-gun battery, the compound dug into the chalky soil and secured by more barbed wire. Three of the big 175mm guns could lob a shell fourteen kilometres out to sea, while a quartet of 105mm cannon covered the closer approaches.

'These are French,' Ortega nodded back at the guns. 'They took them in 1940. The French never fired a shot in anger. This is Ioana, by the way. I can't think of a language she doesn't speak.'

Ioana was a big woman, swarthy, with a broad smile and a huge chest. A knotted scarf protected her from the afternoon sunshine, and she was picking her way carefully towards them over the uneven turf.

'She's Roma, *hombre*. Lives on a patch of land behind the town. Three kids, three fathers, no husband, and half a dozen chickens. She comes up here most days with eggs. Most of the men are Polish or Czech, plus a couple of Russians. She's strong as an ox and the last couple of weeks they've taught her how to serve the guns. They think it's a game they're playing but I'm not sure she does.'

The woman had come to a halt before them, a basket on her arm. She spared Schultz a passing glance but her eyes were on Ortega. Schultz spoke primitive Spanish, unlike Ioana. She pressed two potatoes and a head of lettuce on Ortega before giving his ruined cheek a playful pinch and treating him to a volley of what sounded like endearments. He might, thought Schultz, be one of her family, and it wasn't hard to imagine her largesse extending to the artillerymen. According to Ortega, there were more than a hundred troops manning the clifftop position, and barely a couple of dozen were German.

'These people are effective?'

'Very. We're spoiled for ammunition and we bang away at targets every week. All we need is a glimmer of dawn.' He gestured seawards. 'The guns will take care of the rest.'

'We?'

'We. The gunners have adopted us both. One day the officers may do the same. We're all strangers, *hombre*, in a strange land.'

Schultz nodded, his eyes still on the woman. With most of the *Wehrmacht* away on the Eastern Front, or in North Africa, positions the length of the French coast were manned by garrisons like these, pockets of conquered foreigners who'd been pressed into service with the Greater Reich. Ortega, for reasons that Schultz understood only too well, seemed to have become a sort of mascot, the living evidence that war could wreak terrifying physical damage yet still leave a man's spirit intact. As they stepped into the compound, Ortega shook hand after hand, greeting men by name, introducing his friend from Paris. Finally, Schultz met the officer in charge.

'You're *Abwehr*, Herr *Major*?'

Schultz nodded, watching two men dismantling the breech of a nearby gun. The wheels on the gun carriage were huge, the long barrel aimed at the distant horizon, and a neat pile of shells in their gleaming brass cases lay nearby. Given Schultz's uniform, the officer wanted to know what he and his men might expect.

'It's June, Herr *Leutnant*. After September you can all go to ground and hibernate. In the meantime, beware of a full moon and a high tide.'

'You really think they'll come?' the officer asked.

'I do, yes. And when that happens, I know you'll kick their arses.' He gestured at the readied shells. 'Good shooting, eh? Enjoy yourselves.'

From the clifftop Schultz and Ortega returned to the *Kubelwagen* and drove west to Puys, barely a mile from the town's harbour entrance. Here, a narrow valley lined with holiday properties descended to a tiny beach. Pillboxes mounting heavy machine guns overlooked the grey pebbles, and Ortega led the way to the last villa before the seawall. From a new-looking pillbox in the garden, Schultz had a perfect view of the beach and he listened to Ortega as he gestured towards other machine-gun nests embedded on the nearby clifftop, or in the caves that honeycombed the whiteness of the chalk.

This, thought Schultz, was Linder's schoolroom map made flesh, every position perfectly sited, every arc of fire carefully interlinked, until the beach and the shallows had become a killing zone with nowhere to hide. To storm a place like this would be an act of mass suicide, an ugly surrender to the properties of aimed fire and near-limitless ammunition, and when he shared the thought with Ortega the Spaniard simply nodded.

'You'd have to be crazy to even try,' he muttered. 'On paper, war is always straight lines and split-second timing and nothing ever going wrong, but paper lies. Men on these beaches would be wise to say their prayers.'

It was the same story on the main beaches in front of the town itself. Schultz and Ortega were back on the steeply shelving banks of pebbles the French called *galets*, agreeing once again that even tanks would make no difference to the slaughter. Most of them would dig in, the prisoners of their churning tracks, digging deeper and deeper until a mortar or an artillery shell finished them off, and even if the braver souls managed to make it over the seawall and into the town itself, they faced yet more obstacles: sandbagged firing points for snipers and machine-gunners in the properties overlooking the promenade, yet more machine-gun posts spaced along the seawall running west towards the looming bulk of the castle, and finally a jigsaw of anti-tank barriers, reinforced with more cannon, sealing the roads that ran inland towards the town centre. Since the last time Schultz had stood on this spot, *Kapitan* Linder and his engineers had thickened the town's defences until nothing on the seaward side – neither armour nor flesh and blood – could remain intact.

'Crazy,' Ortega was shading his good eye against the sun. 'Not proper war at all.'

*

Nearly a week later, at O'Donovan's quiet invitation, Hogan made his way to Bridport, a sleepy town inland from the Dorset coast. They'd met two evenings earlier, sharing a hasty drink at the Beaver Club. O'Donovan looked tired.

'This is anything but official,' he'd said at once. 'Can you get a couple of days off?'

'Why?'

'I need you to take a look at what's happening. This is just you and me. I trust you, George. That's all I'm prepared to say.'

At the time, Hogan had simply nodded. He liked O'Donovan a great deal, admired what he was doing for Canadian reputations, but it wasn't hard to detect something else in the man, something new, something close to alarm, and he was flattered by the older man's invitation.

'Any news from Achnacarry?' he'd asked as they parted in the street.

'None.' O'Donovan was looking for a taxi. 'But I'm working on it.'

Now, Hogan stepped off the train at Dorchester to be met once again by O'Donovan's ADC. The area around Bridport was designated a secure zone but O'Donovan had managed to acquire an official pass which the ADC pressed into Hogan's hand. He used it twice, once at a checkpoint midway between Dorchester and Bridport, and once on the outskirts of the town itself. The ADC dropped him at a pub called the Passage where he found a room booked in his name and a scribbled note from O'Donovan, promising a conversation later.

The conversation, when it finally happened, was all too brief. O'Donovan ghosted into the empty bar, declining Hogan's offer of a drink. Tomorrow's exercise, he said, was codenamed *Yukon 1* and was due to kick off at dawn. Four thousand men, most of them Canadian, would be landed at beaches along the nearby coast, and would practise elements in the grand plan that would shortly take them across the Channel.

'Where to, Frank?'

O'Donovan didn't answer. Instead he settled briefly on the scuffed leather before beckoning Hogan closer.

'Combined Ops?' he muttered. 'Linking up with the Air Force? The Navy? Commando units? Even a bunch of American Rangers? Everything timetabled to the second? Everything depending on darkness and surprise? This is all new, George. No one's ever done it before and, believe me, it isn't easy. We're supposed to think multiple phases, each one dovetailing into the next. We're supposed to be getting on top of a million things at once but if you want the truth we simply haven't had the time. Everything's been too rushed. We've been too eager, too hasty. On the Isle of Wight we never had enough ammunition for live firing, and there was never enough of the ancillary stuff. The men are keen as mustard but speed marches, and clambering up cliffs, and jumping out of landing craft only takes you so far. All-arms co-operation, and multiple fire support, and sequenced assaults look fine on paper but doing all this for real is far from easy. Tomorrow will be the test, believe me.'

'And that's why you've invited me down?'

'I've invited you down, George, because I need someone I trust to understand what we're all up against. This is a huge risk from my point of view, exactly what I *shouldn't* be doing, but just now I can't think of a better way.'

'Of doing what?'

'Of covering our ass. That's crude, I know, but me and the Colonel lead a bunch of fine men and I'd hate to let them down. We're looking at a disaster, George, and the Army's instinct will be to cover it up.' He got to his feet and smothered a yawn. 'That's all you get for now. We'll talk again tomorrow night if I can find the time. Otherwise it might have to be London again.'

Disaster was a very big word indeed, but Hogan knew O'Donovan well enough to be certain that he was sparing with terms like these. At the door of the pub they exchanged a slightly awkward handshake. In the darkness of the street, thought Hogan, this could could be an adieu before a proper battle, the real thing, not the eve of a carnival of landing craft headed for empty beaches. Dieppe, he thought again. Has to be.

'You need to be ready for dawn, George,' O'Donovan had found the keys to his Jeep. 'You'll be picked up at five. What size boots do you take?'

Back in the pub, Hogan found the landlady behind the bar, drying a line of glasses. When he asked for a knock on his door at half past four, she shot him a strange look and then nodded.

'Do my best,' she said. 'Come down for the entertainments?'

Hardly. It was raining as well as dark when the ADC called to pick him up next morning. They had a brief reunion in the street, then a muttered conversation in the front of the Jeep as Hogan wrestled with the proffered boots. They were at least a size too small, pinching his feet, and Hogan began to dread the day to come as they sped through the town, the ADC crouched over the wheel, peering through the windscreen.

'There's a greatcoat in the back, too,' he murmured. 'I'm guessing you might need it.'

The Royals were due to attack the beach at Eype, due west of the town. The ADC dropped him beside a footpath on the road out, then fetched the greatcoat and a torch from the back of the Jeep.

'Just follow the path until you get to the clifftop,' he said. 'There may be some Home Guard guys around but I can't imagine they'll trouble you.'

They didn't, not at first. With the aid of the torch, Hogan made his way towards the cliffs as a thin, grey light stole in from the east, the path muddied by the overnight rain. Glad of the boots, despite the lousy fit, he splashed through puddle after puddle, beginning to enjoy himself, remembering summer mornings like this beside the Miramichi River back in the Maritimes with not a soul around for company. According to O'Donovan, four thousand young soldiers were wallowing out there in the Channel but so far there was no sign of them. Would the Germans be taken equally off-guard? Did invasions appear from nowhere? A brief flurry of movement in the shallows before the Canadians presented their credentials and kicked the door in?

In truth, Hogan had no idea. He'd been summoned here by a fellow countryman and a good friend who was trying to do his best by his men. Plans had been laid but the clear implication was that none of them would ever work. Quite who would pay for this extravaganza remained a mystery, but for now Hogan could do nothing but watch and wait.

'Stop there.' Two figures in battledress emerged from the half-darkness. Both rifles were levelled at Hogan's chest. The older man demanded papers. Hogan handed over his pass. A torch settled briefly on the official stamp.

'Mr Hogan?'

'That's me.'

'You're Canadian? Yank?'

'Canadian. On assignment.'

'You mean the exercise?' The beam of the torch found Hogan's face. 'You're a reporter?'

'I am, yes.'

'Paper?'

'*Daily Express.*'

The older man studied him a moment longer, then returned the pass and waved him on his way. As Hogan left, he heard muttered instructions to write the name down. Young man from Fleet Street. Seems to be limping.

Minutes later, Hogan found himself on the clifftop. The patrol, he guessed, had been the expected Home Guard but below him the beach was empty and there was no sign of movement out in the dark sweep of the bay. He pulled the coat around him, beginning to shiver in the chill of the wind off the sea, and finally he sought shelter in a nearby copse.

There he stayed for the next hour or so, glad of the first thin rays of the rising sun, listening hard for any sound he might associate with battle but hearing nothing. Then, in the distance, he caught the faintest throb of marine engines and he returned to the clifftop to watch a flotilla of tiny landing craft heading for a beach at least half a mile away. He must have walked too far in the darkness, he thought, and overshot the assault zone.

The temptation was to make his way back for a better view but already there were men in battledress spilling out of the landing craft, tiny black dots running towards the base of the cliffs. From positions on top of the cliffs, strangely remote from this distance, came the sharp bark of small arms fire, presumably blanks, and Hogan decided to stay where he was, out of harm's way, watching the toy soldiers positioning ladders against the cliff face and clambering awkwardly upwards.

In some respects, he thought, this was an elaborate replay of the exercise he'd watched on the Kawartha Lakes the first time he'd met Larry Elder. Each man carried a rifle, as well as a heavy pack, and Hogan followed their progress until they could go no further. By now, the ladders were bowing under the sheer weight of bodies, and Hogan followed the troops' slow retreat back down to the beach, rung by careful rung as smoke – released far too late – hid the landing craft from view.

A little later, the smoke gone, he watched a line of Hurricanes coming in low over the bay and roaring over the clifftops before bigger landing craft appeared and deposited a number of tanks.

By now he'd ventured closer. The beach was occupied by a mill of aimless troops wandering around as the tanks prowled up and down on the pebbles banked by the rising tide. To Hogan, there seemed no plan, no co-ordination, no thrust at the enemy's throat, and by early afternoon, with both the troops and the tanks re-embarking, he decided to close the curtains on this little piece of theatre. For one thing, he was parched. For another, he was starving hungry. But most important of all, he could make no sense of what had unravelled beneath him.

*

'I'm not the least surprised. The bloody thing was a shambles from start to finish.'

It was early afternoon, and Hogan was back in the Jeep in the depths of Bridport, sitting beside O'Donovan while his ADC enjoyed a cigarette on the pavement. In a very short while, Hogan would be taken back to Dorchester station for the long train journey home but for now one of the Canadian Second Division's more senior officers had a couple of things to get off his chest.

'You want the charge sheet, George? Here it is. For a start, the naval guys were useless. The South Saskatchewans were landed a mile away from where they were headed, and my boys were even further adrift. They were late anyway so this was broad daylight. The tanks on the LCTs got lost in the dark and took forever to arrive. Some of the ladders were too short to make it to the top of the cliffs and when the Hurricanes turned up, the so-called enemy just went to ground which gave our guys totally the wrong idea. If it happens for real, the Germans will be firing back, big time, Hurricanes or no Hurricanes. This was a pantomime. If I'd paid good money for my seat, I'd want it back.'

With that, O'Donovan reached for the door and got out. Hogan leaned across.

'So what next?' he asked.

'I guess we run the damn exercise all over again,' O'Donovan shrugged. 'Or do the sane thing and put the whole wretched plan back in its box.'

19

The latter never happened. Eleven days later, Operation *Rutter* returned to the Dorset coast for a second go at landing the right men on the right beaches at the right time, and although *Yukon 2* wasn't quite so chaotic, there still remained a vast checklist of items to get right. Hogan knew this because O'Donovan hadn't finished with him. Their conversations were now far too sensitive for the Beaver Club and so they met – at O'Donovan's invitation – on a bench in London's St James's Park. By now, it was nearly the end of June, and three hundred Canadian officers had yesterday attended a top-secret briefing at Second Division headquarters.

'So where are you going?' Hogan enquired.

'They wouldn't tell us. They're trying to play cute.'

'But you've hazarded a guess?'

'Better than that, George. I *know*. They've made a nice job of the relief map. It's not small, maybe ten foot by six. Harbour in the middle. Six landing beaches, all colour-coded. Chalk cliffs. Look at any map, at the shape of the coast, and the name stares out at you.'

'Dieppe?'

'Right. How did you know?'

Hogan shook his head, wouldn't say. Instead, he wanted a date.

'The tides are good until 9 July. After that, all bets are probably off.'

'And what about support? Softening up? Bombardment from the sea? Air attacks?'

'That's still not clear. I get the impression there's some token help but not much. I gather the Navy aren't keen to risk capital ships in the Channel. As for the RAF, I've no idea. No doubt we'll be told in God's good time. The guy who took the briefing will be in charge on the day. He's a General, 'Ham' Roberts, Canuck-born and bred, one of ours. He talked of momentum and running over the Boche defences. He also used the word "party", which is an image he might live to regret. There's a para drop to knock out the big guns, and then full-frontal assaults. The latter isn't something you'd like to think too hard about. The guy you should really be talking to is Larry Elder but he and the men will be the last to know. God help Canada, George. And I mean that.'

God help Canada.

The phrase shook Hogan, all the more so because it came from someone as level-headed as Frank O'Donovan. This wasn't a guy who would ever make such a judgement lightly. On the contrary, he'd taken a hard look at the facts, tried to align them with what might await his men on the other side of the Channel and decided that the entire project was an essay in recklessness. Reckless because it wasn't properly thought through. Reckless because the likely weight of opposition would squander countless young lives. And reckless because Operation *Rutter* seemed to have acquired a fatal momentum of its own.

That word again: momentum. For longer than O'Donovan could probably afford, they sat in the warm late-June sunshine and mused over the lethal logic of plans laid, assessed, reassessed, but never formerly abandoned. In O'Donovan's view, the senior

Generals and politicians were all hedging their bets. Montgomery, who was in charge, had reviewed the plans after *Yukon 2*, and had issued a cheerful affirmation that good weather and what he called 'average luck' might pull the Canadians through, while Churchill was said to be dreading another catastrophe after the fall of Tobruk. In O'Donovan's view, the Prime Minister would be wise to call Mountbatten to Downing Street in a last bid to give the plan a thorough shake, but he was unconvinced that this would ever happen. What would be worse, he muttered, was Operation *Rutter* departing into the unknown, propelled by nothing more than Mountbatten's blind conviction that it *had* to work.

'It won't,' O'Donovan said again. 'And that's a promise.'

Hogan could do nothing but nod. He'd stood on the clifftop overlooking Lyme Bay barely a week ago. He'd watched the tiny actors in this drama trying to make sense of their roles and he'd been only too aware of the challenge of choreographing a fiercely opposed landing like this. But just now, just a handful of yards away on another bench in the sunshine, someone else had caught his eye. He was tall, early middle-age, fit-looking, with an outdoors complexion and a hint of gauntness in his face. He had an open copy of *The Times* on his lap, but there was something slightly stagey about the air of studied concentration. From time to time, he'd glance up, seeming to enjoy the sunshine, but Hogan wasn't fooled. For whatever reason, this stranger was here to watch them.

'I suggest we move on, Frank,' Hogan murmured. 'It might be best for both of us.'

They parted at the gates of St James's Park on Horse Guards, conscious of the figure on the bench now twenty yards behind them. He followed Hogan for a while but in the end he disappeared among the rush-hour crowds flooding along Fleet Street. Back in the newsroom, Hogan started to work the phones for a story he was due to file, then looked up to find Betty Bower beside his desk.

Betty was young, pretty and immensely able. She'd joined the paper's proprietor when Beaverbrook was Minister of Production and had stayed on after his resignation to look after his private office. In many ways, Betty reminded Hogan of Annie. She had the same confidence that she could weather any kind of storm, and she also had the looks and the gamine spirit that men of power, headline figures like Beaverbrook and Mountbatten, found irresistible. The few times they'd met, Hogan had always sensed that she regarded the young Canadian scribe as a fellow outsider, keeping a wary distance from the giants who were running this war, and he felt it now as she bent to whisper in his ear.

'He wants you down in Cherkley, George.'

'The Beaver?'

'Yes.'

'When?'

'Tonight.'

Hogan eased his chair back, staring up at her. Cherkley Court was his boss's country house in Surrey. Cherkley was where the names that really mattered gathered nightly around his dinner table. Hogan had never been to Cherkley in his life.

'Why now?' he said. 'Why me?'

'Maisky's due a visit. He read that piece you did on the big rally in Birmingham and the boss wants you to pop it back in the oven and warm it up for him. There's another rally in Trafalgar Square next month. You know about that?'

'I do, yes. In this place, that's all we're supposed to talk about. Second Front Now? *Again?*'

'Jenkins will pick you up at seven sharp,' Betty laughed, her hand on Hogan's arm. 'I'll be the one serving the drinks.'

Hogan watched heads turn as she left the newsroom. Ivan Maisky was the Russian Ambassador, a gifted little survivor from the days of Stalin's show trials. Always impeccably informed, he cast a sharp eye on the smallest print of London politics and Beaverbrook had always looked after him.

'Cherkley, eh?' A journalist across the table had heard every word. 'Lucky boy.'

Thanks to Jenkins, Hogan descended on Cherkley in the Beaverbrook Rolls. It was early evening by the time they arrived, the air still warm, the light golden. To Hogan, the vast building had little grace. It was too big, too overpowering, too pleased with itself, but the views south across the ridge of wooded hills excused any vanity on Beaverbrook's part. You'd buy the place for this alone, Hogan thought, lingering briefly on the terrace, gazing down at the spread of ornamental gardens, enjoying the last of the sun on his face.

Inside, the house was equally oppressive: too grand, too opulent, the boast of an owner who couldn't resist making a point or two about the blessings of wealth. Money had seeped into the very fabric of the building, into the dramatic sweep of the staircase, into the portraits on the walls, even into the enormous stag's head that might have been a trophy from some previous squire.

A maid met Hogan in the entrance hall. Lord Beaverbrook, she said, was a little under the weather at the moment, another attack of asthma, but she was sure that a little extra company might do him the world of good. Extra company? Hogan followed her into the depths of the house. She knocked twice at a door beside the smaller of the two dining rooms and stood back to let Hogan pass. He found himself in the library: high ceilings, thousands of books, and another unforgettable view across a landscape softened by heat haze.

'Bloody summer,' Beaverbrook was on his hands and knees on the carpet, blowing his nose. He was wearing a pair of grey trousers that belonged to a suit and a white shirt open at the collar. Beside him, Betty Bower was delicately rearranging a line of balled tissues that strayed towards the very edge of the carpet. 'That one,' Beaverbrook indicated a particular tissue. 'A bit to the left.'

Betty did his bidding, squatting on her haunches while her boss tossed another tissue onto the carpet after blowing his nose yet again. Hogan was counting the balls of tissue. In all, there were seventeen.

'It's the French coast,' Betty sat back. 'We're staging an invasion.'

'Second Front Now?'

'Exactly. Terrific for asthma, too. Better out than in, as my mother used to tell me.'

Hogan nodded. His boss, he knew, had never learned how to behave but this litter of fresh germs was close to grotesque.

'Anywhere in particular?' Hogan gestured towards the skirting board.

'His Lordship likes to keep his options open. As long as it's French and serves a decent omelette, we'd like to think they're ready for us.'

'And you, son?' Beaverbrook was glaring up at him. 'Any ideas? Any preference?'

Hogan shook his head. The temptation to suggest Dieppe was overwhelming but the watcher on the park bench had unnerved him and now, he suspected, was the time to keep his opinions to himself.

'Not the first idea, sir,' he muttered. 'What would you like me to tell Mr Maisky?'

'Maisky?' Beaverbrook was frowning now. 'Blow lots of smoke up that tight Soviet arse of his. The man needs to be needed. Any stories you can muster, son, from those travels of yours, and none of them has to be true.' His watery eyes suddenly brightened. 'Tell him the Brits love Mother Russia. Think you can handle that?'

*

The Soviet Ambassador arrived shortly afterwards. Ivan Maisky was eager and cheerful and pumped Hogan's hand. The news that Hogan came from the same Maritimes township as their host sparked a roar of laughter.

'Does everyone get out of that place? Is there anyone left? I thought we had problems with Siberia but maybe I'm wrong.'

Beaverbrook ignored the gibe. He was keen to get them a drink, get them into dinner, get them talking about the brave Russians and the never-ending Beaverbrook largesse that would keep them all fighting, while for his part Maisky had eyes for nothing but the taunting hint of Betty's *décolletage*.

The four of them ate at the end of the long table, pheasant with game chips and a medley of vegetables. Beaverbrook held court, a growing pile of tissues at his feet. He introduced Hogan as the young cub who'd sharpened his claws on the Second Front Now movement, a turn of phrase that prompted a nod of approval from Maisky.

'And what did you find, Mr Young Cub, among all those sons of toil?'

Expecting exactly this question, Hogan launched into an account of the interviews he'd conducted, the families he'd met, the raw enthusiasm for the stand that the USSR had taken against the invading Germans, plus a kind of shared pride in what the Russians were starting to achieve.

'In the end, we'll invite our new friends to go home,' Maisky said mildly. 'And by then we'll have killed so many that the rest will probably say yes.'

'Perfect,' Beaverbrook banged the table and shot a look at Betty. 'We especially like "invite". Make a note, my dear. Russian guts. Russian lead. Russian *manners*. If all of that was good enough for the Tsar, I dare say the Germans have no chance,' he swung round in the chair. 'Your thoughts, son?'

Hogan was watching Betty scribbling in the notebook beside her plate. Never off-duty, he thought. Not with a man like this.

'I agree, sir.'

'Of course you agree. That's what you're paid for. But this evening is different. This evening we find ourselves in the company of the real thing. I've met Stalin, son, and believe me that man is not for the faint-hearted. He's a wolf. He recognises weakness at a thousand yards. He can smell it, even if the wind's in the wrong direction. Am I right, Ivan? And if so, what does it take to emerge in one piece?'

Maisky, to Hogan's surprise, was roaring with laughter. Insulting your country's leader was obviously an old Beaverbrook trick.

'You flatter me, Max. Flatter me with your food, flatter me with your women, and now flatter me with this wonderful young man you seem to have rescued from that sleepy little icebox of a childhood you all grew up in. I'm guessing that's what you have in common, lots of fir trees, lots of logs, lots of those big, big rivers, and probably wolves, too. Is this host of ours good to you, George? Does he pay you well? Look after you properly? Make sure you don't get lonely in the evenings, or lack for anything else? Truth is beauty, George. You should remember that because one day my *Vozhd* may step into some nightmare of yours and demand an explanation. In our game, you must always be ready, George. Ready with a smile, and a compliment, and maybe something to eat, and better still something to drink, and above all an explanation. Am I right, Max? Or is this just *dacha* talk?'

Beaverbrook, for once, had been silenced by this latest twist in the conversation. He was looking from one face to another, from Maisky to Hogan, from the seasoned ambassador to the callow scribe, and he seemed to have concluded that Hogan had got beyond this little Russian hedgehog's normal defences and touched something important in his soul.

'More stories, son,' he murmured. 'Tell him more stories.'

Hogan left them to it a couple of hours later. Maisky, by now, was halfway through a bottle of rare Kentucky bourbon, one of many Beaverbrook's trophies from his recent American visit, and he got up to cling unsteadily to the back of his chair as Hogan said his goodbyes. He looked deep into Hogan's eyes, some wordless compliment trying to form itself on his lips, then he enfolded Hogan's tall frame in a bear hug, his balding head brushing Hogan's jaw.

'My friend,' he managed finally, 'evenings can sometimes be perfect.' He reached up, kissing Hogan on the lips, then offered a deep sigh and sank into his chair again.

Beaverbrook, too, was fulsome.

'Fine job, son,' he murmured, escorting Hogan to the door of the dining room before telling the maid to find more tissues.

Hogan nodded, said it had been a pleasure. Wiping his mouth, he walked through the house and into the gathering darkness. Betty was already in the back of the Rolls, making yet more notes. They sat in silence as the big car purred away, and only when they were on the outskirts of Leatherhead did Hogan remember the word that had so puzzled him.

'*Vozhd?*' he queried. 'Have I got that right?'

'You have, yes. It means Leader, the Great One, the All-Powerful.'

'Stalin?'

'The same thing.' She was smiling in the darkness. 'In this war, George, everything begins and ends with that one word.'

'Leader?'

'Power.'

*

The flat was empty when Hogan got back. He checked his watch. Way gone midnight. He looked in vain for some kind of note. Normally, Annie was punctilious about letting him know when he might expect her but tonight, for whatever reason, there was nothing but the drip-drip of a rogue tap from the bathroom and the measured tread of the local air raid warden as he passed the front window.

Hogan brewed himself a pot of tea and settled himself in the battered armchair in the living room to wait. By one in the morning, when nothing had happened, he got to his feet, checked his pockets for loose change and then returned to the street. With their own phone mysteriously out of action, the nearest call box was a two-minute walk away. He dialled the operator and asked for the police.

'This is an emergency, sir?'

'I think it might be, yes.'

A series of clicks on the line took him to a male voice, slightly gruff. Hogan explained his concerns.

'This is your wife, you say?'

'A good friend.'

'And she hasn't come home?'

'No.' Hogan spelled out Annie's name and added a brief description. The voice promised to contact a number of local hospitals and phone back.

'On this number?'

'I'm afraid so, sir. Unless you have another.'

Hogan nodded, said he could think of no alternative, and hung up. Time passed all too slowly. Alone in the unlit phone box, Hogan gazed into the night, peopling the imagined streets with some of the faces he'd met recently. O'Donovan's ADC, the soul of patience. Ivan Maisky, bewitched by Betty's cleavage. The Rage, the little imp-wizard who so loved to set dinner guests at each other's throats. And finally, the tall, gaunt stranger on the bench at St James's Park who'd tried to hide away behind the columns of *The Times*. Who did he work for? What had brought him to the park? And, most important of all, what on earth might he do next?

Hogan was still trying to answer the question when the phone began to trill. Same male voice. None of the hospitals contacted, he said, have any record of admitting a Miss Annie Wrenne. Neither have various police control rooms had any dealings with the said lady.

The said lady. Hogan offered his thanks and left the number of one of the phones in the *Express* newsroom in the event of any further developments. Making his way back along Gower Street, Hogan half expected to see a glimmer of light around the edges of the blackout curtains but the flat was still empty. Anxious now, Hogan lay in the darkness, pushing his imagination harder and harder. Had she decided to leave him? Had she cast off her moorings and turned her back on the life they'd shared? Was it something he'd done? Something he'd said? Or should he be wondering about the face in the photo up in Achnacarry? This afternoon, he'd meant to press O'Donovan again for a name from the archive but thanks to their friend on the neighbouring bench, it had never happened. Tomorrow, Hogan thought, drifting off to sleep.

He awoke earlier than usual, reaching for the emptiness of the bottom sheet that was Annie's side of the bed. He took a moment or two to still his racing brain and then he was out of bed and padding along to the bathroom. A perfunctory shave, a cup of lukewarm tea and he was bumping his bike out of the house and setting off down the street.

His first call tried to find the police operator he'd talked to last night. It was a different voice but the same outcome: no trace of a Miss Annie Wrenne. By now, it was nearly eight o'clock. Reaching for the phone again, Hogan wondered whether it was wise to make contact with Combined Ops. Only once had he bothered Annie at work and her reaction on that occasion told him that the intrusion was far from welcome. This morning, though, he knew he'd surrendered all control. One way or another he had to find this woman of his, if only to be sure she was safe.

The Combined Ops switchboard was manned twenty-four hours a day, and a woman's voice wished him a very good morning. When he enquired about Miss Wrenne, she asked him to repeat his name.

'Hogan,' he said, his spirits lifting. 'You mean she's there? In the building?'

'Since sparrowfart, sir,' the woman was laughing. 'Away all yesterday but back in harness first thing. You want me to put you through?'

Hogan nodded, saying nothing, then came another voice on the line, guarded certainly, but unmistakeably hers.

'Annie?' he said. 'I've been worried.'

'No need. I'm still here. Nothing's changed.'

'What do you mean?'

'I'll tell you later. Thanks for the call.'

Hogan spent the rest of the day at his desk, working on a couple of stories he'd been putting off. A phone call from the Soviet Embassy told him a case of premium vodka with his name on it would be shortly delivered to the *Daily Express*, and another from Betty Bower confirmed that his Lordship was deeply grateful for his company last night. A compliment this unguarded within Express Newspapers was very rare indeed and put a very big smile on Hogan's face. He was back at the flat in Gower Street by six in the evening to find Annie lying fully clothed on the bed, her eyes closed.

Hogan settled beside her, trying to work out whether she was really asleep.

'You,' she murmured.

'Me,' he agreed. He watched her perfect hand crabbing towards his, and then the soft touch of flesh on flesh.

'You mustn't worry,' she said. 'I didn't mean to upset you.'

'So what happened?'

'It doesn't matter.'

'Wrong. It does. Where on earth were you?'

'God...' she turned onto her back, looking up at him. 'Why all the questions? Why not just trust me?'

'Because you're right, I *was* worried, really worried. In fact I even phoned the police.'

'Jesus,' she was frowning now, 'tell me you're joking.'

'I'm not. I did. And you would, too, in my position.'

'You think so? You really think so? You don't think I'd trust you? You don't think I'd give you just that little sliver of freedom?'

'Sliver?'

'Taste, maybe?'

'Is that what you were after? Freedom? Be frank, Annie, no games. If you want to be away from all this, if you've had enough, just say. I'm a grown-up, Annie. I do language for a living. I understand how it works. I've even got a brain in my big fat head. That's all you have to do. Just say. Just tell me.'

'You mean that?'

'I do.'

'Finished? Gone? Over?'

'Of course. If that's what you want.'

She was staring up at him now, colour in her face and a hint of moistness in her eyes. It might be anger or it might be something else but either way he knew he'd taken her by surprise. The older woman, he thought. And the young cub.

'What's happened has gone away,' she said at last. 'Don't ask me why or where or who or whatever else, just take my word for it. It's just you and me, Mr H.' She did her best to summon a smile but failed completely. 'You think you might be able to cope with that?'

The evening largely passed in silence. They each took great care not to raise the subject of her absence again, which simply made things worse. Hogan, for his part, wondered whether or not to tell her about the landing exercise he'd watched down in Dorset, or the friendship he'd renewed with O'Donovan, or even the creepy attentions of the listener on the bench. Over a glass of pink gin he knew she didn't want, he did his best to describe his visit to Cherkley but the moment he touched lightly on the faces round the dining room table he sensed her lack of interest. She's come back, he told himself. And for that I should probably be grateful.

The next few days, far from offering some kind of return to normality, achieved exactly the opposite. Conversation, comparing the small print of each other's days, the tiny intimacies that had always oiled their relationship, had simply died. And so they sat in near-silence, polite, overcautious, like some long-married couple who'd simply run out of ways of breaking the silence.

Then, on the evening of Monday, 6 July, she returned to the flat an hour or so later than usual and Hogan knew at once that something had changed. By now, he'd half decided to leave, to ring the bell in the saloon bar of their shared lives and call time on whatever it was they'd enjoyed. He'd pedal his ancient bike back to Limehouse and resume his life alongside Evie and her child and all the other tenants. He'd wobble his way back and forth to Fleet Street, doing his best to avoid the deeper potholes, and forget all about Annie Wrenne.

But here she was again, fully alive, lightly drunk and demanding to be taken to bed. Once again he badly wanted to know what had happened, what had sparked this sudden turn of the key in her door, but he buttoned his lip. She wanted him back, every last inch of him, and he was very happy – as well as relieved – to oblige.

Afterwards, she turned into him, closer than ever, and offered her congratulations.

'For that?' He nodded down at their naked bodies.

'For not asking,' she kissed him again. 'Self-control is everything, Mr H. I'm glad you haven't lost the knack.'

*

The following morning, an hour or so after dawn, a farmer on the Isle of Wight was inspecting a field of barley with a view to making a decision about early harvesting. His land rose towards the south of the island and from the top of his sixty acres he had a near-perfect view of the anchorage off the little port of Yarmouth. For nearly a week now, this patch of the Solent had been dotted with a sizeable flotilla, including a couple of landing ships that had the look of cross-Channel ferries. Local gossip had put this gathering down to some kind of exercise, maybe a rehearsal for the still distant day when our boys would shoulder their packs and check their weapons and take the war back to where it belonged. True or not, the farmer found a sense of comfort in the sight of so much shipping. Intent, he thought. That's all it takes.

Then came a familiar cackle of engines and four silhouettes appeared against the rising sun to the east. He'd seen these planes before. They were the new Focke-Wulf fighters and at least one of them paid the Solent regular visits, always early in the morning, normally a good deal higher, presumably to take photos. But this was no photo recce. One by one, they dropped out of the sky, heading for the gleaming expanse of the Solent, and he watched the two lead aircraft closing on one of the landing ships. Each of them carried a bomb, and he followed the fall of the tiny black eggs as they plunged into the waiting vessels. Curiously, there was no explosion, no smoke, no sign of damage, and neither – within minutes – was there any evidence that aircraft had even paid the Solent a visit.

*

In *Kapitan* Linder's office in Dieppe, *Major* Schultz answered a *Luftwaffe* summons to the big airfield across at Abbeville. There he was taken to the photo-reconnaissance lab and shown a series of images still wet from the developing tank. The best of them showed the sleek lines of a two-funnel ferry, its upperworks gleaming in the low slant of the sun. Attached to the print was a name: the *Princess Josephine Charlotte*. Also present across the display table was one of the Focke-Wulf 190 pilots who'd attacked and bombed the anchorage shortly after dawn. He unfolded a map of the English Channel and indicated the pencilled course that had taken him from Abbeville to a stretch of water north of the Isle of Wight.

'Lots of shipping,' his finger strayed to a town called Yarmouth. 'Ferries, landing craft, all sorts,' he picked up one of the photos. 'We concentrated on this one, but they gave us shit bombs. They penetrated the deck but didn't explode. We took another look a couple of hours ago.' He was grinning now. 'No more boats, Herr *Major*. We never sank the bastard but we chased them all away.'

Back in Dieppe, *Kapitan* Linder welcomed Schultz's news. The weather had been kind to his little garrison of defenders for days – a big Atlantic depression driving huge waves onto the beaches of Dieppe – and now, thanks to the Abbeville boys, any element of surprise had been lost. The Führer was still roaring about the English appetite for nuisance raids across the Channel, but it was surely inconceivable that they'd try again. Linder, though, still needed persuading.

'You saw the *Luftwaffe* photos yourself? And you're sure this fleet will never sail?'

'Not this month, Herr *Kapitan*. I guarantee it.'

Last word on the subject fell to Carlos Ortega. As unit after unit of the town's garrison enjoyed a stand-down in the blustery sunshine, he insisted on taking Schultz to a late lunch. He chose a restaurant overlooking the unfashionable end of the harbour, partly because he knew the owner always laid hands on the freshest fish, but mainly because he liked the look of her and detected the beginnings of a *tendresse* on her part. Her husband had been away for months, working twelve-hour days in some factory in the Ruhr, and he knew for a fact that girls from Madame Lili's had been spreading the word about his many talents.

'This is she?' Schultz was watching the woman as she approached the table, two plates in one hand laden with fillets of *merlan* and steamed potatoes, a bottle of chilled Sancerre in the other.

'Gabrielle...' Ortega got to his feet and offered a courtly kiss before introducing Schultz. Schultz did the same, scenting the curls of fresh parsley on the fish.

'Glad of the peace and quiet, Madame?' He gestured out at the harbour.

'*Parfait, Monsieur*. Me? I'm thanking God and Berlin for the weather. We never used to get a wind like this in July. Let's hope it lasts,' she shot a look at Ortega, 'eh?'

*

The news that Operation *Rutter* had been cancelled reached Hogan in the *Express* newsroom moments before he'd planned to leave for the day. It was O'Donovan on the phone, and under the circumstances Hogan didn't blame him for using a crude code.

'The party's over, my friend,' Hogan could hear the relief in his voice. 'Thanks to the weather and a couple of other hiccoughs, the bloody thing's dead and gone.'

'No chance of getting together again?'

'None at all. Even this lot can't be that crazy.' He chuckled at the thought, and then asked whether Hogan had a pen. 'Achnacarry? That face in the front row? His name's Giles Roper, and just now he's a serving Lieutenant with 3 Commando.'

Hogan left the *Express* building shortly afterwards, a spring in his step, knowing that in some way this information must offer the key to Annie's recent disappearance. Maybe there'd been some kind of relationship involved. Maybe Giles Roper had been heading for danger. Maybe, after all, you didn't have to be Canadian to find yourself in Dieppe.

He was out through the big glass doors, plunging into the rush-hour swirl of Fleet Street, when he felt the lightest pressure on his arm. He stopped at once and turned to find himself confronted by the tall stranger he'd seen only days ago in

St James's Park. He was offering an ID pass, and one of the two uniformed policemen was already slipping a pair of handcuffs around Hogan's wrists.

Hogan was staring at the pass. Major Tam Moncrieff. Security Service. Also known as MI5.

'We thought we'd spare you arrest on the premises, Mr Hogan' He nodded up at the towering black façade. 'This needn't take long.'

Book Four

20

Hogan had never been a prisoner before. It was a new experience, and far from welcome, but as the hours ticked by and nothing much happened, he told himself he'd nothing to worry about.

He was Canadian by birth, by accent, by instinct. He'd shipped over in good faith to add maybe a different voice to the clamour of debate as the war lurched from disaster to disaster, and he'd naturally been interested in the fate of his country's young soldiers. He'd asked perhaps a question too many from time to time, but what hungry young reporter didn't try to fill his boots? He'd tried a little of this bluster in the aftermath of his arrest, out there in the middle of Fleet Street, but it had cut no ice. Instead of listening, they'd bundled him into the back of a police van and driven him for miles and miles until he'd arrived at God knows where.

Emerging from the van, he'd glimpsed a sprawling red-brick property shielded by a screen of trees. The grounds were extensive and there were rolls of barbed wire on top of the surrounding brick wall. On either side of the drive that led to the main house were temporary hutments, each guarded by an armed soldier, and it was in a small, bare room in one of these huts that he now sat. Bars at the single window. A curling mat, crusted with food stains, on the wooden floor. A single cracked hand basin in the corner and the faintest hint of carbolic soap hanging in the warm air.

There'd been a brief period back in the Maritimes when Hogan had fallen half in love with certain kinds of adventure fiction, plots which suddenly ghosted a book's hero into a never-never world where he could be sure about absolutely nothing, and he felt some of that terror now, hopelessly disorientated, wondering how and when Annie might finally raise the alarm. In a country like this, still a beacon for the world's democracies, it shouldn't be possible to simply disappear, yet here he was, the prisoner of his worst fears, snatched from a busy street in broad daylight while everyone looked the other way. The blessings of raw power, he thought glumly. Betty Bower had been right.

They came for him hours later. Hogan heard the clump-clump of boots on the wooden boards in the corridor, then he caught the scrape of a key in the lock. A burly figure with Sergeant's stripes on his Army uniform ordered Hogan to be handcuffed again. Two other soldiers manhandled him out of the hut and into the darkness. They were rougher than they needed to be and shoved Hogan towards the looming shape of the house when he tried to turn round and ask the Sergeant a question.

'You speak when spoken to, son. They never taught you fucking manners back home?'

The house had the feel of a hospital, green paint on the walls, scruffy blackout curtains on the windows, not a picture or a plant to be seen. The moment Hogan lingered to look round, hands pushed him towards a flight of stairs. Moments later he found himself in a biggish room off a long corridor: high ceiling, thick velvet drapes at the windows and a hanging chandelier over a long oak table. Hogan was staring up at the chandelier. Only a handful of the dozen or so bulbs appeared to work, and all of them were heavily cobwebbed.

'Sit.'

Hogan did the Sergeant's bidding. His request to have the handcuffs removed, or at least loosened, was ignored. Across the table, he was looking at two empty chairs. Hearing the stir of the Sergeant behind him, he wanted to know when he could make a phone call. The Sergeant told him to shut the fuck up.

At length, the door opened. The older of the two men wore a pinstripe suit and a regimental tie. He had a monocle in his right eye and his hair, sleek with Brilliantine, was swept back from a high forehead. He dismissed the Sergeant with a wave of his hand and barely spared Hogan a glance as he settled at the table and carefully opened a file of papers. Hogan, meanwhile, was staring up at the other man. The same tweed jacket. The same flannel trousers. The same check shirt, the tie knot slightly awry.

'You were in the park,' Hogan said. 'You followed me afterwards.'

'I was, and I did. You were clever to lose me. That doesn't happen often, young man.' Light Scots accent.

'And Moncrieff's your real name?'

'I answer to Moncrieff.' A thin smile. 'Might we leave it at that?'

This exchange appeared to amuse the older man. He was fingering a sheaf of paper, adjusting his monocle, checking some fact or other, then he looked up.

'First things first,' he murmured. 'Your name, please. And the basics.'

Hogan gave his name and his date of birth. He was back in the pages of pulp fiction. Should he offer a service number? And volunteer his plans to tunnel out?

'This is crazy,' he said instead. 'What am I doing here? Why are you bothering?'

Hogan's question raised the faintest smile with the older man. He placed his pencil carefully beside the file and sat back in the chair. The monocle slightly magnified his right eye, an effect Hogan found unaccountably disturbing.

'You're a reporter, Mr Hogan. Can we agree on that?'

'We can, yes. The *Daily Express*. I have numbers if you want to check.'

'That won't be necessary. Your job, as we understand it, is to unearth stories, to ask questions, and all of this to keep the rest of us amused. Am I getting warm here?'

'That's part of it, sure. We sell papers. That's what pays our wages.'

'And what else do you sell, Mr Hogan?'

'Nothing.'

'So why have you earned six bottles of vodka from the Russian Embassy?'

Hogan stared at him. Christ, he thought. What don't these people know?

'You're suggesting they were in return for some...' he was angry now '... favour?'

'I'm suggesting nothing. I'm simply asking. It's a question, Mr Hogan. We understand the vodka is Moskovskaya. It's very hard to get hold of and very expensive. I have chums who would kill for a glass of Moskovskaya and our Russian friends never waste it on anyone they regard as a lost cause. So let me ask you again. What prompted such remarkable generosity?'

Hogan shook his head in disbelief, telling himself to calm down, to trust his better instincts, to deal in nothing but the barest facts. He described his recent visit to Cherkley. He'd done his master's bidding by entertaining the Soviet Ambassador. And in return, much to his surprise, he'd been gifted the vodka.

'For making the man laugh?'

'For obeying orders. Lord Beaverbrook says jump, I jump. I was there to talk about the Second Front Now movement and that's what I did. Mr Maisky must have taken a shine to me. The bottles came out of the blue. The truth is I never touch the stuff. They're yours, if you want them. Call it a contribution to the war effort. Call it what you like. They're still at the *Express* building, by the way, if you want to pick them up. Me? I'd quite like to go home.'

The older man nodded and made himself a note before an exchange of glances brought Moncrieff into the conversation.

'This Second Front Now movement...'

'It's a bee in the old man's bonnet,' Hogan said at once. 'He's fallen in love with the Russians and it's our job to indulge him.'

'That I think I understand. What's less clear is your relationship with these two men.' Moncrieff produced a photograph and slid it across the table. Hogan was looking at Elder and O'Donovan bent over plates of fish and chips in the pub beside Freshwater Bay, with Hogan himself in the third seat.

'You were there that evening?' Hogan asked. 'Took this photo?'

'We were, yes. Not me in person but you'll understand that it boils down to the same thing'

'But why did you bother?'

'Concerns were raised about your presence on the island. I can't offer any details, I'm afraid, but the basic principle is clear. That exercise was strictly off-limits, access strictly *verboten*, yet of all the reporters in this wonderful country of ours, you seem to lead a charmed life. Not just the Isle of Wight but here, too.'

Hogan was suddenly looking at another photo. It was Dorset this time, and a lone figure in a poorly fitting greatcoat was huddled on a clifftop overlooking Lyme Bay.

'May we assume that's you, Mr Hogan?'

'It is, yes.'

'And, once again, you find yourself at the heart of the action? Extraordinary. The Home Guard Captain, incidentally, thought you looked less than keen.'

'It was bloody cold. And muddy, too.'

'So we gather. The issue here isn't *how* you gained access. We know the answer to that. It's *why* you've kept going to all this trouble. There has to be a reason, doesn't there? And if so, might it save us all a lot of time if you cared to share it?'

Hogan felt himself nodding. They've talked to Frank already, he thought. They've been down to wherever he's camped with the Royals, probably Elder, too, and taken them both aside, and subjected them to a session like this. So where were these people heading next? And what was he, George Hogan, the fabled Miramichi Express, supposed to have *done*?

'I'm confused,' he said slowly. 'I'm a reporter. It's my job to ask questions. I happen to be a Canadian, too, and just now our boys are on standby for some big operation. Why would I not be interested? Why would I ignore a story like that?'

'Ah...' It was the Monocle this time. 'On standby for what, exactly? We need to take our time here, Mr Hogan, we need to be sure.'

'Of what?'

'Of how much you know. And exactly what you did with that knowledge.'

'You're asking me about the operation?'

'We are, indeed. And very specifically, we have something else in mind.'

'Like what?

'Like where those boys of yours might be off to. Do you know, as a matter of interest?'

'No, not the first idea.'

'Really? Even when you know the operation's been cancelled?'

Hogan was off-balance again, trapped by the silkiness of the questions, the careful tabling of key facts. They know, he thought. They've tapped the phone I use at work. They've been listening to my every word, watching my every movement. They know everything, the whole story.

Except. Except.

There was a long silence. Hogan caught the low whine of a distant trolley bus. Then the Monocle stirred.

'Would you like to start again, Mr Hogan? Might that be wise?'

And so Hogan did their bidding, taking this story of his back to the moment when he first met his future employer in the Colonial Hotel at Fredericton. How he worked hard on his adolescent journalism. How he found himself on the Toronto *Globe and Mail* and secured a perch on the big news desk. How meeting Larry Elder secured his first proper break, and how his friendship with Frank O'Donovan survived the outbreak of war and their passage across to the UK.

'Friends, you say?' Moncrieff this time.

'Yes.'

'Good friends?'

'I like to think so.'

'Despite the age difference?'

'Probably because of the age difference. I think Frank saw something in me.'

'And you?'

'I liked him. Admired him. And I still do.'

'Why, George?'

'*Why?*' This was the first time either of them had used his Christian name. Was it a peace offering? Or simply a ploy?

Might there be something else going on here? Something he'd yet to detect let alone understand?

'I like him because he's an intelligent guy, and because he cares.'

'About?'

'His men, chiefly. He's with the Royals, you'll know that, the Royal Regiment of Canada. He's spent years teaching them how to take care of themselves, how to survive. These are young guys. Some of them aren't that bright. They need protecting, they need nurturing. Frank has always done that and, from where I've been standing, he's bloody good at it.'

'And Elder?'

'Elder is different. He comes from a different place. The man is full of violence, or maybe rage. That can be useful in a soldier, as Frank knows.'

'And you're close to these people?'

'Frank?' Hogan nodded. 'I like to think so. Elder less so. Frank is a listener. Elder hears no one but himself.'

'Good,' Moncrieff nodded, making another note. 'Very good.'

The Monocle stirred. He wanted to change tack.

'Tell us about Miss Wrenne,' he said.

By now Hogan had abandoned any bid to hide. These people, he'd decided, ate guys like him for breakfast. They could smell a lie, or some half-baked evasion, at a thousand miles. That's what they did for a living. That's the way they strove to keep this strange little island in one piece. And so his only salvation lay in making the most of this story of his.

'Her name's Annie,' he said. 'I met her first at Denham Studios where Noël Coward has been making a movie. To the best of my knowledge you guys weren't there.'

Moncrieff acknowledged the sarcasm with the ghost of a smile. He wanted to know what happened next.

'We started an affair.'

'Her doing? Yours?'

'Ours. Sometimes you have to believe stuff for real.'

'And this was for real?'

'Yes.'

'You're sure?'

'On my part? Absolutely.'

'And hers?'

Hogan was faltering again, wondering what else they knew, how they knew, where it might take them all. Just now, Annie Wrenne felt the only thing he had left in the world.

'I love her,' he said simply. 'She changed everything in my life, everything about me.'

'And you trust her?'

'I do, yes.'

Another silence stretched and stretched. Finally, the Monocle took up the running.

'We understand this young lady of yours works for the Combined Operations people.'

'She does, yes.'

'Specifically for Lord Mountbatten?'

'I believe so, yes.'

'I suspect that would give her access to a great deal of sensitive material. Might I be right?'

'Yes.'

'And does she share that material?' A thin smile. 'Pillow talk, maybe? Office gossip? Prime cuts from the Combined Ops table to help that career of yours along?'

Hogan held his gaze. The interview had softened into something closer to a conversation, but he sensed that they'd reached a point of no return. Whatever he said now would probably determine whether he'd ever get out of here.

'She told me one thing and one thing only,' he said carefully.

'And what might that thing be?'

'She told me about an operation called *Rutter*. And she told me where all those guys would be heading.'

'Dieppe?'

'Yes.'

'So you *did* know? That's what you're telling us?'

'Yes.' Hogan nodded. 'Frank told me, too, a bit later. He thought the whole thing was crazy, and he still does.'

'And your lady friend?'

'She wouldn't say, though lately she's been a bit odd.'

'Odd, how?'

'Upset. Disturbed. I think she might have someone else on her mind.'

'You have a name? For this person?'

Hogan closed his eyes. This was very deep water indeed and he could feel the waves lapping over his head. Then, from the other side of the table, came the sound of Moncrieff clearing his throat.

'We need to be candid with you, George,' he murmured. 'We have grounds for believing that you might have been feeding information to the enemy.'

'You mean the Germans?'

'Yes.'

'About Dieppe?'

'Specifically? Yes. We suspect that someone brought the *Luftwaffe* to the Solent yesterday morning, and that someone might well be you. The Abbeville boys dropped some bombs and threw *Rutter* to the dogs. That would be a capital offence, George. We execute people for less.'

'Christ.'

'Exactly.' He paused. 'The consequences of any of us getting this thing wrong don't bear contemplation. You may be guilty of treason, you may not, but it's our job to be certain either way. Our job is to find the enemy within and then take the appropriate steps. Time should be on our side but alas it isn't.'

'Meaning?'

'Meaning there's every reason to believe that this Operation *Rutter* will be somehow resurrected in a different form.'

'You mean now?'

'I mean within the next month or so. After that, it begins to become impractical.' He glanced at the Monocle, and then got to his feet. 'All the windows are locked, George, and the Sergeant will be back to keep an eye on you. My colleague and I will return as soon as we've made a decision.'

'About what?'

'You, George. I'd offer a cup of tea but I understand the kitchen's closed for the night.' A smile briefly warmed his face, and then they were both gone.

Hogan sat with the Sergeant deep into the night. He was leafing through a copy of *Austin Magazine* and for that Hogan was grateful. The last thing he wanted was a conversation, and as the Sergeant carefully ringed a series of car adverts, Hogan did his best to anticipate what might happen next.

If MI5 didn't believe this story of his, he knew it was probably over. They'd look for more evidence, or simply invent it. There'd be a trial of some kind, and doubtless a headline in the *Daily Express*, and in God's good time he'd be taken to the gallows. On the other hand, he'd recognised how little he really knew about these people, about who they trusted and who they didn't, about all the little sub-plots that they had to untangle, about their real agenda when it came to that central issue of power.

What he'd just witnessed, he thought, was nothing more than a skirmish on the very edges of the battlefield they were tasked to patrol. In the end, a young Canadian interloper on the third floor of the *Express* building was of little real consequence. If it suited them, he'd be put to death. If it didn't, they might have something else in mind.

It was nearly two in the morning when Moncrieff returned. To Hogan's surprise, he was alone.

After the Sergeant had left, Moncrieff took the chair across the table, produced a pad and flipped the pages to a fresh sheet. Was this the way you learned whether you were to live or die? Surreal, Hogan thought. And utterly terrifying.

'We've had a bit of a think, George,' Moncrieff began. 'And you'll be glad to know we have a proposition in mind.'

'For?'

'You. I'm afraid it's not altogether perfect from your point of view but given the circumstances it might spare your life.'

The proposition, in essence, was a great deal simpler than Hogan had expected. He would be released that very night and driven back to central London. He'd need a decent cover story for Miss Wrenne, but after that, life would go on as normal. He'd depart for work every morning. He'd sally forth on various stories. And he'd be back home in Gower Street as often as he could manage it.

'And that's it? That's all I have to do?'

'Not quite, George. In some respects, security at Combined Operations isn't all it should be. In other respects, especially when it comes to an agency like ours, they're tight as the proverbial clam. Some people call it turf wars, George, or fallings-out in the councils of the mighty. I've never used that phrase myself but it has some salience.'

'You want me to spy on Combined Ops?'

'We want to get you into the heart of their operation. Your ear to the ground, George. Pillow talk. Other conversations with your good lady. Little snippets that might seem to be of no consequence. We have other sources, of course, and a reputation for putting the whole bloody picture together. Everything must be reported back to my good self, George, so here's my card. There are two numbers on the back. The top one's the best, and the line is always secure as long as you keep using different public boxes.'

'Not the one at home?'

'The one at home will be working by tomorrow. In extremis you might use that, too, though with Miss Wrenne around I imagine that might be tricky. It would be better for all concerned if she knew nothing of any of this. Do I make myself clear?'

Hogan nodded. He was staring at Moncrieff's card, face-up on the table. The flood of sheer relief had gone now, making way for something infinitely more troubling.

'You want me to rat on a woman I love,' he said slowly. 'That's what this is about.'

'We want you to help out an important agency of state. If you say no, then I'm afraid we'll still be considering the other option which might, alas, be terminal. Either way, I'm afraid it boils down to betrayal. That's rather a quaint word. A better one might be treason.'

Hogan gazed at him, shaking his head. At the very back of his mind, where he stored his darkest thoughts, it was beginning to occur to him that he'd fallen into a carefully laid trap. What to really believe was anyone's guess but he suspected that Moncrieff was in the business of leaving him no choice. One way or another, these people had to find out what was really happening inside Richmond Terrace, and part of that task now appeared to fall to him. This was a logic he could follow just so far before it became distinctly problematic.

'I'm a believer, Mr Moncrieff. There are things I will and won't do. Ethically, I'm quite fussy. Should that make a difference to this conversation?'

'Not at all,' Moncrieff was on his feet now, his hand extended. At last, the smile looked unforced. 'We understand you're a Baptist, George. Lately, dare I say it, you've become a stranger to chapel-going but now might offer the perfect opportunity to attend to that conscience of yours. Do I sense we have a deal? Or at least an understanding? Or must we go through this whole tiresome debate afresh?'

Hogan was back in Gower Street by half past three. He let himself into the flat, listening carefully for signs of life, but when he slipped into the bedroom, Annie was asleep. He undressed in the dark, trying not to wake her, but his sudden presence in the bed caused her to stir.

'Where on earth have you been?' she mumbled. 'I've been worried sick.'

'Out,' he said. 'I've had a problem or two. Work stuff.'

'And?'

'Resolved, thank God.' He kissed her softly and told her he loved her. That bit, to the best of his knowledge, was still true.

21

The rest of July was a fine month on the Normandy coast. The big spring tides receded, and with them went any immediate prospect of invasion, but *Kapitan* Linder was taking no chances. Labourers from half a dozen different corners of the Greater Reich set to in the sunshine. Stripped to the waist, they consulted the carefully drawn diagrams they'd been handed by Divisional engineers and added the finishing touches to the protective web of emplacements and strongpoints that had been thrown over the seafront and the promenade. Dieppe, they knew, had already been parcelled tight against intruders. Now came the celebratory ribbons and bows.

For his part, Carlos Ortega had been officially recruited to the ranks of the artillery unit dug into the high ground above the beach at Berneval, eight kilometres east of the harbour mouth. A couple of the officers had shared evenings with him at the local café-bar, listening to his stories from the Spanish Civil War, and recognised the many talents a man like this might offer if it ever came to a proper fight. He understood combat, he knew the price that modern warfare could exact, and you only had to look at the man to know that very little in this world would ever frighten him. Madame Lili was someone else who thought the world of him, as did a handful of her girls. His visits to the brothel were rare now but Mme Lili was the first to congratulate Ortega's new *belle* on her good fortune. You needed more than a fish café and a popular menu in this world, she said, and in the shape of Dieppe's favourite Spaniard, no matter how beaten up he might look, she'd found herself a real man.

Schultz, meanwhile, had returned to Paris where, on 15 July, he and Zimmermann attended a top-level meeting at the Majestic Hôtel. *General* Carl-Heinrich von Stulpnagel was in the chair, mildly berating a representative of the Vichy civilian police for not cracking down harder on the previous day's Bastille Day riots in Marseilles.

'We shot two women, Herr *General*,' the Frenchman pointed out. 'I understand the crowd was enormous. Any more bloodshed and we'd have lost control.'

'But they had flags, tricolours. They were singing the Marseillaise. What's the point of having laws if no one pays any attention?'

The envoy from Vichy mumbled an apology. One day soon, he suspected, the Germans would lose all patience and occupy the entire country, thus saving him the chore of taking the train north across the demarcation line and subjecting himself to humiliations like these. A proud man, with country roots, he badly needed France's new masters to be looking the other way.

'Shouldn't you be worrying about the British, Herr *General*? Your Führer seems to think the British may be heading for Normandy.'

Heads lifted around the long table. Those in the know looked first at Zimmermann, and then at Wilhelm Schultz.

'I think you'll find the matter's in hand, Monsieur,' Schultz grunted. 'Our flyers wrecked this month's little party, and I doubt very much they'll bother us a second time. Even the British aren't foolish enough to knock twice at the same door.'

Schultz said something very similar to Odile. With her young Somali no longer in Paris, she'd had to settle for her *Abwehr* lover again, a decision she told him that had been long overdue. Her husband's gift from the Addis Ababa souk had been a revelation in all kinds of ways but novelty and some breathtaking gymnastics had never been quite enough and, everything considered, she was happy to be back with her old curmudgeon.

Schultz was glad to hear it, not least because she'd learned a couple of tricks at the hands of her infant lover and was eager to practise them again. Afterwards, commendably exhausted, she enquired about the Italians who'd turned up to kill him.

'My Spanish friend got there first,' Schultz was examining a minor flesh-wound she'd just inflicted. 'After what that man's been through, they were foolish even to show up.'

He told her a little about Ortega, though it turned out she knew a great deal already.

'I heard about what happened at the Edouard VII,' she murmured. 'Gasquet can't stop talking about it. He thinks your friend deserves a play of his own at the very least, and I suspect he's busy writing it.'

'Gasquet's never met him.'

'Why should that matter? That man makes everything up. Is your Spanish friend really deformed? *Mutilé?* I only ask because there are still lots of those masks around, the ones they gave our heroes from the last war. Half a face, and you could hide away forever. Will you be seeing him again? I can lay hands on a couple. What size might he be?'

'My size. Maybe bigger.'

'That's enormous. It must be horrible. The man definitely needs a mask. How does he ever cope without one?'

'Oddly he copes very well. Certain kinds of women can't help themselves. One look, and they're smitten. First, they mother him. Then he ends up ravished. I put it down to luck but it's more than that. He has the face of a gargoyle. His mouth doesn't work anymore. Give him a drink, and most of it ends up on his lap. Yet women still find him irresistible. Can you believe that?'

'No. Herr *Major*. You lie for a living. It's seeped into your bones. As it happens, I don't mind in the least.'

She was propped on one elbow, running a moistened finger down his chest, pausing to play among the tiny whorls of hair. Schultz could smell coconut, and something earthier, both a tribute to her departed Somali *beau*.

'You've finished in Dieppe?' She was on her back now, reaching lazily for a cigarette. 'My husband and I went there once. We booked for a weekend and stayed a fortnight. A lovely hotel overlooking the sea. It was rather wonderful.'

'High summer?'

'August. The English were everywhere but most of them were rich so they knew how to behave. What do you think? A week maybe? Same hotel? Same view?'

Schultz smiled, said he'd think about it, then rolled over and took her lit cigarette from her fingers.

'August might be busy,' he tipped his head back and expelled a long plume of smoke. 'Ortega's invited me down for the revels, just in case.'

'Just in case what?'

'Nothing,' he returned the cigarette. 'Let's say September.'

*

That same afternoon, returning to the flat to finish the first draft of a difficult story in peace and quiet, Hogan found Annie in tears.

'You're supposed to be at work,' he had his arms around her. 'How can you possibly save the free world in a state like this?'

'You think that's funny? All those fucking people? The mess they're making?'

'I think you need to tell me what's wrong.'

'Why should you care? Women cry all the time. It comes with the territory.'

'Not yours. Not for a while, anyway. So…?'

He held her at arm's length and suggested he pour her a stiff drink. When she asked for a pink gin, he knew she meant it. He fixed her the drink in the kitchen, adding an extra slurp of Gordon's. It was nearly a week now since he'd been so briefly detained by MI5 but not once had she volunteered anything about Combined Ops, which had come as a source of some relief. Now this.

Back next door, she made room for him on the ancient sofa. The sight of the balled tissue in her tiny hand reminded Hogan of Beaverbrook on his hands and knees, plotting armed raids across the Channel. Betty Bower had phoned him only this morning, enquiring what he might be up to around the middle of August, but when he'd asked why, she'd simply told him to keep that week free.

Now, for whatever reason, Annie's patience appeared to have snapped. She tipped the glass to her lips. Seconds later, most of it had gone.

'Thirsty?'

'Desperate. There's a man called Casa Maury. He's one of his Lordship's set, nice enough in his way, but totally out of his depth. He's a Spanish Marquis. He used to do something clever in the theatre world and I think he once drove racing cars. Lately, for whatever reason, the RAF have made him a Wing Commander but that's probably another story. He's also married to a woman called Freda Dudley Ward, who used to sleep with the Prince of Wales before he became King. Connections count for everything in my little world, Mr H. They shouldn't, but they do.'

'Did you have a drink on the way home?'

'Yes. Several. You're telling me it shows? A woman drinking alone? Oh, Christ, I'm hopeless, aren't I?' She began to cry again, sobbing this time, struggling to catch her breath. At length he managed to calm her down. She blew her nose and dabbed at her swollen eyes and then sat motionless on the edge of the sofa.

'Casa Maury's our intelligence bod,' she said quietly. 'But no one takes him seriously except me. And you know why? Because I speak Spanish. Because we can talk like human beings. He's not the brightest man I've ever met but he has a heart of gold. Seriously. Nine carat. Twenty-four carat. A million carat. That lovely man doesn't deserve us, and we don't deserve him. The service chiefs laugh behind his back. They turn up from their own little corners of Whitehall and put their fat heads round our door and roll their eyes. They think he's trespassing. They think he's a dago. Simple question, my love. What does any of that do for our next little adventure?' She paused, staring at him. 'You haven't heard? It isn't up there in lights? Our glad tidings? Our great joy? Even the fucking name's a joke. *Jubilee?* How sick do you have to be to dream up a codename like that? Talk to anyone who's ever fired a gun in anger. Talk to some of the Navy people. Talk, if you're really desperate, to Casa Maury. He's done his best to put the whole intelligence thing together, and I'm not sure even he believes it. We call it the CB, the Confidential Book. We've become people of blind faith, my love. We're a lost little tribe wandering around in the desert and the Confidential Book is our bible. All the answers we'll ever need. Just as long as there are any of our poor bloody men left standing.'

'This is Dieppe, still?'

'This is Dieppe for ever and ever. It's written on my heart. I used to dream of those times with my mum in the sunshine. Now I'm wasting a whole bloody summer plotting to blow the place apart. I remember Dieppe. I weep for Dieppe. And I weep for the poor sods who have to make our precious Operation *Jubilee* happen. None of this should take me by surprise. None of it. Hand the world to a bunch of men, and this is what you get.'

'Casa who?'

'Maury. If you want to play the reporter, Mr H, write it down. You want to quote me? You want to put your game little mistress on the front page? See if I care. M-A-U-R...' She shook her head and began to cry again. Then she reached for his hand and pulled him closer. 'Something else, Mr H, before that bloody God of yours strikes me down. It's Casa Maury again. He just got word from some Resistance network in Paris, came in via the MI6 rabble in Broadway. It's too late to figure in his precious Confidential Book but that's probably just as well. Apparently, the Germans have neglected to defend Dieppe, just forgot, or maybe scribbled themselves a little note and then lost it. It's a plant, my love. It's transparent. I don't think even Casa believes it but that doesn't matter because there are always bigger things at stake and just now the biggest of them all is bloody *Jubilee*. Getting it wrong once is hard to credit. Giving it a new name and trying a second time is beyond all belief, especially if you stoop to believing duff gen like that.' She peered up at him through a shimmer of tears. 'Do you understand what I'm trying to tell you? Does anyone?'

Hogan phoned the number Moncrieff had given him from the box down the street. He'd told Annie she needed to calm down, put all the Dieppe nonsense behind her, forget about Combined Ops for just an hour or so. A pot of tea might help and he'd rejoin her as soon as he'd laid hands on one of the rumoured bags of black market sugar from a pub called the Star and Garter several minutes' walk away.

'It's me. Hogan.' He was standing in the call box, watching rain pebble the tiny panes of glass.

'George. Good to hear you.' The voice was muffled. Moncrieff evidently had a cold.

'I hate this,' Hogan said. 'You need to know that.'

'I'm sure you do. To be honest we were expecting a call a little earlier. It's been nearly a week, George. Time waits for few men in our business.'

'But that's the point. I'm not in your business.'

'I'm afraid you are now, George. We have an agreement, you and I. I'm afraid backing out isn't an option we're prepared to entertain.'

'You'd arrest me again?'

'Of course.'

'And then what?'

'It's best we don't trouble you with the details. Just now, George, you're free as a bird. If things go well, you may even get a mention in despatches. We can be surprisingly generous when the spirit moves us.' He paused for a moment, and then asked what Hogan had for him.

Hogan mentioned the Marquis, spelled his name.

'And you say this man's running the intel desk?'

'That's what I've been told.'

'By?'

'Annie. She mentioned something else, too. She says a directive went out this morning to all the Combined Ops senior commanders over Mountbatten's signature. He's telling everyone that the chiefs of staff have ordered Combined Ops to stick a new label on *Rutter* and have another go. She saw the directive herself. In fact, I suspect she may have typed it.'

'Have another go at Dieppe?'

'Yes.'

'She has a date?'

'August. Next month. I don't know the exact date.'

'And they have a codename, these people?'

'*Jubilee.*'

'Very festive,' Hogan heard a throaty chuckle. 'And you're telling me that lady of yours is upset? I'm not surprised. We rarely make promises in this game, George, but I've a feeling we won't be letting you down. Keep pressing, George. For your sake, as well as ours.'

With that parting shot, Moncrieff was gone.

Hogan returned empty-handed to the flat, but thankfully Annie appeared to have forgotten about the black market sugar.

'The bloody phone's working again,' she gestured vaguely towards the table in the hall. 'God knows why.'

She told him a Frank O'Donovan had been on the line. Canadian accent. Lovely voice. She seemed calmer, more at peace with herself. When Hogan asked whether she wanted to talk about work again, about what had upset her so much, she shook her head. O'Donovan, she said, would appreciate a call back.

Hogan phoned him the following morning from the office, using the number he'd left with Annie. To his surprise, it was the ADC who answered. The Lt-Colonel, he said, had been summoned elsewhere. Hogan badly wanted to know whether he'd had any dealings with MI5 but didn't know quite how to phrase it. When he asked whether the Royals were still on standby for some kind of operation, the ADC wouldn't give him a straight answer.

'The Lt-Colonel's the guy you need,' he said. 'I'll make sure he gets in touch.'

He didn't. Not that day, nor for the full two weeks that followed. Then, at the very end of the month, Hogan took a call at his desk in the newsroom. It was Betty Bower again. The Beaver, she said, had been delighted with the coverage of Monday's rally in Trafalgar Square. Hogan had been one of the editorial team reporting on the event and now the boss had another assignment in mind. Might Hogan pop round to the Park Lane apartment ASAP? Hogan scribbled the address and then put the phone down. Sixty thousand people had attended the Second Front Now rally in teeming rain. He had a memory of hundreds of raised umbrellas and the crowd bellowing the Internationale. He'd been to previous rallies but nothing on this scale. The speeches had been rousing. Harry Pollitt, a leading Communist, had reproached the crowd for wondering whether they could live with greyhound racing only one day a week while still expecting the Red Army to keep killing the Nazi dogs month after busy month. The taunt had drawn a roar of applause across the Square, clenched fists thrust upwards as the night drew in, and Hogan had retrieved his bike and made his way back to Fleet Street, convinced that something profound was happening under the skin of this sleepy old country.

Hogan tried to share a little of this feeling with his boss when he finally made it to Park Lane. Beaverbrook had just been served lunch. He was picking at an omelette with a boiled potato and a single carrot and he waved Hogan into a spare chair at the dinner table. He half listened to Hogan's account of the rally, and then told him the battle was over.

'You've won?'

'We have. All of us. Don't tell me this is news, George. You know it and I know it and thanks to a lovely girl at Combined Ops, we've got you a seat at the main attraction. The PM's heading for Moscow very soon, and you know what he and Uncle Joe will be discussing? The Second Front, George. It's coming true. It's gonna happen.'

'You mean an invasion?'

'Kind of. More an armed raid. Curtain-raiser for the real thing.' He paused for a moment, putting his fork down, shooting Hogan a long, hard look. 'We're Canadians, George. We're paying our dues. We might even have to shed a little blood. But whatever happens, it will be one of the great stories of this goddam war. Do I hear a thank you, son? Or is that my poor blighted Maritimes imagination?'

That night, Annie admitted that she'd taken a call from Lord Beaverbrook, and put him through to his Lordship. The conversation over, Mountbatten had appeared in the outer office and left a name on her desk to be added to the approved list of correspondents cleared to report on *Jubilee*. Thirteen places had been allotted to journalists and cameramen across the fleet, and Hogan would be one of them.

'You're on a destroyer called HMS *Calpe*,' she said. 'You'll be at the heart of everything.'

'And this is thanks to my boss?'

Annie shook her head, wouldn't say. When he pressed her a little harder, trying to get through the door that had led to Casa Maury, she said she regretted ever mentioning the bloody man.

'You told me you felt sorry for him.'

'That's true. I do. His position is impossible but that isn't his fault. I was drunk. I was upset. In fact, I was bloody angry. You happen to be the one man left in my little world that I trust but I let out far too much and, if you want the truth, I regret it.'

'You're telling me the truth doesn't matter?'

'I'm telling you there's just so much a girl should say. I was getting it off my chest. I thank you for listening. And I thank you for letting this whole thing drop. No more, George.' She put one perfect finger to her lips. 'Not a single word.'

'That's absurd.'

'You're right. It is. Probably more than you realise.'

'Meaning what?'

'Meaning we never mention any of this nonsense again. Not if we care about each other.' She paused, biting her lip, turning her head away. 'Things are moving very fast, Mr H. You're an enlisted man now, thanks to your pushy boss, but it's not too late to back out, and in some ways, my darling man, I hope you bloody do.'

Hogan held her gaze, sensing that she meant every word.

'That bad?' he asked at last.

'Probably worse,' she stepped closer, reached up for him. 'That nice Canadian friend of yours? Ask him.'

*

Hogan spent the days that followed trying to get through to O'Donovan but none of his calls were returned. Finally, on a damp Thursday afternoon with the subs desperately editing copy reporting on Churchill's arrival in Moscow, Hogan lifted the phone to hear the familiar Canadian voice on the other end. By now it was the middle of August, and O'Donovan was in London for one last visit before returning to the Royals. He'd just left his final meeting and Hogan, he said, should get himself to Waterloo Station within the hour.

'Half past four, George. Look on the board for the Portsmouth train and then wait for me by the ticket barrier.'

'We'll have time to talk?'

'I'm afraid so.'

Afraid so? Hogan wanted to press him further, but the line had gone dead.

Waterloo was busy by the time Hogan arrived. A number of trains had been cancelled, and services to Portsmouth were among them. Crowds milled aimlessly around, hundreds of passengers looking for advice.

'Someone dived onto the line at Woking,' a weary porter was explaining to a little knot of servicemen. 'You'd think people would know better during a bloody war.'

It seemed it would take a while for the bits to be tidied up, and Hogan was still listening to the porter describing the way an engine could sever a man's head at the neck when he felt a pressure on his arm. It was O'Donovan.

'An hour at least,' he gestured towards the empty platform. 'Where does a guy eat around here?'

A passer-by who'd overheard the question suggested a café across the road from the station entrance. There was a rumour they'd laid hands on a consignment of black market offal, chiefly liver. Hogan and O'Donovan exchanged glances. They left the station and found the café, where the rumour turned out to be true. Not just liver but rashers of fatty bacon and enough fried onions to satisfy O'Donovan.

'About time,' Hogan settled at a spare table in the steamed-up window. 'You're fading away.'

O'Donovan shot him a look. He was in full uniform, a raincoat folded over his arm, but his jacket hung loosely on his thin frame and he looked drawn and exhausted under the peaked cap.

'You're gonna ask me what it's been like,' he sank into the other seat. 'Lately I've almost ceased caring.' After a precautionary glance at neighbouring tables, O'Donovan beckoned Hogan closer. 'I gather you'll be sailing on *Calpe*. I saw the assignment lists.'

'That's right.'

'Then you've definitely got a dog in this fight. Larry sends his regards by the way. He thinks the trip will do you the world of good which proves something I never suspected about the man.'

'Like what?'

'Like he's got a sense of humour. What you need just now, my friend, is a word or two in your ear. The people at Combined Ops live in a world of their own. They've stepped through the looking glass. This is fantasy on a gigantic scale. We won't be kidding the Krauts for one single moment but we've sure been kidding ourselves.'

Hogan blinked. He'd never seen O'Donovan like this before, so angry, so emphatic. He'd laid his brown leather gloves carefully beside his glass of water and reinforced each point by stabbing the table with his forefinger.

'Number one, it's madness to even think about reviving the bloody operation. Montgomery's off to North Africa. He wants nothing more to do with it. Churchill's hiding away in Cairo, en route to the goddam Kremlin. For the life of me, I can't work out who's now in charge.'

'Mountbatten?' Hogan suggested.

'Sure. He's done the lyrics and the music but who put the show on the road in the first place? The people who matter, George, are all running for cover. You know when a show's gone rotten. You can smell it. This last month we've all been confined to camp. No extra training. Not necessary. Why? Because the men are supposed to be tuned up already. You were down for *Yukon*, George. Did we look battle-ready? Be honest.'

'I understand there was a second exercise.'

'You're right. *Yukon 2*. Marginally better, but not much. Mountbatten's a slave to the clock. As long as he assigns a time to every manoeuvre, to every breath a man takes, then his job is done. The whole thing just knits itself together, absolutely can't fail, because on paper it works. This is nonsense of course because no battle ever invented obeys the rules. Six thousand men floating around in the dark? The Krauts dug in, ready and waiting? No softening up? No pre-dawn bombardment? No heavy bombing? Since when did any invasion boil down to mere flesh and blood? This is negligence, George, on a gigantic scale, and everyone's looking the other way. Except the Germans.'

Hogan had produced a pad. When O'Donovan told him to put it away, he asked why.

'Because this is for your ears only. Call it a favour. Call it whatever you like. But you're one of us now, George. They've called you to the colours. You have a stake in the action and I'd be only half a Canuck if I didn't warn you what to expect. It's gonna be your life on the line, too, and let's hope you don't lose it, but should that happen you at least deserve to know why.'

This was the moment the waitress chose to deliver O'Donovan's liver and bacon. The smell turned Hogan's stomach as he watched O'Donovan carve a slice of the liver, pink with blood, and then pick at a curl of bacon. He chewed at a thread of gristle for a moment, a frown of intense concentration on his face, and then pushed the plate aside.

Operation *Rutter*, he said, had called for a parachute drop on both flanks of the landing to silence the big guns. That, at least, had been sensible but a month later they'd be dropping in the dark and so First Airborne Division had now backed out. Same with Bomber Command. Churchill had issued a diktat about keeping French civilian casualties to the barest minimum. Bombsights were still primitive, with no guarantee of accuracy, and so there was no prospect of a prior bombardment to keep German heads down.

'Battleships?' Hogan asked. 'Way offshore? Those huge guns?'

'Out of the question. After *Prince of Wales* and *Repulse*, the Navy won't take the risk. The best they can manage is a bunch of destroyers. Four-inch pop guns. Limited range. You'll see it for yourself, George. The Krauts will barely know we've arrived, but God knows that may be the whole point. Surprise sometimes has its uses.'

'You don't believe that.'

'Of course I don't. The Germans have been expecting us for months – 10th Panzer Division has just moved to Amiens. Do the sums, George. Twelve thousand men. A hundred and sixty tanks. They could be in Dieppe in time for tea. The whole thing is madness.'

Madness. Annie had said exactly the same thing and, thinking back, Hogan remembered a similar headline in the *Daily Express* the morning after Japanese dive-bombers had sunk *Prince of Wales* and *Repulse* off the coast of Malaya barely months earlier, the rudest shock to a nation depending on its battleships. O'Donovan was right. The face of war was changing by the day.

Hogan wanted to know about the big German gun batteries on the flanks. These, he imagined, had the range to make life very uncomfortable for the fleet offshore and this conversation had suddenly become intensely personal.

'So what's the plan? Instead of the para-drop?'

'Two commando landings, one on either flank. They'll be the first boots on the beach. These guys are good, very good, but they can't work miracles. The marines on the eastern flank are crossing in tiny little landing craft. There are twenty-three of them in all, with a bunch of commandos in each. I'm on top of the figures because I just attended a briefing. These boats are thinly armoured. By the time you hit the beach you've probably spent hours puking your guts out just getting across. All you've gotta do now is climb a sheer cliff which has been wired and probably mined. You've got a ton of kit on your back. There are guys on top with machine guns waiting to kill you. Anyone who survives, all he has to do is blow up the guns, take a prisoner or two and conduct an orderly retreat. Piece of cake, my friend. You heard it here first.'

O'Donovan returned briefly to his meal, stabbing at the fatty disc of liver. The onions, swimming in a pool of grease, were beginning to congeal. Then, struck by another thought, he looked up.

'That's the big picture,' he said. 'Here's what my guys have to do. We land in three waves. It's dark so the Krauts can't see us coming. We rough the bastards up, capture all the guns, get on the high ground, then one company goes into town to look after the demolition guys when they start blowing stuff up. Like I say, piece of cake.'

Hogan nodded, memorising the phrase, trying to imagine men like Larry Elder seizing this challenge. He wanted to press O'Donovan further. He wanted to know how the men would measure up when the real fighting began, but O'Donovan hadn't finished.

'Something else you should know,' he grunted. 'That Giles Roper of yours? The guy in the photo from Achnacarry? He's with 3 Commando in one of those little landing craft. A brave soul, George. But probably doomed.'

Hogan phoned Moncrieff from a call box back at Waterloo Station. He'd seen O'Donovan onto the Portsmouth train. To his surprise, the Canadian said he'd had no dealings with any of the Brit intelligence agencies, and now – waiting for the operator to put him through – Hogan was wondering why. Was this simply carelessness on Moncrieff's part? Or was the plot even more opaque than he'd imagined?

Moncrieff had little time for conversation. All he wanted were the facts. Hogan tallied them one by one, depending wholly on O'Donovan's account. This flew in the face of every journalistic rule he'd ever been taught – demand corroboration from at least one source – but Hogan no longer cared. He could sense the hot breath of events on the back of his neck. He felt hopelessly exposed, horribly vulnerable, and if he could have some small hand in getting this whole adventure abandoned then so much the better.

He told Moncrieff about the lack of inter-service support, about the cancellation of promised bombardments, about the contradiction that lay at the heart of the phrase 'Combined Operations'. Combined Ops was one of Whitehall's orphans, cast away at birth, mistrusted by its older siblings and left to fend for itself. It was taking on far too much with far too little, and in the shape of 10th Panzer, as well as the local garrison, it was facing one of the finest armies Europe had ever seen. *Jubilee*, Hogan told Moncrieff, was an act of blind faith, a gamble of enormous proportions. If any operation had been bred to fail, then here it was.

'This is you speaking? Or O'Donovan?'

'O'Donovan. I'm just there to watch.'

'You've been assigned?' This appeared to be news to Moncrieff.

'I have. We sail on Sunday.'

'That's three days away.'

'I know. I'll be there, of course, but I just hope O'Donovan's wrong. What I don't understand is how any of this has ever happened. Frank says it's still half-baked. He says it needs to go back in the oven. And even then, he doesn't think it would be worth eating.'

'He's a pessimist, this man? Some kind of depressive?'

'He's a Canadian, Mr Moncrieff. We Canucks have a real nose for bullshit.'

'Nicely put.'

'Thank you.'

'And good luck, too. We're impressed, by the way. You're not overgenerous with these reports of yours but you keep it simple, which is far rarer than you might think. If you ever make it back, we might be talking about a proper job.'

For the first time, Hogan laughed.

'Thanks a bunch,' he said. 'You don't think I've got one already?'

If you ever make it back. The phrase wouldn't leave Hogan alone. For reasons that he still didn't fully understand, he seemed to have surrendered all control of his life. Surviving countless air raids and all the other perils of life in the blackout was one thing but putting himself at the tender mercies of two organisations out of control, possibly three including MI5, was quite another.

He'd always known that the *Daily Express*, even now, was still the plaything of an ambitious, mercurial Canadian press baron with far too much money and absolutely no patience, but attendance at huge Second Front Now rallies, plus all his other journalistic assignments, had never felt physically dangerous.

The same went for Combined Ops. Until he'd met Annie, the name had meant nothing, but now he was about to trust it with his very life and the deeper he dug, and the harder he listened to the likes of Annie and O'Donovan, the more he realised how men in their thousands could be slaughtered for no good reason. Not because the Second Front wouldn't, in the end, happen. But because the right time, despite all the hoopla and the bullshit, was still years away.

All that was bad enough but in the shape of Tam Moncrieff he'd found himself suddenly shackled to an organisation that could evidently put him on trial for his life. Mercifully, his dealings with Moncrieff had so far been at arm's length, and there were comforting signs that these people were beginning to take to him, but coupled with everything else he couldn't remember living with a darker sense of menace. In three days' time, he'd embark on an RN destroyer to do battle with the enemy. By dawn the following morning, he might well be dead.

Annie was waiting for him at Gower Street. One look at his face told her something had happened. When she asked exactly what, he shook his head.

'You don't want to know. You told me to drop it.'

'That was a while ago. I'm a woman remember. I'm fluffy. I'm hopeless with time and directions. I have no memory. I never understood logic as a proposition and I never will. But I'm brilliant in bed and one day I might even corrupt you with a big fat gin, so just tell me...' She touched his face. 'Do I hear a yes?'

Hogan accepted a beer and settled on the sofa. It was a tonic just to look at her in moods like these, so playful, so boyish, so frankly available. He told her about meeting O'Donovan at Waterloo, how worn out he'd looked, and then – item by item – all the ways in which Combined Ops bravado could spill into a bloodbath. Before they'd left the café, he said, O'Donovan had drawn the outline of Dieppe in the puddle of gravy on his plate. Six landings on six beaches, each one timed to the minute. An armoured push deep into the town with the new Churchill tanks. Demolition teams blowing up the gasworks and the town's power plant. Snatched trophies to carry back to Mother England. Not a single opportunity missed to bloody the German nose and stiffen French resistance and send a message of solidarity to Moscow. Except none of it would happen because the plan, in O'Donovan's brisk phrase, was the purest crap. At that point, he'd wiped the plate clean with his last slice of bread, a single movement that seemed to sum up the uncertain magic that was Combined Ops.

Hogan sat back on the sofa, Annie beside him, knowing he'd done justice to his conversation with O'Donovan.

'If I was writing this up for a story,' he was staring at the window, 'I'd be taking a hard look at Mountbatten. Something's gone wrong with the wiring system.'

Annie nodded, then reached up and turned his head towards hers.

'Loose connections, you think?'

'Very funny.' Hogan wanted to kiss her, to hold her, to tell her that one day – if he managed to survive Dieppe – they'd put all this nonsense behind them and invest in some other life, but one look at her face told him she hadn't finished.

'I mean it, Mr H. You're Canadian. You don't really know the English. You've no idea how power works in this country, how precious it is, how protected, how it passes from hand to hand, a nod here, a smile there, the lightest pressure on your arm one moment, then gone the next. I see it every day at Richmond Terrace. It begins and ends with connections, Mr H. Plug yourself into the right networks and you can get away with anything.'

'Mass murder?'

'Even that. I don't suspect for a single moment that his Lordship intends anything of the sort. *Au contraire*, it wouldn't surprise me if the poor deluded man thinks he's going to take the Germans and the world by storm. He has lots of Hollywood friends. He's very close to Noël Coward. He loves what's happening at that huge water tank out at Denham. Maybe those are the clues we should be looking at. Maybe he still believes it'll all work out by the time the credits roll.'

'Because the credits matter?'

'Of course they do. He's a man in a man's world, Mr H. And it's men, all too sadly, who will be paying the price.'

Hogan nodded. There were two images he couldn't get out of his mind. One of them was a morsel of half-chewed liver on O'Donovan's plate. And the other, deeply terrifying, was a severed head lying on a railway line, the grossest evidence of an act of suicide. All too soon, Hogan thought, that could be me. Along with thousands of others.

'Tell me about Giles Roper,' he murmured. 'Because time may be short.'

The name froze the smile on Annie's face. Brilliant, Hogan thought. A single misjudged sentence to turn something so promising, so *true*, to ashes.

'You know about Giles?'

'I know what he looks like. I know he went to Achnacarry. And I know exactly what he's going to be doing on Sunday night. Friend? Colleague? Lover? All three?'

'None of the above. We had an off and on affair. Once I thought I loved him but I was wrong.'

'How come?'

'You really want to know?' She was staring at him.

'I do, yes.'

'Why?'

'Because it matters.'

'To you?'

'To both of us.'

Annie considered the proposition for a moment, then nodded.

'He's married,' she said quietly. 'Nice woman, I expect, out in the wilds of Shropshire. Slightly older than Giles but that's often the case, isn't it? Men need women in all kinds of ways, Mr H, especially when there's a war on.'

'Kids?'

'Two that he owns up to. God knows about the rest.'

'He told you from the start?'

'He told me nothing. Except how pretty I was, and how clever, and how sexy, and how he couldn't live without me. Giles wanted to fill his boots, and frankly so did I. On reflection, I might have been more curious about his private life but at the time it didn't seem to matter. We were in Spain. This was a while back, 1937, the Civil War. He was fighting with one of the International Brigades. I was helping out at a rather grand house called the Villa Paz. It had been converted into a hospital during the fighting at Jarama. That was another bloodbath, by the way, though nothing compared with what his Lordship might have to cope with. Giles came in with a belly wound and we sort of bonded. Men like him are trained to eat people alive, sometimes the enemy, sometimes not. Me? I can be as cannibal as the next gal. Except he began to matter, especially when he began to get better, and that was a bad sign.'

'For who?'

'Me. I was deluded enough to take him at his word. It didn't last long, thank Christ, and I should have known it at the time because all the clues were there, but after the Civil War was over and we were busy with the next one he had the nerve to get in touch again. He was up in Scotland, trying to become a Royal Marine. In the end we wrote to each other. He was good on paper, too.'

'And you got together?'

'Not until the end of last year, when I was back in London. To be frank, I'd given him up for lost. I even thought he might be dead. Then he wrote me another letter with a little something inside, a phrase he'd once used, and then turned up out of the blue, at work of all places.'

'Combined Ops?'

'The very same. He was a fully trained commando by now and wanted to buy me lunch, and maybe a little dessert for old times' sake. For whatever reason, I was very happy to say yes to both.'

'But you just told me he was married.'

'He is. That I discovered recently from an ex of his at work. I think she'd taken pity on me. This is a guy, Mr H, who doesn't belong to your world. He'd led me a dance in Spain and years later I should definitely have known better than get involved again. Giles bloody Roper, it turns out, is a fantasist. He loves falling in love. He's very, very good at it and most of us ladies are very, very happy to enjoy the ride because he's brilliant at spinning stories about himself. When it comes to women he presses all the right buttons, does himself more than justice, and then – in his own good time – moves smartly on. He's absolutely made for Combined Ops and the bastard knows it.'

'And yet you still met him? Still went through with it? Regardless?'

'I did. I told him I knew about his wife, and his family, and he swore it was all over, finished, done, and so we coupled again, Mr H, we flung caution to the winds and did it. Was I thrilled? Yes. Were we good at it? Exceptionally. Did it happen again? Yes, as often as possible. And did I believe all those lies he was telling me? Sad girl that I am, yes. Then the same woman, the same ex, told me his wife was pregnant for a third time, and Giles was taking me for a fool, and so I told him to shove off.'

'And did he?'

'Yes. And that probably hurt most of all.'

'Why? How come?'

'Because I realised his ex was right. He'd used me like he'd used all the other women. Not only that but he'd done it twice. On both occasions I thought I was someone special for him and both times I was wrong. He took advantage, Mr H, simple as that. I was just another notch on his belt. Happy now?'

Hogan didn't answer. Not at once.

'The day you wore that suit,' he said at last. 'The one I'd never seen before. I'm guessing that's when you met him again.'

'You're right.'

'And told him to beat it.'

'Right again.'

'But you were really upset afterwards. When you turned up at the pub.'

'I was.'

'Why?'

'Because I went to give him a piece of my mind. I wanted to tell him about you, about meeting someone I could trust, someone who could make me very happy without cheating.'

'And?'

'He laughed in my face. Told me I was wasting my time. Told me he knew exactly what I wanted in life. Told me I needed a real man.'

'Him?'

'Of course.'

'And what did you say?'

'I walked out. Next thing I know I'm sitting in a different pub.'

'With me.'

'Yes.'

'So why didn't you tell me? Why didn't you trust me? Why weren't you *honest*?'

For a long moment she said nothing. Then she shrugged and ducked her head, a gesture that suggested regret or even shame. Moments later, she was looking up at him again.

'If you want the sordid truth, Mr H, me and honesty have never been best friends. There's a time and a place, but certainly not then, not the way I was feeling.'

Hogan nodded. A chill he barely recognised had settled deep inside him.

'So after everything we'd had,' he was frowning now, 'everything we'd done, you were lying to me.'

'By omission? By not telling you about Giles? Yes, you're right. In here?' Her hand closed over her chest. 'No.'

'But why should I believe you?'

'Because it's true, Mr H. This isn't something a girl should say to any man but you're truly someone apart. I've sensed it from the start. When God put you together, I think he had a fit of the giggles. Nothing in that lovely body of yours should work but somehow it does. That's not the point, though. You're awkward, and stubborn, but there's goodness there as well, and sincerity, and the very best of intentions. This, believe me, is extremely rare. In fact, it was weeks and weeks before I began to believe it, began to trust my own luck. Your Beaverbrook has seen it, too, which is why he's sent you to war. I don't know whether he's praying to have you back in one piece, but I most certainly am.'

'And Giles?'

'Giles is with 3 Commando. His Lordship has tasked them to storm a gun battery on the eastern flank which probably means the bloody man's half dead already. I know that cliff. It's at a place called Berneval. Even without the Germans trying to kill you, it's a near-impossible climb. One other thing, my adorable scribe.' She leaned forward and kissed him on the lips. 'I've laid hands on a battledress for you to wear to the revels. It's on our bed. You might like to try it on afterwards.'

She got up, extending a hand, nodding towards the door, but Hogan shook his head.

'Something else,' he muttered. 'That night when you didn't come home. Was that Giles, too?'

'Christ, no. Half an hour in his company was quite enough.'

'Then what was it?'

She gazed down at him, then shook her head.

'I can't.'

'You can. And you must.'

'Otherwise?'

'Otherwise, it's over.'

'You mean that.

'I do, yes. I want you forever. But that means all of you. No more games.'

'Is that you speaking? Or that God of yours? Games can be fun.'

'Not like this. Not given Dieppe. I need to be sure, Annie. I need to know exactly where we are with each other.'

'You're telling me you need to believe?'

'Exactly. Call it faith. Call it whatever you want.' He hadn't taken his eyes off her face. 'So what happened that night you never came home?'

She studied him for a long moment, and then shrugged. She's made a decision, Hogan told himself. Maybe, after all, truth has its uses.

'I was summoned to a hotel,' she began. 'It's in Knightsbridge. No one would give it a second look, which was always rather the point. The meal on this occasion went on longer than I was anticipating. They had a lot of questions, far more than usual, but for once they'd been nice enough to book me a room. By the time we were done, I needed it, believe me.'

'They?'

She looked at him for a long moment. Then reached for his hand again.

'MI5, Mr H. They needed me to tell them you weren't spying for the Germans, something I was very happy to do. You rather strayed into my life and I think that rather confused them. I told them we'd fallen in love but that didn't help matters at all.'

'You said *far more than usual*. What does that mean?'

'It means we've been buddies for a while, for years in fact. I first worked for British intelligence in Spain a while back but that's another story. It's over now,' she gave his hand a squeeze. 'You have my word on that.'

'This is MI5?'

'It is. They recruited me in Madrid just before this bloody war broke out. They had a lively interest in a German plan to kick us off the Rock. For whatever reason, I was happy to say yes.'

'The Rock?'

'Gibraltar.'

'And was Giles involved?'

'Never. He'd never admit it but he's not bright enough. We were together in the Villa Paz but that was years earlier. After the Civil War was over I went to Madrid and got myself a job in the university'

'Doing what?'

'Translation work, mostly, plus a little research. I'd fallen in love with Goya. You know Goya?'

'No.'

'Extraordinary artist, part visionary, part war reporter. He drew a series of pictures, almost cartoons. *Los Desastres de la Guerra*. If you want the truth about warfare, look no further. I had a book in mind, *homage* really, but I still needed to pay the bills. Then a rather nice man from MI5 turned up with a better offer. I said yes, and they sent me further south.'

Los Desastres de la Guerra. The hanging corpse in Roper's letter, watched by the cavalry officer. It all links together, Hogan thought. The hideous cartoon. And the Spanish quote so carefully transcribed on the back. *Love that is not madness is not love.*

'You want to tell me more?' he muttered.

'About what?'

'About working for MI5.'

'No, not yet. Later maybe.'

'Like when?'

'Like when you get back from Dieppe.'

'You mean if?'

'I mean when.'

Hogan nodded, letting each element of this conversation settle in his teeming brain. Giles Roper. The Villa Paz. Goya. The hanging man. Roper again. MI5. Then, for some reason, he remembered Annie's passport lying in a nest of silk underwear.

'You're much older than I thought,' he said.

'You're right, Mr H.' She nodded towards the bedroom. 'And a little wiser, too.'

22

On Sunday, 16 August 1942, Mountbatten's force commanders in charge of Operation *Jubilee* consulted their weather charts and ordered a twenty-four-hour delay in proceedings. Hogan got the message in a telephone call from Combined Ops, standing him by until the following morning. Leaving Annie asleep in bed, Hogan stole out of the house and made his way to the Bloomsbury Central Baptist Church. He arrived late, the service already in progress, and sat on a bench at the back of the building.

The past few days with Annie had been the happiest they'd ever spent together, and he wanted to give thanks. He had no illusions about what awaited him and thousands of other men, but he was – at last – entirely at peace with himself. The news that Annie Wrenne had been working for British intelligence shouldn't have come as a surprise and looking back he could only acknowledge that all the clues had been there: how much Moncrieff had known about him, how conflicted she'd sometimes been, how she'd never quite turned their Gower Street pied-à-terre – an MI5 safe house – into a home of her own.

In the end, it was *Rutter* she'd failed to cope with, *Rutter* that had unsealed her lips, *Rutter* that had disgusted her with its recklessness and its dark promise of huge casualties, and the fact that it had now been rebadged and recycled as *Jubilee* had simply thickened her disgust. Hogan, of course, had promptly passed various titbits on to Moncrieff, one of many ironies the intelligence world doubtless feasted on, but the fact that he and Annie had now come clean with each other felt like a kind of deliverance, and as the service in the Baptist church came to an end, Hogan bowed his head and gave thanks.

That same day, a sizeable part of Dieppe also went to church. Formal belief extended to neither Schultz nor Ortega, who spent the morning with *Kapitan* Linder. In the windy sunshine, the three of them toured the town's seaward defences, impressed by the latest crop of gun emplacements, and comforted by the boisterous crash of surf on the mountain of slate-grey pebbles. Twice over the past forty-eight hours, lone RAF Spitfires had appeared over the town, tiny specks against the blue of the sky, too high for the barking ack-ack from the neighbouring clifftops. They could only have been despatched on photo reconnaissance missions, a sign – said Schultz – that the Brits had lost the knack of writing off their losses. One abortive expedition should have been quite enough. A second smacked of insanity. If the enemy was really bent on a blood sacrifice, then so be it.

On the Monday, back in London, came a second postponement, again due to bad weather, but word circulated that *Jubilee* would definitely set sail at 20.00 the following evening. Hogan badly wanted to spend this last night with Annie but Combined Ops were insisting that key staff remain at Richmond Terrace overnight ahead of the operational launch. This diktat extended to Miss Wrenne, a small but important victory for Mountbatten and his team which rankled with Hogan.

Goodbyes, he'd decided, whether informal or otherwise, were an important paragraph break in the grammar of real life, and after dawn had broken the following morning, he took care to pen a goodbye note which would, he hoped, go some way towards expressing the way he'd come to feel about her. 'It's been a revelation,' he'd written at the end. 'Whatever happens next, you've had the best of me.'

A plain black car, modest in every respect, called to pick him up at the promised 14.00 hours. The driver was a middle-aged naval reservist with little interest in conversation, which suited Hogan just fine. She threaded her way through the southern suburbs and out onto the Portsmouth arterial road, while Hogan sat in the back, trying to get used to the prickliness of his uniform. By late afternoon, having shed his war correspondent tabs in the interests of security, Hogan was stepping onto the quayside at Portsmouth Harbour where he was met by a Canadian press officer. Hogan had been officially assigned to the headquarters destroyer HMS *Calpe*, but the press officer, on Lt-Colonel O'Donovan's orders, invited Hogan to an imminent briefing for the Royals aboard the *Queen Emma*, a Landing Ship (Infantry) requisitioned for the crossing.

Hogan followed him up the gangplank, picking his way over a clutter of stores and other equipment, standing carefully to one side at the head of a flight of steel steps that led to the troop deck. Below him, in the oppressive heat, there was a sea of upturned faces among the hammocks, and weapons racks, and trestle tables, and Hogan could smell meat and potatoes from the men's dixies as they forked their way through their evening meal. Of Frank O'Donovan there was no sign, but the regiment's commanding officer appeared to address the men. Sergeants called for hush, and the CO launched into a passionate call to arms, promising combat against the Boche at Puys and a chance at last to strike a blow for freedom.

Blue Beach at Puys, he said, was the key to the whole operation. Unless the Royals stormed the position and silenced the guns, the fighting on the main beaches in front of the town would be all the harder, with untold consequences for the troops involved, including the Calgary Tanks. A huge responsibility, said the CO, thus lay in the regiment's hands and speaking personally he had absolutely no doubts that the Royals would measure up. No quarter. No retreat. Just a glorious chance, at last, to take the battle to the enemy.

The men roared their approval, and Hogan felt the thunder of boots against the metal deck. A last salute, and the CO had turned on his heel and disappeared, but looking down, Hogan caught sight of Larry Elder. He had a towel in one hand and he was mopping his face. He glanced up, recognising Hogan at the top of the steel steps. Then came a rare smile before he drew his forefinger across his scrawny neck.

'Mr Hogan, sir?' The press officer was tapping his watch. Time to go.

Aboard HMS *Calpe*, space – once again – was at a premium. Hogan was one of only two reporters on the destroyer, both assigned to a young Lieutenant called Boyle, whose twenty-first birthday happened to fall tomorrow. He led Hogan upwards through a warren of passageways until they finally made the top deck. Here, he was briefly introduced to General Roberts, the Canadian in charge of the assault. The legendary 'Ham' cut an impressive figure among his gaggle of radio operators. With his greying hair and firm jaw, he'd direct the landing from this tiny space. The radio operators were already passing a stream of written messages, but Roberts somehow found the time to enquire briefly about life in the Maritimes.

'Any further east, son, and Canada would start to run out. Ever think about that?'

Back on deck, still nursing his kitbag, Hogan stood at the rail. Below, on the quayside, he recognised the figure of Mountbatten. He was wearing the uniform of a Vice-Admiral, and he was surrounded by pressmen and a camera crew. Hogan recognised some of these faces from previous assignments, and he marvelled at Mountbatten's nerveless self-possession as he moved easily among them, a word of encouragement, a pat on the arm, a murmured good luck before they embarked on their respective ships. This performance took Hogan back to the canteen at Denham Studios. He remembered the moment he'd first set eyes on Mountbatten and seeing him in action for real – real combatants, the prospect of a real battle to come – fostered something close to respect. Reckless? Undoubtedly. Vain? Yes. But loved by the men he was sending into combat.

At half past seven, an RN limousine swept to a halt on the quayside beside the destroyer and a senior officer got out. He spared HMS *Calpe* a single glance before hurrying up the gangway and disappearing below. This, explained Boyle, was Commander Hughes-Hallett who would be in charge of all naval assets. Already, matelots had gathered to prepare the mooring ropes fore and aft for departure, and moments later Hogan felt the throb-throb of the ship's engines. She sailed on time at 20.00, and Hogan lingered at the rail as the dockyard and then an older Portsmouth slipped by. From the harbour narrows, Hogan could see the sudden spread of the Solent, flanked by the Isle of Wight, and *Calpe* paused beside the Spithead anti-submarine boom to salute the entire fleet as it sailed east towards the darkening sky. Perfect formation and bang on time, he thought. First blood to Combined Ops.

Down in the wardroom, Hogan finally dumped his bag. He'd be snatching an hour or two of sleep later, curled in the corner on the thin carpet, but for now Boyle had one more port of call in mind. Three sets of steel ladders led to the bridge. The lighting was already dimmed but Boyle talked him through the displayed map of Dieppe. Each of the six landing beaches were colour-coded, including the flanking commando attacks on the big gun batteries, and the map was covered with pencilled annotations. Hogan took a step closer, squinting in the half-darkness: 'possible light gun', 'roadblock', 'anti-tank position', 'house strengthened'.

'This is recent intelligence?' Hogan had his pad out.

'No comment,' Boyle was smiling. 'We've learned to trust our elders and betters'.

Hogan nodded, turning his attention to three sheets of typed paper which appeared to serve as a script for the coming hours. Every next action was carefully timetabled. At 05.10, Hogan was to expect ten minutes of bombardment from seven of the fleet's eight destroyers; 05.20 was designated zero-hour for the main landings, while 11.30 would see two squadrons of Flying Fortresses and a busy swarm of Spitfires bombing and strafing nearby Abbeville airfield.

Scarcely a minute of the coming day had been left to its own devices, and in the face of such confidence Hogan was left with a feeling that nothing could possibly go wrong. Because it was written down, because it had a presence on the page, this schedule of events was surely foolproof.

Before he turned away from the typed schedule he noticed an abbreviation he didn't understand.

'NT?' he asked Boyle.

'Nautical twilight, Mr Hogan. Navy-speak for the darkness before dawn.'

A couple of hours later, deep in the English Channel, Hogan was ordered back on deck for an issue of Mae West life jackets. The Isle of Wight was behind them, a darker mass on the starboard quarter, and Hogan was glad of the life jacket because now it was much colder. The bosun appeared. A narrow channel had been cleared through the approaching belt of mines and he needed to brief them on what to do in the event of what he called 'a stray'. Hogan listened to his list of dos and don'ts, all of them doubtless good advice, marvelling at how calm he felt. Fatalism? Resignation? The hand of God in the darkness? He simply didn't know.

As the first of the lit green buoys slipped past, Hogan caught a murmured confidence from his immediate neighbour. He was wearing a Royal Navy uniform and he was nursing a mug of cocoa. 'The greatest invasion of its kind ever attempted,' the officer gestured back towards the fleet. 'Bloody privilege to be here.'

Hogan nodded. He could hear nothing but the hypnotic sluice of water folding back from the destroyer's hull as she knifed through the blackness of the water, and for a moment he tried to imagine the bosun's stray lying in wait, just a tethered pimple of high explosive lurking beneath the surface. Would it blow the bows off? Would he find himself suddenly in mid-air, bracing for the icy shock of the water?

In the event, he needn't have worried. *Calpe* led the fleet through the cleared channel and everyone on desk retreated to the wardroom for celebratory drinks. Hogan settled for a thin orange juice that tasted of nothing. When a toast was proposed to the Air Commodore who'd masterminded the clearance of the mines, using a top-secret navigational aid not yet in service, he modestly dismissed the applause. 'We watched German E-Boats heading home,' he said. 'What's good enough for them is good enough for us.'

A little later, on the point of claiming his scrap of carpet, Hogan found himself face-to-face with Boyle again. By now it was way past midnight.

'Happy birthday', he pumped the Lieutenant's hand. 'Twenty-one's the key to everything.'

'Glad to hear it. Message from General Roberts, incidentally. He expects to be landing in person around zero-eight-thirty. He says you're welcome to join him.'

*

After Willi Schultz and Hans Zimmermann had conferenced on the phone, Carlos Ortega had elected to stay the night with his new mates in the heavy-gun battery at Berneval. He'd shared a bottle of wine with two other officers last night, and now he was sitting in his borrowed greatcoat metres from the clifftop, nursing a cigarette. It was colder than he'd anticipated, with the wind funneling up the cliff face from the sea, and he was debating whether or not to return to his shared tent when he caught the distant blossom of a flare way out to sea. Half a minute later, maybe longer, came the faint crackle of machine-gun fire, carried on the wind, and then the deeper boom of a heavier weapon.

Ortega waited for a minute or so, just to make sure, then doused his cigarette, struggled to his feet and made his way back through the gap in the wire to report what he'd seen. Five kilometres west, from a concrete bunker overlooking the beach at Puys, Willi Schultz was witness to the same faraway spasm of violence. With access to the battalion radio, he tuned into one of the maritime channels and found himself in the middle of a firefight. It seemed that a convoy inward bound for Dieppe had bumped into a sizeable enemy force, dozens of landing craft with a convoy of warships. Their heading put them on course for a landing beneath the cliffs at Berneval, though sustained fire from German escort vessels was already thinning their ranks.

'They've arrived,' Schultz's gaze found the machine-gunner in charge of the key pillbox. 'Can you believe that?'

*

339

Hogan awoke to a chorus of snoring and the play of a flashlight on the wall of the wardroom. He checked his watch: 03.41. Knowing he'd never get back to sleep, he reached for his borrowed duffel coat and made his way carefully through the jigsaw of slumbering bodies. Up on deck, it was cold again and he fastened the wooden toggles as he made his way forward, peering into the darkness, hunting for some hint of the shapes he'd seen earlier on the Dieppe master map. NT, he thought. Nautical twilight, inseparable from proper dark.

Then came a sudden burst of light away to the left, and the crackle of gunfire. Nowhere on the masterplan had Hogan seen mention of an episode like this and he stood rooted to the deck as another star shell exploded and hung against this huge expanse of black. This was theatre, he thought, one of those fifth-act moments when the script does a sudden somersault and every conclusion you've so cleverly reached is turned on its head. Then came a movement at his elbow and he glanced sideways to find an officer with a pair of binoculars trained on the distant fireworks.

'Shit,' he grunted. 'Just what we don't need.'

*

Schultz was in his element. He'd been planning for this moment since the turn of the year. The debates he'd shared with Hans Zimmermann about the Brits trying to offer some kind of support to the beleaguered Soviets. The likelihood of armed cross-Channel raids to keep the Germans off-balance. The scouring of maps and troop dispositions before settling on Dieppe as the likeliest honeytrap. The careful nurturing of a backchannel to a trusted Resistance network. The stealthy refortification of a little seaside town already, thanks to nature, as secure as any castle. And finally this, the incontrovertible proof that the enemy had swallowed the bait entire and whole. The radio rarely lied, and neither did Schultz disbelieve the evidence of his own ears. E-boats were feasting among the landing craft. Already the Brits were bleeding.

Away to the east, at the gun emplacement at Berneval, men were running to their allotted stations. Gunners from the 571st had been rehearsing for the next few hours since early spring, and face after face told Ortega that the training hadn't been in vain.

'You think the E-boats will leave any scraps for us?' The battery commander was looking apprehensive. To be denied a turkey shoot by a bunch of pirates from the *Kriegsmarine*? Unthinkable.

'There'll be plenty on the table yet,' Ortega was rubbing his ruined face. 'And some left for dessert.'

Aboard HMS *Calpe*, commanders were doing their best to keep the schedule intact as all surprise was lost in the eruption of violence on one flank of the landings. Already, there were the first hints of a thin grey light in the east, and from the chill of the deck Hogan could just make out the humped shapes of infantrymen on the decks of neighbouring ships, patiently awaiting transfer to the landing craft. One by one, these little vessels began to fill, readying for the moment when the destroyer fleet opened fire and they headed for their target beaches.

Hogan borrowed a pair of binoculars and watched the men clambering patiently into their allotted landing craft. However hard he tried, he couldn't forget the sudden blossom of star shells and gunfire just an hour or so earlier. It had been Mountbatten himself who'd recommended a thorough reading of Sun Tzu's *The Art of War* in order to truly understand what had turned Special Ops into such a potent weapon, and Hogan had managed to lay hands on a copy. The emphasis on catching the enemy off-balance, on arriving unannounced, was there on every page. Stealth. Cunning. The lethal impact of the unexpected. Now this.

The bombardment from the fleet, as scheduled, opened at 05.10. *Calpe* herself was spared participation in case it interfered with communications, but Hogan still retreated back inside a companionway, his hands to his ears, already deafened by the blast from neighbouring vessels. The roar of the 4in. guns went on for the full ten minutes, then it was suddenly silent again, except for the answering bark of artillery away to the left.

'Berneval,' Boyle again, appearing from nowhere with a pair of binoculars to try and part the swirling curtains of smoke. 'Where the hell is 3 Commando?'

*

Carlos Ortega had the answer. In his borrowed greatcoat he'd found a perch with a machine-gun crew dug above the narrow ravine that zigzagged up from the beach at Berneval. Three of these men were true professionals. They'd served in that first push into Poland, they'd survived a winter on the Eastern front, and now they were going to teach the Tommy commandos a lesson they wouldn't, alas, live to remember.

The key was nerve. To wait. To preserve that key element of surprise. To hang on until the man leading the ascent was high enough to be exhausted, but too far down to waste a grenade. It was a fine judgement, much debated in messes across the Greater Reich, and Ortega had spent enough time in the company of these men to know that first declaration, that gorgeous initial pressure on the trigger, would be key to an encounter like this.

The spasm of violence would be brief. The fierce impact of a round from this range would knock a man into oblivion. Then a second of the Tommy commandos would tumble into the thin dawn light. Then a third. And afterwards, as long as you took care, you might choose to peer over the cliff edge and mark the bodies dimly spreadeagled on the tide-washed pebbles below. That's what bullets did to flesh and blood. That's what machine guns were for. High explosive, in whatever quantities, never lied.

The lead climber was an older man. Already, he looked exhausted. Did he have a wife, this guy? Kids? A mum, a dad, sepia photos in an album in some drawer or other? Had he led a blameless life? Or were there darker secrets behind that snarl on his face as his battledress snagged on yet another loop of barbed wire?

His hands were bleeding, Ortega could see the tears in the flesh. Then the climber dug his boots into the chalkface to steady himself and began to fumble for a grenade, and Ortega and the machine-gunner exchanged glances, and the machine-gunner raised an eyebrow, and Ortega nodded, and the machine gun chattered on its metal tripod, and suddenly there was nothing but emptiness and chalk dust and the tang of seaweed carried upwards on the wind.

*

Hogan was in the wardroom aboard HMS *Calpe*. On his hands and knees among a litter of half-tidied possessions, he was helping the Mess Steward, whose name was Joe, unpack the contents of several cardboard boxes. Inside, neatly stowed, were nests of bandages and dressings, as well as sundry bottles, mainly brown. Joe sifted quickly through the contents, asking Hogan to clear a space ready for when the first of the lightly wounded arrived alongside. Until this moment, Hogan had devoted little thought to what might happen to battle casualties, but watching Joe lay out his collection of forceps and scalpels, and give both kidney bowls a final wipe, it occurred to him that *Calpe* was about to become a hospital ship.

'This stuff is antiseptic?' Hogan was looking at one of the bottles.

'Yeah.'

'So what happens if you run out?'

Joe rocked back on his haunches and then nodded at the line of optics behind the bar.

'We start on the proper stuff,' he said. 'When God felt sorry for the wounded, he invented brandy.'

It was a nice line, and back on deck Hogan scribbled it down. The morning was windless, the water flat calm. The chalk cliffs rose sheer from the banks of mist along the shoreline, bone-white in the light of dawn but fringed across the top with patches of green. Ignore the roar of battle and the scurry of landing craft heading for yet another beach and a line of Hurricanes swooping low over a distant headland, and the scene could have belonged on a picture postcard, and Hogan tried to imagine a younger Annie Wrenne, here with her mother, looking forward to another day on the beach. Then, drifting towards them, came the acrid, chemical smell of smoke laid by a destroyer. It settled on the offshore fleet, a rolling blanket of grey, but the steady bark of artillery from the eastward flank of the landings never faltered, the falling shells throwing huge plumes of water skywards.

A stir of movement brought one of the officers from the bridge onto the deck. A muttered conversation despatched a seaman to organise a landing net for men to clamber aboard. When the officer paused to gaze briefly shorewards, Hogan asked him how it was going.

'There's a problem with Blue Beach,' he was frowning. 'Bad place to be.'

*

The tiny village of Puys lay a kilometre or so east of Dieppe's main beaches and Willi Schultz had devoted a lot of thought to choosing the best seat in the house. His new comrades-in-arms belonged to 12th Field Company. There were over a hundred of them, many from the Greater Reich, a gipsy band of stalwarts much to Schultz's taste. They were intrigued by his *Abwehr* connections, by his access to secrets none of them could possibly know, and the previous evening, gladdened by the possibility of impending action, half a dozen of them had spent an hour or so walking from strongpoint to strongpoint, trying to settle on the most promising view.

The beach itself, to Schultz, had always looked tiny, the grey pebbles banked by the spring tides. At the top of the beach lay a seawall, metres high, topped with dense thickets of barbed wire, and behind the seawall was a long, low building that had been converted into a casino for the summer crowd who vacationed in the villas above the beach. The casino commanded the entire length of the seawall, and it had been the work of the long winter months to fortify the building with sandbags, extra embrasures and secure storage for near-limitless ammunition.

The little apron of beach was the key to the position at Puys, but it was further defended by heavy mortars firing at carefully pre-set ranges from a field hundreds of metres inland, and from machine-gun crews operating from the safety of caves in the face of the cliff. The latter had been an early favourite with Schultz but the view down towards the beach was near-vertical, and it would be all too easy to get cut off should the Brits somehow manage to squeeze inland.

And so, in the end, Schultz settled for a small concrete bunker that had been installed in the garden of a brick-built villa at the end of the lane that led down to the beach. From here, he had a perfect view of the banks of pebbles as they rose towards the seawall. All but the last half-metre or so beneath the wall itself lay at the mercy of a well-handled machine gun, hence the new name for the beach – 12th Field Company called it the *Todeszone*. In English, the Death Zone.

There were four of them in the bunker. It was an undeniable squeeze, but they liked this gruff stranger from the world of intelligence and were happy to despatch the long night with ersatz coffee and thick sandwiches of gherkin and sausage. After the excitements of the small-hours firefight out to sea, there was no question that the English were on their way, but in what strength and to what exact purpose was still unresolved. Then came ten minutes of steady bombardment just after five in the morning, small-calibre guns that did little damage. Schultz and his new comrades crouched in the bunker, gazing seawards, trying to part the thin curtains of mist that hung in the stillness of the night air, and it was Schultz who first mistook the looming shapes for a bunch of E-boats that had protected the convoy.

'So how come that flag, comrade?' The machine-gunner was indicating a Union Jack on the lead boat.

By now, the naval guns had fallen silent and, as Schultz watched, a wave of tiny landing craft appeared from the mist, the busy chugger-chugger of their engines clearly audible. Behind them, some distance back, was a larger vessel. Through binoculars, Schultz took a closer look. In the first wave he counted nine landing craft and he could clearly make out the hunched bodies as they closed the shoreline and prepared to jump.

The machine-gunner, a Pomeranian with a half-Polish mother, had yet to open fire. In moments of high excitement, he had a habit of talking to himself, and now he was urging the little craft closer, the way you might retrieve a wayward puppy, and then suddenly the bunker became the echo chamber from hell as the gunner hosed bullets seaward and the man beside him fed the belt of gleaming rounds into the breech.

The smell of cordite, coupled with a raw excitement, took Schultz back to the days when he'd accompanied combat units spearing into the belly of France. At a hundred metres, he knew a machine-gun bullet could go through two men, and Schultz watched Tommies getting to their feet as the first landing craft grounded on the pebbles. The moment the bow door went down, these troops offered the perfect target, momentarily poised to jump ashore, and as the first rank fell Schultz became aware of the panic that swept through the men behind.

There was nowhere to hide, nowhere to go, except forward into the torrent of lead. Hedgehog figures, dwarfed by their packs, scrambled over the carpet of bodies on the ramp and in the shallows, only to fall as they made the beach. Some dug desperately into the grey pebbles, using their bare hands, a final convulsive twitch as another bullet killed them. Others started to clamber over the sides of the landing craft, dropping into deeper water. A handful drowned, face down in the surging tide, arms and legs thrashing hopelessly before all movement ceased. The handful left somehow made it to the beach, while the Pomeranian paused for breath before despatching them with a new belt of ammunition.

The minutes went by. More boats grounded. By now, to Schultz, the beach had become the kind of stage you might find in the smaller Parisian theatres, an intimate space where the devil was staging a grotesque entertainment scripted for blind courage and countless deaths. Little vignettes were everywhere. An officer briefly crouched over a radio set, sending God knows what message to God knows who before the machine gun tore him to pieces. A Tommy crawling towards the tideline on his belly, then scooping handfuls of seawater into his mouth. A matelot desperately trying to manoeuvre his landing craft out through the litter of floating bodies, only to be flung sideways by yet another burst from the Pomeranian.

By now, the snipers were at work from neighbouring strongpoints, looking for signs of life amid the carnage, finishing off the wounded. One Tommy had managed to produce a grenade. The sniper waited for him to pull the pin, then shot him through the head before he could raise his arm for the throw. The resulting grenade explosion killed two of his mates. This, Schultz knew, was the true beauty of warfare, violence neatly dispensed by men who knew their trade. Another sniper was concentrating on backpacks. Some of them, as everyone knew, contained bombs for the mortars, and after four duds, a bullet found the right pack. The bombs exploded, leaving a tangle of flesh and blood and a thin pink mist that drifted slowly seawards.

The killing went on. Gunners from 12th Field Company appeared on the clifftop, lobbing down stick grenades to finish off the little nests of wounded men, while snipers in the cliff caves watched for signs of movement among the bodies floating in the lap-lap of the brimming tide. Bombs from the heavy mortars were exploding on the beach, sending lethal shards of pebbles in every direction, and Schultz watched an officer trying to blast a hole through the barbed wire on top of the seawall before a bullet found the explosive and he was gone. To survive on a morning like this, Schultz thought, you had somehow to get off the beach. But thanks to 12th Field Company, that option no longer existed.

Slowly, minute by minute, the intensity of the battle for Puys began to slow. A handful of Tommies had found sanctuary in a recess beneath the seawall where two flights of steps descended to the pebbles. They crouched there, not daring to move, temporarily

·spared. Smoke hung in the air. Everything stank of cordite, the sourness laced with the tang of seaweed. The retreating tide was thick with bodies, the water scarlet where it washed onto the pebbles, and further up the beach a bare-chested Tommy lay face down in the sunshine, appearing to be asleep. Below the waist, he'd simply ceased to exist.

The firing finally stopped. One of the surviving Tommies beneath the seawall produced a white handkerchief and got slowly to his feet. A German officer accepted his surrender and lingered for a few words before turning to share the news with his men.

'Not Tommies at all,' he shouted. 'Canadians.'

The first casualties were arriving alongside HMS *Calpe* and Hogan was on deck to do what he could. In the skies above, a screen of Spitfires had appeared to keep marauding German bombers at a safe height and Hogan bent over the rail, watching two stretchers being lifted aboard before the other men, lightly wounded, were helped up the scrambling nets.

The stretcher cases were manhandled to a doctor waiting in a smallish room two decks below. Hogan had lent a hand with the heavier of the two stretchers and now, at the doctor's insistence, he stayed beside the operating table while two orderlies scissored the injured man's battledress trouser leg, exposing a hideous wound. Beneath the knee, the leg was barely attached at all, and while the doctor gave him an injection, Hogan did his best to comfort the man.

His face was a mask, his eyes fixed on some point in the middle distance. He seemed oblivious of his surroundings, not even in pain, and his lips were moving in some half-remembered account of what he'd just been through. Bending over him,

Hogan caught the odd word – 'tanks', 'barge', 'mortars' – and then the man's eyes were closing, and his breathing seemed to ease, and Hogan watched his chest rise one final time before he stopped breathing completely.

'Gone,' the doctor was already gesturing towards the corridor where the other stretcher case was waiting. 'Get the next one in.'

The Mess Steward had appeared at the door, beckoning Hogan into the companionway outside. He had more casualties to deal with, most of them Canadian, and thought that a familiar accent might brighten their morning. Hogan followed him into the wardroom, numbed by what he'd just seen, wondering what possible reassurance he could offer to men exposed to this kind of violence. His faith didn't help, and neither did his recent conversations with Annie, but he knew that somehow he had to be of service. In the wardroom, he found at least a dozen men trying to struggle out of their soaking battledress. A couple were British marines from 3 Commando but neither of them matched the face in the photo from Achnacarry. The rest were Canadian Royals, returned semi-intact from Blue Beach at Puys. Some of them were trembling with cold, or maybe shock, and all of them had that same glassy-eyed stare that spoke of an encounter none of them had expected.

'They got us all,' one of them muttered. 'Every goddam man standing. We never had a chance.'

This made little sense but Hogan knew he was in the presence of men who would probably take years to recover, not from the flesh-wounds the Mess Steward was busily attending to, but from the sights and sounds of whatever had happened on the beach. At the Mess Steward's suggestion, Hogan fetched a bottle of brandy from behind the bar and circulated with a handful of teacups. By now, most of the men were naked, hand after hand shoved out for one of the cups, and in years to come, Hogan knew that this image – the cocktail party from hell – would never leave him.

'Larry Elder?' he asked one of the Royals. 'Frank O'Donovan?'

'Larry I last saw on the beach. The Lt-Colonel…?' the man shrugged. 'Fuck knows.'

A little later, the Royals comforted with towels and more brandy, Hogan climbed the three sets of ladders to the little office beneath the bridge from where 'Ham' Roberts was trying to direct the battle. The last half-hour had given Hogan a taste of the scale of the developing tragedy, all of it predicted by O'Donovan, and now he was becoming conscious of his own role in whatever might follow. Somehow, from the chaos of the operation, there had to emerge a coherent account, and if he could contribute a handful of small pieces to that jigsaw then so much the better.

The door of the office was open, and to Hogan's surprise the General appeared unflustered. He was sitting at his tiny desk, an ear cocked to the crackle and fizz of the voices on the radio, chain-smoking cigarettes and nursing a large mug of tea. A tally of transcribed messages, most of them incoherent, lay on his lap and he was going through them one by one, dismissing the more pessimistic as probably the work of the Germans. Soon, he told Hogan, he might have to commit his floating reserve, a body of troops from the Fusiliers Mont-Royal, to stiffen the thrust across the beaches, but in the meantime – with some regret – he guessed that life was too hectic to risk a personal trip ashore.

'Shame,' he gestured down at the messages. 'I was kinda looking forward to it.'

*

At Puys, the fighting was over. The 12th Field Company had emerged with some caution from their strongpoints and Schultz stood behind the seawall, his face tilted to the sunshine. The sky was still full of aircraft, desperately tangled in dogfight after dogfight, and the heavy guns over at Berneval were still shelling the offshore fleet, but on this one beach, the battle had come to an end.

One of the unit's officers had found a camera and was stamping across the pebbles, photographing body after body. The handful of Canadian prisoners who'd survived the landing had already been put to work pulling the bodies of their fallen comrades out of the water and carrying them up the beach. From the clifftops, machine guns and heavier cannon were still pumping out fire but Puys itself – after all the fury and carnage – was strangely quiet. Schultz remembered something similar from a recent conversation with Carlos Ortega. After nearly dying in Madrid, the Spaniard had said, there came inexplicable pockets of sudden peace, just another of the many ways that war could take you by surprise.

*

But the war hadn't finished with HMS *Calpe*. Hogan was back in the chaos of the wardroom, helping the Mess Steward deal with yet more casualties. Most of them were suffering from shrapnel wounds, and Joe was doing his rounds with an armful of bandages and yet another bottle of brandy. The bandages were thick pads, about four inches square, with stickers at each corner, and it was Hogan's job to pour neat brandy on wound after wound before Joe secured the bandage. The injured troops, horrified by the waste of brandy, accused Hogan of being a teetotaller, an accusation that had once been true, but the bulk of the men seemed resigned to whatever fate would bring them next.

The fleet was still under attack, especially from the air, and from time to time a bomb would fall close by, and the ship would heel and creak and there'd come the shatter of breaking crockery as plates and cups, unsecured, fell to the deck. The knowledge that these men were far from safe was written on every face, and Hogan began to wonder when General Roberts might declare the whole adventure over. A carefully timetabled evacuation had always been part of the *Jubilee* master plan, and Hogan happened to know that the trigger codeword was 'Vanquish'. In the light of events, he thought, the word was far too close to the truth.

Minutes later, back in the open air, Hogan was astonished to find every inch of the upper deck occupied by yet more wounded. A mess orderly was circulating with packets of cigarettes the men called Sweet Caps, and hands reached uncertainly upwards as he made his way through the tangle of bodies.

Some of these men, Hogan realised, would never make it down to the wardroom, even if there was enough room left to accommodate them. Their eyes blazed in the grey pallor of their faces. They'd lost all focus and when they tried to move, their limbs had the slow imprecision of men on the point of drowning. Beside one, Hogan crouched to try and offer just a moment of comfort.

The man was wearing the badge of the Calvary Tank Regiment. His voice was barely a murmur but there was something in his face that told Hogan he had something important to impart.

'*Regiment,*' he whispered.

'*Regiment?*'

'The Colonel's tank. Colonel Andrews.' The man was struggling to sit up. 'Second off the ramp.'

'This is the landing? On the beach?'

'Sure,' the faintest nod.

'And?'

The man shook his head, exhausted by the effort of trying to pursue the story to its end. Then his hand fluttered in the sunshine, a kind of palsy, and Hogan eased himself a little closer, his ear to the tankie's mouth.

'So what happened?'

'Back. Shifting back. Into deep water. The Colonel never knew. The Colonel gone. All of them gone.' He collapsed slowly backwards. 'Inside the tank. Off the ramp. Way, way down. Gone.'

'The Germans did that?'

'No, buddy,' his eyes closed. 'We did.'

Hogan rocked back on his heels, helpless, appalled. Yet more wounded were being hoisted aboard, more wrecked bodies, more scalding memories. A handful were tankies. Most were plain infantry. But all of them had fallen into that yawning gap between expectation and the nightmare from which they'd just returned. This, Hogan realised, was the end of the journey many of them had started on the Kawartha Lakes, that long-ago Canadian afternoon they'd stormed ashore in a make-believe landing. At the time it had all seemed so easy, so risk-free, a mere game. Now this.

Hogan blinked, shaking his head, suddenly aware of the drone of a two-engine Dornier bomber, flying much lower than usual. Then came the yappy bark of countless ack-ack guns from neighbouring ships, followed by a heavier explosion, and Hogan looked up to watch a destroyer maybe four hundred yards away take a direct hit.

Her name, according to a matelot, was HMS *Berkeley*. She was listing to port, and looked oddly out of place, but already a posse of other vessels were hurrying to rescue survivors. Hogan watched men throwing themselves into the sea to be picked up minutes later. Then came the slower transfer of the wounded before the little fleet backed away, leaving the stricken destroyer wallowing in the water. Minutes passed, then, for the first time, Hogan felt the blast of the forward guns as *Calpe* sent her sister ship to the bottom. More casualties, thought Hogan. More Sweet Caps. More brandy. More dying bodies jigsawed on the warming deck.

*

The order to withdraw finally came at 11.00. Landing craft crammed with wounded men were still heading away from the beaches, harried by fire from the clifftops, and from positions along the promenade. By now, Ortega and Schultz had left their respective posts and reunited behind the shelter of the seawall overlooking one of the main Dieppe beaches. Just a handful of tanks had made it into the town itself while the rest had either been destroyed on the beach or had dug themselves into the unforgiving pebbles. That the Brits were on their way was incontestable. Everywhere, dozens of boats had turned tail and were heading for the open sea.

Schultz spotted the bow wave of an approaching destroyer. Through his binoculars, he identified it as HMS *Calpe*. They've come for a final check, he thought, a final glimpse of a battlefield that has brought them nothing but shame. Aware of the forward guns trained on one of the breakwaters at the mouth of the port, he heard the blast of the Brits loosing a final salvo before the destroyer made smoke and disappeared with the remains of the fleet towards the open sea. With late morning, as usual, came the beginnings of an onshore breeze and Schultz watched the smoke rolling towards him before his binoculars drifted lower, onto the wreckage of burned-out tanks, abandoned landing craft, and hundreds of bodies sprawled on the grey pebbles.

As the smoke engulfed the two men, Schultz gestured towards the beach, and the vanished raiding force.

'*Auf Nimmerwiedersehen*,' he grunted. Good riddance.

23

Most of the battered invasion fleet returned to Newhaven. HMS *Calpe*, in convoy with another destroyer, sailed north-west to Portsmouth. By the time the two ships slipped in through the harbour narrows, it was pitch dark. *Calpe* berthed a bare twenty-four hours after her departure from this same quayside. Waiting orderlies boarded the ship to pick up stretchers and accompany the walking wounded to waiting nurses. A long line of ambulances inched forward, two of the biggest reserved for the dead. Full of bodies, they drove slowly away while officers carrying tiny flashlights established order and summoned reinforcements. Two ambulances weren't enough. *Calpe* had ferried fifty dead and seven hundred wounded across the Channel. That was bad enough, but the Canadians had left more than half their embarked force in Dieppe.

Stumbling off the ship, Hogan was beginning to understand what had happened during that brief, bloody encounter with mainland France. It would be days before anyone in real authority was prepared to acknowledge the sheer scale of the losses, but he'd seen enough to recognise that something avoidably tragic had taken place. At the foot of the gangplank, he came face-to-face with the young Lieutenant who'd looked after him. Even now, after everything that had happened, it was still Boyle's twenty-first birthday. Hogan gripped his hand, then turned away. The last time he'd tasted the saltiness of tears in the back of his throat, he'd been a child.

Boyle indicated a nearby car. Rooms, he muttered, had been reserved at a Southsea hotel. Hogan sat in the back, wedged between two others, as they drove out of the dockyard and through the darkened streets. No one spoke.

Not a light showed from the looming bulk of the Queen's Hotel. Getting out of the car, Hogan could smell the sea in the rising wind. The reception area was beginning to fill with arrivals from Operation *Jubilee* but heads were down and no one made any attempt at conversation. All his life, Hogan had done his best to avoid organised sport but this felt like a team returning to the changing room, shamed by the heaviness of an unexpected defeat. He collected an envelope with his name on and trudged up the staircase to the first floor.

The room, when he stepped in, was pitch black. He fumbled for the light switch on the wall, knowing the blackout curtains were tight shut, but when he finally found the switch, nothing happened. He inched into the room, his hands extended, a blind man determined to turn his back on a day he badly needed to put behind him, and finally bumped into what had to be a bed. Not bothering to undress completely, he shed his service blouse and his serge trousers, and stooped to untie his boots before sliding under the covers. Flat on his back, his eyes began to close, then he felt a movement beside him. For a moment, he froze. Was this some ghost he'd shipped back from northern France? Would Dieppe never leave him alone? Then he became aware of naked flesh, and a slim hand finding his, and warm breath inches from his ear.

'You're freezing, Mr H.' It was Annie. 'Come here.'

By the time Hogan awoke next morning she'd gone, leaving no trace except a note telling him they'd hopefully be able to meet later back in town. 'Later' meant nothing. 'Later' belonged to a world that had gone. Hogan splashed cold water on his face and then opened the curtains, standing at the window and gazing out across a vast expanse of common land towards the seafront. Beyond lay the Solent and the Isle of Wight, gateway to the Channel crossing, and Hogan closed his eyes before turning away, determined not to cede an inch to those terrible memories.

Downstairs, in the big restaurant, the management had done its best to soften their guests' landfall with a proper breakfast, but diners had no taste for anything but their own company. Men sat alone at individual tables, picking at their powdered eggs. Conversation might happen later, but not yet.

After a while, Boyle appeared with an armful of newspapers, moving gamely from table to table. The headline in the *Daily Mirror* read BIG HUN LOSSES IN 9-HR DIEPPE BATTLE, while the *Toronto Star* declared that CANADIANS HELP SMASH NAZI OPPOSITION. Hogan read the copy beneath the headlines, angered by the lies. This wasn't misplaced optimism, he thought, or even sloppiness, but probably the start of something a great deal more sinister. Every conversation he'd shared aboard *Calpe*, every survivor from the bloodbath ashore, had confirmed that the Germans had been impregnable, dug in, impossible to get at. The enemy had been faceless, invisible, killing whomever they chose at a speed which had confounded every calculation. Victory, in short, had been cheap and easy, yet already an entire nation was waking up to a different story. Hogan caught the eye of a naval officer at a nearby table. He, too, had been reading the *Mirror*. He shook his head in disbelief and then shrugged, a gesture – Hogan thought – of despair.

After breakfast, all the correspondents and cameramen were gathered in a downstairs lounge and warned not to discuss what had happened over the last twenty-four hours. Copy submitted to respective editors was to be strictly limited to what the suited representative from Combined Ops called 'the facts of the matter'. That a giant taskforce had crossed the Channel to raid an important French harbour. That landings had taken place on countless beaches. That the operation had called for split-second co-ordination, and outstanding courage. That 4 Commando, led by Lord Lovat, had stormed an entire German battery and spiked their guns, saving untold lives. The latter episode Hogan knew to be true but the rest of it, including a withdrawal in good order, was fanciful. The tally of lives needlessly lost was enormous but the British public, it seemed, should be denied a detail like this. Dunkirk all over again, Hogan thought grimly, except far, far worse because a simple cancellation would have spared so many men.

Another car took Hogan back to London and dropped him at the *Express* building. He mounted the stairs, still in his battledress, unable to shake off a sense of overpowering weariness. His first real taste of war, of what it could do to a man's view of himself, had aged him in ways he'd never anticipated and the moment he stepped into the big newsroom he knew that coming back to work so soon had been a mistake.

Heads lifted around the table. Sub-editors he knew well studied him with that kind of mute curiosity that suggested he might have arrived from outer space. One of them got to his feet and extended a hand but it was a gesture of sympathy, not congratulation, because these men were too cynical, and too experienced, to be taken in. Rumours were already seeping out of Newhaven pubs after the return of the taskforce and Fleet Street obviously suspected that something had gone terribly wrong, but looking round at the faces in the newsroom Hogan knew he couldn't cope with the barrage of inevitable questions. And so, with a curt nod, he turned on his heel and fled.

Back at the flat in Gower Street, because he had no choice, Hogan surrendered to something that felt close to paralysis. He couldn't think properly. He couldn't make the simplest decisions. The challenge of running a bath, of sorting out the taps, of trying to find a towel, was totally beyond him. And so, still fully clothed, he climbed beneath the covers and tried to trick himself to sleep.

Sheep by their thousands. A favourite sunset. The sermon he'd heard only days ago in the Baptist church. But none of it worked and he lay there all day, fending off countless images as his racing brain fought and refought the hours he'd spent off the beaches. He hadn't, of course, been exposed to the pitiless violence at the sharpest end and as the day crawled by it slowly dawned on him that what he was really feeling was guilt. Guilt that he hadn't ridden shorewards in the landing craft. Guilt that he hadn't been properly shot at. Guilt that he'd survived.

Annie, arriving late in the afternoon, had a word for it.

'You're in shock, Mr H. And I'm afraid getting better might take a while.'

Really? Hogan, at last, wanted to talk about it, wanted to shift this terrible weight in his gut, wanted to tell her what had really happened.

'We're quite pleased on the whole,' she said brightly. 'It could have been much worse.'

'We?'

'Combined Ops. The usual suspects. Everyone's staying mum, of course, but we got there and we got back, and all told, that's a pretty good show.'

'And you really believe that?' Hogan was staring at her.

'Of course I don't.' At last she settled on the side of the bed. 'And you, Mr H, are going to tell me why.'

They talked long into the night. Hogan had always had a gift for bringing a scene to life, one of the many reasons he'd become a journalist, and a little of that talent began to return, fighting its way up through his subconscious, offering a glimpse of a man's face here, a shred of conversation there, trying all the time to picture wave after wave of carefully applied violence that had overwhelmed them all. Not because war should be a surprise, but because absolutely nothing had gone to plan.

'It never does,' Annie was picking at a loose thread of cotton on the hem of the sheet. 'And men never understand why.'

*

On the beaches in Dieppe, Canadian prisoners were pressed into service to collect the bodies of their fallen countrymen, four men per stretcher, and great care was taken in carrying the parcels of flesh and bone up the unforgiving pebbles to the promenade. There, they were loaded onto wooden carts the fishermen used to take their catch to market, and local *Dieppois*, women especially, stood at the wayside crossing themselves as the carts rumbled past.

One or two of the women tossed flowers onto the sodden uniforms, and outside a café a little girl dashed into the road to leave her favourite rag doll in the pale hands of a dead Canadian. This earned her a pat and a ten Reichsmark note from Carlos Ortega, who fell into step beside the Canadians and accompanied the cortège to the mass grave where hundreds of other bodies already lay beneath the thin August drizzle.

Only yesterday, to his quiet delight, Ortega's new woman had been officially notified of the death of her husband in a factory accident in Essen, and in a week or two, once she'd got over the worst of her grief, he'd be offering to take the dead man's place. Dieppe, in ways he'd never expected, had seeped into his bones and when he'd recently confessed to Schultz that he could spend the rest of his days here, he'd meant it.

*

Two days later, Annie returned to the Gower Street flat with the news that *Jubilee* force commanders and various members of their staff had got together to try and work out what had really happened at Dieppe.

'I get the feeling they want to end up with a version they'll be happy with,' she said. 'And that might be easier than you'd think because most of the people who'd really know turn out to be dead.'

It was true. But as the casualty figures mounted, beach by beach, it began to dawn on the reading public, especially in Canada, that the cream of their brave little army would never be coming home. By now, a little steadier, Hogan was working on an account of his own tiny corner of Operation *Jubilee*, writing longhand on a foolscap notepad Annie had brought home from Richmond Terrace. The challenge was to capture the moment that *Jubilee* had bumped into a passing German convoy and squandered the element of surprise, to match expectations against the grim chaos that had enveloped 'Ham' Roberts' little command cell under the bridge of HMS *Calpe*, to understand how quickly a disaster on this scale can unfold, loading every corner of the headquarters destroyer with bodies, either badly wounded or dead.

'There was a Mess Steward called Joe,' Hogan was staring at the window. 'That man worked miracles.'

The following day, Annie brought more news from Richmond Terrace. Mountbatten, she said, had cabled a preliminary report of the raid to Churchill, who was in Cairo, still recovering from his visit to Moscow. It seemed that the Prime Minister had read between the lines of the report and decided that *Jubilee* should take the prudent course and retire behind the cover of smoke.

'He cabled back a couple of hours ago,' she said. 'The phrase we use from now on is "reconnaissance in force". One gathers we were there not to win but to do better next time.'

Hogan was busy revising his copy. He looked up.

'Neat,' he grunted. 'And complete bullshit.'

*

Major Wilhelm Schultz was back in Paris by now. Zimmermann, delighted by the scale of the victory at Dieppe, had summoned Schultz to *Abwehr* headquarters to plot ways to further humiliate the British. The real blame, he pointed out, lay not with the Canadians who'd done the dying, but with the planners at Combined Operations who'd conceived the operation in the first place. The more bitter the taste that Dieppe left in Canadian mouths, the looser the ties that would bind the alliance, and so Schultz set out to lay hands on the best of the photos available from the carnage.

Finally, from a vast selection, he chose just twenty-nine and had them pasted into a four-page leaflet designed to look like an album of photos you might bring back from the holiday of your dreams. The black and white images were overwhelmingly graphic, an unsparing collage of dead bodies sprawled on the pebbles, of more bodies floating in the shallows, of ruined tanks, of abandoned landing craft, and finally of shocked Canadian soldiers, their hands in the air, pleading for their lives.

The leaflets were mass-printed on a press belonging to a major Parisian newspaper and shipped to an airfield in Normandy. Under cover of darkness, a Dornier bomber crossed the

Channel and thousands of the leaflets fluttered onto Canadian encampments inland from the coast. The authorities did their best to collect and suppress this evidence of what had really happened at Dieppe, but word was already out in the pubs and the market squares of Sussex and Kent and the images from the beaches spoke louder than any government minister.

Schultz took one of the leaflets back to Odile. She thumbed through it, listening to Schultz's account of the Canadian invaders cut down on the pebbles at Puys, her eyebrows raised at the sight of so many bodies at the foot of the seawall.

'That took minutes,' Schultz was peering over her shoulder. 'They queued up to be shot.'

'It looks nice,' Odile's attention had been caught by another image, showing a line of villas in the background. 'I know it's not Venice but are we still planning a visit? After all this?'

'Of course. We've given the mayor ten million francs to put the place back together again. It's a little *douceur*. Late September might be best.'

*

Hogan was back at work by the start of the following week. By now, thanks to Annie, he knew that a long list of names was under preparation at Richmond Terrace for the award of medals for outstanding gallantry. They were to include more than sixty Military Crosses, and Military Medals, twelve DSOs, and probably two Victoria Crosses. While Hogan had no doubts that the medals had been hard-earned, he also suspected they were part of the bid to recast defeat as a kind of victory. It was the Dunkirk story all over again, he thought. Allied daring. Allied fortitude. The enemy left in charge... but only for a while.

By now, Hogan's own account – heavily edited – had been published. He'd paid careful tribute to the efforts and courage of the troops who'd hit the beaches, especially his own countrymen, but nothing in his account that even hinted at the real picture had survived the official censor. He knew from a long conversation with Betty Bower that The Beaver was raging about the waste of Canadian blood, but it seemed that even the country's most powerful press baron was helpless in the face of a government determined to rewrite the story of an operation that had gone so badly wrong. Soon, went the whisper, Allied troops would be landing in North Africa. After that, in God's good time, we and the Americans would find somewhere suitable to mount a proper cross-Channel invasion, for which Dieppe would doubtless serve as an invaluable dress rehearsal.

Dress rehearsal? On a transatlantic telephone line, Hogan shared the thought with a reporter on his old paper, the Toronto *Globe and Mail*. The reporter had been assigned to talk to as many Canadian officers as possible. These phone conversations were off the record, and some had been extremely difficult, but it was impossible not to question the official line.

'Nothing justifies that kind of slaughter,' the reporter said. 'You arrive with more than six thousand perfectly fit men? More than half of them never come home? And all this in a matter of hours? These guys, the ones I talk to, are bitter as hell. They've had it with the Brits. They were promised a walk in the park and the way it turned out none of them will ever be the same again. We're taking a stand here, buddy, because someone has to. Recklessly conceived, poorly planned and wholly avoidable. How's that for a headline?'

*

That same afternoon, Moncrieff invited Hogan to dinner at the Ritz. The call came out of the blue, finding Hogan at his desk. Moncrieff enquired first about his health, which under the circumstances made a great deal of sense.

'I survived in one piece,' Hogan said drily. 'If that's what you're asking.'

'No flesh-wounds?'

'None that I've discovered.'

'And upstairs?' Hogan could imagine Moncrieff tapping his head. 'I understand the going got rough.'

'Upstairs isn't so pretty.'

'Sleeping OK?

'No.'

Moncrieff said he sympathised. He'd been a Royal Marine himself, knew what combat could take out of a man.

'I wasn't fighting,' Hogan pointed out. 'I was watching.'

'Watching's probably worse. Fighting tends to swallow you whole. You never get a moment to yourself. Think too hard and you end up dead. Seven o'clock OK? Main restaurant? Early doors tonight.'

The line went dead and Hogan was left holding the phone.

The Ritz, when he stepped in through the door, seemed full of Americans, mainly men. Most of them were in uniform, newly arrived from the look of their suntans, and they crowded around the bigger of the bars, loudly demanding a certain brand of Kentucky bourbon.

'A taste of our collective future, George,' Moncrieff was watching them from his table in the corner of the restaurant, 'This is Mr Liddell. Be nice to him because he's my boss.'

Liddell was the other figure at the table, a little older, a little more rumpled. His hair was beginning to thin and his only concession to formality was a battered tweed jacket leather-patched at the elbows, and a Garrick Club tie with a hint of soup stain halfway down. The slow smile lent him a kindliness that Hogan didn't entirely trust.

'Call me Guy.' He got to his feet and extended a soft hand. 'It's good of you to join us at such short notice.'

Hogan nodded, said nothing. These were the people who'd enlisted Annie Wrenne in Madrid, who'd doubtless despatched her to Gibraltar, and who'd afterwards retained her services to give themselves a peek inside Combined Ops. Worse still, barely weeks ago, these were the people who were threatening to have him strung up. Now, Moncrieff was thrusting a menu at him and recommending the *blanquette de veau*.

Liddell wanted to know about *Jubilee*. All too sadly, he said, excitements like these had passed him by, and now, to be frank, he was too old to be even considered for active service.

'You should count yourself lucky.' Hogan had yet to bother with the menu. 'The thing was a mess from start to finish.'

'And whose fault might that be?'

The question, so blunt, caught Hogan by surprise. Is that why he was here? To stick the knife in Mountbatten and give these spooks some return for their hospitality?

'I'm not sure fault's entirely the right word,' he said carefully. 'Because I'm not sure it takes us anywhere worthwhile. You're looking at a series of events. All it needs is for people who should know better to take their eye off the ball.'

'Not his Lordship?'

'Not at all. As far as I can judge, Mountbatten stepped into a void of someone else's making. Ambition isn't a capital offence, even in this country, especially with his connections. You won't find a Canadian with a good word to say about him, probably not for years to come, possibly not ever, but you don't string a man up for vanity, or even incompetence.'

'So he shouldn't worry us? Mountbatten?'

'The freedoms he grabbed should worry you. The sheer number of men he sent to the butcher's block should worry you. If you were a republican, I dare say his very existence should worry you. But laying a disaster of this magnitude solely at his door...' Hogan shook his head. 'Unfair. Mountbatten was out of control. That should never have happened.'

'So where might one be looking? Any ideas?'

'Churchill,' Hogan said at once. 'Montgomery, too. They went missing in action. When Canada needed them, they were nowhere to be seen. *Jubilee* was a gamble from start to finish. Had it come off, the glory would have gone to Mountbatten, no question. He knew that. That was the wager he made. But Churchill and Montgomery would have been at the same campfire, warming their hands. That won't happen, not now, not after last week.'

'Defeat is an orphan,' Moncrieff said quietly. 'No one wants anything to do with it.'

'Exactly. And looking back, defeat was the only possible outcome.'

The two men exchanged glances, and watching Moncrieff permit himself the ghost of a smile, Hogan had the feeling he'd passed some kind of test. He was here, he decided, to perform for the benefit of Moncrieff's boss. The menu, still untouched, lay at his elbow and the waiter was casting a look in their direction.

'One favour,' Hogan said. 'Just one.'

'Of course,' Liddell again.

'What do you want from me? Why am I here?'

Another exchange of glances, more troubled this time. At length, Liddell fingered his tie before reaching for a bread roll.

'It won't come as any surprise, George, to learn that we might have a serious problem with some of your countrymen. Our little outfit deals with the threats from within. It falls to us to take care of any trouble and we hear murmurings from behind the arras that all might not be well.' He offered a grave nod, and then began to nibble at his roll while Moncrieff took up the running.

'Your people are very angry, George,' he said.

'People?'

'Fellow Canadians. Don't get me wrong, *Jubilee* was a débacle, a total Horlicks. We're not blaming them in the least for having opinions on the subject but there's a line beyond anger that we don't want anyone to cross, and there are indications that certain individuals may be prepared to take the law into their own hands.'

'By doing what?'

'By concocting some crazy plot to – as they see it – apply due process.'

'To whom?'

'Mountbatten.'

'How?'

'By killing him.'

The suggestion hung briefly between them. Hogan was in deep water again, not believing this charade for a moment, but then he gave the proposition some thought.

'I guess it's possible,' he admitted. 'But what does any of that have to do with me?'

'We're putting together a taskforce and we need someone, to be blunt, with the inside track when it comes to dealing with Canadians.'

'Because I am one?'

'Because you know how these people think. What matters to them. What might drive them to do something very foolish.'

'Like kill Mountbatten?'

'Indeed. We will, of course, make you very welcome inside our little band of brothers. In fact, we may even have a permanent post in mind.'

Yippee, Hogan thought. Very carefully, he folded his napkin, put the menu to one side and stood up. The clincher was the word 'people'. *What matters to them. What might drive them to do something very foolish.*

He stood behind his chair, aware of the two faces peering up at him. Liddell's expression was unreadable but there was just a hint of admiration in the way Moncrieff's gaze drifted to the abandoned menu.

'You have something to get off your chest, George?' he murmured.

'I do, yes. First it turns out my girlfriend has been working for you all along. Did you ask her to seduce me? Did you ask her to spy on me? I have no idea. Next, you lock me up and make a plausible case for sending me to the gallows before letting me go. Did you need to check up on Annie Wrenne? Were you trying to gauge whether she was worth keeping on in that flat of yours? Again, I don't know. But now is very different. Now is broad daylight. Why? Because at last you've paid me the compliment of making a direct offer. You'd rather like me to pass judgement on my fellow Canadians. Not because they've done anything wrong, but because you've killed hundreds of them, probably thousands of them, to no good purpose. I'd like to pretend I'm flattered. I'd like to say thank you.' Hogan offered a cold smile. 'But that, gentlemen, would be two more lies.'

Annie was waiting in the flat when Hogan finally made it home. He'd stopped at the Star and Garter en route, downing two large gins, curious about the way it scorched down his gullet and into his belly. Now, a little lightheaded, he settled in the armchair beside the window, wondering vaguely about the pile of paperwork on the low table Annie usually reserved for a bowl of fruit lifted from Richmond Terrace.

'You've turned me into a proper thief,' she nodded at the paperwork. 'I stole this lot from our Registry. Tomorrow I'll have to smuggle them back in, but you've got all night to make whatever notes you need.'

'And why should I make notes?'

'Because I believe you, Mr H. Because I know how this disaster came about, and because now's the time that someone told the whole story.'

'And that someone is me?'

'Correct. I can give you the bones. The flesh is in those documents. We have a deal?'

Hogan shook his head, taking his time, trying to puzzle out what he really wanted to say.

'They'll kill you,' he muttered at last. 'They'll make you complicit. They'll find out you stole the documents and arrest you and put you in a court of law. They'll charge you with treason and string you up.'

'Who will?'

'My friends from the Ritz.'

'The *Ritz*? What on earth were you doing there?'

Hogan contemplated the possibility of an answer but decided against it. The weariness and the sense of swimming hopelessly against tides he didn't understand had returned. Betty Bower had told him The Beaver wanted a word. As vindictive as ever, he was demanding a full exposé of Mountbatten. MI5 wanted him to spy on his fellow Canadians, simply because he shared the same accent, the same birthright. And now the woman he loved, herself corrupted by MI5, wanted to turn him into the scourge of a government he knew would stop at nothing to get their way. The curl of half-chewed liver on O'Donovan's plate, he thought. And a litter of dead bodies in the thin *Dieppois* sunshine.

'No,' he said.

'No what?'

'No, thank you.'

'You don't want even a look through?' She nodded at the pile of documents.

'No.'

'Why on earth not?' She seemed astonished. 'But you *care*, Mr H. That's why that God of yours put you on earth with us mere mortals. You even care enough to turn someone as feeble as me into a believer. We *have* to do this thing.'

'Why?'

'Because we're lesser people if we don't.'

Lesser people. Hogan closed his eyes. Something had been preying on his mind, demanding an answer, and only now did he realise what it was.

'That friend of yours,' he said. 'Your commando lover.'

'Giles?'

'Yes. What happened to him?'

'He was killed on the cliffs at Berneval, leading the climb.'

'You know that for certain?'

'That was his assigned role. I've seen a photo of him. As has half the nation.'

'He's on that leaflet the Germans dropped?'

'He is. Third page, halfway down. He was flat on his back and someone had stolen most of his clothes. You could see the scar he carried from the Spanish Civil War but he looked very dead.'

'Did that upset you?'

'Not in the least.'

'And me? Saying no?' Hogan gestured vaguely at the paperwork on the low table. 'Does that upset you?'

Annie was gazing at him. After a moment or two she slipped off the sofa and knelt before him on the carpet.

'You've been drinking,' she said at last. 'I can smell it.'

'Gin,' he said.

'You lie.'

'I don't. That's my problem. I never lie. I don't know how to. That's why...' He looked around him, at the worn MI5 furniture, at the tatty second-hand rugs, at the huge typewriter Annie had borrowed on his behalf, at her ancient suitcase, lying open beside the pile of documents, then he shrugged. 'Lies are beyond me, always have been. Maybe I should try harder. Or maybe there's another way.'

'Like?'

'Us being just us,' he was frowning now, trying to concentrate, trying – as ever – to get the right words in the right order. 'So what do you think?' He reached for her. 'Agnès?'

AFTERWARDS

Four years later, the war won, the coldest winter in living memory descended on Western Europe and gripped Britain by the throat. Nationwide, heavy snow fell for day after day. Pipes froze, a handful of skaters used canals in London to get to work, while a bitter, scouring wind drove everyone else indoors.

For his part, Hogan simply hung more and more layers of clothing on his lanky frame, invested in a thicker coat from the Salvation Army stores and walked the three miles from the family home in Kensal Rise to Paddington Station. A new outpost of the Baptist church was about to open in Somerset, and he was to be the first of the guest preachers.

The train was unheated and he joined it late, lucky enough to find a seat in a carriage near the engine. He settled down, gathering his coat around him, and reopened the book Annie had just given him for Christmas. He'd never read Flaubert, barely heard of him, but he'd been happy to believe his wife when she'd told him that *Madame Bovary* had seen her through a difficult adolescence, and now, seven chapters in, he thought he could see why. The recklessness of the woman. Her wild sense of abandon. And most revelatory of all, the many ways she knew how to manipulate men.

The train left on time. It began to snow again, yet another layer on the deadness of the landscape, clouds of white flakes disturbed by the busy passage of the engine, and Hogan lifted his head from the book, gazing out at the thinning suburbs, wondering what text he'd explore for his sermon. In ways that still surprised him, the Bible had become a best friend, a limitless source of challenge and reward, offering a solace and a consolation he'd once thought beyond his reach.

At Reading, yet more passengers were standing in the snow at the end of the platform. A handful got off the train, including a couple from Hogan's compartment, and he was watching them wade gingerly through the crusting ice when he saw a man in a wheelchair. He was middle-aged, slight, bundled against the freezing wind, and he had a plaid blanket tucked around his legs. A burly porter was pushing him towards the next carriage, and as the wheelchair drew level with Hogan's window, he realised he knew this man. Four years was a long time, especially these days, but there was absolutely no doubt. He was looking at Larry Elder.

Hogan pocketed his book and left the compartment. The corridor was already filling with new passengers complaining about the cold and the lack of seats and Hogan nodded back towards the compartment he'd just left.

'Seat by the window,' he smiled. 'Help yourself.'

The carriage next door contained the guard's van. The porter was wrestling the wheelchair up the steps and into the train and Hogan recognised Elder's low growl as the chair collided with the edge of the door. Moments later, Elder was sitting in the metal cage that contained half a dozen mail sacks and an untidy scatter of other items.

'OK, mate? All right, there?' The porter, heading for the still open door, didn't wait for an answer.

The train began to move and Hogan stepped inside the cage. Elder had his back to him and to the nearest window and was doing his best to turn the wheelchair around, but Hogan spared him the effort.

'Allow me,' he murmured.

It was mid-afternoon by now, and dusk was beginning to fall outside. There were no lights in the guard's van but something in this stranger's voice had caught Elder's attention, and as Hogan eased the wheelchair around he peered up at the face beneath the knitted cap.

'Fuck me,' he said softly. 'It's you.'

'Me,' Hogan agreed. 'I thought you were dead.'

'Nearly right, buddy. Put it there.' He extended a thin hand from beneath the blanket, and Hogan felt the sharpness of the bones as he gave it a squeeze. 'Steady, my friend,' Elder was wincing in pain. 'We live by different rules now. This fucking weather never ends, does it?'

Hogan found a box to sit on and settled beside the wheelchair. Elder was right about the weather. The temperature in the guard's van had to be close to freezing, and Hogan took off his coat and draped it over Elder's bony shoulders.

'How come the fancy dress?' Elder was staring up at him. 'And why the cross?'

'I'm a minister. A man of God. Nothing changes, Larry. Not in my world, anyway.'

'So what about the papers? The job? We all read those pieces you did for the *Express*. You're telling me all that's over?'

'Dead and gone. I'd tell you about revelations but that would be preaching. Dieppe, Larry. Tell me what happened.'

Elder nodded. Still shivering, he was obviously glad for the coat. He said he'd landed on Blue Beach at Puys with the Headquarters Group alongside the CO. Pinned down from every angle, a Sergeant had somehow managed to cut a hole through the barbed wire blocking a route up the cliff at the western end of the seawall. A party of maybe twenty guys had scrambled up the path until they got to a big house towards the top. On the way, he said, they'd stopped to clear two other properties.

'They were occupied?'

'They were.'

'So what did you do?'

Elder was grinning. He gazed up, then drew a bony finger across his throat.

'Sitting ducks.' He nodded. 'Every single one of the fuckers. Grenades for starters. Then a bullet in the head for the ones who needed it.'

Back on the beach, he said, the Germans were still helping themselves.

'To what?'

'Our guys,' his skinny hand slapped the arm of the wheelchair. '*Bam-bam*.'

'Including O'Donovan?'

'No.'

'He survived? He's still alive?'

'Christ, no. He'd blown himself up on a Bangalore torpedo trying to make a breach in the top of the seawall. Nothing left of him. Bravest move I ever saw.'

Hogan nodded, then briefly closed his eyes and crossed himself before looking at Elder again.

'So what happened with your lot?'

'We were no match for anyone. We were a handful of guys with rifles and Sten guns and a couple of grenades. We found a bunch of trees behind a gun site and hid up for the rest of the morning. We had a perfect view of the beaches. Believe me, you'd never want to see anything like that again. It was murder in plain sight. Should never have been allowed.'

Should never have been allowed.

Hogan was back on the destroyer, back on the deck of HMS *Calpe*, watching fit young men die. It was almost dark now in the guard's van as the train pitched and rattled through the snow but where it mattered, in his head, it was mid-August once again, and the war was far from won, and he felt that same brimming anger that had accompanied him back across the English Channel. Murder in plain sight, he thought. Unforgiveable.

'So how come?' Hogan was nodding at the wheelchair.

'I took a bullet or two in a firefight before we had to surrender. Both legs.'

'And?'

'The Krauts took me to Rouen. Good hospital. Great nurses. There were hundreds of us stretcher cases and the surgeons had no time.'

'So?'

'Double amputation, one leg below the knee, the other above. They've promised to get me walking again but patience is something I've never quite figured. One day, maybe. Who fucking knows?'

'And that lovely wife of yours?' Hogan was trying to remember her name. 'Back home?'

'Juanita thinks I'm dead. Maybe it's best that way.'

'Meaning you've found someone else?'

'Yeah. Traudel. Lives down in Bristol. Lovely woman. She says she's Swiss but she never was. She came to this country before the war. She's older than me, and much nicer than me, and she bakes a mean strudel. She also knows how to look after a man. In real life, she's German.'

'And that's OK by you?'

'Everything's OK by me.'

'*Everything?* You really mean that?'

'Sure. Even fucking Dieppe,' Hogan caught a flash of broken white teeth in the darkness of the freezing guard's van. 'We took a proper pasting over there. Wouldn't have missed it for the world.'

Hogan nodded, then reached out for his hand.

'A while ago,' he said softly, 'you told me about Teruel. I have a good memory, especially when a quote makes sense. You want me to tell you what you said?'

Elder frowned for a moment, trying to retrieve the memory.

'I told you none of us can ever change any of this shit,' he said at last. 'Not you, not me, not anyone. Then I told you to write it down, and make sure you used it.' He paused, steadying himself in the wheelchair as the train hit a bend. 'So did you? Have you? Will you?'

'No.'

'Why not?'

'Because it turned out you're right. Wars are probably forever. Like any kind of madness.'

Elder stared at him, then nodded. 'You're on the money, *padre.* So here's another thought. *Cuando el amor no es locura, no es amor.* You remember any of that Calderón shit?'

'I do.'

'And?'

'Love that is not madness is not love,' Hogan smiled. 'Have I passed the test?'

ACKNOWLEDGEMENT

This book owes a very big debt to Patrick Bishop. I've admired his work for many years, but nothing prepared me for *Operation Jubilee*, his recent account of the genesis of the Dieppe Raid and the hours of slaughter that left so many Canadians dead on a foreign beach. By the time I laid hands on *Operation Jubilee* I'd read dozens of accounts for a novel of my own, many of them contemporaneous, but Patrick Bishop managed to synthesise both history and incredulity in ways that confirmed my own determination to shed yet more light on one of the darkest days of the Second World War. A superb book. Highly recommended.

ABOUT THE AUTHOR

GRAHAM HURLEY is an award-winning TV documentary maker and the author of the acclaimed Faraday and Winter crime novels, two of which have been shortlisted for the Theakston's Old Peculier Award for Best Crime Novel. His Second World War thriller *Finisterre*, part of the critically acclaimed Spoils of War collection, was shortlisted for the Wilbur Smith Adventure Writing Prize.

Follow him on @Seasidepicture

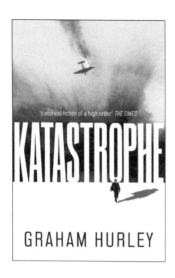

GRAHAM HURLEY

'A taut, detailed and
compelling read'
Sun

'A penetrating, compelling,
and skilfully vivid slice of
historical fiction'
LoveReading

'Inventive and
thought-provoking'
Crime Time

**Confidant of Goebbels. Instrument of Stalin.
What's the worst that could happen?**

January 1945. Wherever you look on the map, the Thousand
Year Reich is shrinking. Even Goebbels has run out of lies to
sweeten the reckoning to come. An Allied victory is inevitable,
but who will reap the spoils of war?

Two years ago, Werner Nehmann's war came to an abrupt
end in Stalingrad. With the city in ruins, the remains of General
Paulus' Sixth Army surrendered to the Soviets, and Nehmann was
taken captive. But now he's riding on the back of one of Marshal
Zhukov's T-34 tanks, heading home with a message for the man
who consigned him to the Stalingrad Cauldron.

With the Red Army about to fall on Berlin, Stalin fears his
sometime allies are conspiring to deny him his prize. He needs to
speak to Goebbels – and who better to broker the contact than
Nehmann, Goebbels' one-time confidant?

Having swapped the ruins of Stalingrad for the wreckage of
Berlin, the influence of Goebbels for the machinations of Stalin,
and Gulag rags for a Red Army uniform, Nehmann's war has taken
a turn for the worse. The Germans have a word for it:
Katastrophe.